GRIN

A DEPARTMENT OF SECOND CHANCES NOVEL

ANGELA BREEN

This is a work of fiction. All of the character, organizations, and events portrayed in this novel are either products of the author's imagination or are used fictitiously.

Grin

Cover by Aaron Bolduc

www.aaronbolduc.com

eBook ISBN: 978-1-955331-10-4

Hardcover ISBN: 978-1-955331-05-0

Paperback ISBN: 978-1-955331-11-1

First Edition

To my unconditional friends,
you're the best

ACKNOWLEDGMENTS

A big shoutout to my editor, Jake Watrous! He went above and beyond on this one and I owe him more than one lunch for pulling this off!

PRAISE FOR ANGELA BREEN

"Wow. Talk about a captivating, edge of your seat, and suspenseful story. If you love a good mystery that can keep you glued to your book, this is it. I was pulled in from the very first page and as the story continued to develop it got harder and harder to put the book down."

~*Goodreads Reviewer*

"Loved the book, the suspense was killing me!"

~*Goodreads Reviewer*

"WOW this one was good! Breen's first novel was a perfectly paced rollercoaster of emotion. A blend of real human emotion - ranging from romance, to maternal love, to incredibly complicated and painful familial relationships - and action that keeps you on your toes, this book sunk deep into my mind…"

~Amy Spitzfaden, Author of *It's Funny You Mentioned Chloe*

"This book was good, a crime thriller filled with suspense, mystery and romance."

~*Goodreads Reviewer*

JOIN THE CLUB

Forced to face her painful past while dodging a target on her back, will crime reporter Paige Quill choose justice-or the law?

Join the club now for a free ebook
https://dl.bookfunnel.com/w72xco0dvt

PROLOGUE

Indianapolis, Indiana
Spring 2019

"I took my first life in high school."

The declaration drew his eyes from Hatter to the Hare. Code names were the only way to get through this without anyone running to the cops. Leaning back in his recliner, he observed his living room. The people around him. It wasn't often he was around this many like-minded folk. He took a drag off the hookah that sat next to him. None of his companions shared this particular vice. But that was for the best. How was he expected to play the part of the Caterpillar if the Mad Hatter or March Hare wanted his hookah?

"I was sixteen," the Hare went on. "I stared into her eyes as she died. Three people saw me do it and are still too scared to talk."

His eyes slid from the Hare to the Hatter. They were growing more animated. More determined to prove that they were the worst devil in the city. A grin pulled itself across his lips. They were almost ready. Of course, the White Rabbit and King of Hearts sat back. They were pathetic. They could mess everything up. He'd have to watch them as this story progressed.

"I lost count," the Hatter countered with a laugh, unable to control himself as he relived some dark encounter in his mind. "I don't do it for numbers. I do it for the women. Gosh, I hope they're all too scared to talk!"

Meanwhile, the Cat, sat back, watching and listening. More out of curiosity and to learn their temperaments than out of weakness. He'd use that against them later. The Cheshire Cat was his greatest accomplishment.

"And that makes you better?" the Hare raged, pulling him from appreciating his work back to the exchange.

"You said it, not me." The Hatter gave a hearty laugh this time.

"I know how to solve this," he said, setting his hookah on the table and standing. "How to figure out who the biggest bad is. If you're all up to the challenge?"

Murmurs filled the room as curiosity took hold. The Cat grinned from his place, perched on a dresser in the corner. He'd been so patient.

"I propose a little wager, a test of prowess and cunning," he said over the din of side conversations.

Silence greeted him as the Hare and Hatter eyed each other. Both laughed after a moment. Grinning from ear to ear, he laid out his plan. This was going to be the bloodiest summer Indianapolis had ever seen.

ONE

INDIANAPOLIS, INDIANA
Summer 2019

DETECTIVE TANVI NIGHTINGALE ARRIVED AT THE PRECINCT A LITTLE after two in the afternoon. Pushing her straightened, black hair behind her ear, she moved briskly through the familiar halls. Her heels clicking as she made her way to the coroner's office. Her stomach did somersaults at the prospect of what she was about to find. A friend of the family had gone missing ten days prior, and the body currently lying in the morgue was eerily close to her description.

"Nightingale?" John called to her from down the hall, pulling her out of her self-induced panic. The idea of telling her mother that Tamika had died was daunting. She turned and waited for him to catch up. "I'm glad I caught you."

The crime scene tech was out of breath as he jogged to catch her. He was tall, with dark hair and darker eyes. He'd asked her out on more occasions than she found appropriate, but he was still able to do his job, which was all she really cared about.

"When was she found?" she asked as they continued toward

the coroner's office, not leaving time for pleasantries. Her boyfriend of seven years broke up with her, and the assault started almost immediately. Not only did she have to move in with her parents, she had to field advances from other officers, lawyers, and even medical personnel. But if Henry had taught her anything, it was that she didn't need a man right now. As a rookie detective in a male dominated unit, she needed to stay focused and keep her eye on the prize. Solving cases was the way to impress her boss and help her community. Nothing else mattered right now, much to her mother's dismay.

"Early this morning. There was a festival in the park last night. I live in the apartments across the street."

"Hear anything suspicious?"

"Honestly, I had ear protection in." He looked ashamed. "It was a music festival, and I was on call."

She nodded. The old ear protection and phone on vibrate situation. "Who found her?"

"Some festival goers," he said as they turned the corner. "Woman named Tawny lost her wallet. She and her friends went back to the park to try to find it. Found our vic instead."

"Was the wallet ever recovered?"

"That and several others," he said.

"So, their story checks out."

"Yes."

"You photographed the scene?"

"Yes," he confirmed, handing her a folder. "This is everything we know so far and everything we're testing. DNA and so forth."

"She was raped?"

"She was positioned in such a way that makes us think it's likely. Melinda should be done with the preliminary report."

She nodded, opening the file. Her heart sank. "Shit."

"You know her?"

"My sister went to school with her. My family has been connected with hers for a long time."

"Shit."

Melinda Walker stood at her computer typing in data when Tanvi and John entered. Of the four coroners in Indianapolis right now, she was the most thorough.

"John, good," Melinda said with a nod as they entered. "I have some more samples. Could you take them to the lab for me?"

"Of course." He picked up the evidence bags and headed back out the door.

"What have you got for me?" Tanvi asked as they walked over to the sheet-covered body.

"Enough to get you started," she said, pulling the sheet back. "This girl went through hell. I want this guy off the street."

"You think he'll do it again?"

She nodded. "And I doubt this is his first. He left little to no evidence. What I did find—" She shook her head and took a deep breath. "It's almost like it was left on purpose. I ran all the standard tests to see if I was missing something, but I wouldn't hold your breath."

"I understand."

"He beat her, raped her, and then strangled her."

Tanvi frowned. "In that order?"

"Yes," Melinda nodded. "Then he stripped her down and tossed her in the park. The thing is, her body looks like it was thrown out of a moving vehicle. The postmortem bruising, the position of her body, all of it. But her clothes were neatly folded and placed by the park entrance. Her wallet and keys were left on top of them."

"That is odd," Tanvi said, studying Tamika's face. "Tamika Jackson."

"How'd you know?"

"My family has known hers for years. Our mothers are pretty close."

"I'm sorry." Melinda watched her with added concern. "Are you sure you should be working this case?"

"I have to," she replied. "I didn't know Tami well, but I know her mom."

Melinda nodded her understanding.

"So raped, murdered, and discarded. That's everything we have?"

"He used a belt to strangle her. It had an interesting pattern." She handed over the photographs of the bruising.

"Studded?"

"Or something."

Tanvi nodded. "Thanks, Melinda."

"I'll shoot you a message if anything helpful comes from the lab."

"I appreciate it." Tanvi turned to leave. "Hey, did John tell you where he put the other wallets found near the scene?"

"Copies should be in the file he gave you. He's pretty thorough."

She nodded. John was the most thorough tech they had on staff. Not that she chose favorites, but he was definitely hers.

"And Detective," she said, "I don't know what's going on in this city, but we already have more deaths than normal. Something is happening."

TANVI SAT AT HER DESK WITH A PERPETUAL FROWN AS SHE READ through the file John had given her.

"Anything interesting?" Foster's voice startled her. She hadn't noticed her boss approaching her.

"Lots," she replied. He didn't like her, and she wasn't sure why. Part of her didn't care, but she also knew how much easier her job would be if he'd come around. "I have a few leads to check out while we're waiting on the lab."

"Melinda thinks this guy is dangerous," he said. "You need help?"

Her brows knitted together, and her lips thinned. The other detectives didn't really want to be saddled with the rookie. They'd made that very clear. They didn't care about her training or skill. She was still green, and they wouldn't touch her with a ten-foot pole.

"Before you answer, there's a guy over at State Police Headquarters. He focuses on cold cases, but he's a great teacher and has taken down more than a few serial offenders."

"Who?"

"Frank Tench. Former FBI profiler. I could reach out to him. I know this unit hasn't been the most—welcoming."

She huffed. "That's one way to put it."

"He'd show you the ropes. Mentor you. I've mentioned you to him a few times now."

She blinked. "A few times?"

"He likes Cherry Land, over on South Missouri Street," he added. "If you need guidance, he's there almost every night for an hour or two before he heads home to the wife."

"Really? An hour or two?" she gave a laugh. "Surprised he still has a wife."

"You can't take this shit home with you. And if you rush home after your shift, that's exactly what you'll end up doing."

She nodded. She wouldn't know. Her boyfriend of seven years had ended things because she wasn't home often enough. But Foster looked like he knew something about it.

"I have to go notify the family," she said, packing up her files.

"What do you have so far?"

"She went missing about ten days ago. I can't find her missing person's report, though. I know she'd just gotten out of rehab and was doing well."

"That's not a lot," he said.

"Well, once I talk to her parents, I can get more information about her last known whereabouts and what her mindset was like. She was raped and strangled to death. I'd be foolish not to check the boyfriend out. If she had one."

He gave a nod. "Look Frank up. When you get stuck."

"*If*," she corrected. "I'll look Frank up *if* I get stuck."

"If you don't get stuck at least once, you're not doing it right."

TWO

Virginia

Summer 2019

Metallic scent of gun smoke permeated the air as the man hit the ground. Supervisory Special Agent Lucas McGinn of the BAU stood frozen, gun still aimed at the body. The young woman the suspect was attacking wriggled out from underneath him. Curling herself into a ball in the corner, knees tucked into her chest, she shuddered. Her steadfast eyes on her assailant.

McGinn kept his weapon trained on the body as he approached. Kneeling beside his suspect, Lester Tompson, he felt for a pulse. None could be found. He stood, holstering his weapon as sirens approached the house. He moved to the door to greet them when a hand caught his. The tear-stained face of the girl looked up at him. She couldn't be more than sixteen.

"Don't leave me with him."

He helped her up, removed his jacket, and slung it over her shoulders. They walked toward the door.

"You're safe now."

As they reached the edge of the lawn, so did the local cops.

They ran past him, inside. His boss, Supervisory Special Agent Teresa Prentis, stepped out of her car, her head shaking as McGinn helped the girl into the ambulance and told the officer nearby what happened. When he was done, he turned to face the music.

"How many times do we have to have the same conversation?" she asked. "I'm wondering if I should just fire you or try one more time."

He crossed his arms over his chest, legs wide, knees locked, settling in for what was looking like a world-class ass chewing.

"Oh, silence," she beamed. "That's nice. While you're into the strong, silent routine, let me reiterate. We help the local cops. We are not the heroes. We don't rush in and save the princess. We tell them when we find answers, and we allow them to mobilize as they see fit. That's how this works."

"So, considering that he was over her, with his hands around her neck, and if I was a second later, she could have been dead—that doesn't matter at all?"

She took in a sharp breath. "You know I'm here to help victims as much as anyone, but the way to do that isn't to run ahead, guns a blazing. Lucas, you need to stop turning your nose up at the locals and start building relationships with them. You need to trust them to do the right thing."

"They do it too slowly," he said, exasperated.

"They won't call us next time they need help," she replied through gritted teeth. "How many girls will die then because you couldn't follow basic protocols?"

He glanced away from her, anger brewing in his chest. He didn't know how to refrain from acting on good intel. If he could save a life, he would. Every single time.

She ground her teeth, adjusting her stance and her approach. "I want you to take over the unit."

His jaw hit the floor as he looked back at her. He misheard that. He must have. "What? The BAU?"

"The Behavioral Analysis Unit, yes. Now, Matthew is poised and ready for the promotion, but he doesn't have your leadership skills or your talent. I want you, Lucas. But if you can't get this sorted out, that can never happen. I'm fifty-two years old. I want to retire soon. In the next four or five years. Which would mean you could shadow me for that time, and the transition would be smooth. Also, that would leave me to deal with Matthew's anger instead of you."

"The team hates me," he offered, trying to figure out what the hell she was talking about.

"It's best that way," she said with a tilt of her head. "Honestly, that's part of your appeal. It's easier to make tough calls and put people where they can do the most good if you're not friends."

"You hate me."

"I hate your stubbornness and lack of listening skills."

He watched the house and the police and crime scene techs that were swarming it like ants to a spilled ice cream cone. "What do I need to do?"

"You need to learn to work with people. Make them trust you, respect them, and gain respect in return."

He let out a frustrated sigh. That sounded really fucking slow.

"I have someone in mind, as a mentor. An in-between step for you to take."

He frowned.

"He's a former BAU member, one of the best to ever work with me," Teresa said. "If I can get him to agree, will you go work with him? Learn from him?"

Lucas gave a nod. He'd been a machine gun leader in the Marines, and he'd been looking at leadership opportunities in the FBI. Usually, the fact that everyone hated him was a deterrent.

"Good." She gave a smile that didn't look too forced and clapped her hands in front of her. "Good."

TANVI WAITED OUTSIDE THE JACKSON'S DOOR, HER HEART POUNDING. She hated this part. Mr. Jackson opened the door, a smile on his face until he realized her mother wasn't with her.

"Cheryl!" he called over his shoulder. She was there in seconds. The smile quickly faded from her face as well.

"May I come in?" Tanvi asked. They nodded and stepped aside. Mrs. Jackson led her into the living room, where she sat on a well-worn, green wingback chair across from the couch. The couple sat down, hands and arms locked as they waited for the worst possible news she could bring them.

"This is about Tami?" Mr. Jackson asked.

"Yes," she said, clearing her throat. She'd thought about how to say this a million ways in the car. "A body was found this morning in the park. White River State Park, near the Amphitheater."

"Oh, Jesus," Cheryl sobbed, burying her face in her husband's arm.

"Tamika's wallet and ID were found in the woods nearby," Tanvi continued. "It won't be official until one of you can come to the precinct and give us a positive ID, but we're pretty sure. I saw her."

Mr. Jackson slid his hand over his wife's arm as she sobbed. His eyes drifted to the floor as the words sunk in.

"I have a few questions, and then I'll let you be," Tanvi said. "But I want to find who did this to your daughter, and unfortunately, these things don't last. Sometimes, if you don't put the pieces together right away, they get lost."

"Of course," he said, his voice distant.

"Can you think of anyone who would want to hurt Tami?"

"No," he said.

"There was a girl," Cheryl chimed in. "She thought Tami stole her boyfriend."

"Do you recall their names? The girl and the boyfriend?" Tanvi asked, pulling out a small notepad to take notes.

"I don't know her name, but he was Mike Morgan," she replied. "He seemed to really like Tami."

"Thank you, Mrs. Jackson."

She nodded before her eyes fell on her husband, who looked lost.

"When was the last time you had contact with Tami?"

"Just over a week ago now." Her eyes were still on Mr. Jackson. "It was last Monday."

"How'd she seem to you?"

"She was excited," she said, shifting back to Tanvi. "She'd just signed up for classes to get her GED. She went for a walk. Just a walk, and she promised to be home for dinner."

"When did she leave?"

"I was cooking, so it was around five." She looked to her husband again. "If you'll excuse us—"

"Of course," Tanvi said, handing her a business card. "If you remember anything else you think could be relevant—even things you don't—give me a call. I can see myself out."

"When do we have to ID her?" she asked as Tanvi reached the door.

"I'll be by to pick you guys up in the morning. Around nine. Oh, where did you file Tami's missing person report? I couldn't find it when I did my search."

"With Metro." She stood, then put her hand to her lips.

"What is it, Mrs. Jackson?" Tanvi asked, her hand on the doorknob.

"What if it isn't her?" she asked. "What will that mean?"

"It means she's likely connected to this girl. Or she was in the park. Either way, we have a lead on your daughter. But, Mrs. Jackson—"

She put her hand up to silence any further discussion. She knew what she was about to say. Tanvi nodded. "I'll see you in the morning."

Tanvi tapped an irritated foot as she waited for the missing person report. The one lead Carol Jackson, Tami's mother, had given her had turned out to be a dead end, and her lack of possible suspects, or even people to ask, was starting to grate on her nerves. People didn't just vanish. Someone knew something, and her only hope was the report from when her parents' minds were fresh.

The Desk Sergeant rifled through paperwork. He'd already searched the computer.

"What day did you say it is?" he asked, a bead of sweat trickling down his neck. He was panicking. Why would he be panicking?

Another man, older and much more plump, stepped in from one of the other rooms, a half-eaten sandwich in his hand. "What are you looking for?"

"Tamika Jackson's missing persons report," Tanvi said. "Her body was found this morning in the park, and I'm gathering all the evidence. Since this was filed the day she went missing, it will likely have more facts the parents couldn't recall after being notified."

"Wasn't she the one who was into drugs?" he asked, squinting his beady eyes at her as he chewed what looked like a turkey on wheat.

"Yes," the other officer said. "She was fresh out of rehab."

A smile spread over his face as if he'd won a bet. "That explains it then. I never filed it."

Tanvi saw red as rage swept through her chest and out of her mouth. "What do you mean you never filed it?"

Her midnight eyes wide, lips pressed into a firm line as she struggled to maintain her composure. He scowled back at her through his thick-rimmed glasses. The glass magnifying his eyes, made him look like a bug.

"Ma'am—"

"It's Detective," she snapped again.

"Detective," he shot back. "There was nothing to investigate.

The girl fell off the wagon. She'd be found when she wanted to be."

"Well, as I said, she just was." Tanvi fumed. "Dead, naked in White River State Park."

"I don't know what you're getting all upset over," he said. "Look at her dealer, and whoever killed her will be easy to find."

Tanvi slammed her hands on the plexiglass. She smiled as he jumped, dropping what remained of his sandwich onto the other officer.

"She was seventeen. You haven't heard the last of this."

"Nightingale!" Foster's voice went over her like ice water. Rather than cooling her temper, it ignited it. She closed her eyes and took several deep breaths. No one pissed her off more than her boss.

"Foster?" she asked, her eyes wide and unblinking. A look that made most people shrink away. Not Foster.

"My office," he barked through gritted teeth. "Now."

THREE

Indianapolis

The bar was packed with law enforcement, and there was a group of firefighters around the pool table in the back. The AC was cranking, but the number of warm bodies meant the place was on the warm side. Lucas hadn't changed after his flight, so his black T and jeans meant he stuck out to those around them. It was that or that all these guys knew each other well enough to know a new guy on sight.

A massive man by the bar eyed him with malice. The kind of guy you'd be smart to stay away from. But Lucas wasn't exactly known for his intelligence. "I'm looking for a guy who's supposed to come in here."

"Which guy?" he grumbled, sizing Lucas up.

"Frank Tench."

His eyes widened, and he stepped back out of Lucas's way. Interesting. "He's at the end of the bar. You FBI?"

Lucas gave a nod. "For now."

"I've been thinking about joining."

"Are you a team player?" Lucas asked. The man narrowed his

eyes. "I'm about to get the boot unless I can learn to play well with others." He nodded. Lucas made his way down the bar to an old-timer nursing a blue moon with a ton of oranges in it.

"You're here early," he said, turning and offering his hand. "Frank Tench."

"Lucas McGinn." He gave Frank's hand a shake and sat on the stool next to him. "Teresa wanted me gone. Needed it to look like I got in trouble. I'm a hothead, you know."

"Oh, she told me all about it," Frank laughed.

"Look, I don't even know why I'm here. I don't know why I'm still in the FBI or why she thinks I can lead the BAU."

"How'd you end up in the FBI?" Frank asked. All laughter had left his eyes as he studied the younger man.

"I was told I couldn't make it. So, I did."

Frank's lip quirked up. "You were in the Marines?"

"Yeah, recruiter told me a fuck-up like me couldn't make it. So, I did."

"And you got into the BAU?"

"You're sensing a pattern?"

Frank nodded.

"Teresa told me I didn't have *it*. But couldn't tell me what *it* was, so—"

"You did it." Frank finished off his beer. "You've spent your life doing things you were told you couldn't do."

"Every damn day." The bartender, a pretty brunette, put a beer in front of Lucas with a wink, and he took a swig.

"You're going to be just fine," Frank said.

"Will I be fine in the FBI, or do I need something I can't do first?" He eyed the older man.

"Only time will tell."

"You think I can lead the BAU?"

"Teresa does."

"Yeah, but why?"

"As of right now? I have no idea. You're trouble where the FBI is concerned." He paused. "You might do well in a field office SWAT team."

He laughed. "You have to tell me I can't first."

"I'll leave that to the SWAT team leader. That way, it'll mean more when you land a spot."

"SWAT would never tell a Marine they can't join."

"Oh, yes, they would."

Lucas frowned at the laugh in Frank's voice.

"You aren't the only one to get the boot from the BAU."

"And SWAT didn't want a Saudi Marine?"

"Nope. I was kinda infamous at the time, so it might have had more to do with that than anything else."

He eyed the old man with new respect. "When do we start, and what are we doing?"

"I work cold cases mostly and occasionally consult on new ones. No glory. No rushing in to save the princess."

Lucas rolled his eyes. "Princesses are for rookies."

"Says the guy who can't call in to the guys actually working the case before jumping on his white horse and riding off into the sunset."

"Every second counts." Lucas said before taking another swig.

"Yes, it does."

TANVI STOOD BY THE EXIT, READY TO BOLT IF HER TEMPER GOT THE BEST of her. Her frustration and anger had become a caged animal, rabid and merciless. Foster was old school. He thought women couldn't do the job and assumed she had a soft spot for women who put themselves in danger. When in reality, she valued human life regardless of all the bullshit. She also refused to be deterred by a challenge. A dead prostitute deserved just as much of an investigation as anyone else. Most of the people she ran into in the business agreed. Foster was just a stubborn holdout.

"What the hell are you doing?" he asked as he closed the door.

"That asshole didn't even file a missing persons report for Tamika."

"That's not a crime," he argued.

"The parents thought there was a report."

His face dropped, but she knew it wasn't for the victim—it was for the department. "How can I face them knowing no one was even looking for their daughter?"

"If you have a problem like that, you need to come to me," he stated, sitting in his chair. "You don't need to be taking on the other officers."

"I won't lie for him."

"You'll do as you're told," he roared. "Procedure—"

"Don't tell me about procedure!" she shouted back. "There's right, and there's wrong, and what he did to that family, to an eighteen-year-old girl, is wrong!"

"You want to be the morals police, I hear they're accepting applications," he shot back.

"This is serious, Bill," she said. "I think—I think we have a serial killer."

He grimaced. "What, one druggy kid dies, and you think it's a serial killer?"

Hurt flared behind her eyes, she swallowed back the tears that threatened to overwhelm her. "Because serial killers never target the most vulnerable members of society."

She walked out of the room, slamming the door as he tried to call her back.

Back at her desk, she found a stack of files. Everything they had so far on Tamika as well as other girls' files.

Her brows knitted together. They were all over the city and seemingly random. Everything from suicide to an accident to a solved case of domestic abuse gone as wrong as it can. Four in all. Including Tamika's.

John walked into the homicide unit, and Tanvi flagged him down.

"What are these?"

"Melinda talking about how it looked like this guy killed before got me thinking. These girls are all high-risk, or were rather. Got their lives together just before they went missing—"

"But, John," she said, looking at them. "This one was ruled a suicide—"

"Yes, but hear me out. They were all strangled. They were all reported missing. I mean, how do you accidentally strangle yourself?"

"Apparently, when you're new to erotic asphyxiation," she answered, pointing out the cause of death.

"In an abandoned apartment building?" he challenged. "Who does that?"

She couldn't think of a way to answer. He was reaching, but she knew that kind of desperation.

"I'm sorry, I didn't mean to overstep. I'll take these back." He reached for the files, and something tugged at her chest.

"Wait." She placed a hand on his and offered a small smile. "I'll take a look. A serious, non-judgmental look. And let you know tomorrow."

He grinned from ear to ear. "Thanks, T."

"You shouldn't indulge him," Foster said from behind her, making her jump as John left, heading out of the bullpen.

"Sir," she snapped. "You scared me."

"Sorry."

"But he means well, and he's damn good at his job. I think it's worth a look."

"I meant I'm sorry about earlier." He gave her a look she couldn't place. "The sergeant will be dealt with."

"How?" she asked, brows raised.

"That's between him and his Department Head. But I'll make my position clear."

"Fine."

"Dead end on Tamika Jackson already?" There was a teasing note in his voice she didn't appreciate.

"Not so much an end as it is an unforeseen detour."

"Look up Frank. I'm telling you, you can learn from him, and he'll help. Don't let your annoyance with me stop you from tapping that resource."

Irritation bubbled up in her chest at the fact that he knew why she hadn't gone to Frank yet. That and the fact that he used to be in the FBI meant he was old. She'd had her fill of old assholes telling her what to do.

FOUR

TANVI SAT IN THE LIVING ROOM OF HER FAMILY HOME. ONE LAMP offered light to read and sort her files as the rest of the house slept. She searched, but there was little evidence that these were connected. Tamika's ID with her mother had been beyond emotionally draining. Carol had gone alone and barely gotten the words out before Melinda had to cover Tami up again. Her heart ached for the woman, empathy overwhelming her. She couldn't imagine the pain she was going through. The silent drive back to her house was the hardest Tanvi had ever made.

Shaking her head, she turned back to Carmon González's file. She removed the photos of her home and then her dump site. She then placed them on the coffee table, followed by Jada Jones's, then Felicia Williams's. She stared at the photos. The dump sites were all over the city, the abductions were in different neighborhoods. Each woman was different.

Her phone buzzed on the table top. Carol Jackson shone across the screen, and Tanvi slid the green icon home to answer.

"Mrs. Jackson?"

"Call me Carol, for heaven's sake."

"Sorry," Tanvi looked around the room, feeling like a child being scolded. "Is there something I can help you with?"

"In Tami's things, there was something odd." She was speaking so fast it was hard to understand her.

"Slow down." She grabbed her pen and paper. "What did you see?"

"In her wallet, there was a Post-it Note. It had a smile on it, I know it isn't hers."

"How do you know that?"

"She hated that movie."

"What movie?"

"Alice in Wonderland."

Tanvi sat up. "It was a Cheshire Cat smile, you mean?"

"Yes. And she hated that movie as a kid. Any time it came up, even as an adult, she hated it. I need to go, but I wanted you to know that."

"Thank you, Carol."

The call disconnected, and Tanvi looked through the photos of Tami's belongings. Sure enough, there it was. A yellow Post-it with an obvious Cheshire Cat smile. At least, obvious to anyone who'd seen the Disney film. What the hell was that supposed to mean?

She let out a frustrated sigh and kicked the coffee table as she sat back on the couch.

"Easy," her father said as he entered the room. "That's an antique."

"Sorry," she sighed. He shuffled across the room, two steaming cups of tea in his hands. Even in the dead of summer, he insisted that their evening cup be hot, not iced. His thick, black-rimmed glasses were pushed up on his prominent nose. His once black hair was now silver, and the lines on his face were getting deeper and deeper with every passing day.

"What has you so upset?" he asked as he handed her a cup. His gaze falling to the images on the table. "Oh, we have crime scene photos on the table, that's nice."

She chuckled, and he looked at her.

"When did you say you'd be moving out?" he teased.

"You've seen plenty of crime scene photos before."

"My time at the DA's office was short-lived," he argued.

"You became a criminal defense attorney," she shot back, raising a brow.

"Yeah, but my clients were innocent."

"Every single one?"

"Yes."

"How can you know that?"

He smiled a smile she'd seen a million times before, and she already knew his answer. "God."

She pursed her lips. "I wish he'd help me find the bad guys."

"He is," her father said, looking over the photos. "What are we looking for?"

"I think these crimes are connected."

"That's strange," he said, picking up a photo of Carmon's dumpsite.

"What?"

"The graffiti," he said, pointing to what looked like an eerie grin.

"Can I see that?" she asked. She frowned at the photo. She hadn't noticed the smile. It was on a wall outside the closet she was found in. You couldn't see the entire thing unless the door was closed. "How'd you even see that?"

"I have good eyes," he said, eyeing the other photos through the glasses on the tip of his nose. He plucked another from the table. "She has one, too." He pointed to a cement wall behind Jada's body.

"Tamika had one, too, but it was in her wallet," Tanvi said, pulling out a photo of the Post-it Note Mrs. Jackson had pointed out. "A Cheshire Cat Smile."

"Why do they all have chess pieces in their rooms?"

"What?" She took the photo from him. Putting it back down, she grabbed Felicia's dumpsite photo. Sure enough, there was a smile.

"This is weird." She sat back, looking at the ceiling again. "How do I get Foster to listen with graffiti, chess pieces, and my gut being the only things tying these cases together? Some of these are solved already. Jada's boyfriend has already been tried and found guilty. He's just waiting for sentencing."

"Then you have more victims than just the ones on this table to fight for. Your gut means more than you're giving it credit for."

"Dad." She let out an exhausted sigh and took a sip of her beer. "You don't understand what it's like. I'm new to homicide, I'm the youngest person on the squad, and I'm the only woman right now. There're all kinds of rumors as to why that is—"

He placed a hand on her knee, that same look on his face. "You can't control other people. All you can do is your best. Will you be able to sleep tomorrow night if you don't try to convince them that these are connected?"

She shook her head.

"Then that's what you do. You try."

"What if it doesn't work?"

"You were assigned to these cases?"

She leaned forward, searching out Tamika's file. "Just this one."

"Then you work that one. If you're correct, and they are connected, then you're hunting the same person regardless. You have these files. The information. Do you need permission to investigate them?"

Again, she shook her head as she took in her dad's wisdom. Her dad could always see the way through.

"Don't fall into the sexist-bigot trap," he added. "You don't need to see bad people where there are just people. If something happens to you, then proceed as necessary based on the event. No need to get worked up about rumors and oddities."

"They didn't even file Tamika's missing persons report."

His brow shot up. "What?"

"I went to find it before going to talk to the Jacksons. I couldn't, so I checked in when I got back, and the Desk Sergeant said he never filed it. That she was a druggy, and she'd be found when she wanted to."

"Have you told her parents?"

"No," she huffed. "Melinda said she was alive for a few days. Maybe we'd never have found her. But we should have been looking."

"Will the Desk Sergeant be reprimanded?"

"Foster says he will, but I won't hold my breath."

"Well, again, do what you have to do to sleep at night, T. You've never backed down from a fight. And Tamika and the Jacksons are counting on you to fight for them."

She stared at the ceiling as he spoke. If there was one thing she knew about her father, it was that he was always pushing her to grow. Nudging her outside her comfort zone. And it was always for the best. Walking outside of what makes us feel safe, secure, and comfortable—something outside of our hamster wheel routine—is the *only* way to progress in life. Somewhere deep down, she knew that. How could she fight the entire department? Rather than ask out loud, she decided it was time for bed. "Thanks, Dad."

They were both silent for a while, sipping their tea.

"How's mom doing?"

"She's strong," He sat next to her, but his eyes said he was somewhere else. "Right now is tough, but she's been through tough times before."

"How are *you*?" she asked. "You knew Tamika as well as mom did."

"I've always worried about her. Since the incident with her boyfriend."

"You mean her trafficker," she corrected. The thought of human trafficking had always soured her stomach.

He nodded. "Yes, that piece of work." He gave a heavy sigh. "I really thought she was out of danger."

"You never know," she said over her mug. "You just never know what's going to happen."

"You're right," he nodded. "I can't imagine what her parents are going through right now."

"I know. Mom will probably be making dinners tomorrow."

"Yes, she has a list on the counter of everything she needs. Adina said she'd pick it up on her way from class."

"She's so weird."

"You're mother?"

"Adina," Tanvi laughed. "Who volunteers to take summer courses your first year out of high school?"

"She wants to be in the world of cops and robbers, just like her big sister." He pulled her to him and kissed her head.

She gave him a kiss on the cheek and leaned forward to tidy her files.

"I'm off to bed."

"Good night, baby girl," he said with a smile.

"Night."

THE HISS OF FRESH COFFEE AND THE SMELL OF SCRAMBLED EGGS FILLED the small house as all the occupants congregated in the kitchen to start their day. Adina, one of Tanvi's little sisters, sat in a chair against the wall reading her Criminal Justice textbook while spooning yogurt into her face. Yasmin, the youngest of the four, was eyeing the eggs still in the pan, waiting for their mother to give her the okay to grab some.

Tanvi grabbed the coffee and poured herself a mug. She'd barely slept, going over and over how to talk to Foster this morning.

"Good morning, mama," she said, kissing her mother, Cora, on the cheek. "Did you get any sleep?"

"Not much, my dear," her mother said as she moved the eggs around the pan. Her sadness over Tamika was palpable and added a weight to the atmosphere in the small kitchen.

"You look terrible," Adina said, drawing Tanvi's attention.

"Just wait 'til you're on the force. You have sleepless nights to look forward to, I assure you."

The door opened, and Reina entered, a bundle of flowers in her hands. "Good morning!" she said, kissing their mother and father each on the cheek before finding a vase for the flowers. "These are for you, mama. I'm here all day to help with cooking and anything else you need."

"Aren't those lovely?" Cora exclaimed, brightening a degree, and Tanvi found herself sending up a silent prayer of thanks for her sister's timing and kind heart.

"Only the best for my mother," Reina said.

"Well, thank you," Cora said, a smile on her face. "We'll go over to the Jacksons' while Adina is in class and see what we can do to help. Then come back, and I want to make four dinners. I've reached out to some more women in the neighborhood, and we're all doing them in freezable packaging. I made sure there were no doubles. Too much comfort food is unfortunate. You end up not eating at all."

Their mother was the best when it came to things like this. She'd lost so many family members, she knew very well how to make it easier to bear. Not that it was ever easy.

"Reina," Adina said, eyeing her older sister. "Don't you think we should all go out tonight?"

"Yes!" Yasmin piped up. At only seventeen, there weren't many places she could get into, but she was always up for dancing.

"I can't," Tanvi said. The very idea made her tired.

"Can't is a bad word," her mother scolded.

"You need a break and some fun," Adina argued. "And so do we."

"I think that's a great idea," Reina said. "I only have a few more months to go out before baby-boober-butt arrives."

"You really need to pick a name," Cora frowned.

"Why?" Reina teased. "It's kinda growing on me. You think they'll let me hyphenate it on the birth certificate?"

"Reina," their father chimed in from behind his paper. "Don't tease your mother."

"Besides," Adina said, pulling them back to the conversation at hand. "You haven't gone out since Henry gave you the boot. You need a rebound. You said so yourself the other night."

"I don't need a rebound." Tanvi crossed her arms.

"But you want one," Reina said in a singsong voice.

"Fine, but it's entirely dependent on how today goes."

TANVI PLACED THE PHOTOS AND REPORTS ON FOSTER'S DESK. "THESE are connected," she argued. "See the graffiti?"

"Thin."

"They also each have a random chess piece in their bedrooms," she added.

"Listen," he started, leaning forward, "I'm not saying it's impossible. Lord knows there are plenty of sickos out there. What I'm saying is you don't have enough evidence to investigate this. Have you spoken to the other detectives in these other cases?"

She tilted her head back and exhaled slowly.

"This is not how it's done. Some of these are closed. You don't just steal someone else's cases."

"So I'm supposed to ignore this?"

"Unless you find hard evidence, yes. Stay in your lane, Nightingale."

"This one, Jada, how do her parents feel about the boyfriend being convicted?"

"They aren't on board yet, but the evidence is compelling."

"Lay it out for me," she urged, crossing her arms over her chest.

"You are the biggest pain in my ass—"

"Sure, just lay it out for me. From what I've seen in these files, there's no physical evidence indicating he was involved. They're ignoring the evidence, hard evidence, they have to make this charge stick."

"They make a compelling case. Go let them lay it out for you.

I'm sure they'll be thrilled to hear your take on the situation." He smiled as an idea occurred to him. She practically watched the light come on. "Show this to Frank. You get him on board, and I'll talk to the ADA's and other detectives myself."

She nodded. Collecting her files, she headed for the door.

"Nightingale," he called after her. She stopped and turned back.

If you ever show up with files that aren't yours without speaking to the detectives again, you're fired."

Rage flared in her eyes and fear shot across his face before he could mask it.

CHERRY LAND WAS A WELL-KNOWN COP BAR A FEW BLOCKS FROM THE State Police's offices. Low profile, good food, good beer, and pool tables.

Tanvi wove her way through the bar, looking for someone who looked like a former FBI agent.

She brushed against a larger man on a bar stool, accidentally grabbing his attention.

"Hey there," he said with a smile that told her she was going to have a hard time moving on from this one without being rude. Hopefully, he wasn't Frank. "Can I help you with something?"

"I'm looking for Frank Tench," she said. He leaned in, ear first. She projected into his ear. "Frank Tench, the former FBI agent?"

He nodded. "Down the end of the bar."

She smiled at him, feeling a little guilty for misjudging him. At the end of the bar was a man sitting all alone. The younger cops around him all gave him a wide berth, and she wondered what Foster had sent her into. Frank was stout, with silver-gray hair at his temples and deep wrinkles.

She walked up to him. His gaze swept over her before doing a double-take.

"Don't get a lot of female cops in here?" she asked.

"We do, but I've never seen you before."

"That's because I work too much and have no life," she joked, extending her hand. He smiled and took it. "I'm Tanvi Nightingale."

"Frank Tench," he said. "Have a seat."

"I have a confession--"

"You need help with a case?"

"Happens to you a lot?"

He nodded. "Part of why this seat is always open. The guys want to make sure cases get solved before they hit my desk."

"You're working cold cases now, right?"

"Did your homework," he nodded, tipping his beer back.

"I have some weird cases. I think they're connected."

He squinted at her. "Okay, I'm listening."

She laid out her evidence, showing him the photos of the graffiti and the chess pieces.

He stared at the photos for a long time in silence, she was starting to wonder if she'd offended him somehow.

"I have a few cases I think could be connected, but it's damn thin."

"You're kidding."

"No, I'm not." He shook his head. "Graffiti-connected cases is insane. But it's what we've got."

"You think they're connected."

"I think we have investigating to do. Hard evidence to find. I have an agent coming in the next few days," he said, picking up his beer and ordering one for her. "You'll need to submit a formal request for help from the BAU."

"You think we need it?"

"Never say no to more resources. The FBI will aid in the investigation. Hell, after I left, they probably only hired bookworms, anyway. They need the field experience."

FIVE

Lucas stood by the bar, eyeing the people of Indianapolis as they milled about. Some were drunk, but most were just having a good time. Drinking, dancing and singing along with the Jukebox, very poorly but with great enthusiasm. From what he'd seen in the papers, they had no idea a serial killer was lurking in the shadows.

A laugh emanating from the corner of the room pulled Lucas's attention. The women in the back corner were having more fun than anyone else in the bar. That was, except for one. She sat in a bright, red dress that showed off her curves and light brown skin. Her hair was left to curl naturally around her face, and she was looking at her phone. Another woman elbowed her in her ribs, and she put the phone down. A smile plastered on her face. The one sitting across the table held her hand out, and the lady in red took it before they moved to the dance floor.

Lucas was captivated by them. They spoke often, generally having a good time, but she was still distracted. Her friend tapped her on the shoulder, pointed to him, and said something to her. He'd been made.

She focused in on him and headed straight for him. He swallowed hard as she approached. His heart pounding in his chest.

She brushed up against him, her rosy scent invading his senses, as she sat on the stool to his right and ordered a drink. Her big, chestnut eyes taking him in. The hint of a smile at the edges of her lips. "My sister tells me you've been staring at me." She smiled as her drink was delivered. He held out cash to pay for the tequila sunrise with extra cherries. Her eyes were fixated on him as she plucked one off the top and ate the cherry, stem and all.

"Your friends seem to be having an exceptional time, but you seem distracted."

She spread her lips to show him the cherry stem tied into a knot between her teeth, and he gulped. *Damn. That was smooth.*

"I have a very demanding job." She put the stem on her napkin and took a drink. "And my boyfriend of seven years just left me. I'm living with my parents. At thirty-one."

"That all sounds very distracting," he agreed, his eyes glued to her. She was pushing her breasts up and leaning in towards him, but not quite touching.

"What I need," she began, then paused to touch his chin and get his eyes back on hers, "is someone to help me, take the edge off. For a night or two. And well, you're sexy as hell. Which might just be enough to turn off this big brain of mine."

"I won't be here long," he said. "I'm just in the city to consult on a project. Then I'm out."

She leaned in closer, putting her chin on his shoulder. Was this real?

"I don't care," she chuckled her warm breath rolling over his ear. "Hell, that's even better."

"You're telling me you want to use me."

"For your body," she admitted with a devilish grin as she pulled back, placing her hand on his chest.

"What about my brain?" he teased. "I'm told it can be fun, too."

She shook her head. "Is that what you really want?"

"Well, I'm not saying no, if that's what you're asking."

"So, you're up for the challenge?"

"Not much of a challenge," he boasted.

"You think it'll be easy?"

"I think I'm gonna rock your world," he said, smirking. "You're going to miss me the next time that itch makes itself known."

Leaning in, her breath caressed his ear as she whispered, "I'm going to pop you like warm champagne." She bit her bottom lip and slid her hand down his chest and over to his side. He caught her wrist just as her fingers brushed his gun. She sat up, looking at his belt. His FBI credentials and the grip of his pistol were plain to see. Her face went pale. "You're FBI?"

His brows pinched. "That's not usually the response I get."

She fell slowly forward, resting her forehead on his shoulder for a moment, a light flowery scent surrounded him at her nearness. She sat up, and her face matched her dress.

"I'm Tanvi Nightingale." She offered him her hand. "And I don't normally come on to strangers."

"Well—you're very good at it," he said, taking her hand. "But who—"

"Detective Nightingale."

A smile spread over his face. "Oh, this *is* embarrassing."

"Yep," she hopped off the stool and spoke over her shoulder. "Have a good night."

"Come on," he yelled after her. "I was just starting to like this city."

TANVI GRABBED HER WALLET FROM THE TABLE.

"What happened?" Reina asked, glancing back at Lucas, who raised his glass to her.

"He's the damn FBI agent," Tanvi snapped. "The one I'm supposed to impress tomorrow with how I figured out these cases are connected, with almost no information. And I told him I'd pop him like warm Champagne. Fuck!"

"You went Faith on him!" Reina fought her laughter but failed. "You must have really wanted it tonight."

"I wanted one of those nights where it's all sexy and needy, and then you never speak again, and they can't ruin it—you're just left with this perfect memory."

"Does that exist?" Reina asked.

"I was prepared to find out."

"He looks very impressed," Adina added, looking over to where he was still watching. An arm draped over his lap, hiding the evidence that her words had worked. They roared with laughter. Tanvi squeezed her eyes shut. Part of her wanted to go through with it, anyway. But she couldn't risk the case. Tami's parents' pain was still fresh in her mind.

"I'm heading home. I should know better than to try and have a one-night stand, anyway. I'd just regret it."

"Very true," Reina said as she sipped her virgin daiquiri.

"Then why didn't you stop me?"

"Because sometimes you have to live through shit to know it's true. You've been talking about banging one out since you moved back home. I figured you were a woman on a mission."

"You could have at least tried to talk me out of it."

"She did," Adina interjected. "We all have. Even mom."

"What?"

"See, you're so dead set on it, you didn't even realize you told mom your thirteen reasons why a one-night stand was for you."

"You're kidding," she grimaced. "No. When?"

"Two bottles of wine in, the night before book club."

"Shit. I don't even remember that."

"Don't worry," Reina laughed. "Your words were so slurred, mom thought you were talking about speed dating."

"Does anyone speed date anymore?"

"I don't think so, but apparently, mom doesn't know that."

Tanvi turned to make her escape and ran right into a solid wall of muscle. His drink spilling all over them both.

"If you wanted my attention, you could have just asked," Agent McGinn said with a cocky smile.

"I already told you, it was a mistake."

"Right, because cops and FBI never fraternize. Ever." He smirked, and she wanted to punch him in his perfect, white teeth. Pushing her embarrassment aside, she clung to her anger. "Bonus points for the Buffy reference, by the way."

"Look, I'm going home. I suggest you do the same before you embarrass yourself any further."

"I'm not embarrassed." He raised a brow at her.

"You are so unprofessional!"

"We're off duty," he chuckled again, so she pushed him to the side and headed for the door.

First guy she'd come onto that aggressively *ever,* and it was the guy she needed to impress with her brain, not her body. What was wrong with her?

She'd been working the case hard while her sisters had fun. It would have made her stand out to someone who was paying attention. *Dammit.* That's why he was watching her. He was curious. She should have known to study him more before making assumptions.

He eyed the board with a smile. His little game started off swimmingly. Muffled moans drew his attention to the bed. She'd have to be drugged again. She was becoming resistant to it. *Pity,* he thought to himself. She'd likely OD soon, and he'd need to find another. Or not. If everything went to plan, he'd be busy soon. Too busy for his pets. He gave a resigned sigh as he filled the syringe.

The Cheshire Cat, his protégé, had proven the most useful thus far. He let them get the game started without a hitch. Plus, he managed to make sure the right detective was on a case when things were ready. And the one he'd picked. A chuckle rose in his throat. *Oh, yes*. She was a great detective, but she was blinded to half their game. Her finding the FBI agents so soon was a surprise. But they could work with that, too.

He slid the needle into the girl's arm and looked back at his board. This was going to be the greatest game between a serial killer and the police that was ever played. And no one would be able to stop him. Once he'd beaten them, he'd go to New York and start all over again.

SIX

Tanvi entered the station with a nest of snakes vying for the top spot in her stomach. Foster was always looking for reasons to get her off the squad. Was this going to be it? She squared her shoulders and tried to focus on the good. The FBI Agent would help them today. With that profile, women like Carol Jackson would finally get justice for their murdered daughters. And the daughters that remained would be safe.

"Nightingale?" John said from behind her. She turned, his face filled with concern. "Are you okay?"

"Yeah, I just couldn't sleep." She pulled her buzzing phone out of her pocket, choosing not to share the reason behind her sleep-deprived evening. The girl on the screen was an eleven-year-old who'd gone missing over a week ago. They'd been running coverage all night. "She's eleven, and I didn't even know she was missing. Did you get the Amber Alert?"

"Yeah, the trouble is they have no idea who took her."

"Where was she taken from?" Tanvi asked. "That wasn't in the press release, which I thought was odd."

"Her bed." He cleared his throat and sighed. "The captain on the case asked them to keep it out of the press, so they can rule out friends and family without the media accusations. Remember Elizabeth Smart?"

"Still, someone may have information."

"They plan to release it today from what my buddy said."

She looked at the girl again, a firm frown in place as her problems began to feel small. "Do you know how recent this photo is?"

"A couple days before the abduction. It was her birthday."

Tanvi shook her head as she walked toward the office they'd designated as the Case Headquarters. I'm this way," he said, pointing down the opposite hall.

"I'll see you later," she said. He gave a wave, and she was alone with her thoughts again. The photo of the girl was haunting. Her long, blonde hair hung loose down her back, and she had bangs covering her forehead. Tanvi sent up a prayer that she'd be found safe and continued down the hall. She had her own case to focus on.

As she approached the HQ, voices could be heard. She quieted her steps as she neared the door. Frank sat off to the side, arms crossed over his chest. Foster stood in front of her board as the hottie from the bar stood looking it over. He was tall with broad shoulders and blond hair that was cropped short at the sides and left longer on top, so it could be swept back. A flash of how his muscles felt under hand shot through her mind, and her cheeks burned. *Dammit.* She leaned back against the cold cinder block wall and took a deep breath, listening.

"You think this means anything?" Foster was saying.

"From this, I don't think you have a case. I'd guess the person who put this together *wants* to see a connection. But I need evidence. Any DNA yet?"

"We're waiting on the lab."

Tanvi felt rage boiling in her belly, replacing her embarrassment.

The man turned to Frank. "If it weren't for you, I'd leave right now."

"Good," Frank said. There was zero emotion in his tone, leaving her to wonder what he was thinking. "I can teach you a thing or two before I send you back to Quantico."

"That's funny," Tanvi said as she entered the room before the agent could respond. "I thought the meeting was at eight."

The FBI agent turned to look at her, and the fact that he was even more gorgeous in shitty fluorescent lighting than in a dingy bar was infuriating. As was the fact that his attraction clearly matched her own. He gave her a slow once over she could practically feel. Not that she'd spared him her own visual caress.

"Nightingale," Foster said with a smile that was more fake than the cheese in the Kraft Macaroni her mother fed her as a child. "You made it." Although they sent waves of anger through her body, she was accustomed to office politics and hidden agendas.

She forced a smile that she hoped said she was going to rip his head off as soon as she had a chance. Not that it mattered. He seemed used to her tirades and unaffected by her anger.

"We weren't going to leave before you got here," he said, raising his hands. "Frank wouldn't let us."

"So?" she said, gesturing to the agent. "Tell me what you see."

He pointed to himself, a quizzical look creasing his brow.

"Yes," she said as condescendingly as possible. "Please, enlighten us. You clearly don't care what I have to say."

Frank's body shook as he struggled to stamp down a laugh.

"I see women from different areas of town, all different ethnicities, religions. Different causes of death. I see no connection. Outside your—-well, you."

She gaped. Unable to form words.

Frank stood up and moved between them. He knew more about her in their short time working together than Foster did from years.

"Tanvi recognized what you didn't, Lucas," Frank said. "Detective Nightingale, this is Lucas McGinn. Born and raised in Boston. Lucas, Tanvi left something out of this display. She put it together without this particular clue. We, well I, decided to test you."

The color drained from Lucas's face. "Test me?"

"Yes. Teresa and I go way back," Frank explained. "She said you have good instincts in the field, but you struggle at times to form a picture from crime scenes. I'm also supposed to help you form a good relationship with the local cops. I think I'm failing on that front."

He balked. "Give me all the information, and I'll run it down for you."

Tanvi moved to the board and removed the three cases Frank had brought in. "There. That's all the information I had when I realized we had a problem."

Lucas glared at her. "So, what are you hiding?"

"Do you concede?" she asked, a look of satisfaction working its way across her face.

He glared at her before going back to the board. "All the women are similar ages, all minorities. From low-income housing. Not all have broken homes—" he paused. "None are from broken homes."

Tanvi stepped forward. She hadn't even thought to look at that.

"None of this says serial killer," he said in frustration, looking from her to Frank.

"You haven't noticed the graffiti or the chess pieces," Frank announced.

Lucas moved closer to the board, eyeing each photo. "Not all of them have chess pieces or the graffiti."

"Not all photographed," Tanvi said. "And Josefine Vargas, hers was tough."

"Then, why is she included?"

"She had one—" she paused. "Inside."

"Oh," he said, looking back at the images. "Shit."

"The pieces and graffiti at the dump sites were enough for me to be concerned, but the timeline is what really scares me." Frank said, stepping forward. "A woman is taken every few weeks, with the closest abductions being Tamika Jackson and Jada Jones only twelve days apart. Jada's body was found the day Tamika went missing."

"Have there been any other women reported missing?" Lucas asked.

"So, you're entertaining this?" Foster asked.

"Look," Lucas said, "this is thin, the thinnest evidence I've ever seen. I mean, graffiti? But the only way to know is to investigate. So, we're working. If you have something to contribute, go for it. If not, you can leave."

Tanvi failed to conceal her grin as Foster headed for the door. Not the best plan when it would come to long-term support, but it was fun to watch. Besides, she could handle Foster.

"That's part of the issue," Tanvi said as the door closed. "Tamika was never reported missing. The Desk Sargent said he filed a report, but he never did. These cases aren't always taken seriously because of the neighborhoods and some of their pasts. Tamika wasn't taken seriously because she'd just gotten out of rehab. She wasn't exactly a stranger to the men charged with finding her. I did speak to one uniform. He did search in her usual drug spots, but they assumed they'd pick her up for prostitution or find her in a hospital post OD."

"That's going to make this a hell of a lot more difficult," Lucas said, crossing his arms over his chest. "What kind of press has this gotten?"

"Jada Jones was the most publicized abduction," Frank said. "The only one I saw coverage on. I've been working with Jim Scranton. He's the lead on the Ali Kim case. We were going to go to the press with her case when Tanvi showed up. Kim went missing from her bedroom, according to her parents. There's no way she could have or would have after going to bed. A chess piece left on her pillow confirms it for me."

"Wait, didn't they all have chess pieces in their rooms?"

"Yes," Tanvi confirmed.

"Then why assume she was abducted from her room?"

They exchanged a look. "I guess we don't," Frank said. "Good work. Assumptions like that can lead to mistakes that help our killer escape."

"Are any of them missing a piece, either the smile or the chess pieces?"

"Quite a few. If we didn't believe they were abducted from home, we didn't take photos of the bedrooms. John did—he's very thorough, but he wasn't assigned to all the cases we've connected at this point."

"So, we don't have anything."

"We have enough to keep looking," Tanvi said, her hands placed firmly on her feminine hips.

He looked to Frank, who was staying annoyingly neutral. "Where do we start? There's nothing to profile here..."

"What do you mean, 'nothing to profile'?"

A tick worked in his jaw. "Who shoved a stick up your ass this morning?"

"You did," she barked. "I am connected to these women. I grew up in the same conditions, and knowing that my murder or the murder of one of my sisters might not be taken seriously because of where we live pisses me off."

"Are you telling me none of these were investigated properly?" he asked, shifting on his feet. His eyes wild, but she was too angry to let it bother her.

"No."

"In fact, they all look pretty standard with the exception of Ms. Jackson," he continued, looking back at the wall. "Would you say that's correct?"

"Yes," she said through gritted teeth.

"Then what should have been done?"

She stared into his eyes, knowing he was right. But she also knew it was all too possible to get a shitty cop or one having a bad day who might not take her parents seriously. He couldn't understand that.

"You have no idea what you're talking about."

"I don't know what it's like to be looked at as trash," he corrected. He gave her an angry nod, begging her to take the bait. She wondered what he was hiding. "That's your argument."

Her brown eyes searched his. They were full of pain and anger. She doubled down. He's going to cry horrible upbringing with his nice suits and shoes and expensive haircut?

She opened her mouth to spew venom, but Frank stepped in the way.

"Enough!" he glared at both of them. "We have a press conference to get to. Not to mention a serial killer who will not stop until we find him lurking in the streets and apprehend him. He's probably already picked out who the next victim will be. We can't get wrapped up in personal bullshit. Our job is too important."

She crossed her arms over her chest and looked at the floor. "Sorry, Frank."

"Yeah, sorry." She looked up to see Lucas's eyes locked on hers, rage still burning within them.

TANVI LEFT THE ROOM, AND FRANK TURNED ON LUCAS. *HERE WE GO.*

"So, about working with locals," Frank started.

"Don't piss them off?" Lucas offered. "Yeah, I've heard that one before. It's the dismount I seem to struggle with."

"I'd say it's the entire move, but yeah."

"It's not my fault she came on to me last night and is embarrassed about it now."

Frank bit back a laugh. "That explains so much. But that's not all that happened here."

"I know what it's like to be seen as society's outcast. The town pariah," Lucas snarled.

"I know you do. But does it matter?"

"If she's letting it color her view of me or the case, then yes, it does."

Frank pondered that a moment. "Okay, better communication skills could go a long way."

Lucas huffed. He wasn't cut out for this shit. "Maybe Teresa made a mistake."

"Maybe you need to man the fuck up and step outside your comfort zone."

"Okay, someone came to play."

"I read your file. I know your history, including your time in the service. Oorah, Marine. Let's do this fucking thing."

Lucas nodded. "You too?"

Frank nodded. "Little different. My stepdad killed my dad."

So, not that different.

"Come on, we really do have a press conference. I set it up this morning."

SEVEN

LUCAS AND TANVI STOOD ON EITHER SIDE OF FRANK AS HE ADDRESSED the audience. They'd decided his history of teaching and doing events such as these made him the best person for the job. Lucas stole a glance at Tanvi. She was equal parts gorgeous and infuriating.

"Are you telling us there's definitely a serial killer in Indianapolis?" a female reporter in the front row asked.

"We're investigating the possibility," Frank announced, sounding diplomatic. "Several of the women were out celebrating in clubs and bars the nights they disappeared. We'd like to ask everyone to be extra vigilant while out and to report anything suspicious. We're especially interested in the night Chloe Tran went missing from Wilbur's, its blues club on fifth. If anyone saw anything at all, please call our tip line."

"That's it?" the woman demanded. "There's a madman on the streets, and you just want people to call a tip line? What's being done to keep the young women safe?"

"The possibility of a madman," Frank corrected.

"Pardon?"

"Nothing is confirmed. When we have more information, we'll

share it with you. In the meantime, stay vigilant and call us about anything strange."

Lucas bit his lip, trying not to smile. He was good.

"Thank you, that's all for now." He nodded as questions came hurling at him from all directions. They were moving out the side, and Lucas could tell by the way Tanvi's fists were clenched that she was less than impressed.

As soon as the doors closed behind them, Tanvi whirled on Frank. To his credit, he seemed to know it was coming.

"Why didn't you give them the information?" she asked, her brow knitted together. "There were three girls taken from bars. Not just the one Chloe was taken from. Why wouldn't we talk about that?"

"Because," Frank began calmly, "everything we tell the people, we also tell the perp. And I don't want him to know all the details we have. It's the same reason I didn't list all the victims' names. We have no evidence yet. We have a pretty solid MO, and I feel confident about where the investigation is going. But the public doesn't get it, nor do they care. And the families all need to be notified prior to being mentioned at a press conference like that. Not to mention the cases we're about to derail. You spring that on the wrong ADA, and they'll dig their heels in."

They reached the room for the tip line, and it was all hands on deck. Everyone had a phone between their ear and their shoulder as they took notes. John waved them down, phone still to his ear. Lucas wondered how the tech had ended up here instead of in the lab.

"Okay, yes, we'll need you to come down to the station and work with a sketch artist," John was saying. All three of them perked up. "The sooner the better. Okay, I'll have someone lined up. See you soon."

He hung up the phone and looked wide-eyed at Tanvi. "Holy shit, that was a rush. I've never worked the phones before on these. I was just coming to bring you the list of registered sex offenders Frank asked for."

"Who was it? What did they see?" Tanvi asked, ignoring his excitement.

"Oh, right," he picked up the paper. "Guy's name is Joe White. He saw Miss Tran being led out to a car. He assumed it was with a rideshare company but he didn't look for the sticker. The sketch artist will work with Mr. White once he gets here. White claims the perp is an 'older, Indian-looking guy.'"

"When's he coming in?" Frank asked. "We'll need to speak to him after he sees the artist."

"He's on his way down now."

Lucas wasn't going to get his hopes up. He'd seen enough poor police sketches to know this was a long shot.

Joe White sat with a cup of water as he looked at his watch again. Tanvi and Lucas stood, arms crossed over their chests, observing from the other side of the one-way glass.

"What are you guys doing?" John asked as he approached. "Aren't you supposed to go in there?"

"Look at his leg bounce," Lucas said. John took notice.

"And he keeps checking his watch." Tanvi added.

"You guys know people have lives, right?" John scoffed. "Most people don't want to spend their whole day in the police station."

Tanvi cocked her head to the side. "Yeah, but this is more than a simple inconvenience."

"How can you tell?"

"He's either the most nervous man I've ever seen, or—"

"He's an addict looking for a fix."

"We didn't offer a reward," John offered.

Tanvi glanced at him. "Why would you bring that up?"

"Why would a junkie come here if there is no reward?" John asked.

"Because he actually saw something, or—"

"He wants attention," Tanvi finished for Lucas. "Let's go."

She grabbed the sketch off the desk behind her and led Lucas into the room. "John, can you go get Frank? He was getting coffee. Just tell him we're going in."

She opened the door and entered, Lucas at her back.

"Hello, Mr. White. Do you mind if we call you Joe?" She approached the table and sat across from him. His hair was ghostly white despite him not being more than fifty. His mustache twitched as he looked from her to Lucas, who stood next to her. "I'm Detective Nightingale with the IPD. This is Agent McGinn with the FBI's Behavioral Analysis Unit."

"It's about time. Do you have any idea what will happen if I'm late?" He pointed to his watch and stood.

"Easy, Joe," Lucas said, placing a hand on the man's shoulder. He recoiled from Lucas's touch but sat back down. "We just have a few questions. We appreciate your patience."

"What do you need to know?"

"We need your account of what happened the night Chloe Tran was abducted."

"I was in the bar. I noticed her because she was telling everyone she'd gotten into Harvard Law. It was impressive, so I paid attention. I never got into any schools. So, I just observed."

"Did you notice anything odd in the bar?" Tanvi asked. "Anyone giving her more attention than you thought they should be?"

"Any overly aggressive people around her?" Lucas added.

"No," he shook his head. "But she had one beer and was acting drunk. Like blackout drunk. She was falling into people, laughing, stumbling. A man showed up—the one you had me create the sketch for. He said he was her ride and took her out of the bar, and that was it."

"No one seemed concerned about this man taking her?"

"No, she went with him. Asked him to take her home. No one seemed too concerned at all. I didn't even know she was missing until I caught the end of the press conference."

"Thank you," Tanvi said. "We'll need you to write that out and sign your statement, please."

"Of course, I just need to hurry."

Tanvi pulled a statement form out of her file and slid it over to him, while Lucas offered him a pen.

"We'll be back in a few minutes," Tanvi said. They both stood and went back to the observation room. Frank stood, watching.

"Anything weird?" he asked. "I got here a few minutes ago."

"He's nervous."

"But it could be anything," Lucas added. "He could be worried about losing his job, could have a jealous wife. We just don't know. Anyone run a background check on him?"

John popped up once again. "Yeah, he's divorced, works at the post office. He lives with his mother, who is immobile, and he can only pay for a nurse to be with her part-time. So, I suspect that's the problem."

"You're kidding. Why didn't he say so?"

"Maybe he's embarrassed," Lucas said, his lip curled.

"There's nothing wrong with taking care of your parents."

Lucas looked at her. "Nope, there isn't, but I'd still rather have my ass scrubbed with a toilet brush than live with mine ever again."

"You're disgusting," she spat.

"Careful," he wagged a playful brow at her. "You hurt my feelings enough, and I'm gonna start thinking you're sweet on me."

She rolled her eyes, but a smile tugged at her lips.

"What's next?" she asked Frank as he was packing up his briefcase.

"We go home," he said, looking at the clock.

It was after five, sure, but they had a killer to find. "We have the Sex Offender Registry."

"If you want to take that, figure out who has been in the area, and match MOs, you can go right ahead. My wife has a steak out for me, and I'm not going to miss it."

"Hey, Frank," Lucas said. He was eyeing the map of dumpsites.

"Yeah?"

"I think we need help," he said, continuing to stare.

"What are you thinking?"

"There's a guy in the BAU, he's one of those kids who graduated from high school at sixteen and then got two PHDs before he was twenty. But he's great with numbers and patterns. I could be wrong, but this looks like something to me. He'd be able to tell us for sure."

"Make the call."

"Thanks, can you wait just a minute?" Frank frowned but nodded as Lucas took out his phone and dialed.

"Nash?"

"Luke?"

"Yeah, I'm in Indiana, and I could use some backup."

"I'm in Vegas, visiting my mother," he said.

"Stop in on your way home? It'll be worth your while."

"What've you got?"

"I'm not sure yet. This is getting big fast, and we could use someone with an eye for patterns." It sounded crazy when he said it out loud.

"You're pulling my leg."

"I'm not."

"This is like the escort thing again."

"No, it's really not."

"How can I even begin to trust you?"

Lucas looked around the room at the people staring at him. "You don't have to."

He passed the phone to Frank, who covered the receiver with his palm.

"He's insanely smart, and I may or may not have pulled a prank or two on him in the past. But he can help us here. We need him."

Frank took the phone. "Frank Tench—yes, I'm that Frank—I was fired for ignoring orders regarding a trafficking case. I saved the girl and lost my job for fucking up an operation that had been ongoing for years.—Yes, by all means, now that I've gotten to relive some of the worst parts of my life, let me do you a favor.—I understand, kid, it was a joke—yeah, get your ass here."

Frank handed him the phone back.

"You in, little buddy?" Lucas asked, unable to hide his excitement.

"I can't believe you get to work with Frank Tench."

"You can, too, if you get your butt on a plane, train, or automobile."

"I have a few days left still, so I'll call Teresa and let her know."

"So, we'll see you—?"

"Tomorrow. Pick me up from the airport."

He hung up and looked back at the map.

"Who was it?" Tanvi asked.

"Tobias Nash," Lucas said with a wink. "He's twenty-two, and he knows everything."

EIGHT

TANVI STOOD ON THE STOOP OF A MODEST HOME IN THE SUBURBS. A white, picket fence lined the backyard, and a floral wreath hung on the door. As she leaned forward to knock, a car pulled up behind her. She turned to see who it was as Lucas stepped out of the passenger seat with a bottle of wine. He thanked the rideshare driver and walked toward her. Her eyes fell from his face to his hips. The man had swagger. Too bad he was a shithead.

A half-smile tugged at his lips as he approached. "Good evening, Detective."

"I didn't realize you were invited," she admitted.

"And I didn't realize you were invited," he chuckled. "Frank's pulling out the big guns."

"A sit-down meal is the big guns?"

"For us, it was. My grandfather made a point to have us sit down to dinner every night. If something needed to be said or worked out, it happened around dinner."

She frowned. Grandfather?

The door swung open, and a beautiful redhead smiled up at them. "Welcome to our home! I'm Rachel, Frank's wife. He's in the backyard, cooking. You can't eat pork, right?" she directed the question at Tanvi.

"I try not to, but I'm not as strict about it as some of my family members. Don't put yourself out."

Her lips pinched together in a straight line. "Could you not say it like that to Frank?"

Lucas laughed.

Tanvi glared at him over her shoulder. "I really shouldn't eat it."

Rachel smiled. "Come on in."

"What's so funny?" Tanvi whispered to Lucas as they followed Rachel.

"Married people."

"What's wrong with being married?"

"Nothing," he replied, looking into her eyes. "I just thought that was funny. Why are you so uptight?"

"I'm not. You know nothing about me."

"Whatever you say, Detective."

She frowned, realizing the biting truth of his words. Maybe it was from the job or stress. She didn't know, but it felt as though she'd been holding her breath and had a knot of anxiety in her chest. It would be wonderful to laugh again—loosen up and let go. It had been so long since she'd really laughed, she wasn't even sure she knew how.

Rachel led them through the house and out a set of French-style patio doors. Frank was wearing a 'kiss the cook' apron, barbecue fork in hand, as he seasoned some thick steaks.

"Those are beautiful." Lucas stood over the grill.

"I can take those if you'd like," Rachel offered, indicating the flowers in Tanvi's hands. Tanvi handed them to Rachel, who placed them in the center of the outdoor table.

"This is a great little spot," Tanvi said, looking about the backyard. There were swing sets and a playhouse tucked into the corner. "You have kids?"

"Mine are all grown up," Rachel beamed. "Four girls. The oldest, Charlotte, is expecting her first. Our first grandbaby. Frank is beyond excited, which sort of surprised me. I wasn't sure how he'd feel about the girls having kids."

"Why wouldn't he want them to have kids?" Tanvi asked. Her dad never said he wanted grandkids like her mother, but she saw the look in his eye when Reina said she was pregnant.

"He never wanted kids. The stuff he sees day in and day out, it was just too scary."

"But he had four?"

"No, you'd think. The way he looks after my girls, but they aren't his. They're my first husband's."

"Oh, I'm sorry."

"No need to be sorry," Rachel smiled. "But it ruined his first marriage. To Teresa, from the FBI."

"That explains a lot." Tanvi shot a glance over to Lucas, who was drooling over the steaks. "What do you know about Lucas?"

"He had a rough childhood. He has issues with authority, probably something to do with the upbringing. And he's really close to getting the boot."

"Why?"

"He's hotheaded. Reacts without thinking, which has resulted in many lives saved, but it can also put people in danger. And he's not a team player. But, Teresa wants him to take over for her. She sees something in him."

"Teresa tell Frank all that?"

"She mentioned some of it. He put the rest together." Her emerald eyes flicked from person to person. "You are too in the job and have no life, hence, dinner."

"You sound like my mother."

"You have to have balance, or you'll burn out."

"I can't just stop caring because I'm off the clock."

"It's not that anyone stops caring," Rachel's eyes fell to Frank as she spoke, "it's that you can do more when you're on the clock if you take a break while off the clock. I can't tell you how many times he's come home, feeling defeated. Like the bad guy was going to get away with it. Rather than obsessing, he'd ask the girls if they wanted a movie night. Spend the whole time with them, watching *The Princess Bride*, or *The Three Musketeers* for the evening. Joking with them and having fun. And then, he'll wake up in the middle of the night with some revelation that breaks the case wide open. Sometimes, you need the downtime, to see the answers that are right in front of you."

Tanvi followed Rachel's gaze to Frank. He had an impressive close rate. It's why he handled more cold cases than new ones. But Tamika Jackson's face burned into her mind. The other's, too, but Tami was closer to home on a few levels. Tanvi's eyes and her mind fell back to Lucas. She knew he could make her forget. Even if just for a little while. Nevertheless, his presence still angered her. Perhaps she was resenting herself for the embarrassment at the bar, or maybe she resented him for trying to make her look foolish about the case in front of her superior.

Lucas popped open a beer and offered it to Tanvi, brows raised. His version of an olive branch? She shook her head, so he put it to his lips and took a sip. He was strange. But not the kind of strange she could just ignore. Waves of frustration and excitement swirled in her whenever he was close by. Yes, he could be infuriating, but she constantly found herself wanting to figure him out.

"These are ready, Honey," Frank announced. "You have the rest?"

"Oh!" Rachel ran inside without another word.

"Have a seat, you two," Frank said, placing the platter on the table. He put a large steak on Tanvi's plate.

"There's no way I can eat all that," she admitted awkwardly.

"Cut off what you like, and then put it back on the platter," Frank smiled. "Rachel eats about half of one of these."

"Just put it right on my plate," Rachel smiled as she placed a steaming pile of corn on the cob on the table. "We also have potato salad if anyone wants it."

"I want it," all three said at once. She smiled and headed back in. A few moments later, she emerged with a bowl and spoon.

"How do you like Indianapolis, Lucas?" Rachel asked after the initial silence of everyone digging into their food.

"So far, I've mostly seen the inside of the police stations, but my first night out was very--" he eyed Tanvi— "welcoming."

"That's great," Rachel smiled as Tanvi's face flushed. As the burn spread, she imagined herself throwing the bowl of potato salad in Lucas's face. "What did you do?"

"I went to a bar, met some really friendly locals."

"So, about the case," Frank coughed. Tanvi sent him a silent 'thank you' with her eyes. And Rachel looked from her to Frank, trying to figure out what she'd missed.

"The DNA will help us get others to see the connection," Tanvi said.

"And make sure we're on the same track. We can't make mistakes in a case like this. Even one victim who doesn't belong could throw everything else, profiling wise, off base," Frank said before scooping more potato salad into his mouth.

"Speaking of," Lucas said, swallowing a chunk of steak to continue, "I don't think Carmon González should be excluded. The graffiti is weak. It barely looks like a smile, and there are so many other tags in the area. I think it's too thin."

"She fits the rest of the MO," Tanvi argued.

"Owning a chess piece doesn't make you a murder victim. So, test the DNA, sure, but leave her out until it's confirmed."

"What makes you say that?" Frank asked.

"The other smiles are clearer, and she could have just made a mistake. I still think we should rule her out officially with DNA. But with limited resources and time, maybe we need to focus on the ones that were clearly murdered."

Tanvi glared. She hated that he could be right. "We should keep her in, until DNA says otherwise."

Lucas put his fork down and looked at her. Irritation blazing. "Why are you so attached to this? If one of those women wasn't killed by our unsub, and we pin it on him, that means a killer goes free. Never having to pay for what they did. Most murders are not serial murders. There have to be other cases in this city that are just everyday, jealousy, accidents, or vengeance. If you're not careful, you're exactly the kind of cop who'd end up putting an innocent person in jail, while not even entertaining the thought the actual perp was the one who did it."

Tanvi rose from her chair, resentment boiling in her chest. "Rachel, Frank, I'd like to thank you for a lovely dinner. I need to be going now."

She left over the sounds of protests. Tears stung her eyes. There was no way she was going back into that room and letting him see he'd gotten to her. She was a good cop. She knew she was right. But if the DNA said otherwise, that would be that. She wasn't one of those cops who rejected evidence. She wasn't.

Lucas ran his tongue over the sharp edges of his teeth and sucked in a breath as he stared at the door Tanvi disappeared through. He knew there were two glaring people at the table with him and wasn't ready to deal with their shit until his steak was gone.

"I'm not saying you're wrong," Frank started. "But you have to be able to work *with* the local cops to do your job."

Lucas gave him a look and was surprised to see a knowing smile on Frank's face instead of the anger he was expecting. Rachel munched on her food with an odd expression on her face. Again, it wasn't anger.

"What should I have said?" he asked.

"In that situation, I'd just have waited for the evidence. We have reasons for including each and every case. But we don't know anything for sure until hard evidence is discovered."

"Working on a case with red herrings boiled in could cause us to excuse or zero in on the wrong people. How do we proceed in the meantime? DNA is not a fast process. Nor do you want it to be.

Rushing labs make mistakes. I'd rather arrest no one, then arrest the wrong person."

"And Tanvi needs the killing to stop," Frank said. "The victims are people she knows, seen around, or went to school with. Not all of them, but enough of them to give her an edge."

Lucas sat back. He knew he should have downed the steak before this conversation, now his stomach was revolting. "I didn't know that."

"How could you?" Frank offered. "She didn't even tell me. I figured it out while investigating."

"How you talk to people is also key," Rachel added, fork full of potato salad poised. "Cops who ignore evidence are the worst kind. Why would you accuse her of being that if you *have* no evidence? Including a case isn't ignoring evidence—it's working with what you have."

Lucas gave a heavy sigh as he considered her words. "How do you see someone eyeing a dangerous and harmful road and not say something? Tanvi is desperate. Which is exactly what you cannot be and do this job."

"You said it yourself," Frank said.

What are they talking about?

"Wait for the evidence," Rachel said, clueing him in.

"Her family has a barbecue every Saturday. Her mother invited me, but we had plans. You should go, apologize to her once she has a chance to cool off. Build a relationship as she starts down that path—the dangerous one you see her to be flirting with—then you'll be in a position to pull her off it rather than push her down it."

Shit. He was right. Being strategic in these relationships was important. He needed to know the cops in order to have effective communication. Kicking himself, he realized he knew this already from his time in the Marines. And yet, he'd seen cops as some other entity. Not his partners. He'd been so busy judging them as incompetent, he missed the point of his being here in the first place. That's what Teresa was talking about.

NINE

Tanvi's smile faded as she stepped out the back door for their weekly Saturday barbecue. The assembly in her backyard was not what she expected. She'd thought to find Kenyan-Indian aunties and uncles and the one Jewish cousin and aunt who lived close enough to attend. They were all there. Well, most of them, anyway. Her father's sister was absent, but that wasn't what worried her. The slew of handsome, single men in their mid-to-late thirties was disturbing. She placed the bowl of pasta salad on the picnic table, kissed her father on the cheek, and stomped back inside.

"Mama?" she said, hands on her hips as she stopped in the doorway to the kitchen.

"What?" Cora asked, large, brown eyes blinking innocently.

"You know *what*."

"They had no plans. Why shouldn't they come spend the day with my beautiful, unwed daughters?"

"Daughters or daughter?"

"Well, I had hoped that crime scene guy would go for you, but look!" She pointed with her potato salad-covered spoon through the window. Adina and John were chatting under their apple tree. "He and Adina seem to be having quite the time."

"Mama," she said, getting the older woman's attention.

"You need to let us lead our own lives. Reina got married and is pumping out grandchildren just as fast as she can, so you'll leave the rest of us alone."

"She's married and is living a fulfilling life—because she listened to me," she put the spoon back in her salad. "Take this to the table, try to talk to some of them. You see him?" she pointed to a tall, handsome man who was speaking to her father. "He's a Jamaican immigrant, excellent work ethic, and he's so funny." She started to laugh, clearly remembering something he'd said before.

Tanvi shook her head as she took the bowl. She walked back outside and placed it on the table. Approaching her father, who, to her mother's credit, was laughing with the would-be suitor.

"Did you know about this?" she challenged as they sobered.

"What?" her father asked.

She gestured to the man he was talking to.

"Oh, I'm only here for the food," he declared, offering her his hand. "I'm Jamil."

"Nice of you to lie for my mother," she said sardonically. "Be honest, I'm a detective, and I'll know if you're lying. Did she show you my photo or all of our photos?"

"It was a group photo," he admitted. "But she pointed you out." He bit back a laugh.

"What did she say?"

"You needed humor in your life. You're too serious. Which is why I'm here for the food."

He and her father started to snicker.

Glaring she made her way to the picnic table and plopped down next to Yasmin, whose nose was stuck in the midst of *Pride and Prejudice*. Tanvi crossed her arms over her chest as she watched Jamil and her father, now laughing so hard they were doubled over.

"What's so important about laughing?"

"It's a bonding experience," Yasmin said without looking up.

"There are other ways to bond."

"But laughing is fun, and therefore more memorable and effective."

Tanvi glared until she put the book down.

"You laugh together—it's like you're not alone. You get each other."

Confusion and frustration filled Tanvi. She always felt alone with Henry. They'd laughed in the beginning, she supposed. Before he got too busy with being a doctor and her with being a cop and studying for the detective exams.

"Have you even started *Pride and Prejudice*?"

Tanvi's lips thinned. "I may have read the opening scene with Mr. Bennet teasing Mrs. Bennet's 'poor nerves.'"

"Lizzy and Mr. Darcy have much to teach you, my sister," she replied, staring pointedly at Tanvi.

"Fine, I'll watch the movie tonight."

"Seriously?" Yasmin gaped. "You'll start reading the book tonight."

"Fine," she hissed. Sliding back off the picnic table bench, she went to find Adina, who appeared to be fawning over John. Barely holding back an eye roll, she sat next to Adina and glared at John. "How did my mother get to you?"

"She stopped by the precinct, saw us talking, and then invited me," he answered as his face paled.

"What exactly did she say?"

"Well—"

"You stop harassing my guests," Cora yelled from the kitchen window.

Adina looked at her. Concern creased her brow. Great, now she probably thought Tanvi was interested in John.

"If you hurt my sister, I'll kill you," she said as she stood. "And you won't be here to find the body."

He chuckled as she left to go back to her father. Jamil had promise, even if her mother had roped him into coming.

LUCAS STOOD OUTSIDE THE HOUSE, FEELING LIKE AN IDIOT. FRANK told him to apologize. *Working with the locals was as important as catching the killer. You can't catch the killer if they kick you off the case.* Frank's words buzzed in his mind. He was right, but Lucas wasn't the only one who'd said things to regret. At least, he hoped she regretted them. He had to get this right. It was why he was here.

"Aren't you going to knock?" Nash's voice startled him out of his spiral.

"Give me a second," he barked over his shoulder at the younger agent. As soon as he heard the words 'Barbecue' he'd decided he wanted to hang out with Lucas rather than go to the hotel.

"I'm starving," he bit back, eyes burning in defiance. For a scrawny twig of a guy, he wasn't afraid to piss people off.

The door flew open, and a small, dark-skinned woman squinted up at him. Suspicion clear on her face. "You selling something?"

"No, ma'am," Lucas said as she walked around him. He could feel her eyes examining him. He covered his package by clasping his hands in front of him.

"Gay?"

"No," Nash snapped, stepping forward.

"Not since college," Lucas joked, but when she stopped to stare him down, he cleared his throat. "No, ma'am. Sorry, it's Marine Corps humor."

"Single? Marine?" Her eyes lit up.

"Yes?" he drew out the word, unsure where this was going.

"Perfect, you'll marry one of my daughters. Come quickly." She grabbed his arm and pulled him through the house. "I got a lot of suitors today. If you want a chance, you better get in there."

"Um, can I come in?" Nash asked. She stopped to look at him over her shoulder.

"What do you do?"

"I have a few degrees, and I'm an FBI agent."

"Sure, you can marry one of them, too. I have three. Three unwed daughters to choose from. One is underage though. So don't pick her."

"I'm actually here to speak with Tanvi," Lucas said as they made their way through the house.

"Good, she needs more suitors than the others. She needs some fire in her life, passion. You look passionate. And feel these muscles. Even if she hates you, she'll love you. Perfect!"

"I think there's been a misunderstanding—" His voice caught in his throat as he saw Tanvi standing by the grill. She wore an off-the-shoulder top that showed off her midriff with a skirt that hugged her hips before flowing around her bare feet, her once straight, brown hair hung in tight ringlets. Her face lit up at something the man next to her said, and she laughed. It was the most heavenly sound. A pang of jealousy shot through him. Why couldn't he make her laugh?

He shook his head. He was an asshole, that's why. He looked back to her. A vision of serenity. Not like when they were working the case, and she was filled with uncertainty. That was, until her eyes fell on him. Her smile faded, and a tick worked in her jaw. She stepped around the grill, her white skirt flowing with the swing of her hips as she moved. His heart fell at the change. He really was an asshole. He didn't think he knew how to be anything else.

"What are you doing here?" she asked, crossing her arms, effectively pushing her breasts up. His gaze got stuck for a moment, and she quickly adjusted her stance. Hands on her hips, she waited.

"Your mother invited me," he lied after a minute. "Apparently, you need as many suitors as you can get. And the way you blush--" he sucked air in through his teeth. "I couldn't resist."

Hurt shot across her face, and he hated himself for it.

"Look, I'm sorry. I came here to apologize," he tried again, taking a step toward her. "Can we talk somewhere?"

She stared at him for a long time. Just when he thought she was going to tell him where he could shove his apology, she motioned at the house and led him to her bedroom.

The room was bright, with yellow walls and white window sills and baseboards. Her bedspread had sunflowers on it, and he tried to remember how she looked in the backyard before she'd seen him.

"What did you want to say? I need to get back, or my mother will have a conniption."

"I'm sorry about what I said yesterday," he ran his tongue over his teeth, looking about the room before meeting her angry eyes.

"Oh, you're sorry for treating me like a rookie? Like some bimbo at the bar who's not allowed to have a professional opinion?"

"Look, just let me say—"

"Who do you think you are? Coming in here and acting like—"

"Tanvi, please. Let me get this out." She crossed her arms and pushed out one hip. "I was put on the spot and I lashed out. I'm sorry. Usually, I'm the authority, but Frank is evaluating me. It threw me off, and I shouldn't have taken it out on you. And at dinner--I wasn't trying to say you are a bad cop, I was trying to say —it doesn't matter. You know not to ignore evidence, and I should have just stopped talking."

She looked at the floor, her lips slightly parted, and he had the strangest urge to kiss her. Taken aback. He didn't know what to make of her.

"I'm sorry, too," she said, looking up. "I shouldn't have assumed I knew anything about you when we just met. I was also thrown off. I thought you were going to listen to what I had to say before making a judgment. I realized that's my fault too. I came on to you in the bar."

"No, I should have listened," he admitted. "But I'm an asshole. And the longer I'm here, the more you'll see how true that is."

She shook her head and smiled, making his heart soar. "Quite the apology."

"The best an asshole can do," he said, half of his mouth turning up. She gave him a shy smile as she looked him over. "So, what do you say we go eat something?"

"I suppose," she said with a mischievous smile. "You did weasel an invitation out of my mother."

"I think the criteria was being single and straight."

"Huh, she must have lowered the bar," she jested.

Lucas laughed, but when she joined in, it made everything up to this point worth it. What the hell was wrong with him? He followed her back to the party.

"Come on," she said, heading toward the grill. "You already met my mom, but this is my dad, David."

Lucas offered his hand. David took it, looking at his daughter.

"Daddy," she said, placing her hands and chin on his shoulder. "This is the FBI agent, Lucas."

David's eyes narrowed. "Ah, the one who thinks you're a bad cop?"

Lucas gave a nervous laugh as David released his hand.

"Oh, no, Daddy," she said with a smile. "He apologized for that."

"Good." David's demeanor shifted instantly, and Lucas felt air rush into his lungs. "Luke, tell me, are you a religious man?"

"I was raised Catholic but I can't say that I'm religious," he admitted.

"That's too bad," he said, flipping the burgers and chicken thighs on the grill. "I'd really like my Tanvi to end up with a nice, Jewish boy."

"Who does Tanvi want to end up with?" Lucas asked, accepting the beer she offered him. Her eyes flashed to his.

"Dad, are you kidding me?" Before he could respond, she slipped her arm through his and directed him towards a new group of people, one of whom was Nash. He felt relief at the sight of a familiar face. Which was saying something about the company, since Nash would probably sell him down the river the first chance he got. Not that he didn't deserve it. "I'm sorry."

"Why are they all so obsessed with you getting married?" he asked.

"For them, there's nothing better than marriage. They want me to experience it. But--"

He paused before they reached the group and raised a brow at her. This was okay. He could just be. Here, with her. Until he had to leave. That was okay. "But?"

"But if you get it wrong, it can be the very worst life has to offer."

He gave her a knowing nod as he eyed the people at the party. He could be nice. He could make her laugh. What was it about her that made him want to? "Well, if you want, I can hang 'til everyone leaves. Keep your parents happy, and--"

She cocked her head to the side. "Agent McGinn," she said, a hand on her chest for dramatic effect. "Are you actually trying to help someone else?"

"I always help other people," he said before taking a sip of beer. "I'm just not usually so open about it."

"Well, I do declare!" Reina said as she and her sisters approached. "If it isn't a nice, northern gentleman!"

"This is Reina," Tanvi said as if her sister wasn't speaking in a fake southern accent.

"Yeah, we met the other night." Lucas said with a nod.

Tanvi frowned. "What?"

"After you bailed," Adina said. "He met everyone except--"

"Me," Yasmin said, looking down her nose at him. "I refuse to be on the side of someone until you expressly wish it."

"Well," Tanvi said, glaring at Adina and Reina. "At least I have one loyal sister."

"Once you see him naked, we can revisit this conversation," Adina said with a smirk.

"I'm right here," Lucas laughed. Adina winked at him, and he decided to hide in his beer.

"Well, this is Yasmin," she said. "The baby, she's still in high school."

"One more year, then I'm off to college, where I will study anything and everything until I find something I'm equal parts talented in and enjoy."

"That's one way to do it," he said, rocking back on his heels.

"I know it's expensive. I'm going to a state school on a work study program."

"Have it all figured out then," he said.

"Yes."

"What if the thing you like and are good at is, say, being an electrician? Or working on cars?"

Her jaw dropped. "I can't do various trade schools."

"You could just intern," he offered. "Or go to Job Corps."

She walked away, toward the grill, eyes wide.

"Your dad is going to hate me," Lucas said as he watched him greet his daughter with a scowl.

Tanvi nudged him with an elbow. "It almost sounded like you cared what he thinks about you."

"Your mom is cool," he said, turning back to the group. "I'd hate to have to choose between her and, you know, living."

"He won't kill you," Adina said.

"No," Tanvi agreed.

"He'll do worse," Reina nodded.

Lucas's brow furrowed. "What will he do?"

"Hope you never find out."

He couldn't help a boyish grin from pulling itself across his face. He liked playful Tanvi.

LATE IN THE AFTERNOON, THE LAST GUESTS WERE LEAVING, AND LUCAS stayed behind to help clean up. Something about this place reminded him of his childhood. Before his father died. He'd forgotten what it felt like to just be himself. To laugh and be laughed at. To be completely comfortable with the people around him. Nash headed out shortly after meeting Adina. He'd been in a rush, so Lucas would have to sort that out later. But for now, he was enjoying the family vibes this place was giving.

"You have a talent, Cora," he said as he placed the now empty salad bowls in the sink for her.

She smiled at him, "You like the salad?"

"I did," he smiled. "But I meant you attract good people."

Her smile grew into a toothy grin. "Well, thank you, I made most of them, you know."

He laughed. "I noticed. You made the best ones."

"I like you."

Something shifted in his chest. Something he couldn't place.

"Luke?"

He turned to see Tanvi leaning into the room. She was biting her lower lip, and there was a mischievous look in her eye. She summoned him with one finger. He followed her to her room.

"What's up?" he asked as she closed the door.

"You were so amazing today," she leaned against the door, one leg bent, foot on the door.

"I'm glad you were able to have fun."

Her gaze slid over him slowly. His heart raced at the visual caress. He waited for her to move. She'd made her position clear. He wasn't making a move until she did.

Then her eyes moved behind him to her bed, and the blood drained from her face. Concern replaced the early-stage lust, and he turned to see what had her so worried.

The Post-it Note was innocuous enough, lying on her pillow with a distinct Cheshire Cat smile on it.

"Tell me you're really into Alice in Wonderland," he begged.

"Oh, shit," she reached for it, and he grabbed her arm just before she could touch it. A shockwave shot up his arm at the contact. *Shit*, he was attracted to her, but he was well aware it was a dangerous idea—the two of them. Maybe they were destined to be a cocktail of resentment and attraction, rather than a couple.

"We need to preserve it," he said, releasing her arm.

"John's still here," she said, remembering the CSI tech flirting with her sister.

"Yeah, was he one of your suitors?" he asked before he could stop himself.

"He was supposed to be, but he found Adina more agreeable."

"So, he doesn't appreciate the fight in you," Lucas teased.

"Few men do, it would seem."

A twinge of excitement stirred in his belly. Maybe she was as difficult as he was. Maybe he'd stand a chance. "Maybe you need to find yourself an asshole."

TEN

Ignoring the expression on Lucas's face, Tanvi found John sitting on the steps of their front stoop. Adina, a stair below, staring up at him with stars in her eyes.

"John," A pang of guilt shot through Tanvi for the interruption. "We need your expertise."

"Yeah, sure. Just a min—my what?"

She indicated the house with a nod, but Adina was already well aware. "What happened?"

"There's something I need John to look at. Preferably without our parents finding out, you know, until it's confirmed. And you need to wait out here."

Adina's brows knitted together in a universal, younger sibling 'it's not fair' expression. But Tanvi didn't have time to care. She led John to her bedroom, where Lucas was waiting to make sure nothing was disturbed. His arms crossed, he glared at the tiny, yellow piece of paper like it might disappear if he took his eyes off it.

John's eyes lit up. "Is that—?" He glanced around the room. "Who's bedroom is this?"

"Mine," Tanvi said, taking up a position beside Lucas.

"Shit, you just found this?"

"Yes," they answered in unison.

John turned slowly from the bed toward the pair of investigators. "What were you doing in here?"

"Talking," Tanvi said with an exasperated sigh. "Is it legit?"

"I mean, it looks it, but I'm not magic. There's actual work and protocols I need to follow. The first of which would be notifying your boss."

"Of course it is."

FOSTER AND ANOTHER CRIME SCENE TECHS ARRIVED BEFORE FRANK did. Tanvi sat in the hall, outside her bedroom, while Lucas paced back and forth in front of her. Her mother and father were sequestered in their bedroom. The conversation was not about the success of the party.

Lucas paused in his pacing as she let her head fall into her hands. She didn't know how to feel right now. Scared that a killer was in her bedroom, excited that they had a clue, angry that he was this close to her sisters.... All the emotions and worry left a pit in her stomach.

And then, there was the fact that she'd almost slept with Lucas. Again. She'd told herself she just wanted to talk, but the way he'd taken it was clear. And the benefit of lying to yourself is that deep down, you know you're lying.

Lucas knelt in front of her. She peered at him through her fingers. "Are you okay?"

She thought about it for a moment. "If I say yes, you won't believe me."

He shrugged. "Could you blame me?"

"Nope."

"What are you thinking?"

She chewed her bottom lip. "That this is an opportunity. That I'm angry he was in my house. He was way too close to my sisters."

"This is an opportunity," Frank said as he entered the other end of the hall.

"What are you two thinking?" Lucas asked, his tone full of suspicion.

"If he wants Tanvi--" Frank began.

"We have bait. Now, we just need a hook," she finished.

Lucas stood as a tick worked in his jaw. He didn't like this. Not that she blamed him. Being bait wasn't ideal, but this had to end, and the sooner, the better. She wouldn't run from an opportunity like this.

"This is a dangerous game," Lucas said to both of them before focusing in on Tanvi, "and you're playing with your life."

She looked up at him. "I'd rather it be me."

The anger on his face was unmoving as he glanced down at her. He was terrifying like that. He looked ready to kill at a moment's notice. Still, after a sigh, he nodded to her. "For the record, I don't like this. We don't know enough about this guy. We're flying blind, and you two want to dangle bait in front of him?"

"I've been digging up more cases," Frank said. "Unfortunately, and fortunately, there are a lot more."

"Enough to make a profile?"

Frank nodded.

Lucas still didn't seem impressed. "What does Nash think?"

"He's still studying the pattern. He thinks he can find us a bar to set our trap."

"Of course he would."

Tanvi stood and eyed Lucas. He was acting very strange.

"I'm going to go discuss it with Foster," Frank said before entering her room.

"What are you thinking?" she asked.

He met her eyes, and there was a strange emotion on his face. "I don't like putting people at risk."

"I don't like it either," she said, stepping closer to speak quietly, "but we have an opportunity to catch this guy. I have my training. I can do this. I can catch him."

"And if you can't, Rookie?" her pain was reflected in his gaze before he looked away from her.

"Then you'll have to rescue me, asshole."

A smile broke the seriousness of his features, but there was still something in his eyes she couldn't quite place. Fear?

LUCAS SAT IN THE KITCHEN AS THE CRIME SCENE TECHS AND investigators spoke to the rest of the family. He was fuming. Everyone was acting like a kid on Christmas instead of seeing the danger Tanvi was in. He couldn't understand it. It pissed him off.

Tanvi entered the room, eyes on her hands as she messed with her nails. A nervous habit.

She stepped forward, her shirt rising up to show the edges of a tattoo on her side, just above her hip. He focused on it. Wondering what that little black mark could be, kept his vision clear. "I know you're worried about me. But you have to know, you have to understand. I'd rather it be me."

Her brown eyes burned into him with their sincerity. The rage inside Lucas simmering just below the surface bubbled up. He swallowed it back down.

She waited, but when he didn't speak, she started again. "If it's me, we have a better shot at preventing him from taking another girl or worse."

"What's worse?" he bit out.

"Him taking another girl and us not knowing about it until we find a body."

"We can get the press on it. Then everyone in this city will be looking for him, too. Get the sketch out. I've never seen a better sketch."

"Or we could use what we have," she said, standing up straight. "We use me as bait and end this now. Before he knows that we have a sketch. He's taken seven that we know of. I can't have another dead, young woman on my conscience."

"Then you're in the wrong profession." He stood over her again. "You're going to get yourself and others killed."

"I'm not stupid, Lucas. I know the risks, I just think it's worth it. I'm not putting myself in danger for no reason. Let's use this to our advantage." she placed her hands on his, her eyes begging him to just go along with her.

"Sure, as long as the person who dies is you, right?" his anger was winning. He needed to stop talking. She yanked her hands from his and stepped back. He followed her getting in close. "As long as the rest of us get to shoulder the guilt, it's worth it."

He expected her shrink up, run away. Instead she stepped in closer to him, smiling like she'd figured out a secret. "You'd rather it was you. I guess we have something in common after all."

Rage overflowed his control. "I'm nothing like you, Rookie."

ELEVEN

Tanvi sat in the back of the room as Lucas and Frank addressed the rest of the detectives. Tobias Nash stood behind them, leaning against the wall. He looked like a kid in a white button-down with a gun.

She observed the detectives around her. Each one more haggard than the last. Her gaze landed on Lucas, his lean hips and broad shoulders sucking her in. She crossed her arms over her chest in an attempt to separate herself from him. He was infuriating, and instead of that helping her get over this weird attraction, it seemed to make it stronger. She didn't want to make love to him. She wanted to fuck his brains out. Maybe some spanking could be involved.

"Thank you all, for joining us," Frank began. Lucas was leaning against the wall, looking angrier than usual behind the more seasoned detective. "Some of you know me. I'm Frank Tench. I was in the FBI for years, studying serial killers. Which is why I took Detective Nightingale's beliefs seriously from the beginning." A few snickers rippled throughout the room, and Tanvi had to focus on unclenching her jaw. "It's a good thing, too. Nightingale picked up on something that escaped the rest of us. This is SSA

McGinn and SSA Nash. They are our FBI contacts and will be helping us with the profile and apprehension of this unsub."

Eyeing Nash, she suddenly realized just how thin and pale he really was. He looked like he belonged in a library, not planning an operation that so many lives depended on.

"How old you think that Nash guy is?" the man sitting next to her leaned in and whispered into her ear. "Ten?"

She chuckled. "I don't know," she joked. "He's got to be at least--sixteen?"

Lucas stepped forward, scolding her with his eyes. She swallowed hard. Her mind flashed images of what was under that suit, and it was more than she could handle right now. Maybe it was the possibility of her death, or maybe it was that she'd let her guard down at the barbecue. She wasn't sure, but something in her had shifted toward him. She wanted his approval. And his anger over her decision pissed her off. It was *her* decision.

"Before we get started, let's address the elephant in the room," Lucas said. He gestured to Nash. "Nash is twenty-two, and he has multiple degrees in criminology, abnormal psychology, engineering, and more. Rather than arguing about how a kid can know so much, let alone anything about what you do, just listen to him. It'll save us all a lot of time."

The detective whispered to her, "He's one of the kids who is so smart he's awkward as shit."

Tanvi had never met anyone like that before. She knew people who were smart but never multiple degrees by twenty-two smart.

"Now that's out of the way. Our unsub is a male, mid-to-late forties, he'll have a hard time holding down a job, and will blame others for his problems. He's most likely single, though we are entertaining the idea that these acts are being completed by a pair. If that's the case, there will be a dominant and a submissive partner. They'll always be together. The dominant one won't trust the submissive, but he also gets off on ordering him around. The victims were all raped, held for days. Some were raped before they were killed, while others were raped postmortem."

"You think he's Black or Hispanic?" one of the detectives towards the back asked.

"Most likely, but I wouldn't rule anyone out based on melanin alone," Lucas answered.

"Why not?"

"Because in recent years, several serial killers have been caught killing people of a race other than their own," Nash said, stepping forward. "This is either a new development or we missed killers in the past because of this assumption. That's more likely the case."

"All profiles are to be used as a guide, to take a closer look at someone, and to get through others faster," Frank added. "Use it as a guide, not fact."

Tanvi sat up. "If we come in contact with the dominant partner," she asked. "How should we proceed?"

"You would go about it differently than the rest of the people in this room," Lucas said, his green eyes locking with hers. "As a woman in a position of authority, you may have a unique opportunity to rile him or get him to slip up. With the submissive, you may be able to feign relatability."

"What about the rest of us?" the man to her left asked.

"You need to read the situation. He's not going to believe you're submissive, so you need to get him on your side."

"Are there tells for us to see which is which?" Tanvi asked.

"Let's focus on what we know for sure," Frank interrupted. "We're comparing DNA found on three of the bodies. That will tell us if we're looking at one perp or more."

"What if they aren't working together?" Tanvi asked. "What if it's like LISK, with two different serial killers? One noticed the other and decided to—play."

"Nothing is impossible at this point," Frank said, pacing the front of the room, hands in his pockets. "But LISK is still an unknown. Focus on proven theories."

"What do we know?" the man to her left asked.

"He's after Detective Nightingale," Lucas said.

They frowned as she stood. "This weekend, he entered my

home during a party and left his calling card on my pillow." She held up the Post-it in an evidence bag for everyone to see.

"Is the fact that not all of them have those a further indication that it could be more than one person?"

"Yes," all three said in unison.

"But we'll know more soon."

"How?"

"I'm going to be bait."

"The FBI approves of this?" the man she'd been sitting next to said.

"No," Lucas said, staring at Tanvi rather than the man he was responding to. "We do not and have condemned the idea, but we're just here to aid in the investigation. I can't stop you."

"I've gone over the plan and feel Detective Nightingale will be perfectly safe," Foster added from his place by the door. "If you'd like to volunteer to help, see me."

"I also think this is the best bet for catching this guy and ending this now," Nash piped up. Lucas turned on him, and, to his credit, he didn't back down. "It's risky, but we can take precautions."

"That's all we have, Chief Foster," Frank said. "At this point."

WHILE FOSTER TOOK VOLUNTEERS FOR THE STING, TANVI MOVED TO stand next to Frank.

"Do you think I'll be perfectly safe?"

"Nothing is 'perfectly safe.' We don't know a lot about this guy yet, Tanvi," Frank said honestly. "It's a risk."

"A stupid risk," Lucas said, pushing himself off the wall and sauntering over to them.

"I can handle myself. Even if everything else goes wrong, I know *I* can do this."

"If he's following you and ready to take you tonight." Lucas said. "He knows we had to have found his token. I don't think he's even looking at you now. He wanted to take you at the party or scare you. Neither of those guarantees an abduction. In fact, if he does want to take you, he probably wants to scare the shit out of you first."

"So, I'll act scared," she replied between her teeth. He'd gotten closer to her, so close they were almost touching now.

"Break it up, guys," Frank scolded, putting a hand on each of their shoulders and forcing each to take a step back. "You're scaring the kids."

Tanvi glanced over to see the other detectives, who were still in the room watching them.

"Besides," Nash added, putting his files in his bag, "what choice do you have? We have no DNA, no idea how he's choosing victims, and a sketch that may or may not even be relevant to the case."

Lucas shot him a glare.

"You asked me here for my help," Nash snapped back. "I found you the most likely places for an abduction to take place, and I'm being honest about what I think is the best move right now. You can glare at me all you want. Those things won't change."

Lucas left the room, and Tanvi let out a breath she didn't know she'd been holding.

"He's like that when people are put at risk," Nash said. "Don't worry about it. Once we have our guy and you're safe, he'll be his normal pain-in the ass self again. Pranks, drinks, and laughs."

She offered Nash a smile and placed her hand on his forearm. "Thanks, Nash."

TANVI LEFT THE STATION TO SEE LUCAS—FACE TURNED UP TOWARD THE sun, eyes closed like he was hoping answers would come from the sky, from a higher power. Or maybe he was trying to soak up some rays. "Will you just get on board with this?" she said.

His eyes opened, and he looked at her.

A chill shot down her spine. "I'd feel better if I knew you were on board."

"I don't want you to feel better."

"Look, I have to do this either way. It would be nice if I knew you had my back."

"I have your back, Rookie." he answered.

"Why are you being like this?"

"You already know the answer to that."

"Luke--"

"What?" he pushed himself off the wall to stand in front of her. "You want me to say everything will be fine, like Foster? I won't lie to you. This is a stupid risk."

"Come on," she yelled. "I have no choice. You heard Nash and Frank."

He nodded. "You know what they aren't saying?"

She waited.

"You can't save anyone if you're dead."

"If I was a man, what would you say to me?" she asked.

He stepped in closer, holding eye contact as he spoke slowly, as if she couldn't understand him otherwise. His nearness sending shivers all over her body. "The same, damn thing."

TWELVE

Once again, Lucas found himself outside the Nightingales' door. And once again, he felt like an idiot thanks to Frank and all his wisdom. This time, he'd simply pointed out that Tanvi needed to be able to trust the people around her to make it through this. And of course, he was right.

David answered the door.

He looked less than pleased to see Lucas darkening his doorstep.

Lucas offered a smile, "Mr. Nightingale."

"Mr. McGinn," he said, reciprocating with a forced smile. "I suppose I have to let you in, but if I may say something."

Lucas gave a heavy sigh. "Shoot."

"If you're going to send my daughter into a tailspin tirade, remember, you're not the one who has to listen to it all night after working hard in a law office all day—*I am.*"

"Of course, sir," he said. "But I can't promise it won't happen again. She brings out the asshole in me."

"Well, try," he barked before walking away from the door. But he left it open, so Lucas took it as an invitation.

"And then, do you know what he said?"

"Yes," Adina was saying from her place on the couch. "You've told all of us multiple times. So, yes. We know. Just let it—wait, he's here."

Lucas gave a small wave as he leaned against the doorway. Tanvi whipped around to glare at him.

"Who keeps letting you in here?" Tanvi asked. She stood next to him, leaning to see who'd let him in, but her father was already safely tucked away in his study. She moved forward, and her breasts nearly brushed his arm. He took a deep breath and tried to focus on baseball until she took a step back. "What do you want?"

"To apologize."

"You know, if you stop being a jackass, you won't have to apologize so much."

"Better a jackass than a dumbass."

"Are you done?"

"Are we good?"

"No," she scoffed.

"Then I'm not done."

"Holding my family and me hostage is not going to get you into my good graces," she stated, nostrils flaring. Lips pursed.

He glanced around the house as he heard cursing coming from the kitchen. He held a finger up. "Hold that thought."

He moved into the small kitchen to see her mother on the floor with bleach and a mop bucket. She was pulling everything out of a lower cupboard.

"What's going on?" he asked. She looked at him for a moment.

"You can't marry my daughter. You blew it."

"Thanks," he chuckled, kneeling down beside her. "But that's not what I meant."

"I have rodent. It won't go in the trap. I've caught mice before, but this is different."

He leaned in to see the critter scat. "Oh, that's a rat."

"A rat?" she gaped. "How? We're not dirty. Rats are dirty."

"Yeah, they are, but they don't require a dirty place to move in. They'll get into anything. If they're working on the sewers, it can cause a mass exodus, which can result in them moving into your home. Or if a neighbor has an infestation. Happened to my mom. But of course, she's not a great housekeeper, so—"

"How'd she get rid of it?"

"I did," he said. "You have a trail cam?"

"A what?"

"For hunting, a trail cam? It takes photos or videos of the animals while you're not there, so you can see their habits or if they're in the area at all."

"We don't hunt."

"Well, it makes it easier, but it's not necessary. You'll need a bigger trap, though, and you need to leave it somewhere you know he's going. This cabinet could work and not set it. While he's getting used to it, start testing out food. What's his favorite? Once you know. Use that to bait him into the trap."

"This sounds complicated."

"More complicated than a mouse, but it's worth it. They carry diseases, and besides, they make one hell of a mess."

"I know. I have to clean up behind my trash can every morning."

"Exactly," he said. "Notice anything particular in the pile?"

"It cleaned off the chicken bones."

"What are you doing?" Tanvi asked from the doorway.

"What you're too busy complaining to do," Cora said as she struggled to stand. He offered her a hand up, and she took it. "Helping your mother. I don't care if he makes you happy anymore, he makes *me* happy. One of you is marrying him."

"Before you marry one of your daughters to me, you should know I live in Virginia."

"You can move."

He laughed. Tanvi glared.

TANVI SAT DOWN IN THE LIVING ROOM WITH A LARGE WINE GLASS. SHE handed Lucas a beer, which he opened without comment and downed about half of.

"So, why are you here?"

He eyed the bottle in his hands rather than looking at her. "Frank made a pretty good point."

When he didn't continue, she prompted him. "And that was?"

"You have to trust the people around you tomorrow if you intend to get through this. And how likely are you to trust me after the way I've been today?"

She sipped her wine as she considered it. Although she couldn't say the words, today had actually made her trust him more. It was clear from his actions and protests he cared about her. Not that she'd given herself leave to think about it before, just now. "Why'd you say all that stuff? No bullshit."

He picked at the label on his beer. "I work really hard to keep the people around me safe. I can't handle one of the cops or agents I work with being hurt. It sends me right over the edge."

She watched him. There was more to it than that, but at least he was being honest.

"You've lost a lot of people in your life?"

"You lose one, and it's enough," he chuckled.

"What?"

"Nothing." That was it. Whatever had him being open with her was gone, and he'd closed himself back off by shifting in his chair and downing the other half of his drink. He'd built a stonewall around his soul, and she wondered if anyone could tear it down. "I wanted to go over the plan for tomorrow. Your parents agreed to this?"

"They don't know," she whispered. She slid her hand into his and led him out the front door, where they could talk without being overheard.

She stepped out after him and closed the door. He sat on the stoop and looked at her, leaning against the post. "Don't you think, if you're doing something you can't tell your parents, you shouldn't be doing it?"

"Right, because your parents always approve of your choices."

"My parents don't give a fuck about my choices or anything

else," he said so calmly she wasn't sure if he was joking or not. He started to laugh.

"What?" She sat next to him, doing her best to ignore the fact that his shirt slid up, revealing the tawny flesh she'd been dreaming about since the cookout.

"My parents aren't like yours," he said simply. "I could tell my mom I was running for president, and she'd ask how much money I'd be sending her if I got the job."

"You're kidding."

"Nope," his eyes caught hers for a moment, noticing the pity in her gaze. She looked away as anger darkened his features. "I'm not telling you this for your pity. I'm telling you so you can appreciate what you have. Those two love you. Don't hurt them like this."

"I do appreciate it. I just don't think they need to be worrying over me more than they already are. I'll be fine. You said you wouldn't let me get hurt."

"I'll be there. Nothing's going to happen to you." He said it like he was telling himself as much as he was telling her.

"That part, I already knew," she said, before taking a sip of wine.

"You know, you get awfully mad for someone who can dish it out."

"Mine are funny, yours are just mean."

"Okay, define funny versus mean?" he challenged, lightheartedly. "Bearing in mind, I'm from New England, where there is no such thing as going too far for a joke. At least where I grew up."

"It's relative." She nudged him and started giggling.

A boyish chuckle bubbled up in his chest as he spoke. "You just proved my point. Why are you laughing?"

"Don't you ever just like to argue for the sake of arguing? You can be completely ridiculous, no one gets hurt, and you can just—" she paused as she realized what Yasmin was talking about—"laugh."

THIRTEEN

Tanvi sat at the bar Nash had picked out as a likely abduction site. She sipped her margarita slowly. She liked a glass of wine or a beer now and then, but she didn't usually partake of hard liquor. Still, more than a few of the victims were out celebrating when they were abducted. They were more than likely hitting the bottle pretty hard, and she needed to keep up appearances.

"I don't see anything," she said around her little cocktail straw.

"It's early yet," Frank's voice said in her ear.

"Go dance with someone. Have some fun," Lucas offered through the same connection. "If you can have fun."

"I have fun," she snapped before biting her straw.

"You look like the place fun goes to die," he argued.

"I said I have fun," she said, eyebrows raised.

"Prove it."

"I don't give in to peer pressure."

"I think it's a good idea," Frank added.

"Dammit."

"Easiest time peer pressuring a person I've ever had," Lucas snickered.

"Meet me on the dance floor," she sighed, butterflies in her stomach.

"What?"

"I'm not grinding up on some stranger for the sake of a serial killer. He'll think he's going to get lucky or something, and then I wasted his evening. You get your butt down here, or I'm planting my ass in this chair."

"Leave your drink on a table by the dance floor, unattended," Frank interrupted.

"You think he's drugging them?" she asked.

"I think we don't know. Worst-case scenario, we catch a different predator."

She shrugged.

"You look insane," Lucas whispered, his breath on her ear making her jump. "I can tell you're having a conversation, and guess what, so can he."

"I'm sorry, I—" She turned in her seat, and her jaw dropped. He was wearing a tight, black tank that showed off his ripped shoulder, arms, and lean hips, with perfectly cut jeans and a black belt and biker boots. "I'm sorry, did someone say you were going clubbing tonight?"

"I had to blend in," he laughed. "I was at a table right over there."

"You two need to pull your heads out of your asses and do what we came here to do—please," Foster said over the line.

"No freaking fun," she hissed as she slid off her stool.

"You're looking nice and slutty this evening," Lucas said with a smile as he offered her his hand.

"Are you saying I'm sexy?" she asked with a coy smile. "The word slut is mean."

"You need to get over this fear of words you have," he said as she pulled him toward the dance floor, placing her drink and coat on an empty table. "You know you're sexy, and you know I think so."

"Do I?"

"We're all here with you two," Frank said.

"Dude," she said with a smile. "We're acting."

"Wow," a few voices said.

"This is the worst steak—" She put her finger over his lips and shook her head.

"The worst *club experience* I've ever been on."

"Shut up and dance with me, Daddy." She teased.

"Don't ever say that to me again." He begged as she twirled around him. She gave a deep laugh at his discomfort.

IT WAS A STRUGGLE TO KEEP HIS ATTENTION ON THEIR SURROUNDINGS as Tanvi moved beside and against him. Unfortunately, he was losing the battle.

The song tempo picked up, and she moved faster, swinging her head from side to side along with her hips. She put his hands on her waist, then put hers on his to help him get into the rhythm of the music. But the problem wasn't his white man dance skills. It was her. She was all-consuming. He couldn't pay attention to anything else. Not even Frank in his ear when she was touching him like this.

The music slowed as they shifted into a calmer song, and she wrapped herself around him, laying her head on his chest. Her warm, rosy scent taking over his senses. What was wrong with him? They were here to catch a killer, but all he could see was her. Feel her pressed against him. Her presence was intoxicating, and their closeness made him feel both blissful and vulnerable.

Frank's voice came through broken, and he clung to the urgency in the pieces he could hear. Pulling her close to him, his eyes scanned the crowd. She stood on her tiptoes to speak into his ear.

"My drink."

Lucas's eyes found the man at the table. He was an older man with medium brown skin, thick glasses, and a grin plastered on his face. His head was bald on top with white tufts of hair in a horseshoe going from ear to ear. He wore a white, button-up shirt despite the heat of the club. Frank was behind him as they approached.

He glanced over his shoulder. "Everyone came today, I see," he said, looking amused at the pair. "I believe you're looking for me."

"Bag the drink, print everything," Frank ordered as the lights came on, and the music was cut. Everyone moaned their opposition as the man responsible for seven deaths sat in front of her with a smug smile on his face. He looked exactly like the sketch.

"No need to check the drink. I knew you were here. I *would* have to drug one such as this, though. Wouldn't I, Frank?"

Lucas and Frank exchanged a look.

"Oh, I know all about all of you. McGinn, the hothead from Boston. Interesting that you're arresting me instead of becoming me, don't you think? Given your history." He waited for a reaction, but Lucas was careful not to give him one. His face fell as he turned to Tanvi. "And, of course, the beautiful and exotic Tanvi. I can't imagine being half Jew" he spat. Tanvi bristled. Lucas placed a hand on her lower back, and she calmed, at least outwardly. Grateful she understood what he was trying to say, he looked back to Frank.

"What's your name?" Frank barked.

"Carl Singh," he answered. "Am I under arrest? Because I should be."

LUCAS CHUCKLED AS TANVI FOUGHT TO SWALLOW HER SHOT OF tequila. Her entire body convulsed as she forced it down, shaking her head back and forth and sticking out her tongue.

He threw his shot back without incident and eyed her, one brow raised.

"I don't drink," she croaked.

"I can tell."

"I almost fucked it up, didn't I? My first time in front of a guy like that, I let him get under my skin."

"Yep," he answered with a smile as he put his beer to his lips.

"Do you have to be so mean?" she laughed.

"Don't ask me questions if you don't want to hear the answers," he said. "But listen, I was afraid he'd see me trying to signal you. The fact that all I had to do was touch your back was amazing. He didn't even see it."

He thought back to the feel of her skin under his palm and eyed her. Maybe he'd underestimated her. Her plan worked. They'd caught the bad guy, and now Tanvi was all the more alluring. But there was one issue. He looked away from her and held the cold beer against his forehead.

"What?"

"It was too easy," he said. She frowned and shook her head. "It was. He actually sat down at your table and said, 'I'm the one you want.'"

"I mean, yeah, but that does happen. He said he made us. Maybe he wanted to be caught. For the fame."

"Maybe." He didn't look up. "But I think it's something worse."

"Like what?"

"Like he's distracting us."

"From the other unsub?" she asked.

"Or whatever his grand plan is."

"Serial killers aren't really that smart," she asserted. "They all think they're Hannibal Lector, but they're really Buffalo Bill."

"Buffalo Bill killed a lot of women before Starling took him out."

"Yeah, but that's because it's fiction, and it wouldn't be a good story without the buildup. Death stakes. This is reality. It's automatically interesting because it's real. Real women, real criminal. Actual death."

"I have a bad feeling about this," he admitted. She stared at him, trying to figure him out. Usually, a feeling was just that—a feeling. But this was one of the times he needed to not only listen to it, he needed her to as well.

"What did he mean, about your history?"

"Caught that, did you?" he chuckled. "I was—a bit of a juvenile delinquent."

"I honestly can't imagine you as anything else," she teased. He loved the sound.

"Barkeep?" Frank said, weaving his way between them. "Another round."

"What? Wait," Tanvi said. "Aren't we going to talk to him tonight?"

"No, he's being processed." Frank said. "We'll talk to him tomorrow."

"What do you mean tomorrow?" she asked.

"I mean, I want him to stew in his own juices overnight before we talk to him."

"We can only hold him so long without charging him before we have to let him go. We shouldn't waste any of that time."

"Thanks, Rookie," Frank teased. "I had no idea that's how the law works."

"Lucas is a bad influence on you." She narrowed her eyes on both of them.

"Look," Frank said, turning to face her. "He wanted to get caught, he wants to talk, and he really wants to talk to you. And that's about all we know at this point. John is digging up what he can, now that we have his name. Tomorrow, we will go in refreshed and well-rested, and we will nail this bastard to the wall."

"What if he lawyers up?"

"I asked him if he wanted one. He said no," Frank said, waving his hand. "Hence the waiting. No sane person says no to a lawyer when you're connected to multiple murders."

"Even if the only connection so far is his word?" Lucas asked as the bartender put three tequila shots and three beers in front of them. Tanvi winced at the sight of all the booze.

"Even then," Frank said, throwing his shot back.

"Don't worry, Rookie." Lucas took his shot and then grabbed hers. "I got you."

"YOU DON'T HAVE TO WALK ME TO MY DOOR," LUCAS SAID A FEW hours later as he stumbled and fell into the wall. Those hotel hallways could be tricky when you were plastered. She covered her mouth and laughed. She offered him her hand. "Frank can drink."

"I thought you were Irish." She leaned back to try to heave him to his feet. He was so heavy, but somehow, they managed it.

"I am," he scoffed, falling against her. "Don't question my heritage, little lady, I was drinking all of yours so you wouldn't have to."

"I appreciate the thought, I do, but if you'd let me refuse, you would have been able to get yourself home. And Frank wouldn't have to discover the massive dent in his bank account tomorrow."

He was silent as they made their way to the room. When they reached his door, he handed her the key card and stooped over, hands on his knees. "You could have said that like way sooner."

"You're right," she chuckled. "But you were so determined to save me."

He cocked his head to the side, a strange tenderness filling his eyes. "You like when I save you?"

She shot him a quick glance. "Being a detective and a cop before, I rescue people all the time. Sometimes it's nice to be on the receiving end, and you know, for it not to be life or death." She pushed the door open and held it for him as he entered.

"You should probably shower," she said, taking several water bottles out of her bag. "And drink these before you go to bed."

She looked over at him as he flopped onto the bed. His shirt riding up, her gaze moved over the plains of his chest to the v that disappeared under his jeans. She handed him a bottle of water. "Drink."

He pushed himself up enough to comply. "Yes, mother."

"I thought your mom wouldn't care?"

He took a long drink. Which was good since he needed the fluids, but it was also clear he was avoiding the question.

"I think the worst part," he said, sitting up and resting his elbows on his knees, "is that she use to."

Tanvi sat next to him, her thigh touching his as the mattress dipped under their combined weight. "What happened?"

"She had too many kids, and my dad died." He pursed his lips and let out a long sigh. "We should talk about something else. This is really killing my buzz."

He placed a hand on her cheek, and she felt a spark shoot through her body. The sensation was wonderful and terrifying. She stood up and stepped away. "I should be going now. I'll see you in the morning."

He flopped back on the mattress. "Goodnight, Rookie."

"Don't forget to drink water." She closed the door behind her and walked briskly out to her car. What the hell was that? Attraction she could handle. Lust? Sure. But this. This was something else. Something she could not let take hold. He lived in Virginia. He loved his job. And now that they caught Carl, this was almost over. Then, he'd be gone. Gone forever.

FOURTEEN

"WHAT DO YOU MEAN, I CAN'T GO IN?" TANVI SHOUTED.

"Keep your voice down," Lucas begged, though she wasn't sure if it was for the benefit of the man sitting in interrogation or his hangover. "He wants to talk to you. You're our secret weapon. So, sit your ass down, and listen to what's being said in there, so when it's time to bust you out, you're ready."

"You have got to be kidding. This is my case, mine."

"Careful, you'll start to sound like you don't care about the victims."

"You know what I mean," she snapped. "I've been working on this for months, before I was even allowed to."

"Yeah, you're an excellent little problem solver, seer of patterns." He patted her on the head, and it took all her control not to punch him in the stomach. That control was quickly lost as her fist flew before she could stop herself.

"Do not touch me," she said into his ear. He groaned as he started breathing deep. Trying not to lose whatever he'd eaten for breakfast.

"I can't leave you guys for ten minutes," Frank said as he approached, a tray of coffees and a bag of bagels in his hand. "Would it kill either of you to be even remotely professional?"

She pulled an apple crunch bagel out of the bag and tore into it, staring at Lucas.

"We're totally professional," he said, sitting in a chair, his voice strained. "At least I am. Anyone less professional would have lost it all over this nice, white floor. Frank looked less than amused as he handed Lucas a bagel.

"Everything?" he fussed.

"I want your breath to be offensive."

Lucas held up his bagel at Tanvi. "See, and you thought being the secret weapon was a shitty job."

"Is that what this is about?" Frank asked, looking to Tanvi. "You're mad you won't be in the room?"

"Well, yes," she said, eyes wide, ready to make her case. Until Frank held his hand up.

"Do you want this guy to walk?" Frank asked.

"If he's our guy, no," she admitted, shooting a glare at Lucas. *I can follow the evidence.*

"He wants you. He's talked about nothing else. The only thing we know about this guy is he claims to be connected to all the cases *we've* connected, plus one we didn't. We're still trying to verify who he really is and how he fits in with all of this."

"What case?"

"A white girl, Susan Johnson, swiped her sister's college ID to sneak into a bar and see a band. Never seen alive again. That was eighteen months ago."

"You're kidding. White?" she frowned.

"So, as Lucas already said, please wait outside the room, listen to everything. I want your take on everything he says after we're done."

"So, I can't talk to him at all today?"

"That will depend on how the interview goes. He's already extremely agitated because we made him wait all night. If you get to go in, he's the most important person in the room. Understand?"

She nodded. She'd never interrogated someone like this before.

Only low level scum and her usual 'I'm more powerful than you' bit wouldn't work here.

Lucas and Frank entered as Tanvi watched through the one-way window, with Foster to her right. This was probably the first time since they'd met that she was happy to have him by her side.

Carl Singh sat across the table, giving her a perfect view of his expression. The fluorescent lights glinting off his thick glasses, obscuring his eyes from her view, giving him an eerie air. Tanvi couldn't have imagined him being creepier than he had the night before. The thing that set her most on edge about him was that he appeared so benign and trustworthy—like an uncle or the nice, old man in a store she'd help with his grocery bags.

"Sorry to have kept you waiting. You want to tell us why you felt you should be arrested?" Frank asked as he sat down. The man looked from him to Lucas.

"You won't let her in here, will you?" he said to Lucas. Ignoring Frank entirely.

"I don't have a say," Lucas lied. "She has other cases she's working on. I don't know if you've noticed, but this city's crime rate has been increasing over the past few weeks."

A smile spread over his lips. "You're saying *she* wants to wait. To piss me off? Or is that what *you* want, Lucas McGinn? You can handle someone when they're angry. It's the cool calculations you struggle with."

"She wants to stop innocent women from being murdered," Lucas sighed, leaning back in his chair. "If talking to you will do that, then that's where she wants to be. But Carl, you haven't given us anything that can considered proof."

"The murder is the nicest part of what happens to them." His unblinking eyes watched Tanvi, a grin spread across his face. She suddenly felt sick to her stomach. She put a hand over her mouth, and Foster shifted next to her. Despite the urge to look away, she forced herself to look at the suspect. She searched his expression, his posture—everything one could see about him. There was evil in him, for sure, by why did they all look so normal? BTK, Kemper,

Dahmer—not only did they seem normal, they were almost *too* ordinary, like they could put you to sleep just by talking. Only after they'd been apprehended and their evil deeds were made public did they look wicked.

"You want to talk about what you do to them?" Frank asked, closing the files and giving Carl his full attention.

"Sure. But so we're clear," he paused until Frank looked up to meet his gaze, "I didn't kill *these* women."

"I knew it," Foster snarled. "You brought us on a wild goose chase, and—"

"Shut up," she demanded, authority in her voice as she glared. "He's involved, just please be quiet."

"But you saw them murdered?" Frank asked.

"One or two," he smiled. "Good luck figuring out which."

"How do you know all these girls are connected if you didn't commit or witness all the crimes?" Lucas asked.

"Your girlfriend knows."

"Nightingale is not my girlfriend. You're barking up the wrong tree, pal."

"Oh, so you're gay?"

Lucas chuckled, "No."

Carl wanted to piss him off. Lucas's easy going nature would make that difficult. Tanvi smiled. She'd know.

"The way you two danced last night was positively—" he paused, lifting his gaze to the ceiling as if it would help him find the word— "pornographic."

"I thought it was pretty tame," Frank interjected. Tanvi's face scrunched as she listened. Why would he say that? To piss him off? To keep him talking. Frank was learning something from this. She wanted to learn it too.

"I know about you, too, Mr. Tench," he said, sounding self-satisfied. "You've tangled with more than a few like me. So, you think you're the big man in the room. The thing is, though, there's no one like me."

"You're not so different," Frank declared, leaning back.

"How so?"

"You get off on hurting people who can't fight back. You love talking about yourself. And you're not nearly as smart as you think you are. Besides, every serial killer I've ever met tells me the same thing. They're the only one."

A deep, throaty laugh filled the room that sent a resounding chill down Tanvi's spine. "We'll just have to see about that, Frank."

"I guess we will," he said without hesitation. "Now, are you going to help us, or should we send you back to your cell until Detective Nightingale has time for you?"

"She's outside that window," he announced. She froze. There was no way he could see her here, but she couldn't stop herself from feeling his eyes.

"No, she's not," Lucas said. "She has a lot to do since she's one of the best in this department. Hopefully, she'll be here as soon as she can."

His lips thinned.

"She's right there," he said, standing. He shuffled over to the window, chains clanking with each step. Her smile faded. "She's really something, isn't she?"

Lucas stood up and walked to the door. He opened it. "She's not here. See for yourself."

Her heart raced as she held her breath. But the man didn't move. "If you say so."

"You don't have to take my word for it," Lucas said, gesturing for him to step through the door way and see for himself. Instead, he moved back to his seat. Lucas shrugged. "Suit yourself."

"Go in," Foster said as Frank dropped a piece of paper on the floor.

"What?"

"That was the signal, so go in." He gave her a push towards the door.

She took a moment to get in the right mindset and pulled the door open. Striding inside and approaching the table, she looked at her watch. "I have ten minutes. Where are we?"

"Got a whole lot of nothin, so far." Lucas said, his eyes still on Carl.

"You're kidding." She put a hand on her hip, looking at the suspect for the first time. He was so still, watching her through his thick glasses. "I thought you said you were the one we were looking for?"

"I am."

She sat down in the last chair. "Prove it."

"I need to know Nightingale. Who *are* you?"

"I'm not interested in that shit. I wanna hear about the girls, or I'm leaving."

"Are you a Jew? Or are you—what kind of mongrel is your mother? Kenyan? Indian?

"I'm waiting."

"Why did your family change their name from *Nachtegall*? Was the original German too painful for those who escaped the death camps alive?"

"You'd have to find yourself a medium, and ask my grandparents. It never came up at the dinner table. You understand."

"Yes." He looked away from her, back to his hands. "I know who I am. But you're lost. You half-Jew."

She glanced to Frank. This was not how she thought this would go. "Don't worry about me, I'm not lost. I'm right where I'm supposed to be."

"Lost people always think that. Take Tamika Jackson." He turned to Frank, looking for a reaction. "She was lost. She was supposed to die in a ditch like the druggy whore she was. But her parents gave her a come to Jesus speech, and I'll be damned, but it worked. She was on the path to recovery and thought she'd found herself. But I could see the truth. The truth was, who she was before. *That* was who she was meant to be. And how she needed to die."

"How'd you get to her?" Tanvi asked.

"Spiked her soda, once she had a taste she couldn't stop. I

waited until she was drunk, drugged her, and put her in my car. Another young woman even helped me lift her in and thanked me for taking such good care of a woman in need." His smile was sickening. "You have to understand, it's not time yet. But you need to be brought down to normal size."

Tanvi clenched her jaw, and her heart drummed in her ears. What the hell was he talking about?

"You're feeling pretty big, aren't you? Your plan worked, you caught the bad guy. I wish I could watch you shrink when you realize how big your mistake was. Unfortunately, I'm in here, and that will inevitably transpire out there."

"What about the other girls?" Tanvi asked in an effort to redirect the conversation.

"When you find them all, I'll tell you about each one. Until then, I'll tell you about Tamika."

"Why did you put a chess piece on her?"

"Because it's part of the game. If you really want to know, you'll have to figure out who you are, Tanvi *Nachtegall*. Who are you?"

She eyed him and then looked at Frank. "I say we cut him loose."

Frank crossed his arms, a playful look on his face. "You think so?"

"He's useless. I don't think he had anything to do with the abductions or the murders."

"He may know something about them, though."

"We have zero evidence linking him to anything." She looked into Carl's eyes. "All I can see is a wannabe. A boy looking for attention—for a friend to play with. And the only thing more pathetic than a serial killer is a wannabe serial killer."

Carl's lips twisted into a horrible grin. "You're going to regret that."

"Prove it," she egged him on. "Give me one piece of evidence that says you were involved in any of these murders that I can test. Give me *something* to investigate."

"What will I get out of it?" Carl laughed. "You just offered me freedom to keep playing. What do I get if I give you evidence that will lead to my imprisonment and possibly my death?"

She studied him. What did he want? Why was he here right now? Why had he turned himself in?

"What do you want?" she asked.

"I'm disappointed in you, *Nacht*—"

"For starters," she interrupted, "you'll have my full attention."

He nodded, a haunting look in his eyes. "You'll also answer my questions," he mused. His glasses seemed to darken, hiding his eyes. He was insidious.

Frank moved, but she answered before he was able to speak. "Yes."

Carl offered her his hand. She stared at it a moment. The idea of touching him made her sick. She slid her hand into his and he tightened his around hers. Squeezing it, showing her exactly how strong he still was for an older man. She gave his hand a shake and waited for him to release her. He looked to Lucas and then Frank, waiting just long enough to make everyone uncomfortable before releasing her.

"I abducted Tamika, but you won't connect me with any carpet fibers or fibers from her clothes. No touch DNA either. I was too careful for that. What you *will* find is that she was raped twice by two separate men."

"From what I've heard, it was more than twice."

"Well," he sat back, crossing one leg over the other, "the two men are verifiable. How many times is—open to interpretation."

The door flew open. An angry, young woman with red and light-brown hair in a gray skirt and jacket stood there, looking as if she'd run in from the parking lot. "What are you doing speaking to my client?"

"He refused counsel," Frank argued.

"Oh, did I forget to mention I'd used my phone call last night?" Carl said, holding up one finger. "By the way, before you decide

I'm not worth your time, Detective *Nachtegall,* check out my house."

She looked to Frank.

"You have an apartment," Frank said, looking over the files John collected.

"Yes, and a house. Look under Carlton Lional Singh jr. You'll want to find it fast."

FIFTEEN

Leaving Carl in the room with his attorney, the three investigators headed to the observation room. Foster stood right where Tanvi'd left him. By his side now, though, were Nash and the ADA, Fiona Kincaid. She was a tiny woman with a big reputation. And based on the scowl on her face and the white knuckles she wasn't bothering to hide, she was not pleased. She tapped her four-inch heel—that only made her a measly five-five.

She didn't even look at the investigators. Instead, she turned to Foster.

"First, the DA's office learns about a serial killer in our city through a public press conference. And then, I get a front row seat to *this* shit show?"

"With the exception of the lawyer we were unaware of," Frank said, stepping forward, "this actually went pretty well. Nightingale played him beautifully. We can check on the information he gave us today and go in again—"

"Information that will likely be ruled inadmissible," she snapped.

"It wasn't a lot of information. He didn't tell us who's DNA we'd find, just simply that there were two sets," Tanvi tried. She looked to Lucas, who's jaw clenched and unclenched as he looked at anything but the tiny lawyer in front of them.

"And if the judge rules the DNA isn't admissible at all?"

"Unlikely," Frank barked. "We had the DNA in the lab before he mentioned it. The only thing you won't be able to use is that he pointed us in the direction of two unsubs."

She leveled her glare on Tanvi. "What the hell were you thinking letting a rookie take the lead in there?" she looked back to Frank "You better pray you're right."

"I don't have to," Frank said. Lucas placed a hand on his shoulder. "I've been around this shit since before you were born."

"Kincade?" Foster's calm voice penetrated the argument, drawing them all back down to earth. "Please come with me. We'll discuss it in my office."

Foster led her away, as panic swelled in Tanvi's chest. She hid it well but the feeling was threatening to take over. What the hell was she doing here? She was a rookie, she'd never talked to a serial killer let alone interrogated one. A warm heavy hand landed on her shoulder. She looked up to see Lucas eyeing her.

"You were great," Lucas said. His eyes burning with something she couldn't quiet place.

"I messed up everything. And opened myself up to a psycho."

Frank did a little bob with his head as if weighing the options. "Yeah, you did."

"I won't tell him the truth," she offered. "Police lie in interrogations all the time."

"Yeah," Lucas said, "but there's a good chance he'll know."

Frank stared at the floor. "He was sure Lucas was lying."

"And I'm pretty good," Lucas said. She eyed him, unsure how she felt about his being a good liar. And realizing he would have been lying about how he felt about her.

"Maybe not something you should be proud of," she chastised.

He gave her a cocky grin. "You afraid I'm gonna lie to you, Rookie?"

She turned back to Frank, ignoring him. "You really think we're good on the DNA?"

"Yes, I'd be shocked if that got thrown out based on a conversation that took place after it was collected."

"Maybe someone should help miss tightly-wound relax," Lucas offered.

"Ew, Luke," Tanvi snapped.

"What?" he asked innocently.

"You can't just suggest people have sex with other people they work with."

"I was talking about bowling. But now that we know where your mind is—"

"Would you just stop?" she growled.

He threw his hands up in the air. "If she does need sex, John is totally into you."

"He's with my sister."

"If you say so," Lucas said, eyeing the box of doughnuts near the coffee maker to avoid her gaze. "He's been keeping a close eye on you."

Frank shot a look from her to Lucas, which told her more about what he'd discovered than Lucas's statement had.

"I'm surprised you wouldn't volunteer." She walked up to Lucas, cocking her head to the side as she stood close enough to feel the heat from his body. "You like me, don't you?"

He took a bite of a doughnut. "I'm just observant."

"And trying to get John away from me. Someone who you don't have to worry about. He's close with my sister, *and* he's never getting into my pants. Ever. He already tried."

"You rejected him, and he went for your sister?"

"Yeah," she realized what he was getting at. "She doesn't need to know that."

He raised a brow at her.

"Back to Tanvi lying," Frank said, reeling them back in. "He's going to want to know about you."

"He already knows about me. My family history, anyway. I'm not exactly open about my grandparents and the holocaust."

"Looking at you, I'd have thought you were middle eastern," Lucas added.

"So, he did research," she mused, staring at nothing.

"Knew stuff about *my* childhood," Lucas realized out loud. "In the club, he said he was surprised I was on your side, given my history."

Tanvi looked him over. He said it like it was nothing, but she knew all too well what serial killers went through before snapping. Before they gave into the masochistic fantasies and became true monsters.

"How could he know you were even in town?" Frank asked. "We live here. With my connection to the FBI, I'm the only one he could have anticipated being on the case, but he was completely focused on you two."

"We did the press conference," she said. "We didn't speak, but we were there. A quick reverse image search would turn us up."

Frank's brow furrowed. He didn't buy it, but he didn't argue the point either.

"Look," Lucas said, drawing their attention. "Either way, this is a win. The team needs to celebrate."

"Seriously?" she challenged. "We need to work."

"We're waiting on DNA and background on Carl. Come on, we have to keep morale up."

Frank nodded, and she bristled. "Morale is important, Tanvi. These cases are never over quickly. It could be the difference between someone reaching their breaking point or being the key to unlocking this mystery."

Foster entered the room looking irritated. Nash was right behind him, looking like he also had urgent news. So much for morale boosters.

"John found the house, Fiona is getting the warrant now," Foster said.

. . .

A FEW HOURS LATER, FRANK STOOD IN FRONT OF THEM AGAIN. Everyone was tired. Coffee cups littered the work space. Nash and Tanvi were still staring at the wall of abduction sites, looking for a pattern, while Lucas tossed crumpled up pieces of paper at the trash can.

"I've been working with John and Fiona, we found the house in question. We spoke to the neighbors. Carl definitely lives there. Fiona should have the warrant soon, but we will not be going in tonight."

"Why? There could be a victim inside." Lucas argued. "He said we needed to find it fast."

"Exactly. He wants us in there. We need to take every precaution. Once we've swept for bombs and other traps, we can proceed. In the meantime, we have plenty to do. Tanvi, what did you learn?"

She eyed Lucas a moment, noting his anger before answering the question. "There were indeed fibers on Tamika's body and clothing, but when compared to those in Carl's vehicle, they were not a match. We also received confirmation on three more of the victims having received Cheshire Cat smiles prior to their abduction. He's been breaking into their houses."

"Or he was invited in," Lucas added. Tanvi met his gaze, offering him a nod.

Everyone dispersed as Tanvi marked each confirmed clue on the board. Nash stared, working the problem in his mind rather than out loud like the rest of them.

"I feel like the answer is right here, and we just aren't seeing it."

"I know," she grumbled. "You were supposed to come in here and put it into focus for us."

He cocked his head, and his brows pinched together. Then, he tipped his head farther to the side.

"I'll be damned."

"What?" she asked, following his action.

"Each abduction—" He pointed to them, grabbing the map and shifting it. "We need a new map."

"What are you seeing?" she asked, excitement radiating off of him and into her.

"These are each within a certain number of city blocks. Look." He grabbed a highlighter and outlined the different blocks. "Now, if we look at where the bodies are found—"

He continued making squares until there were three rows drawn sloppily on the map. Now, Jada, see this, and then Felicia, they're chess pieces."

Her stomach dropped, and she felt bile rise up in her throat. "That means--"

"We only have half the game."

Lucas was next to her, looking at the findings. "That means more people. More killers."

"More murder victims."

John approached her with a smile. They all turned to him as the seriousness of the case weighed them down.

"And Kincaid was just here," he said.

"The warrant?" Tanvi asked. Lucas stepped forward.

"We've got it. Frank said the teams will take a few hours to get together."

Her eyes flicked to the warrant sitting on his desk. The weight of more victims pulling her toward a decision she wouldn't normally make.

"Whatever you're thinking, it's a bad idea." John said.

"If we wait and they already have a victim, she could die." She looked from John to Lucas. He gave a slight nod of agreement.

Lucas turned to Nash. "Give us a twenty-minute head start, and then tell Frank we're stupid."

Nash nodded. "As long as you know it's stupid."

SIXTEEN

THEY EYED THE TWO-STORY HOUSE WITH NO YARD AND NEIGHBORS right on top of it, the front illuminated by their headlights as they approached.

"No way he's keeping them here," Lucas said as they stepped out of the car.

"Areal Castro kept three women and their children in a home much like this. You overestimate the good will of your fellow man."

"And you underestimate it," he said. He got a strange look in his eye as he made his way up the step to the front door. He tried the knob, and it opened. Fear shot through Tanvi's chest as they slowly leaned inside the doorway. An awful image of Lucas tripping a bomb flashed through her mind. She held her breath and placed a hand on his bicep. he paused, eyeing her hand.

"Maybe we should wait for the bomb squad," she whispered, squeezing his arm.

He looked through the door. Pulling out his phone, he turned on the flashlight and peered inside, scanning for tripwire and any weapons waiting to fall or be shot at trespassers. He took a tentative step inside, when nothing blew up, she followed, stepping where he'd stepped. The main floor looked normal enough. A living room, kitchen, dining room, and one bath.

"Upstairs or basement first?"

She thought about it. "Bedrooms are always weird. Plus, the computer may be upstairs, and that's on the warrant."

"Upstairs it is." He crept forward tactically, placing one boot slowly in front of the other. Tanvi placed her hand on his hip as she followed him, and he froze. She quickly withdrew it.

"Sorry," she said.

He took a deep breath and continued. She couldn't get a bead on this guy. One minute he's undressing her with his eyes and making comments, and now he's opposed to being touched? The stair he stepped on creaked—they both froze. When nothing happened. Lucas let out a nervous chuckle and continued. The landing at the top of the stairs was open to the front door. There was a bathroom in front of them, what looked like the master to the right, and two other rooms to the left. Lucas went right first. He made his way to the closet while Tanvi looked in the dresser.

"Ugh," he grunted from his place in the closet. A look of sadness on his face.

"What?" she asked, looking at him. He met her with a pained expression on his face. He put a shoebox on the floor. "Kiddie porn."

Her heart sank. That was not something she could handle. She'd do it for the victims if she had to, but there were people who specialized in the clues offered in those materials, so she'd leave it to them.

Finding little else, they moved to the next room, directly across from the master on the other side of the bathroom. It was a simple guest room. Nothing special, so they entered the last room. Again, Lucas went first.

"Jesus, Mary, and Joseph," he said as he stopped in the doorway.

"What now?" she asked, trying to peer over his shoulder. She wasn't tall enough. She shoved at him but his larger frame wouldn't budge. So, she squirmed through the doorway under his arm. As soon as she was in, she glared at him. His eyes were still wide as he took in the room. She followed his gaze to the shelves and posters. It was wall-to-wall *Alice in Wonderland*. The books, movie posters, dolls. One of the posters was even just the Cheshire cat smile and his stripes as he left a confused Alice behind. A hookah sat on the small table in the corner by a recliner.

"Holy—"

"Yeah—" Lucas added for her. He swallowed hard, his face a mask of disgust. "The girls in the photos were prepubescent blondes."

"Then why is he taking late teen, early twenties women of color?"

"The other people involved must prefer older women. But—"

"But what?"

"They might not know about this," Lucas said. "Even among criminals, children are off limits. It's why so many pedophiles die in prison. If word of a pedo spreads, someone takes 'em out."

"What if it was a lie?" she asked.

"It happens. You cross someone in there, and the next thing you know, you're labeled and waiting to die."

"Criminals are weird," she said, looking about the room.

"Why? Because they have rules and consequences?" he asked, raising a brow at her.

"Well, they don't believe in 'innocent until proven guilty' when their own future depends on it as much as anyone else's."

"Two things. First, if you're in prison for pedophilia, you've been proven guilty." She nodded her agreement. "And second, when you grow up a criminal, dad is a criminal, uncles, mom. It's different. There's less right and wrong and more do what you have to in order to survive."

"You want to tell me what Carl was touching on in there," she asked. "With your family?"

He looked at her, and her breath caught in her throat. There was so much fear in his eyes.

"No."

"Can I ask why?"

"Because I hate when you look at me like that, and if I tell you, you'll never look at me any other way."

"If he can use it against you—"

"Did I give him that indication?"

She stayed silent. He'd been cooler than she was, but she worried that wouldn't stay the case. Instead, she just followed back out of the room.

They found the computer in the next room but couldn't find anything on it, so they'd have to send it to the lab.

Lucas pulled the basement door open, and they were assaulted by a strong chemical odor.

"Bleach," Lucas said, his emerald eyes locking with hers. They made their way down the stairs slowly, despite the lack of traps or danger thus far. A blue glow from a room in the back pulled her in.

He was right behind her as she entered. It was a large room set up for entertaining, like an in-home theater. Three monitors were set up on a table in the corner. Behind them, there was a sitting area with a couch and two armchairs around a coffee table. A projector was set up, pointing at the far wall.

She swished the computer mouse, and the screen turned on. A chat was open on the screen. The handle speaking to Carl AKA "Caterpillar" was "The Mad Hatter."

Lucas touched the projector, and the lights went out. Images of Tamika Jackson flew up onto the wall. Lucas's face was grim as she was assaulted in front of them. He closed his eyes and turned the projector off.

"He was right," he said with a heavy sigh. "This proves we can't let him go."

The computer chimed, pulling their attention back to the screen. A message from "The Mad Hatter" popped up.

MadHatter: Ready on your command

Please advise.

"He thinks we're 'The Caterpillar.' What should I say?"

"Meet at this place?" he suggested as she placed her fingers on the keys.

Caterpillar: Gather everyone.

Meet at the viewing room.

"What do you think?" she asked, stepping back so he could take a look.

"Why'd you say it like that?"

She pointed to the older communications in the chat history. "They talk weird. I don't know?" She shrugged at him, "You think it matches?"

He took a minute to look over the past messages. "Looks damn good to me."

She hit send, and they waited as the Hatter typed back.

MadHatter: What is the least important chess piece?

"Shit. He's testing me." Tanvi said.

"I just don't know. I was never a chess player," he said as the tension in the room rose steadily.

"Me either," she frowned.

TheCaterpillar: The pawn

. . .

She hit send, and suddenly, the screen went blue. Then, files were being pulled up on the screen and deleted. Lucas pulled the plug.

"Fuck," he said, looking at her. "I guess pawn was the wrong answer."

"Should have called Nash," she realized.

He nodded. "Hopefully, disconnecting it will save it."

"There's another room down here," she pointed out of the room.

He followed her lead across the basement to what looked like an illegal addition. They'd broken the cement of the foundation to add the room. Lucas went in first, using his flashlight to look around, his face grim.

"There are claw marks on the walls."

She stayed back. Fear tugged at her as she struggled not to imagine being trapped here would be like. An insidious chill ran down her spine, and she felt the hair on her body stand at attention. Taking a deep breath, she took a step inside. She was next to Lucas before he noticed what she was doing.

"Shit," was all he got out before the door to the room slammed closed, sealing them inside.

SEVENTEEN

TANVI SLAMMED HER FISTS AGAINST THE DOOR, RAGE AND PANIC fighting for control of her. "No!" She fought to put air in her lungs, but it kept getting pushed right back out.

A large, rough hand slid over her fist on the door. She turned to see Lucas in the glow of his phone's flashlight.

"We need to remain calm," he said. His tone was serious yet held a soothing edge.

Normally, she'd yell at him and do the opposite just because. But he was right.

"Do you think it's airtight?" Panic nudged rage out of the way in the fight for her top emotion.

He placed a hand on her chest. The weight helped to calm her, and she decided to ignore how close he was to her breasts. "Easy, we don't know one way or the other. So let's proceed like it is."

She was starting to hyperventilate. Her honey-colored eyes pleaded with him. "I'm claustrophobic."

"I hadn't noticed." His whispered sarcasm didn't go over her head or help keep her calm. His eyes shifted over the door, then back to her. He put his hand back on her chest, this time pushing her shirt aside for skin to skin contact. The warmth and power were grounding as she fought to breathe.

"What are you doing?"

"Just focus on slowing your breathing," he grunted as he slid his other arm around her back, pulling her into his palm. She closed her eyes, forcing her mind to focus on the feel of his hands on her. Images of Frank finding their dead bodies flashed through her mind.

"Shit!" she pushed him away as a sob broke free from her control. She knelt on the ground, pressing her hands into the cold earth. Before she could even try again, Lucas grabbed her arm, turned her to face him, and planted a kiss on her lips. Her lips parted in a gasp, and he slid his tongue inside, gently probing her mouth. His hand wrapped around her, pulling her into him as he laid her down on the cold floor. Placing his body on top of hers, she reveled in the weight of him. He nipped her lip as he explored her mouth. She slid her hands into his hair as his hand slipped down to her hip. Once her breathing had settled, he pulled back, his green eyes peering into her midnight gaze.

"Better?" he asked.

She swallowed hard. "How did you do that?"

"Distraction is the best way to stop panic." He nuzzled her neck as he spoke. "I'd be lying if I said I hadn't been thinking about this since you promised to pop me like warm champagne."

She looked away from him, her cheeks burning. But as she saw the surrounding walls, she gave a sharp intake of breath.

"Easy," he said, putting a finger under her chin and pulling her back to face him. He kissed the corner of her mouth. "Focus on me. Feel me."

She slid her hands up under his shirt and over his soft skin. As he kissed a trail along her chin and down her neck. He nipped and sucked just above her collar bone, and she shuddered as pleasure shot through her. She couldn't remember the last time she'd been touched like this. She wrapped her legs around his lean waist, pulling him closer, wanting to feel more of him.

"Easy, Rookie," he chuckled. "The idea is to keep you calm, not to get me worked up."

She whimpered, and he pulled back to look at her.

They both jumped as someone started pounding on the door.

"Guys?" Frank's voice washed over them like the first rain after a drought.

"We're in here!" they yelled.

"It was a trap. Be careful," Lucas added.

"We've swept the place."

Tanvi pulled Lucas to her, giving him a tight hug. "Thank you."

He smiled. "You're welcome."

They stood, brushing themselves off as they waited for Frank. "All right, stay back!"

A drill poked through the metal door, followed by a flame as they burned an arch until it fell into the room.

"This is why you don't go off half-cocked!" Frank chastised as he entered. "You two could have died in here."

"I can't speak for her, but I'm always fully-cocked."

Tanvi laughed, and Frank glared at them. "Did you find anything?"

Tanvi told Frank about the room with the computers, what they'd seen before the virus was activated, and what they'd found on the projector. By the time she'd finished, they were safely outside, where she could breathe easy and see the night sky.

"So, we have no evidence, no proof."

"We know Carl is leading them. And that he's incredibly careful. I think we saved the computer, but only the tech guys can say for sure. We also know Carl's deviancy points towards prepubescent girls with blonde hair and blue eyes."

Lucas and Tanvi locked eyes. "It was too easy to get in here."

"Shit." She ran her hands through her hair. "We didn't get anything he didn't want us to."

Lucas was silent as he stood with his arms crossed and one hand on his chin. "We need to look for cameras."

Tanvi whirled around. "What?"

"I bet there were cameras in that room we were trapped in. If not, other places."

"I'll get the tech guys on it."

"Shouldn't we just do it," Tanvi said, unable to hide the nervousness in her voice.

"What's the matter, Rookie?" Lucas asked with a smirk.

Frank stared at them, eyes shifting from one to the other. "What happened?"

"Nothing," she snapped.

"Nothing?" Lucas said as he placed a hand over his heart. "That hurts."

"Whatever it is, there's a good chance it will come out," Frank said. "Tell me now. If it comes out, I'll handle it, and if it doesn't, I'll take it to my grave."

"He kissed me," she spat, throwing up her hands and shooting Lucas a glare.

"She kissed me back," Lucas added playfully. "She was panicking, it was that or slap her."

She gaped at him.

"What?" Lucas asked. "I chose kissing. Doesn't that count for anything?"

"I *hate* you." she smacked his shoulder and stormed off.

"Funny, a few minutes ago, with your hands all over me, you could've fooled me!" he yelled. All work around them ceased, and all eyes fell on Lucas and Tanvi.

"You're an animal!" she shouted.

"Damn it," he said under his breath.

"You really stepped in it on that one," Frank criticized.

"I stepped in it on day one," he admitted. "And every time I try to make it better, we get in a fight, and then she hates me more."

Frank eyed him. "Try not being an asshole."

Lucas's face scrunched. "It just comes so naturally." He gave a sigh as he searched for the words. "I don't know how to be nice."

"Then stop trying to get the girl," Frank shrugged.

"I'm not trying."

"Bullshit," Frank laughed. "You've been after her since she put you in your place on your first day here."

EIGHTEEN

ANGER FLARED IN HER CHEST, KNOWING FRANK AND LUCAS WERE OFF having a good time with everyone who should be working this case. Sure, morale was important, but so was actually doing the work. Her fingers traced her lips as the memory of Lucas on top of her flew through her mind. Was she mad he was out or mad he wouldn't rather spend the evening with her? She shook her head and focused on her report. He was trouble. With a capital T, and that was one thing she didn't need right now.

"You did good today." Foster's words pulled Tanvi out of her haze as she tried to fill out her report.

"Thanks," she said after his words sunk in. She eyed her report, fear and uncertainty plain on her face.

"This guy is sick, and he's off the streets because of you. Don't worry about Kincaid. I can handle her."

"Did you get information back on Carl?"

"I went to check on how it was coming. It's not good. We have the guy in custody and are still struggling to find any information on him." His face was grim. There wasn't a lot that could shake a seasoned detective. "That's another reason for the morale booster evening. You should be out with everyone else. I heard McGinn say he was buying drinks down at Cherry Land. You deserve it."

"You aren't going to reprimand me?" she asked, nerves tingling below her skin.

"Didn't I hear Frank chew you out already?"

"Yeah, but you seem to enjoy it so."

He looked away. "Well, given your history, I'm sure you'll give me another opportunity. Now, get out there and celebrate. We have the computer in the lab, the kiddie porn to charge Carl, and the evidence that he's involved with Tamika. Today was a good day. Not perfect, but good."

She looked at her watch. "I should get home, though. My mom will worry."

"Shoot her a text and go. This is your chance." When she gave him a confused stare, he added, "To get in good with the guys. You've been an outcast since you got here. And bringing in the FBI didn't help you out at all. So, go, be one of them."

He was right. Her bed was calling to her, but getting in good with her fellow officers was a long-game move she desperately needed. "Thanks."

Noise engulfed Tanvi as she entered the bar. It was packed with cops, techs, and detectives, and exactly one FBI agent who was doling out shots like they'd actually made progress today. He saw her from across the bar, and his eyes lit up. Her heart fluttered, and she swallowed hard in hopes that the feeling would pass.

"There she is!" he said over the crowd. The surrounding group followed his gaze to her. He lifted his drink. "To Nightingale!"

They all copied the chant and downed their drinks as she scooted onto a bar stool next to Frank. It was karaoke night, and an off-key version of *Eye of the Tiger* was threatening to send her running for the hills.

"Tell me again how important this morale thing is?" she asked, slipping her jacket off. Her navy tank top much more appropriate for the temperature in the bar.

"This can sustain them for the rest of the case if we do it right. And Lucas is doing it right."

"Totally," she teased. "Put a bunch of borderline alcoholics in a bar and feed them shot after shot. That'll help."

He chuckled. "And get them to sing and dance." He waved his Blue Moon at those brave souls lined up to sing and the group on the dance floor. She couldn't help but smile as she watched. They looked happy, and it was the first time she'd seen most of them smiling.

Her gaze moved back to Lucas, his carefree happiness contagious.

"Rachel said you adopted her girls," she said, looking to Frank. "That's pretty special."

"I love those girls more than anything." The conviction in his voice something she'd heard in her own father's. She frowned, unsure if she should ask her next question. Curiosity won out.

"What happened to their father?"

"He OD'd shortly after attacking Rachel for the last time."

Her brows raised as her Spidey Sense tingled. "OD'd?"

"I have my suspicions about how he really died. But the official report says overdose. And it saved me from having to kill him, so I didn't feel the need to look into it. I suspect his brother, though."

"That's messed up."

"Abuse is rarely clean."

She nodded. "I have no personal experience."

"But you wonder. When you get called to the same house month after month, year after year, why doesn't she just leave? Why doesn't she care about herself? Can't she see how bad it is for her children? Are they safe?"

Tanvi sighed and ran a hand over her tired face.

"The manipulation and control in those relationships is so fucked up, we can't understand it. We know healthy, normal relationships. They think that jealousy means he loves them. They think it's their fault. He wouldn't hit them if they were better." He shook his head. "McGinn grew up in worse. Teresa thinks it's clouding his judgment."

Tanvi looked at the happy-go-lucky guy throwing back shots. "Define worse."

He shook his head. "I don't know the details. But have you seen his forearms?"

She frowned. "What about them? He's covered in tattoos."

"Take a closer look when you get a chance."

Tanvi's frown was impossible to shed. She glanced at Lucas. His sleeves rolled up past his elbows in the guy equivalent of a low-cut blouse. "And his judgment?" she asked, knowing she'd be in the field with this man. "What do you think about that?"

He peeled at the label on his beer. "Me?" he stuck his bottom lip out and raised both brows. Nodding his head, he contemplated the question. "I think he has an advantage. He just hasn't figured out how to use it yet."

"Is this old man bothering you?"

Tanvi turned and jumped up. "Rachel! What are you doing in a dive like this?" she laughed as the woman pulled her into a hug.

"Trying to drag this old man home!" she draped her arms over Frank's shoulders.

"I'll be ready in five," he said.

A brunette who looked like she was about to pop out a baby any second pushed her way through the crowd, three other girls in tow. Their light brown skin shining in the bar lights. At first glance, they looked nothing like their mother. After a more thorough look, though, Tanvi spotted Rachel's lips and nose.

"Dad?" the brunette said, a look of concern coming over Frank's face. "Let's go. My feet are killing me."

"You shouldn't even be out here. Where's your husband?"

"He's at home," she said, rubbing a hand over her belly. "Putting the crib together. You know as well as anyone he has no say over what I do. If I want a last hoorah with my mother, I'm taking it."

"Please," Frank scoffed. "You and your mom can go out any time. You have three sisters, a husband, and a dad who will gladly take the rugrat."

He downed his beer and stood. "All right, let's get this show on the road. See you tomorrow, T."

The family surrounded Frank, and he led them out the door. The looks they exchanged reminded her of her own family.

As they left, a warm hand landed on her bare shoulder. She jumped and turned to see Lucas, mischief in his eyes.

"Sorry, I've been calling your name," he chuckled.

"I was lost in thought," she said. "You think families—" she stopped, remembering what Frank had said about Lucas's history.

He cocked his head, waiting for her to finish the question.

"Never mind."

"What?" he asked, signaling for the bartender to bring him another beer.

"Don't you think you should slow down?" she said. "This isn't over yet."

"Right now," he said, sliding money to the bartender as he took the beer, "there is nothing we can do to move this case forward. We're waiting on DNA, and we're talking in circles with a psychopath. That means, I have—" he looked at his watch— "three more hours to have fun before I have to crash and be ready to do this all over again tomorrow. I'm going to enjoy it. I suggest you do, too. This case feels like a long one."

She looked at his beer. He slid it over to her. She smiled at him but didn't take it. "What's his game?" she asked. He shrugged and shook his head. "Carl. Why did he turn himself in? Why cut a deal with me?"

"Detective," he said in a scolding tone. He moved close to whisper in her ear. His breath sending shivers over her as she remembered how his lips felt against her skin. Dammit, why couldn't she stay mad at him. "I'm having fun. Let the case go, and have fun with me. Things will click tomorrow if you have fun tonight."

"That can't be—"

"It is true. Your subconscious is working the puzzle even when you're not actively thinking about it." He raised his beer as the opening notes of *Welcome to the Jungle* blared. "Let's have fun!"

She pursed her lips. His gaze fell to her lips, and a hunger showed in his eyes. Her own eyes widened as she realized what he was thinking about, and she felt her cheeks flush. His lips pulled into a smirk.

"You wanna dance?"

"To Karaoke?" she balked.

"Sure," he shrugged. "Why not?"

"Mostly 'cause all the songs aren't great to dance to," she offered a small smile. Did she enjoy teasing him? Yes. Did she want to have sex with him? N—yes. Was it a good idea? Definitely not.

He pouted at her. "All right, but please loosen up."

She ran her fingers through her hair. "What do you suggest?"

A smile spread over his lips. "If you want to dance to Karaoke, that leaves one option."

"Ha, no."

"Have a drink with me," he scoffed. "You think I look like the type to sing? No fucking way."

She gave him a playful grin.

"No."

"You sing one song of my choosing, and I'll have as many drinks as you think I need to have 'fun' within reason."

"Within reason. Of course." He looked at the stage as a young woman belted out *Single Ladies*. "How many are 'within reason'?"

"I'm not having more than six drinks. I like a beer after work, but I'm not a heavy drinker. In fact, six feels like a lot. Four, definitely not more than four."

"How about one shot and a few beers?" he asked.

I'm a lightweight. Maybe this is a bad move, she thought.

"Three beers."

"Unless you feel you need to stop at two," he offered.

She held out her hand.

"I get to pick the song, though," he smiled.

"No deal," she pulled her hand away.

He looked around the bar. "You take the shot before I do it, so I'll sound better."

She put her hand out again, and he slid his hand into hers. The warmth spread through her body and she barely contained a shiver. What was it about this guy?

"Don't make me regret this," he said sheepishly.

"Honestly, I'm surprised you don't *already* regret it," she laughed.

"Okay, go sign me up, I'll order your shot," he paused. "Preference?"

"Jack Daniel's," she said with a sigh. Tequila would definitely make her clothes fall off if he sang a song of her choosing. Hell, Jack might make them fall off, too. *If* he did this with any kind of confidence, but at least she'd stand a chance.

She made her way to the sign-up as the man on stage gave a fairly true rendition of *Heaven's on Fire* by Kiss. The crowd was getting into it. Singing along and having a great time. Tanvi looked over the song list, unaware of Lucas's music preference, but the crowd was enjoying Rock. She looked back at him, he was lip syncing the song. Remembering his BBQ attire. She pegged him for a rock guy, but new or old? He raised her shot and cocked his head to the side as he noticed how she was studying him.

She looked back at the list. As much as she'd like to make him sing, *Girls Just Want to Have Fun,* she was curious to see what he'd do if she gave him a song he could get into.

After signing him up, she strutted back to where he sat at the bar.

"What did you do to me?" he asked as she took the shot and threw it back.

She forced it past the lump in her throat that was vehemently opposed to hard liquor. Shaking her head back and forth before answering.

"You'll just have to wait and see."

"It's not *Girls Just Want to Have Fun* or something, is it?"

She spit out the beer she'd been using as a chaser. "Get out of my head!"

"But," he paused, handing her a napkin and giving his head a quick shake, "you didn't do it, right?"

Seeing him this insecure was a first. A smile forced its way over her lips.

As if her thoughts had been broadcast for him to hear, he stood a little taller, wiping the worry from his face and said, "Because I would have nailed that song."

"Now I wish I had. Think they'll let me change it?" She stood, looking towards the sign-up.

He placed a hand on her arm. Shaking his head. "It's against Karaoke doctrine. You do not want to upset the Karaoke gods."

"I'll admit," she said, looking from where his hand was on her arm up to his eyes, "I'm impressed. The lengths you're willing to go —what you'll do just to drink with me. You could have just not been an asshole and asked me out."

"It's less about the drinking and more about spending time with me," He shook his head as if to rid any remaining sentimentality before continuing. "Besides, I am an asshole. It's not an act. It's just me."

"You're an asshole… by nature?"

"Yes," he nodded very matter-of-factly.

His name was called to sing next, and she began clapping and gave him a whoop.

"Time to face the music," he said, throwing back a shot. She laughed as he ran up to the stage. Of course, he'd be a cocky bastard even when forced to sing in front of a room full of cops. The other women in the room took notice. She felt a strange pang shoot through her at their whispers. *What the hell was that?*

"Howdy, folks," he said, looking at the song. "I'll be performing, *Animal I have Become* by Three Days Grace this evening, which I'm a little surprised about. My lady friend and coworker over there signed me up. Half-expected something terrible. Very cool of you, Rookie. Very cool." He gave her a wink before looking at the DJ. "Whenever you're ready."

The song opened with a strong bass guitar riff that reeled in the crowd. Maybe this was a bad idea. They'd crucify him if he messed this up. Not that she needed to worry. When he opened his mouth, everyone in the bar went silent to listen. Tanvi felt her jaw hit the floor, and John came over to sit beside her as Lucas sang.

"He can't really be FBI, can he?" he asked.

She shook her head. "He's something."

"He's too much fun. I thought the FBI guys were always stuffy pencil pushers. He's been in more firefights than most in the department. I can't believe the number of times he's pulled his gun."

She pulled her eyes away from Lucas to John. "What are you saying?"

"He's saved a lot of lives. He's great on his feet. Apparently, it's the behind-the-scenes stuff he struggles with."

"He told you that?" she asked.

"No, I did some digging. It was weird he was here before the formal invite. Anyway, I'm going to get a beer."

As she followed his movements to the other end of the bar, Nash caught her eye. He looked nervous as he approached. Her gaze was drawn back to Lucas. There was something about the performance. Something she needed to figure out.

"You know when an artist can capture something no one else can?" Nash said to her. She didn't take her eyes off Lucas. What was it about the way he sang? It was primal, daring, captivating. It wasn't that he was good, particularly, which he was; it was something else. "When you can feel the pain in a painted person's eyes or when you hear someone sing a song and know they've been there."

Nash's words hit her like a tsunami. She looked at him, his gaze drifting from her back to Lucas as he broke into the chorus. Lucas's eyes were fixated on her. He closed his eyes and gave it his all as he sang the final notes of the song.

The bar erupted around them in applause.

"Thanks," he said with a laugh. "My shower curtains never really appreciated my talents." A chuckle rumbled through the room as he leaped off the stage.

"Be careful with him. He likes people to think he's a selfish bastard—which he is—but he's also been through more than his fair share." Nash lifted his drink to her before heading back to the other end of the bar. Lucas high-fived him on his way back to her.

"Ready to get drunk?" he asked, his excitement contagious.

She shook her head at him. "You tricked me, sir."

"It's called a hustle, Rook," he put his hands on the bar, on either side of her. His presence was larger than life, but rather than wanting to escape from him, she found herself wanting to escape *into* him. She could smell the beer on his breath. But what scared her was the twinkle in his eye. The way it made her feel. "Surprised you didn't see it coming."

She leaned into him, whispering in his ear, "I guess I trusted you too much. I won't make that mistake twice."

She gave him a light shove and slipped off her stool, taking a few steps away. The situation was both terrifying and exhilarating—she needed space to figure out what it all meant. What she wanted.

"Aw, Tanvi." The disappointment in his voice made her turn around. "It was all in good fun."

His eyes burned with sincerity. She walked back to him feeling a little guilty about bailing on their deal. Once again, she found herself wanting—needing to be close to him. To feel his touch, breathe his scent, and get lost in his penetrating eyes.

"I'll get you back," she teased. "When you least expect it."

"I'm counting on it." He smiled at her before ordering her a beer.

NINETEEN

TANVI GOT THE KEY IN THE LOCK ON THE THIRD TRY, STIFLING childish giggles as she fell into the entryway. Lucas fell on top of her, his own laughter less stifled.

"Shhhh," she said through her giggles. "Everyone's asleep. And everyone but Reina lives here. That's a lot of ears."

He wrinkled his nose. "And other parts."

"Like mouths," she added, crawling forward so she could kick the door closed. "Mouths that scold."

"Your family is not that bad," Lucas whispered from the corner he'd scurried to avoid getting hit by the door. He locked it and stood, hitting his head on the coat hooks on the wall. She stuffed her face into the crook of her arm to muffle the laughter she had no hope of containing.

"Son of a bitch," he rubbed his head.

The light came on, and her mother stood in a pink robe with matching curlers in her hair, a baseball bat raised above her head. As soon as she recognized Lucas, she lowered the bat, and joy lit her eyes. Her father entered the hall, shotgun in hand and a take-no-prisoners attitude.

"No, no, no," Cora pushed him backwards. "Go back to bed."

He mumbled something, but Tanvi couldn't make it out.

"No, it's the FBI agent and Tanvi. If he gets her pregnant, he'll have to stay."

"Absolutely not!" the door shut and they couldn't hear the rest of her father's argument.

They exchanged a horrified look. Tanvi's laughter bubbled up before she could stop it. Her mother was beyond ridiculous.

"You have condoms, right?" Lucas asked patting his pockets. "I didn't bring any."

"We're not having sex," she said through her laughter, more to herself than to him.

"Just in case, though? You have some right?"

"Yeah," she chuckled harder. "I've got you covered," her voice went up as she finished, unable to hold back her drunken giggling at the pun.

"You're terrible," he scolded through a smile as he offered her a hand. He hauled her up and wrapped his other arm around her waist. Her giggles faded at being so close to him. Pressed against him. She placed a hand on his chest and pushed him back. He released her, but the look in his eyes didn't fade.

"Water," she said, moving into the kitchen. She grabbed two glasses out of the cupboard and ran the cold water from the faucet.

Lucas leaned against the doorway, arms crossed over his chest. His eyes followed her every movement, and she wished she'd had one less beer. Her movements felt clumsy, her thoughts foggy. She handed him a glass of water and chugged her own. He followed suit, and she took his to refill it.

"We're not twenty anymore," she jested as she put the glass under the faucet. Before she'd refilled the second glass, his hands were on her hips. Turning her to face him, she dropped the glass in the sink with a clunk. His eyes burned with desire, and she shuddered under their scrutiny.

"Tell me to stop," he said, dipping his head to her neck. His lips moving over her skin. Pleasure shot through her at the intimate contact.

"And if I can't?" she asked, her voice a husky whisper.

"Then I'm not going to stop," he promised as he moved to capture her lips with his own. She opened her mouth to him and pulled him closer, needing to feel every inch of him. She hated her clothes. She wanted nothing to be between them.

He slid his hand into her hair and cupped her head close to him. She moved away this time, kissing a trail along his jaw to his neck. She bit the tawny flesh, sucking gently as he moaned.

He slid a hand up under her shirt, pushing her bra aside so he could grab her breast, teasing the taught peaks.

A loud scratching invaded their make-out session. Both paused to listen. They exchanged a look before breaking apart to investigate. The streetlight outside was the only thing to illuminate the space. The sound grew louder. It was coming from the counter above the dishwasher. Lucas was right behind her.

"It's your rat," he announced as the realization hit him.

Rage consumed her. She slammed a fist down on the counter top, and they heard the animal hit the ground. Lucas hit the lights, and she shook the dishwasher as much as she could in the small space.

"He must have a hole in the back," she said, trying to peer around the appliance. "My poor mother. She keeps this house so clean, and the little bastard is getting in the trash."

"They can cause a lot of damage," he said. "And fires."

"He's going to die," she said, just as the rat flung itself out from on top of the dishwasher and landed right on her foot. It's wet, soft, flabby belly sliding over her foot as its tiny claws scrapped her skin in a desperate plea to escape. She screamed, lifting her foot off the ground and standing on her tip-toes on the other. The rat scurried across the house and up under a different cabinet.

"Holy shit," Lucas laughed as he wrapped her in his arms. She couldn't put her foot down, so she leaned against him, barely resisting the urge to hop completely into his arms. "You're okay. We'll catch it."

"Why? Why was it wet?" she asked as her mother came back into the room with the baseball bat.

"The rat," Tanvi said with a deep frown.

"You saw it?" she asked, looking around the kitchen.

"It was on top of the dishwasher, trying to chew a hole into the trash compartment." Tanvi grimaced as she relayed the news.

Tanvi sent Lucas to her room before getting her mother's mind settled on something less invasive, and then followed her savior down the hall. Her bed was calling to her. Her eyes were barely able to stay open as it was.

Back in her bedroom, she found Lucas remarkably still vertical. He was making his way around the room, looking at all the posters on her walls of boy bands and other teen girl things.

"Did you find the toothbrushes?" she asked, handing him his glass of water.

He offered up a toothy grin, showing her his freshly-brushed pearly whites before turning back to her wall display and sipping the water.

"All of that stuff is from high school."

"What? You mean you're not into the Backstreet Boys anymore?" he teased.

"Truth be told, I wasn't into them then, but my mom started to think I was gay. And she was adorable, trying to be supportive and everything, but I'm not. So, I tried to act more like other girls my age where boys were concerned. Thus the posters."

"High schoolers didn't do it for you?" he winked.

"Nope. Only two ever have, and I wasn't really into them so much as they were convenient."

"Ouch," he teased, placing a hand on his chest.

"I suppose you've had many women," she joked, lying back on her bed and spreading her arms.

"Nah," He sat down on the other side and lay back as well. "A few. My childhood—my life wasn't exactly wholesome. I didn't ever want to bring a woman into it. And then, I was in the Marines and the FBI. It was more, get what you can when you can and then back to training and studying."

"How'd you end up in the FBI?" she asked.

"What? A white kid from the wrong side of the tracks?" He laughed, but she just listened. "After my four years in the Marines, I was worried about my brother, so rather than re-upping, I joined the FBI. Fully intending to end up in Mass."

"You have a brother?" she asked, still looking at her ceiling. If she looked at him lying on her bed, she might do something she'd regret. Mainly jump his super attractive bones. And now that she knew he was a good kisser, she barely stood a chance.

"I have four brothers and seven sisters," he replied as if it were nothing. "My mom had two sets of triplets and three sets of twins."

"Holy shit." She rolled to look at him despite her better judgment. He couldn't be serious.

He puffed his cheeks and exhaled slowly. They were spent. Still, her fatigued eyes hung on his every word. "Yeah. I think I would have stopped after the first set of triplets."

"Are you a twin or a triplet?"

"Triplet," he said. "But Dustin is the one I worry about. Matt was always fine on his own. He was amazing at staying out of trouble. Dustin was the opposite. If he was present, he was in trouble. Still is actually."

"Which were you?" she asked, propping her head up on her hand. He turned his head to face her, her heart skipping a beat as they locked eyes.

"I was whatever either of them needed me to be." There was something strange in his voice. Almost painful?

"That sounds tough," she prodded.

"I'm fine. It was fine."

"I totally believe you," she smirked.

"Liar." The dimple in his right cheek became more obvious as his grin grew.

"Wait!" she sat up to look at him. "Identical or fraternal?"

His smile widened. "We don't share women, don't get too excited."

She grabbed her pillow and hit him in the face with it.

He blocked the pillow, grabbing it and pulling it from her hands. Tossing it away, he grabbed her wrist and pinned her to the bed rolling on top of her. The weight of him was undeniable and he had that hungry look in his eyes. She felt a shiver of anticipation shoot through her. She was helpless against his charm. And worse? She was perfectly fine with it right now.

He dipped his head down and kissed her. But this was different. It wasn't the needy, strong kisses she'd come to expect from him. It was tender and filled her with longing. He was going to be the death of her sanity. Just when she knew she'd never be able to say no, he pulled back, his green eyes drinking her in as if this was the last time he'd ever see her.

"If we do this," he said, looking down her body. "We're both going to be sober."

She pouted. "You're stopping?"

"I'm stopping," he said, touching his nose to hers. Her heart melted at the gentle gesture from a man who could be so rough. "I don't want to. But I do want to remember every detail when this happens."

"You're awfully cocky," she teased. "Maybe the only reason you're here now is the booze."

He rolled off her and she felt his absence to her core. "Then we definitely can't do this." His eyes got serious. "I couldn't live knowing I was nothing more than your regret."

She put a hand on his cheek as she searched her mind—her heart—for the right words. This all seemed to be happening so fast and excruciatingly slow all at the same time.

Pulling away, he hopped off her bed, and she went into her bathroom to brush her teeth and wash her face. By the time she returned, he was asleep on the floor. She would have gladly shared her bed with him. A pang shot through her chest at the loss of time together. Draping a blanket over him, she turned out the lamp beside her bed and tried to sleep.

LUCAS'S EYES FLEW OPEN, AND A LOOK OF DISGUST PULLED ITSELF INTO place as he stared at a 98 Degrees poster on the ceiling. How did he not notice that the first time he was in here? The night before came flooding back as he sat up. Other than a deep fog he'd love to sleep off, he felt okay. Tanvi lay sprawled across her bed. A pair of lacy sleep shorts cupped her perfect ass. Her matching camisole was pulled just enough to the side to gift him with an eyeful of flesh, her partially-exposed breast showing from the side. He rubbed his eyes and looked at the door. Coffee. He needed coffee. But first. He slid his hand into his pants and tried to adjust the morning wood so it was less noticeable.

"Jerking off to a sleeping woman is creepy." He turned to see Tanvi looking at him, but not her cami wasn't just showing side boob. It was the whole boob. He blinked a few times before turning back to the door.

"It's just," he paused. "The morning."

"Shit," she must have noticed her wardrobe malfunction.

"I'm going to get coffee."

"Mom will have coffee and breakfast ready," she said as she pulled something over her head.

"Great, I'll just go make small talk with your mother while I have a raging boner."

"Well, get a handle on it, McGinn," she slapped his ass on her way by. She was wearing an IPD sweatshirt, but those damn shorts meant there was no way he was getting a handle on anything.

He sat on her bed. "I'll be a minute."

"Don't jerk off in here," she pointed a finger and raised a brow at him. "Go in the bathroom, like a gentleman."

After a moment of staring at Nick Lachey's ridiculous pouty face, he was cured and headed out to the kitchen.

Cora held a game cam in her hands as she sifted through the photos and videos.

"You got one!" Lucas snatched a piece of toast from Yasmin's plate on his way to Cora in the far side of the kitchen. Yasmin growled at him as he bit into it.

"Yes," she winced. "I'm not sure I want to see it, though."

"Well, look," he pointed to the second photo, "see, he's coming out over here. To get to the trash, so he doesn't have direct access to the trash yet. That's why he's trying to chew above the dishwasher."

"So, now what?"

"Look at the rest of the photos." Lucas took control, looking for something they could use. "See? Here he goes in after your crackers. Place your trap in there, bait it with his favorite food, and bye bye, ratty."

"That easy?"

"Nothing is easy with rats," Lucas said. His eyes drifted from Cora to Tanvi, who was on her tiptoes trying to reach a glass. She leaned over the counter, pushing her beautiful yoga ass out and tempting him with a perfect view. Her mother jabbed an elbow into his stomach.

"Don't just stare," she whispered. "Do something."

Just one problem. He *really* liked the way she was doing it. Tanvi turned around to glare at him and her mother. Feeling sheepish, he stepped forward. "Let me help you." He grabbed the glass and handed it to her.

"Thanks," the word dripped with suspicion.

"Well, I promised to get you home safe, and it appears I did that." He headed for the door.

"Luke?" Tanvi called after him. "You don't want food? Or coffee?"

"I have to get back and shower. We have a busy day catching psychopaths, remember?" Without another word, he slipped out of the house. His head pivoted left to right. Where did he leave his car?

The door opened behind him, and he turned to see Tanvi walking out onto the front path. He looked around at her neighbors.

"You shouldn't be out here like that," he said.

She looked at her shorts and snorted. A most becoming sound. He felt a laugh bubbling up.

"You're such a prude. They're PJs."

"They're *sexy* PJs," he said, stepping closer to her.

"I keep them in the closet for when gentlemen bring me home and pass out on my floor."

"Happens to you a lot, does it?" he teased. "So, our cars?"

"At the bar," she nodded. "We ordered a car. And you insisted on paying the bill, just in case we decided to have sex. It was very chivalrous of you."

"What can I say?" he asked. "I'm a chivalrous guy."

She smiled at him, arms crossed.

"Well," he said, giving her one last look. "I'll see you at the station."

"I'll be there," she saluted playfully. "If you wait a minute, I can get Adina to drive us to the bar."

He looked out over the neighborhood. He needed to get away from her long enough to clear his head and figure out what the hell he was doing. Their kisses had not been forgotten in the fog of beer and liquor. "Yeah, I'll wait on the step."

"I'll be quick." She ran back into her house. He sat on the step. What was it about this chick that had him so thrown? She's fun, she's smart, she's insanely sexy and extremely—off limits. He looked back toward the house. She'd just said goodbye to a messy relationship—or boring relationship—according to her mother. The door opened, and Adina flopped down on the stoop next to him. Still in her sweats, hair matted, she leaned against him, eyes closed behind large, round glasses.

"Are you even awake?" he asked.

"Nope."

"Want me to drive us there? Maybe grab you a coffee on the way?"

"You're the best," she said through a yawn.

"Hey, can I ask you something?" He eyed her. She opened one eye.

"You're suddenly *less* the best."

"It's about your sister, or I'd wait until after coffee."

She sat up, eyes alert and trained on him. "What about my sister?"

"She ever have casual relationships?"

"Nope," she shook her head. "She's been with two guys, and they were both serious. Dated for a month before they kissed serious."

"You're sure?" he asked. "There couldn't be someone you don't know about?"

"No way. We're an open family. We *all* know all. And Tanvi is the commitment type. We were all surprised when she decided to hit on you."

"She did hit on me, though."

Adina looked at him through narrowed eyes. "Are you trying to bang my sister and then leave? 'Cause my mother might like you right now, but if you hurt her child? She'll cut your balls off and feed them to the rat."

"Noted."

"You two ready?" Tanvi asked as she bounded out of the house and between them. She turned to look at them, the morning sun bouncing off her hair and face, making her glow. He wanted her more than anything. And not just in a one night kind of way. He could see himself with her for the long term. A lifetime. He needed to get away from this woman as fast as he could. And the only way to do that would be to catch the killers.

"Let's go," he hauled Adina up with him. She handed him the keys, and Tanvi frowned. "You could have at least given her coffee first."

"Yeah," Adina fussed. "You animal."

Tanvi shook her head, laughing, and Lucas let himself smile at the sound. But that was it. He would not get tangled up in this woman. He was here to learn and do a job. Then he'd go home. But as he opened the car door and placed Adina inside, he wondered, *did he even have a home?*

TWENTY

LUCAS WAS SIPPING HIS COFFEE WHEN FRANK AND TANVI ARRIVED. She looked great. Her hair hung loose around her shoulders, and her cheeks held a natural blush that showed off her spirit. She really did need the night of fun. He smiled to himself, happy to have given it to her.

He held coffee up for them, and they both took it greedily, though Frank was a little slower.

"Feeling those shots, Frank?" Lucas teased.

"Shhhh," Frank pleaded with his eyes closed as he drank the coffee. "We're all right here, so there is no reason to yell."

"Did Rachel make sure you drank water?" Tanvi whispered, placing a daughterly hand on his shoulder. Lucas's face pinched. *How did people just form those attachments?* He couldn't even form them with his family, let alone someone at work.

"She was busy," he replied over his cup. He was determined to drink every drop while it was still scalding.

Tanvi's brow furrowed as she considered what he could mean. Then it struck her. She popped Frank in the shoulder.

He chuckled as he made his way to the bulletin board they were working on.

Nash entered the room looking chipper, rested.

"How was the rest of your evening?" He asked.

"I was assaulted by a rat," she snapped.

"I passed out on her floor," Lucas answered, stretching his neck until he cracked. He offered Nash the last coffee on the tray. "What about you?"

"I went home alone, so nothing as exciting," he blinked. "As a rat or a night on a hard floor."

"Guess Frank had the best time then," Lucas chuckled.

Frank grabbed the file on Carl Singh, ignoring the conversation. "Looks like Carl grew up in the US, but his parents were immigrants, his dad had a—firm hand. Mom had a firmer hand."

"Yes, he has a pretty normal history for these offenders," Nash concurred over his coffee.

Tanvi leaned in to read over Frank's shoulder.

"There's something weird about his history," Lucas added as he joined them by the board.

"What?" Frank asked.

"It's like someone took an abnormal psychology book and wrote it out." He pointed to a specific piece. "See, bed-wetting, animal mutilation, and fire starting all mentioned in the same sentence? Did John dig this up?"

"Yes," John said from behind them.

Lucas turned and thought he saw anger in the younger man's eyes. "Where'd you pull it from?"

"His school records, mostly. He saw a psychologist for a time as a teen because—"

"He started peeping," Lucas finished for him. *Yep, that was anger. Interesting.*

"I found some things that don't seem to be included in here," Nash said, eyeing the file. Lucas watched as John's anger was replaced with something else for a split second.

"You guys should see this," John drew their attention away from Carl's file, handing Tanvi a report.

"The DNA results," she said. "How'd you get them so fast?"

"Put a rush on down at the lab. I know a girl there, and she owed me a favor."

"Thank you!" Tanvi gushed. Lucas watched as John beamed. Was he trying to get in good with Adina—or Tanvi? And was Lucas jealous, or was he actually seeing what he thought he was seeing. He glanced at Nash, but he was engrossed in Carl's file.

Tanvi studied the DNA results. Her face went white. Lucas stepped forward, and John gave him a look. He ignored the tech. "What is it?"

"There are three different DNA samples. None from Carl Singh."

"No hits on the database for Carl or the others either," John added.

"Four people involved?" Frank asked. "And Carl is what? Pulling the strings?"

"If he picked Ali up, he should have touch DNA on her," Lucas hypothesized.

"Unless whomever he delivered her to, washed her," Tanvi said, disgust clear in her voice. "We have to stop this."

"We will," John stepped up and put a hand on her shoulder. She offered a smile, and Lucas felt a jolt of jealousy shoot through him. He stamped it down. His heart raced as he tried to gain composure. He was being ridiculous. There was no use getting attached. After all, he was leaving once this was over. Even as the thought crossed his mind, he knew the truth. He was already attached.

A jingle from Nash's phone drew his attention away from the conversation.

"You need to see this." Nash grabbed the remote and turned on the TV in the corner. It was a press conference.

"… if you have any information about the whereabouts of my fiancée, please call the number at the bottom of the screen. My family and I have put together a twenty-five-thousand-dollar reward for any information that leads to her safe return. Thank you…"

The man looked like he'd been gutted. Lucas felt for him. He glanced to Tanvi, her face pinched in anger as she shook her head.

"This is going to overshadow our case," she spat.

"I think this is *part* of our case." Nash stepped between them as Lucas fought to understand her anger.

"She's white," Tanvi said. "That doesn't match our MO."

"We'd need more information," Lucas countered, putting his thumbs in his belt. "Carl did point us to one white woman. The high schooler who stole her sister's ID."

"That's just it," Nash moved back to the board, "I found the bodies of three other white women who fit the victim's profile. Broken homes, prostitutes, or poor, homeless, and they bettered themselves. At which point, they were abducted and then found murdered or dead. Same deal—some look like suicides or accidental deaths. Look."

He laid the photos out on the table. Each one had a Cheshire cat smile in the background. They were small or barely visible, though. Hardly the clear signs like at some of the other sites.

"She may be our newest victim in whatever they're doing."

"I agree," Frank nodded. "We need to talk to the detective working the case."

"It's a waste of time," Tanvi said. "Time we don't have. One of Carl's buddies might have the next victim chosen already. Those smiles could be anything. They're barely smile-shaped."

"So, I'll do it," Lucas barked. She took a step back.

"We need to keep an open mind," Frank interjected, shooting Lucas a scolding glare. "We don't know much for certain yet. Carl is still a mystery, as is this game."

"Yes," she whispered, staring at the floor.

"I agree," Frank said. "We need to talk to the detective working the case."

"I'll give the number a call after and make sure there were no chess pieces or smiles left at her house. Then, we can move on or investigate properly." Lucas said.

Frank turned to Tanvi. She nodded her agreement.

TWENTY-ONE

"Where is Detective Nightingale?" Carl asked as soon as he was brought in. He sat opposite Lucas at the table with his lawyer, a pesky defense attorney, Jennifer Taylor, to his right. She glared at Lucas like she expected the worst.

"She'll be here," Lucas said casually, ignoring the daggers being flung at him from Ms. Taylor. "Another woman went missing. Haven't you heard?"

"Yes, but she's not on that case." He jingled the chains on his cuffs. "We had a deal."

"We have to rule out a connection," Lucas said. "Especially since we got the DNA back."

He leaned forward to stare at Carl.

"Oh?"

"Yeah, guess whose wasn't present on any of the victims?"

He grinned. "Mine, of course. I already told you that."

"So, for all we know, you're completely full of shit."

"Tell me, Agent McGinn, when will Detective Nightingale be coming in?" He said her name like he was savoring fine wine, letting it rest on his tongue. His eyes flew up from the table, and a grin pulled across his face. He called himself the Caterpillar, but damn, that smile was like the cat.

"You can see her when I say you can," he said. "You might not have killed these women, but you sure do have an odd fascination with Nightingale. And I don't like it."

"You like her."

"Tell me about Ali Kim."

His grin fell. "You fucked her, didn't you?"

"Ms. Kim—"

"You ruined her," he said through clenched teeth, slamming his hand on the table.

Lucas fought the urge to strangle the man across from him. "That's not how women work."

"You did, or you want to. You'll defile her soon enough."

The door opened, and Tanvi entered. "Let's talk about Ali Kim," she said, pulling the chair next to Lucas out and sitting down.

"I want to talk about the FBI agent," he said, watching them calmly. "Has he wormed his way inside you yet? I need to know. It will greatly affect my plans. Besides, you're late. You owe me."

"I apologize. Agent McGinn wasn't supposed to start without me. If you give me information about Ali, then we'll see," Tanvi smiled at him. He sat back as if weighing his options.

"I drugged her, played the fatherly type. Same as Tamika No one questioned it. Then I delivered her to the person who killed her."

"Why?" she asked. Lucas would have gone with *who,* but he hadn't gotten anywhere with the guy.

"Because I can," he declared. "Now. *Tell me,* how easy was it for him to get those legs apart? Did you fight back? Did he have to take it?" He licked his lips, and Lucas felt rage boiling in his belly.

"That's a little vulgar for you, don't you think?" Tanvi asked. "That's not really you. The sophisticated caterpillar."

He sat back. "I don't play it well, do I?"

"No," she said. Lucas shot her a concerned look. He'd missed something. "I've sat across from more than a few creeps who wanted a piece of me. You're laying it on way too thick."

"Very good, Detective *Nachtegall*. Very good."

"Now, let's talk about Tamika."

"No, you owe me still, and I need to know if he's had you," he licked his lips but this time he looked bored. "An associate cares very much about who you're with. Even if I don't."

"An associate?" she asked. "Tell me who, and I'll consider answering."

"I know him only as… the Cheshire Cat."

She exchanged a look with Lucas.

"Yes, there's no doubt you've seen his work."

"What does he want with Tanvi?" Lucas asked, barely containing his panic.

A small smile tugged at his lips. "There it is again. He keeps calling you by your first name. Does that bother you? It would bother me. If I were a mere woman, to be demeaned and disrespected like that."

"No," Tanvi said plainly. "He doesn't mean any disrespect. And that's what matters."

Lucas eyed her. Did she think it was disrespectful to call her by her name? He knew he shouldn't do it in here, but it slipped out.

"Answer the question," Lucas barked.

"He wants to devour her. Every inch of her. Body and soul. And then leave her for you to find." He looked at his nails and started picking at them. "Kind of inspiring really. For someone to embrace what society sees as their dysfunction. You'd never know him if you saw him on the street. But all the while, he's planning how to hurt you the most. It's why I chose him. I saw his potential. I've been teaching him for a few years now. He may even surpass me."

"Then turn him in," she said. "He can't surpass you if he's in jail."

"That's cheating," he barked. The sudden vitriol in his words made her jump. "The rules are set. We play by them, or we're nothing more than savages."

"Wouldn't you say murdering and raping women is savage?" Tanvi asked.

"That's a matter of perspective. But you need to understand your place. These women didn't. So, we showed them."

"This interview is over," Taylor said as she glared at him.

Lucas followed Tanvi toward the door.

"You haven't found my house yet? I practically gave it to you."

They exchanged a look. Lucas smiled. "Yeah, we found your kiddie porn. We're handing you off to the ADA for speedy trial and a long stay in Gen Pop. Best of luck Mr. Caterpillar."

His eyes widened momentarily before he regained his composure. "If that's all you found, you didn't go deep enough. Maybe that's why Nightingale doesn't want to talk about it. Maybe *you* didn't go deep enough."

"What did you want us to find?" Tanvi asked.

"Something to take you down a peg or two. Women need to know their place." He narrowed his gaze on her, and Lucas couldn't stay back anymore.

He walked to the table, staring Carl in the eye.

Carl laughed. "If we were in Boston, you'd have hit me already. How is your father? In prison still? Does your brother feel the same amount of guilt? For not being there? Or is he too busy playing the criminal?"

"You think knowing about family means something?" he laughed. "You don't know shit."

He turned and walked out of the room, leading Tanvi out with him. The door clicked shut, and he moved straight past the people gathered and buried his fist in the wall. Pain replaced rage as he pulled his hand from the drywall. He focused on the stinging in his knuckles, the smell of blood as it spilled down his arm, letting everything else fall away. There was only this, only pain.

"What the hell was that?" Tanvi barked. He couldn't answer right now. When his eyes opened, he saw Frank staring at him. The old coot would know his history soon enough if he didn't already.

Stinging in his hand pulled his gaze from Frank to Tanvi. She held a towel to his hand, nudging him to the sink, so she could wash the drywall out.

Frank barked orders, but Lucas was lost in Tanvi's gentle touch and the pain radiating through his hand and wrist.

"So we're clear," Frank said as he approached, "you two aren't sleeping together?"

"No," they said in unison. Their eyes locked, and Lucas wanted nothing more than for that to be a lie.

"Keep it that way." Frank gave them a stern look before settling his glare on Lucas. "You can tell me, or I can find out."

Lucas's gaze fell on Tanvi. He didn't want her to know. Didn't want her to look at him like she was right now. Like he was broken. Snatching the towel, he wrapped it around his hand.

"Figure it out yourself then." She walked away from them both.

"I know the gist," Frank said. "I don't need the details, just how this is affecting you."

He looked away. Saying it was like reliving it. Reliving his failures to protect his family. He wasn't sure he was strong enough to go through it again.

TANVI SAT IN THE BREAK ROOM WITH HER GRILLED CHICKEN SALAD IN front of her. She couldn't find the will to eat it, though. She shouldn't care that Lucas didn't want to talk to her. It didn't matter. He wasn't hers and she wasn't his. They were just two people with an undeniable attraction. Nothing more. But she still had this incessant need tugging at her heart. Urging her to know everything about him, to comfort him when the pain and sadness leached into his eyes. He was all-too accustomed to masking it, but she'd seen it a few times now. Briefly, but it was there. She wanted him to trust her with the truth.

"You look like someone chewed up and spit out your heart."

She looked up to see John entering. He poured himself a fresh cup of coffee and sat down across from her. "You want to talk?"

"Not really," she said, flipping over a piece of chicken.

"Spill," he said as he sipped the hot beverage in his hands.

"What would you do if you were into someone, and they were going to leave in a week or so? Maybe longer."

"There's no way out of it? Them leaving?"

"No."

"I'd make the most of it."

"Would you tell them? How you were feeling?"

He shifted in his seat. "How strong are the feelings?"

"Stronger than I'm willing to admit to myself," she winced.

He leaned forward and placed a hand on hers. "What's the worst that can happen?"

"Everything will get super awkward and mess with the case, risking innocent people's lives with my drama. You know. The usual."

"First of all, you're not risking anyone's life by being honest with yourself and Lucas."

Her eyes shot up from her salad.

"Please," he laughed, leaning back. "Everyone knows you two dig each other."

"Dig?" she grimaced. "That's the word you're choosing? Seriously?"

"You want me to be overheard?"

"Oh, yeah, okay." She grinned. "I dig it."

He rolled his eyes at her. "I can't believe I was into you."

"Hey!" she swatted at his arm.

After talking to Frank for an hour, Lucas was more than happy to get out of the precinct. The call from Ramirez couldn't have come soon enough. On his way to the garage, he found Tanvi and John in the break room. She was picking at a salad, and he looked like he was on the edge of his seat listening to her problems. She smiled and swatted at his arm. Lucas felt a pang at their ease. She always seemed so guarded around him. Rarely carefree.

"Rook," he said, her eyes shifting to him and the smile fading from her face. His heart sunk. "I'm going to see Richard Geller, Julie Martin's fiancé. Do you want to come?"

She nodded and stood. "Thanks, John. For listening."

"Remember what I said," he called after them. Lucas pushed away the feelings of hurt that she'd gone to someone else and headed for the parking garage.

THE DRIVE TO RICHARD'S HOUSE WAS LONG, AND LUCAS WAS ABOUT ready to crawl out of his skin. He couldn't be this close to Tanvi for this long and not touch her. His hand itched to slip over the center console and pull her hand into his. She didn't even like him. She'd made that abundantly clear. He was only in her room the other night because she was drunk.

"What were you and John talking about?" Lucas asked before he could stop himself.

"Stuff," she said as she checked her blind spot before merging into the left lane to pass a semi.

"Was I part of the stuff?" he asked, irritation brewing in his chest. He flexed his sore hand, allowing the pain to draw him in.

"Are you going to tell me what happened in the interrogation room?"

He looked back out the window. "No."

"Then you can stop whatever this is." She glared at him, and it hurt his soul.

"Sorry I asked."

She turned up the music, so conversation would be impossible, and anger festered in his belly. By the look of her, he wasn't the only one. *Fucking great.*

TANVI PULLED UP TO THE HOUSE, THOUGH MANSION WAS A BETTER word for what this was. Deep within the gated grounds, and surrounded by lots of outbuildings and gardens, the place was impressive.

"Tell me again what this guy does for a living?" Lucas asked as he stepped out of the car and buttoned his suit jacket.

"He's in politics or something," Tanvi huffed as she looked around the property.

Richard stood in the doorway and waved them in. His eyes were bloodshot, and his skin splotchy from crying.

"Mr. Geller?" Tanvi asked.

"Is this about Julie?" he asked, his pink eyes wide, an air of hope lifting his features.

"It is," Lucas said. "I'm SSA Lucas McGinn with the FBI. This is Detective Nightingale with the IPD. We're investigating a possible serial killer. Detective Ramirez was supposed to be here to go over everything with us? We want to rule out your fiancée's disappearance as part of our case."

"So, this is just procedure."

"Well," Tanvi said, looking to Lucas for reassurance, "there are certain similarities between the other cases and Julie's. There is a possibility that she's involved. But we were hopeful it's unrelated."

"Hopeful," he said as he led them through the entryway, toward the open-concept kitchen and dining room. He gave a chuckle as he reached the couch and seating area on the other side of the dining room. Detective Ramirez was already seated. A cup of coffee in hand and a pastry abandoned on the table in front of him. "I'd love some answers."

"Thank you for contacting me," Ramirez said. "I hope this is all for nothing, though. You understand."

"Of course," Tanvi nodded.

"What do you need to know?" Richard asked.

"Where she went missing from," Tanvi said. "And if she found anything strange in her room prior to her disappearance."

Richard frowned. "Like what?"

"A smile or a chess piece," Lucas offered.

"She went missing from the Wal-Mart Plaza just inside the city limits," Ramirez said.

Tanvi's heart sank. "That's right where Ali Kim was found."

Lucas gave a heavy sigh.

Richard was white as a ghost.

"What is it?" Lucas asked him.

Richard stood. "You need to come with me."

They followed him down the hall to the master suite. In the corner by the window was a vanity, a Post- it Note on her mirror and a chess piece on the edge of the table.

"I thought... Well... I didn't think anything of it. She leaves notes all over the house. All the time. Sometimes she codes them if she's trying to surprise me."

"We need to lock down your house. Check for a break-in," Lucas said.

"Yes, of course, whatever you need."

"This means?" Ramirez asked.

"She's part of our case," Tanvi said.

"We'll need your prints," Lucas said. "For exclusionary purposes. And we'll need to talk to all of your staff."

"He'll come down to the station tomorrow," The woman who spoke was covered in shadows as she stood in the doorway to the room. "I'm Richard's mother."

"I'd say nice to meet you, but—"

"The circumstances, yes," she said, finishing Tanvi's thought.

"We'll need your notes on the case," Lucas said to Ramirez. "You're welcome to join us as well. A few of the other detectives have already."

"Thank you. I'll see you tomorrow."

TWENTY-TWO

LUCAS WALKED INTO THE PRECINCT AT SIX A.M. THE DAY BEFORE HAD been full of tediousness. None of Richard's help around the house had seen anything strange. They didn't find a window or door that looked tampered with or so much as a hair out of place. Despite his mother's protests, they all came down to the station to give statements. All was neatly put away with little to show for their effort.

He turned the corner into the HQ. Tanvi was already there. He ground his teeth at her, bent over the desk. Despite his best efforts to forget how Tanvi's body felt beneath him, he'd had a restless night—tossing and turning with images of her flashing in his mind.

"Afraid someone else is going to catch your worm?" he teased. She looked up, displeased. Ignoring him, she put a pin on the map she was working on. "You're here early," he tried again.

"I couldn't sleep," she said. Still not looking at him.

"Me either." He eyed her, but she wasn't listening. "I mean, all I could think about was your legs wrapped around my hips while I—"

"Stop," she barked, her cheeks burning. "I'm listening to you, I'm just not looking at you."

He stepped closer to see what she was working on. She had pins on the map with the locations of the abductions and where they were found.

"Well, that's frustratingly familiar," he mused, staring at the pins. There was something about the locations that tugged at his memory.

Nash walked in, chipper as usual. "Good morning, you two."

Neither one took their eyes off the board.

"It's like Chloe, Ali, and Julie are part of something completely different. On the other side of town."

"We know Carl has a weird obsession with Alice in Wonderland," Lucas said. "The posters, but also the codenames they use. What if there are teams?"

Nash pushed between them and grabbed the map, putting it on the table.

"Hey," Tanvi protested.

"You guys are about to feel really stupid."

"Thanks, little buddy," Lucas said in a faux happy voice as he slapped Nash on the back.

"I already feel stupid," Nash admitted as he drew a grid on the map. "It's chess."

Lucas looked at the floor. "Okay, stupid doesn't quite cover what this feels like."

"Have either of you ever heard of a serial killer, let alone a group of serial killers, using people like chess pieces?" Tanvi said, exasperated.

They shook their heads, no.

"Let's not commence with the flogging and accept, this is new to everyone. Then, we can move on and stop them."

Lucas exchanged a look with Nash. "I guess *she* doesn't feel stupid."

They shrugged.

"Hey," Lucas said as he eyed the board anew. "That means Julie is a bishop, that's what her piece is. It was left on her vanity."

"This is a pretty typical opening sequence," Nash said, putting the board back up. It's more than likely she'll be found here." He pointed out the location.

"We need increased patrols."

"It looks like the black team is mimicking white's moves, which is also pretty standard."

"So, we can expect an abduction around here," Lucas pointed to the square with the station in it.

"That's a ballsy move," Tanvi said. They could have made the board so the police station wasn't involved.

"Well, you have the bulk of them at the edge or in the middle. Maybe the edge felt safer. Unless the other team gets a pawn across the board, this square could become inconsequential."

Lucas sat back. "We're only looking at half the game."

"Well, sort of," Nash pointed out. "Ali, Chloe, and Julie—they're white on the board."

"This gets more and more fucked up the more we learn," Lucas said. "They're playing chess by murdering women."

"We need to get Carl to talk about the other players."

"He won't talk. This is his show. He tried to tell us that from the beginning, and we were too cocky to listen." Tanvi said.

"Couldn't sleep either?" Frank said as he entered.

"Check out what Nightingale and our boy Nash put together," Lucas said.

He put the coffees down, along with a bag of donuts, and cursed as he looked over the map.

"He's in complete control," Tanvi said. "And it's pissing me off. I want him to be reacting to us. I'm sick of playing his game."

"That would be ideal, but we need more information. We haven't found any friends or…"

"What?" Tanvi asked.

"Anyone look into Joe White?" Lucas asked. "No one else in that club came forward. Plus, I've never seen a sketch that detailed from a quick glimpse like he claims to have had."

"Worth looking into," Frank said. "They could have planned it. The sketch, getting caught."

"All of it," Nash added.

"We need to find Joe and get back in the room with Carl," Lucas pointed, eyebrows raised.

"Nash and I can get started tracking down Joe. You two go talk to Carl. Try a different tactic. You're gonna have to give him something T. We need him to talk. Even if half of what he says is bullshit—he'll slip up."

They nodded.

"WE FOUND YOUR ALICE ROOM," TANVI POINTED OUT AS SHE OPENED the conversation with Carl. He sat across from her with his lawyer, his smile telling her he was beyond happy she was here. It had taken all day for Ms. Taylor to get down here resulting in worn out patience all around. Additionally, Tanvi's stomach refused to be silent any longer. She should have gone to lunch with Luke, but the plan was to avoid him as much as possible. It was easier this way. She placed a hand over her stomach as it grumbled like Winnie the Pooh's in search of honey.

"Ah, yes, I do hope you put everything back."

"You're never going back to that house. I wouldn't worry too much about it," Lucas promised.

"Don't threaten my client," the smug attorney butted in. The detectives eyed the attorney's suit. Sadly, it probably cost as much as detectives made in a year. "He hasn't been convicted of anything yet."

"Of course," Tanvi said, glaring at Lucas. He was going to mess this up if he couldn't get a grip. "What about the dungeon? Can you talk about that?"

"I'd love to," he smiled. "I made it myself. It was difficult to build the door to close like that. Of course, I had to do it without sacrificing the integrity of the building. Resale value and all. Did you like it?"

"Excellent craftsmanship." Lucas sounded like he'd rather be pulling his own teeth out with pliers. What the hell was his problem?

"Got stuck in there, did you?" The lights reflecting off his glasses made it impossible for her to see his eyes, and she hated that more than anything.

"Yes," Tanvi said, her voice wobbling a bit at the memory of Lucas more than the room itself.

"I know." He opened the folder in front of him and placed a photo in the center of the table.

Tanvi glanced at it, and her heart sank. It was Lucas on top of her in the dungeon. Lucas leaned forward to grab the photo.

"This came out really cool with the backlighting from my phone light." He smiled at her as she fought to take his 'it was nothing' attitude and run with it. "Can I get a copy of this?"

"If you wish." His eyes shifted to Tanvi. "And you, Nightingale? Do you want a copy?"

She plastered a smile on her face, ensuring it reached her eyes. "I'd love one. Thank you."

"Tell me about it," Carl looked as excited as a kid on Christmas making her relive this. "How did you end up under the FBI agent, Detective?"

"I was having a panic attack. I can get claustrophobic sometimes. Lucas chose a kiss rather than slapping me to keep me calm."

"Is that all?" he smiled at her. "I know how you reacted. This is a photo sure, but I pulled it from a video camera."

She looked away.

"The cat wasn't silent about this at all. You should have heard him scream when I played the video for him."

Tanvi's eyes narrowed. How was he in contact with the Cat from a jail cell?

"You two are obviously not professional enough to investigate this or any other case." Ms. Taylor said trying to pull Tanvi's attention away from her clue.

"My close rate would disagree with you," Lucas said to the lawyer.

"What about Joe White?" Tanvi asked, bringing the conversation back to the case. Was Joe the Cat? "Did he help?"

Again, he paused, "I don't know to whom you are referring."

"I think you do," she persisted, staring him down.

"Why would you do this if you don't like—grown women? He likes them, doesn't he?" she cocked her head to the side. "And the others. They must as well. Do they know about your affinity for little girls?"

"Trying to get ahead of me, aren't you, *Nachtegall*," he said. "Trying to cheat me out of my fun. I'm disappointed in you. I guess it's the Jew in you."

"It's the cop in me," Tanvi said, leaning forward with a lopsided grin. "I've got your balls in a vice, and I'm not going to stop cranking 'til they pop."

Lucas shifted uncomfortably next to her, but she stayed focused.

"I'll let you discuss it with your lawyer," she offered. "We'll chat again real soon."

"I look forward to it," he said between clenched teeth.

They stood and left the room. Frank was grinning ear to ear, shaking his head. "I really hope Joe is in on this."

"He is," Tanvi said, shooting Lucas a look. "Or the DNA will prove me wrong. But I'd be surprised."

"Are we going to talk about the elephant in the room?" Lucas asked.

"The photo," Frank said. "How'd he get it."

"I thought we sealed off the house."

"And took everything." Tanvi added.

"Unless it was sending images off site," Nash said around a mouthful of noodles.

A lab tech came running into the room, her black hair in two braids on either side of her head. "Detective Nightingale?" she asked through her heavy breathing.

"That's me," Tanvi said, stepping forward. "John sent me. We have confirmation—Carl's DNA on Ali Kim. It's touch DNA on a piece of her clothing."

"Clothing?" she frowned. "Was it near her body, like Tamika's?"

"No," she said. "It was from her bedroom."

She looked at Lucas and Frank.

"Kim was abducted outside her home," Frank confirmed for them.

"So, he either entered to put the Cheshire Cat smile in there, or he went back in later."

"Why would he, though?" Lucas asked. "He doesn't like adults. It wouldn't be to relive the crime."

"This is his game," Tanvi said. "We're not the only ones playing with him."

"You think the others...," Frank began, "...are being manipulated by him? Why would he turn himself in if this was all his grand plan?"

"So he can manipulate us, too," she nodded. "To prove he's the smartest. Smarter than others like him and smarter than us."

LUCAS WATCHED AS TANVI'S GAZE FELL TO A PACKAGE ON HER DESK. "What's this?"

"Adina brought you dinner," Frank said.

She ripped the package open. Heavenly scent filled the room. Lucas felt his own hunger approaching. He hated the weirdness between them. He wanted things to go back to the way they were before. She noticed him staring and held up another container. "She brought you one, too."

He approached to see what she was talking about. She held out a glass container filled with a homemade meal. Some kind of noodle dish. He stared at it for a long moment. Holding it in his hands, he couldn't believe it. What would make her think of him.

Nash held his up. "She brought me one too, it's delicious."

"You don't have to eat it," she assured him, reaching to take it back. Her tone and eyes angry.

He jerked the container away. "No, I'll eat it."

"What do we know?" Frank said, sounding exhausted.

Lucas looked away from the novelty that was the kindness behind his dinner and back at the board. "Not a lot more than we did this morning. What about Joe?"

"He hasn't been to work since he came in for the sketch," Nash said, eyeing Lucas's dinner. Lucas growled and he stepped back.

"He hasn't been home either," Frank added. "We spoke to his neighbors when no one answered the door to his place."

"Didn't his mother live with him? And she needed a lot of help?" Tanvi asked. She blinked her eyes like they were bothering her, but she was still focused on the conversation.

"Yeah," Lucas jumped in, drawing attention away from her. She took a drink from her thermos before continuing. "He could only afford part-time help or something."

"He has a sister. I spoke to her first thing. Before we found any of this," Nash said. "She didn't mention anything, but I'm not sure she would."

"What do you mean?"

"She said the mother was horribly abusive towards Joe...won't even have a relationship with the woman because of how she treated him."

"But Joe is taking care of her?" Lucas asked, knowing how common that was, he felt his cheeks flush. Ignoring it, he looked at Nash, who averted his gaze.

"Yeah, that's more common than you'd think."

Tanvi wobbled and slid off her desk, rubbing her eyes.

"You all right?" Lucas asked as he approached her.

"I'm fine. I think the food just helped the lack of sleep hit me." She gave a light laugh, but he wasn't convinced.

"Go home," Frank said without looking at her. "You've done well today, we're close to getting ahead of this instead of chasing our tails."

She nodded and grabbed her bag. "Enjoy your dinner, Luke. Night, everyone."

"Night." Lucas watched as she left. Her feet were unsteady as she made her way out the door. "You okay to drive?"

She offered him a smile that stopped his breath and waved. "I'll be fine."

He watched as she vanished around the corner. As he opened the container to his dinner, the spicy aroma pulled him in. Why would her mother think to send him dinner? It was probably some ploy to get him to marry one of her daughters. Smiling, he put the top back on and looked after Tanvi.

"I'm just going to make sure she gets to her car safely."

Frank nodded, studying the board.

Lucas rushed after Tanvi, pushing past John on his way out the door. John made some kind of comment, but Lucas wasn't stopping. John called again and again...Lucas ignored him.

He reached the parking garage for the officers and started looking for Tanvi. His eyes scanning for her red button-down blouse. When he found it, rage swelled in his chest. A man in black was dragging her away from her car. He pulled his gun.

"Hey!" the man dropped her and ran away from Lucas. "Freeze!"

The man was around the corner before Lucas could stop him. He knelt by Tanvi's side. She'd hit her head pretty hard on the concrete. He pulled his phone from his pocket and called for an ambulance.

"Rook? Can you hear me? Are you okay? Open your eyes." he said as it rang in his ear. He pulled her into his lap.

"911, what's your emergency?"

"Officer down, in the parking garage at the police station. She hit her head, and she seems out of it."

"Out of it how, sir?" the operator asked.

"Tanvi?" he said again. She moaned. "She's not speaking...She was acting strange I thought she was just tired..."

"Was she drugged?"

"It's possible. Is the ambulance on the way?"

"It'll be there shortly, sir."

He hung up and dialed Frank.

"Frank, get Tanvi's thermos to the lab. The Tupperware, too."

"Why, what's up?"

"I think she was drugged. Someone was trying to kidnap her."

He hung up again and held her close, looking around the garage as fear and panic filled his chest. If he'd been a second later, she'd have been gone.

TWENTY-THREE

McGinn watched as the doctors worked. One of them, a young man with blue eyes and curly, dark hair, spied him through thin-rimmed glasses. He approached, pulling the agent's attention from Tanvi.

"You need to get blood. I think it's GHB," he said.

The man offered him a condescending smile. "I'm sorry, sir, but I'm going to need you to leave. Only family can be in with her."

"I'm her partner," he said through his hand as he watched them pumping fluids into her.

"Even so—"

"You want to visit the ER as a patient?" Lucas barked, ripping his eyes from Tanvi to the doctor. "'Cause I can rearrange that pretty face of yours for you."

"It's fine, Henry," Cora's voice washed over him as she, Adina, and David entered the room. "He's family."

The doctor, Henry, apparently, backed off. But when he stood by Tanvi, he placed a hand on her shoulder, caressing her skin with his thumb in a way that made Lucas see red.

"Who the fuck is this guy?" Lucas asked. Henry looked up in surprise.

"Please, Lucas," her father said. "At least pretend you care about being civil."

"Okay, who is this clown?" Lucas tried again through clenched teeth.

"He's her ex," Adina said through her tears. "Which doesn't really matter right now. Does it?"

"It's GHB. We're testing for it. And if this asshole would take a blood sample, we could know for sure," Lucas said.

Henry turned back to him. "I think she would like some peace and quiet to--"

"Then you don't know her very well," Lucas barked. "She'd want us to catch the SOB who did this before she woke up."

Cora placed a hand on Lucas's bicep, her eyes pleading with him. "Please, Lucas, come tell me what happened."

"She won't remember anything tomorrow. She'll have a hell of a headache, but the dangerous part is that others can take advantage of you. So, she's out of danger."

"Barring an allergic reaction," Henry added as the nurses left. He stood holding a clipboard. "So far, everything seems normal. She's going to sleep it off, and we'll keep an eye on her until she comes out of it."

"How long?" Tanvi's mother asked.

"By tomorrow morning, she should feel like she has a bad hangover. But then she'll be as good as new. The fluids will help flush her system. How did she come to be dosed with GHB?" He eyed Lucas suspiciously.

"We're hunting a nutbag who's got a hard-on for her," he said. "How do you think?"

"I think if she was still with me, I never would have let her put herself in danger."

"Must be why she's not with you anymore."

"Henry," Cora said, breaking the tension between them, "you need to go. Lucas is here, she's safe. And we appreciate you helping her. But we have it from here."

Henry looked at his feet. "Can I speak with you outside?"

Lucas narrowed his eyes on the doctor and looked at Adina and Cora. They nodded. He followed Henry out of the room and let the door click closed.

"I'm sorry. Our breakup is new, and I'm—"

"I really don't care," Lucas interrupted. "I'm literally her partner, from the FBI, trying to catch a serial killer here."

Henry smiled. "So, you're about as available as she is. I guess that makes you a better fit."

"Funny, I'd think a doctor would understand her commitment to her job a bit better," Lucas shot.

"She was a glorified roommate."

"And you were the World's Greatest Boyfriend?"

"She talked to you about me?"

"Yeah, we braided each other's hair, held hands, and skipped after. Had a real fucking girls' night. No, she hasn't said shit about you. Her family, on the other hand—"

"She hasn't said *anything*?"

"Not a fucking word," Lucas said, taking a bit too much pleasure at the pain in the young doctor's eyes. "Get over her, Bud. She's gone."

He nodded before heading back toward the nurses' station. Lucas raked both hands over his face as the adrenaline started wearing off. He was exhausted and certainly didn't have the patience he needed to deal with this asshole. Taking a deep breath, he made his way back inside the room. Tanvi lay in bed, wearing a hospital gown covered with tubes and sensors. He'd kill the son-of-a-bitch responsible for this.

Adina sat on the bed, holding Tanvi's hand as she slept.

"We're going to go get coffee," Cora said as she tugged her husband along. She gave Lucas a pointed look and then motioned toward Adina on her way out.

Lucas moved to stand beside Adina, unsure about what her mother thought he could do to help this situation.

"You have to ingest GHB, right?" Adina asked through her tears.

"Yes, it's usually slipped into a person's drink."

"So, the food I left on her desk." She turned to look up at him, tears streaming down her cheeks. He wished he could take her pain away.

"You couldn't have possibly known," Lucas shook his head, trying to make her understand. "This guy is ten steps ahead of us. He had someone in the station, waiting for that opportunity. Her food should have been safe on her desk. I wouldn't have thought twice about leaving something there for her, either."

"That's nice of you to say." She wiped her tears and turned back to her sister.

"I'm not a nice person, Adina," he said, realizing that use to be true. But these people had worked their way into his heart. All of them. Her cranky father, her eccentric mother, and every one of her sisters.

"So, what?" she scoffed. "We're just special?"

He smiled. "Yeah."

"Thank you for looking after her," Adina said after a minute. "I can't imagine what would have happened if you'd been even a few minutes later."

Lucas's heart raced at the prospect, sending a new dose of adrenaline through his system. She'd be a piece in these people's game. Not just as Alice, but as a chess piece.

"Can you excuse me?" he asked, pulling his phone from his pocket and dialing Frank.

"McGinn," Frank answered. "How's our girl?"

"Hanging in there like a trooper, but is Nash there still?"

"Yeah, he's tired, though. I was going to send him to the hotel and have all of us meet back here in the morning."

"I'm not leaving her side."

"Understandable. What do you have?"

"She's a piece," he blurted. "Tanvi was going to be black's next move. The police station is in a square on the board, like Nash said. He wants to make his move from the piece on that square.

Increase patrols in the area, check out the map, and ask Nash to see which piece it is and if he can tell us anything about the strategy."

"Good work, kid," Frank said. "I'll be sure Teresa knows how you're doing."

Lucas glanced at the bed. "Why'd you leave the FBI?"

"I was asked to," he replied. "A few times."

Lucas's eyes stayed on Tanvi. "What happened?"

"I couldn't play by their rules. Saving the girl was always more important to me. The FBI looks at the big picture. They have to. They need to think strategically and play the long game. I'm just no good at that. I could never sacrifice the victim in front of me to maybe save ten in the future. That's part of why I like the BAU. You learn about the bad guys, you catch the bad guys, there is no letting them go to catch the bigger bad guy."

"What happened?"

"A little girl was kidnapped. Ten years later, she turned up, trafficked. The FBI was already working the case. They had a man on the inside, and they were getting ready to blow the whole thing wide open, when the mother of this girl went in to get her out. I couldn't walk away from them. So, when the dust cleared, I was fired."

"Do you regret it?"

"Not one bit. I did what I had to do. We saved a lot of girls that day, and the FBI got a lot of inside information that has since saved more girls. Maybe they could have done better their way. We'll never know."

"Thanks," he said, looking at Tanvi.

"Anytime, little brother. Get some rest. I'll call you in the morning."

TWENTY-FOUR

TANVI WOKE UP TO THE BLINDING LIGHTS AND A NAUSEA DEEP IN HER stomach. A chill raced through her as she looked around. Lucas stood at the counter across the room from her bed eyeing his phone. Relief shot through her at the sight go him. What the hell happened?

"You're awake!" her father's hand slid into hers, and she pulled her gaze from Lucas to where her father sat next to her bed. Behind him, Adina was asleep in a hospital chair. "Your mother just stepped out to get coffee. How are you feeling?"

She pushed herself up in bed, every motion causing her head to pound. Lucas was standing next to her bed on the other side. She hadn't even heard him move.

"Like I got hit by a Mack Truck mostly," she looked to Lucas. "What the hell happened?"

"What's the last thing you remember?"

"I was in the station, eating dinner. We were talking about ways to identify… I can't remember."

"Someone drugged you," Lucas said. "Far as we can tell, your thermos was dropped off by Adina around seven. Someone slipped GHB or a similar drug into it before Frank got back in the room at seven fifteen."

Her head throbbed, and various images swirled in her mind as she fought to understand what happened—what was *happening*.

"They would have had to know my schedule. I'm usually home for dinner," she tried to piece together how this could be.

"Frank and I think they have someone in the station. It's the only way. They had to be ready and waiting for the opportunity to present itself."

Her father squeezed her hand and gave her a small smile as she tried to take in the information. His way of comforting her. She was glad he was here and not her mother. She loved her mother, but she was prone to being over dramatic, and right now, Tanvi needed the calm.

"You'll need a protective detail until we can find the mole and catch these guys."

She dropped her head back and hissed as pain sliced through her brain.

"I know it's the last thing you want, but these guys know who you are… They know where you are at all times...It's just not safe. Besides, the way Carl talks about you—"

"The other guys in the department are just starting to see my worth," she said. "I'm not throwing that away because he caught me unwitting once."

"Twice," Lucas said. She looked up at him, trying to figure out what he meant.

"The barbecue. He got into the barbecue," she admitted, looking at her father. "Mom had a number of guys from the precinct there. John, Mike, Stephan I think, and there were more."

"You think one of them is our mole?"

"Not John. Or Mike, actually, but there were a few I don't know as well," she said as the realization hit her.

"We need a list of invitees."

"We can do that," her father nodded to Lucas before looking back to her. "But as for you, you aren't the only one in danger."

She frowned.

"You live with your mother and two of your sisters."

"What if we could meet somewhere in the middle?" Lucas offered. "I worked security for a while in Boston. You stay at my hotel. I keep an eye on you at all times. No one will be the wiser since we've been working together this whole time."

She gave a weak thumbs up.

"One adjustment," her father said, eyeing him. "She gets her own room. Cora might be wishing for a surprise baby, but I prefer all offspring to be planned and born into a marriage."

Lucas laughed. "Of course."

Just as Lucas seemed to be feeling good about that being settled, Henry walked into the room. Tanvi's blood ran cold. Why was he assigned to her?

"Oh, good! You're awake!" he said as he approached the bed. He sat down and pulled her hand into his. "I was hoping you'd be up before my shift was over."

"Hey, Henry," she said, her cheeks warmed as she glanced at Lucas.

"How are you feeling?" he asked, going into doctor mode. He moved to put a hand on her head but she dodged, sending a shooting pain through her head.

"Fine...Well, like I was drugged."

"You can be honest with me." He dropped his hand but his intense stare didn't give up so easily.

"I am being honest." Tanvi stared at him.

"Please, Tanvi, put the walls down, and talk to me. I'm your doctor."

"Look, I'm fine. But I'm tired, and I have a headache from hell. 'Cause I was drugged."

"Is that really what happened?" he gave a pointed stare in Lucas's direction. "You can tell me who did this to you."

"If I knew who did this to me, I wouldn't tell you." She was too tired for his crap. "I'd tell Lucas or Frank or hell, even Foster. So they could arrest them."

"I know you're scared--"

"Are you deaf?" Lucas barked. Tanvi felt a weight lifted at his interference. The last thing she wanted was to argue with her ex while her head was pounding relentlessly.

"I will have you removed from this room," Henry said, turning on Lucas. The agent looked at Tanvi, who nodded. Henry was being an ass, so he deserved whatever he got.

"You can," Lucas said, taking a step toward him. "But I'll have you unconscious before security even gets here."

"Henry, you need to leave," Tanvi said as her father put himself between them. While watching Henry eat shit would be amusing, she couldn't take it if her dad got hurt.

"Thank you, Henry, it's time for you to go. The next doctor on duty can give Tanvi a once-over and discharge her," David said.

"I guess I just wasn't Neanderthal enough for you," Henry shot over his shoulder. Lucas followed him to the door.

"Neanderthal? Really?" Lucas scoffed. "How many years of schooling and the best you can do is Neanderthal?"

"I'm sorry," she said through a laugh. "He broke up with me, if you can believe it."

"He's an idiot." Lucas turned back to face her, calmness replacing the storm in his eyes.

"Besides," David said, looking from one to the other. "You two are just working together, right?"

"Of course," she said, eyes locked with Lucas's. She knew the lie was plain on her face for Lucas but maybe her father wouldn't see it.

"Yeah, I'm leaving once the case is over," Lucas added. Something like guilt in his eyes. "I just don't like pushy doctors."

Tanvi's stomach did a flip, and she dove for the emesis basin on the table, next to her bed. *Great.* Puking in front of the guy she liked was exactly the cherry she needed on the world's shittiest sundae. When her hair was pulled back, she expected it to be her father. To her surprise, David stood at the ready to take the basin to the bathroom. Looking over her shoulder, she noticed the man she'd been trying to deny. The man who insisted he'd be leaving. The one who always made her heart flutter despite her best efforts. His name was stamped in her heart, for better or worse.

He glanced at the clock. "I think shift change has happened. I'll go find someone to have a look at you."

And just like that, he was gone.

"You've got it bad," Adina's sleepy words startled her.

"I'd forgotten you were there," she admitted, pulling the blankets up over her. She was freezing. Her teeth were threatening to chatter

Adina crossed the small space and added her blanket to Tanvi's.

"Not gonna deny it?"

"There's nothing to deny. I'm really into him, and he's going to be leaving to live across the country as soon as this case is over."

"You could work something out," Adina assured her. "After all, it is possible for a woman to settle too close to her family."

Adina offered her a wink, and she had a feeling that was a line from the famed Mr. Darcy himself.

LUCAS LAY IN BED, KNOWING TANVI WAS JUST A FEW FEET AWAY through an adjoining door. One that was left unlocked, just in case. His mind went over a thousand scenarios that ended with him in her room looking like a dumbass.

He rolled over, stuffing the pillow under his head. He went over the day's events. Tanvi's withdrawals had been moderate, lots of puking and chills. And she'd asked him to get into bed with her. For the body heat. He'd have stayed there all night if she'd wanted him to. But the fever broke late that afternoon, and she'd seemed to realize what was happening and banished him back to his room. After showering and ordering new sheets, she was ready for an evening alone. Hell, he should be, too. But being close to Tanvi all day had his head spinning. All he wanted was her touch, her attention. He'd never wanted to hear his name on a woman's lips like this before. Every time she called for him, it was all he could do not to come completely undone. Never before did he need a distraction so desperately— someone to focus on besides the temptress in the next room.

He couldn't think about anything else— only the feel of her lips on his. The way she wrapped her legs around his hips and the sounds she made as he was kissing her neck. He wanted to explore her body, to keep her close and never let her go. That damn kiss had done him in.

Rage flared as an image of the man in black dragging her away raced across his mind. He should have shot the son of a bitch. He shook his head as he paced the small room. Placing both hands on the adjoining room door, he listened for signs of movement. Any sign that she was awake. Just silence. With a sigh, he went back to his bed and turned on the TV.

TWENTY-FIVE

Tanvi paced her room. Every light was on, and the curtains were drawn. She was safe. Logically, she could see it. Lucas was on the other side of the door, they were eight stories up, she had her gun loaded on her hip, and her door was locked. So, why couldn't she stave off the panic? Waves of fear crashed over her again and again. From the moment she'd sent Lucas back to his room, the assault had been nonstop. She couldn't remember anything from her encounter with her would-be abductor. That was the scariest part of all. If Lucas hadn't decided to check on her, she'd be locked away in some dungeon without his kisses to keep her sane.

Brushing her fingers along her lips, she remembered the way he'd pressed himself into her. How she'd felt safe in his arms. She rushed to the door adjoining their rooms, grabbed the handle, and paused. This was foolish. Placing her ear gently against the door, she heard nothing. Then, she heard the TV click on. She carefully opened the door, holding her breath as she slid into the room. He lay on his bed, his button-down left open, showing a tank top underneath. His eyes shot from the TV to her, but he didn't say anything. She moved across his room and tugged the curtains closed. Quietly, she shifted herself onto the mattress and curled up in the bottom corner in an attempt not to disturb him. Her body relaxed, the fear subsided. Her gaze fell to the TV. Lethal Weapon 2 played on the screen, with Martin Riggs hanging from a tow truck as he tried to apprehend the suspect. Glancing up one last time, she was met with a curious stare. He was watching her but didn't move, like she was a wild animal that might run away at the slightest movement. He was wrong. His hands slowly removed his button-down, and he placed his gun on the bedside table.

Tanvi scooted up the bed and placed her head on his shoulder. He ran his hand over her back, and she hated the layers of clothing that separated them. She picked her head up, pulled his shirt to the side so she could lay her head on his bare chest. Tiny hairs tickled her cheek. Following her lead, he tugged her T-shirt up so he could run his rough fingers over her skin, on her side and back. Shivers covered her body at his touch, and she settled into the comfort he offered.

"Are you cold?" he asked.

"No." She gave him a small smile and let her eyes fall back to the TV. "Do you think we'll catch him?"

He shifted beneath her. "We already have one," he said. "It's only a matter of time."

"We caught him because he wanted us to." She looked up at him.

"That was his biggest mistake." He said. "It would have taken us a hell of a lot longer to put this mess of a case into focus without him. But we know the game now, and knowing the game means we can win."

"Can we?" she asked.

His brow furrowed. "We can, and we will."

"What makes you so sure?"

"Because he came after you, and I can't let anything happen to you."

"Can't?" She met his gaze again. He shifted so he was leaning over her. She lay back on the mattress as he moved, her heart pounding against her chest like a drum. His weight pinning her to the bed, she closed her eyes and exhaled slowly.

"Can't," he confirmed before his lips covered hers. She slid her hand into his hair and pulled him closer, his hand moving over her side and back to cup her ass in his hand and pull her closer. She wanted this so badly.

He kissed and nipped a trail down her neck. She gasped as pleasure shot through her body. His hands fumbled with her clothes, and he grunted in frustration, pulling back to grab the bottom of her shirt. As he was about to rip it over her head, he stopped and collapsed on top of her, leaving her breathless.

With a heavy groan, he rolled off of her, sitting on the edge of the bed, running his hands over his face.

"What?" she asked, sitting up. Her lips still tingled from the fierceness of his kisses.

"You're 'strictly a commitment girl,'" he said over his shoulder, using her own words against her. She would have expected the words to be full of venom, but they weren't. Instead, he sounded sad. His wish to give her what she needed burned in his eyes. Or was that wishful thinking?

She looked away. He wasn't wrong.

"I don't want to be one of your regrets. Like Henry."

She ran her hand over his back. "Maybe we can enjoy each other's company and cross that bridge when we come to it?"

He stood, walking away from the bed. "That's exactly how you end up with regrets."

"Maybe," she agreed, but Adina's words hung in her mind. "Maybe not."

"You don't even like me," he spat the words. "You just feel safe with me."

"I do feel safe here," she admitted. "But--" the words caught in her throat. Once she said it, she couldn't take it back. It would be out there—in the universe—but most importantly, he'd know. He'd know he had her heart, and with that knowledge, he could break it.

"But?" he asked, hope glinting in his green eyes.

"You're right," she spat before she could muster the courage to tell him how she felt. The hurt in his eye sliced through her chest. "I'll go back to my room."

She moved off the bed and raced to her door. But then, fear gripped her heart. She didn't want to hide in her room alone. Her eyes locked with his—he was vulnerable, too.

"You can stay," he said. "I won't do anything."

Her voice cracked. How did this hurt so bad? She hadn't even let him in yet. "Could you hold me?"

He offered a comforting smile and sat back down on the bed. She snuggled into his side, and they both pretended to watch the movie.

"I love this one," she said. He kissed the top of her head, and tears pooled in her eyes. He could be the best thing she'd never have.

TANVI WOKE TO THE VIBRATIONS OF A PHONE ON THE BEDSIDE TABLE. Lucas moved to grab it, and she sat up. The TV was on random infomercials, giving her a pretty clear idea of the hour. She moved to the window as he answered the call. Pulling the curtains open, a midnight city met her on the other side. Speckles of light from other buildings, cars, and streetlights illuminated the darkness.

"McGinn," Lucas said into the phone. She turned to listen. "Yeah, she's here—no, in her own damn room—sure thing, pops. — no shit? — we'll be right there.—look she's sleeping finally," he looked over his shoulder at her. "We might be a few, but wait for us."

He hung up the phone and watched her with such longing in his emerald gaze. She knew the feeling. She could have stayed curled up with him for ten more days and still not felt like it was long enough.

"What?" she asked when he didn't share. "What is it?"

"Patrol just picked up Joe White. With a teenager, drugged, in his passenger seat."

"If this is connected—"

"We have one of the players."

"Let's go!" She shot out of the bed, and he fell back into it. "What are you waiting for?"

He gave a heavy sigh and stood, gathering his gun off the bedside table. She rushed to grab work clothes and eyed herself in the mirror. Her hair was a tangled mess, shoved into a bun, and her blouses were all wrinkled from being in her suitcase. *Who cares?* This was the break they needed. Something Carl wasn't expecting.

"Do we think this guy is a submissive?" Tanvi asked as they walked from the car to the precinct. She felt like this was the big break they'd been looking for. Like they could win for the first time since being pulled into this sick game. "How do we approach this?"

Lucas shrugged, his head still foggy. Good lord, he was distracting. This was definitely easier when she hated his guts. Imagining how to gut him like a fish never left her cheeks burning.

"He seems submissive," Frank offered as he joined them on the way to interrogation, pulling her out of her daze. "Based on we know so far."

"Which is what?" Lucas asked as they reached the door to the room. He closed his eyes and rubbed them with his thumbs and forefingers. She could relieve that tension. *God, Tanvi! Get a grip!* Hormones in check, she wondered if he'd gotten any sleep.

"He lives with his mother. John said Joe called her, and she's on her way in. He was playing along when he said he'd seen Carl pick Ali up—"

"That's been confirmed?" Tanvi asked.

"Spoke to the bartender, and she'd never seen him in her life. Also said she only calls rideshare or taxis for patrons. Never an independent driver."

"But that would mean—"

"There's another unsub. We could very well have teams of unsubs being manipulated by Carl." Lucas sounded exasperated and looked exhausted.

"You didn't get any sleep last night, did you?" Frank asked him.

"No, I was at the hospital—" He shook his head, and Tanvi's ears perked up. "I just don't like hospitals. And last night--"

"I was a mess. I kept him up," Tanvi said, guilt racking her chest even as she wondered what he didn't like about hospitals. He'd been agitated, sure, but she thought that was just because Henry was being a dink. Maybe it had less to do with her than she'd thought.

Frank nodded. Did he know Lucas's big secret?

"He's been nervous the whole time but has refused a lawyer," Nash greeted them, coffees in hand.

"You're my favorite," Lucas said, grabbing the one with his name on it. "Never let them tell you any different."

"You're like a dog. As long as I feed you, you love me," Nash said with a chuckle.

"How long did it take you to figure that out?" Lucas teased, hitting him in the arm. Nash took a step to the side and rubbed his bicep.

"Do you guys ever sleep?" Tanvi asked as she sniffed her coffee. She hadn't seen it made, so she wasn't sure she'd drink it, but she could smell it.

"I've been staying in the crash room," Nash replied, pointing over his shoulder to the bunk room, where cops could catch a few Zs between breaks in the case.

"And I went home this afternoon for a bit," Frank assured her. No one here was one hundred percent.

TWENTY-SIX

Lucas leveled a glare at the man across from him. He'd had enough of this horseshit. This depraved game needed to end. He wanted to take out the bad guys and then hide away with Tanvi in a hotel room and not come out until he had his fill. Not that he was likely to ever get enough where she was concerned.

"Do you always do as you're told?" Lucas asked, looking to make sure the recorder was on.

"What?" Joe asked. "I don't know why I'm here."

"You had an underage girl, drugged, in the passenger seat of your vehicle," Lucas answered, folding his hands on the table. "But it wasn't your idea."

Tanvi eyed Lucas before leaning forward, across the table, to get Joe's attention. "He thinks you're too dumb to pull this off on your own."

He frowned. First at Tanvi and then at Lucas.

"I was doing this long before he found me."

Lucas fought back a smile. "Who found you?"

"What were you doing?" Tanvi asked. They exchanged a look.

"The Caterpillar," he replied to Lucas. "Raping women. I never had the stomach for the killing."

"Then why play his game?" Tanvi asked.

"It added..." He glanced to the door and then the watch on his wrist. "...excitement. But make no mistake, I don't need to be told anything."

"What's The Caterpillar's real name?" Lucas asked.

"Carl," he picked at the dirt under his fingernails.

Lucas couldn't tell if this guy was stupid or didn't care that he was giving up everyone's secrets.

"Why don't we take this from the beginning--"

"That will take a very long time," Joe stated. "I'm not going to do that."

"I guess we just throw him back in a cell until he's ready to talk?" Tanvi said to Luke. His eyes never leaving Joe. He wasn't going to let this guy sit in a cell when he could help them end this now.

"We already spoke to your mother—"

"You did what?" he roared, the first animated reaction since he'd been brought in. "Why would you bring that old bat into this?"

"I assumed you were on better terms with her. Living with her and all?"

"Well, I'm not," he spat, baring his teeth. "How'd you like it if I went talking to *your* mother about *your* mistakes?"

"I wouldn't give a shit. 'Cause only pussies care what mommy thinks."

Rage burned in the icy-blue depths of Joe's eyes, and Lucas knew he'd found the nerve.

"You care, though," Lucas taunted. "You live with her, so that's a bit of a different situation, huh? Are you one of those people who just can't grow the fuck up or what? I mean, it's not like you have any debt to speak of. If you hate her so much, why are you still there?"

"You have no idea," he spoke through his teeth, head angled down as he glared at Lucas. "I had to let her move in. She had nowhere to go, and the nursing homes all cost too much."

"Must be a real hardship. Having to look after the woman who used to wipe your ass, make sure you ate, and put a roof over your head."

"Please," he growled, raising a hand for Lucas to stop. "She's no saint. She would have killed me if she could have still collected her welfare checks."

"You poor thing," Lucas mocked, leaning back and crossing his arms over his chest. He saw Tanvi glaring at him out of the corner of his eye, but he had to go here. Hopefully, she wouldn't look at him with pity in her eyes. He hated to be looked at with pity.

"What do you know about it?"

"More than you," he spoke softly so Joe would really have to listen. He pulled up his sleeve to reveal a tattoo of bullet holes in his forearm. "These are where my stepdad used to put out his cigars. My mom and stepdad just loved hurting me. But the icing on the cake came when I was away for the summer. Mom's new beau went after my little sister, and my brother stepped in. Thought it was over, and got stabbed in the stomach. He died slow and painful and all alone."

"And you took the hardship and made yourself into a big, bad cop, didn't you? How long did it take you to get justice for your brother?" Joe's eyes flared.

Lucas refused to meet Tanvi's eyes. He couldn't handle her reaction. "Five years."

"Good for you," Joe nodded. "Meanwhile, *I* turned into a monster. Right? You bore the pain and the hardship and came out like this."

"Because you're weak," Lucas goaded. He stared Joe down unflinching. "Carl saw it. Took advantage of it. You're pathetic."

"Not Carl. I didn't have to be manipulated. I haven't killed one."

"What about abducting and raping?"

He shrugged, as if he couldn't deny it.

The door opened, and a woman in a fitted suit entered. Her wavy, auburn hair framing her narrow face and falling around her shoulders. She slapped a file on the table, glaring. Her blue v-neck stood out under her gray blazer.

"You're in the wrong room, Taylor," Tanvi said. "This isn't your client."

"I'm Mr. White's attorney. This conversation is over. I'd like to talk to my client."

"I didn't ask for an attorney," Joe said, looking furious.

"Please leave, officers," she said, ignoring him.

"You're Carl and Joe's attorney? Don't you think thats kind of a conflict?" Tanvi asked.

"I'll explain it to him and he can choose what to do. But for now, I get a call, I show up and defend. It's kinda my thing. And I'm here now, so you two need to skidaddle."

"I'm not leaving you with him," Lucas scoffed. He'd been playing a big game, but this guy was nuts.

"You don't have a choice," she said.

He stared at Joe. "I'm going to be right on the other side of this door. I'm fast, and I'm lethal. Don't you touch her."

Joe hissed at Lucas as they left the room.

"Stop harassing my client, and leave, Agent McGinn," Ms. Taylor barked.

"Who called him a lawyer?" Lucas asked as soon as he got out of the room, his fury palpable to those around him. He needed it, though. Needed the anger and needed to avoid Nightingale's caring eyes. He could handle being alone. He could handle no one caring if he lived or died. He couldn't handle what he'd see reflected in her eyes.

Frank shook his head.

"I had him!" Lucas slammed his fists on the table, and Tanvi flinched. "He was talking."

"She came in and said she'd been hired by a concerned family member," Frank said. "But that was excellent, Lucas. He would have spilled everything."

"We'll get them. We're making progress despite the setbacks," Nash added from his place in the corner.

"Someone has Julie right now, and Joe may very well know where. We don't have time for setbacks," Tanvi argued.

"So, he has something powerful to bargain with," Frank noted.

When Ms. Taylor came back out, she stood in front of the door with her face pinched.

"Anything he said is inadmissible," she snapped. "You were speaking to him without counsel present."

"He waved the right." Tanvi stepped forward to be between the woman and Lucas. While he appreciated the physical barrier, that she thought he needed it, pissed him off more.

"Apparently not, as I was called."

"We have the recording," Frank intervened. "If the judge agrees with you, then it will be inadmissible. Until then, it's ours."

"So, you are charging him?"

"He had a drugged, underage girl in his car, with a blood alcohol level of point two-nine. So, yeah," Lucas barked, "we're charging him."

"That's all circumstantial. He has a rideshare company."

"No, he doesn't," Tanvi said. "At least not according to any state records or local bartenders we spoke to."

Her lips thinned. "So it's under the table. What are you gonna do, sick the IRS on him?"

"If he can tell us where to find Julie Martin, we'll work out a deal with the DA," Frank offered.

"I'll need an ADA present when making any offers."

"A woman's life is at stake," Tanvi argued.

"So is my client's," she said.

"I'll call the ADA. She's supposed to be here soon, anyway," Frank said in his peacekeeper tone.

Nash signaled Lucas with a wave from the doorway as Taylor went back in with her client. Lucas nudged Tanvi, and they headed out to the HQ.

"I think I've found where he'll strike next. Though it's worth mentioning he tried to take the teen from this square," he pointed to the square with the precinct on it. "He's trying to move his bishop."

"You think he'll keep trying?"

"Depends on the kind of player he is and how attached he is to his strategy. The murders add a layer of complexity to the game. It makes it harder to predict."

"What can you tell us?" Tanvi asked.

"White came out with a standard opening sequence," Nash said, his finger moving along the board Tanvi made on the map. "With this layout, he has control of the center of the board. Which is why Black opened with a mimic. I think White is trying to work a side defense, with this bishop already moved into place. By moving the other one, it will give him a stronger setup. But again, I really can't tell just yet. Now, I suspect that this," he pointed to a cluster of bodies near the black side of the board, "was him moving these out so he could to king side castle."

"What's that?" Lucas asked.

"If you move your knight and bishop, you put the king here, and the rook moves to the opposite side, forming a barrier between the king and the rest of the pieces. It's pretty standard. But they've both almost got their setup. They should be getting ready to play. This is both good and bad."

"Give us the good first," Lucas said, chewing the inside of his lip.

"If they care about winning the game and not just killing," Nash began, "they'll have to take their time between moves. So, abductions and murders should slow down and give us more time to process the evidence."

"And the bad?" Tanvi asked.

"We won't be able to pick out specific squares on the board and catch them like we did with Joe. I can guess which moves they're going to make, but it's just a guess. It would take studying multiple games for me to be able to predict anything more accurately."

"How can they be abducting women when Julie Martin hasn't

been found yet?" Lucas asked, thinking about the teen currently in the hospital.

"If they're communicating with one another outside of the bodies through someone like Carl, they don't need us. They can play their game at their leisure. Not at all dependent on us finding or reporting anything. If that was not the case, I'd suggest lying to the press. Tell them the bodies were found in other places. Mess with them that way. But I think we'd be fooling ourselves and no one else."

"So, we need to continue increased patrols in this area and what?" Lucas asked.

"Pray," Nash said.

"Hopefully, we can catch the bastards before they finish their opening moves," Tanvi sighed, blowing a strand of hair out of her eyes. She pulled her arms tight around herself in a comforting hug, and Lucas wished he could pull her into his arms.

"Julie, is White's king-side castle," Nash pointed out. "If Joe was working alone as the black side, he's the best we can hope for. We need to get him talking."

Lucas nodded, looking at all the work Nash had put in. He'd connected another five missing women to the case, for a total of eleven, counting Julie. "Thanks for coming out."

"This is an incredible case. I appreciate you thinking of me. I still don't trust you, though."

Frank leaned in the doorway.

"I need to borrow Nightingale a moment."

"We'll be right there," Lucas called over his shoulder.

"No, you're fine. I'll send her back in here as soon as I'm done."

"I'm not a child," Tanvi scolded as she followed him.

"She's clearly terrified," Lucas joked as she left. "Can't stay away from me."

"Clearly," Nash laughed.

After a moment, Nash turned to look at him. Not in a casual way, but like he was studying him.

"What?" Lucas asked, barely avoiding the temptation to see if he had food on his face or something.

"You're different."

"What?" Lucas asked again.

"You've changed since being here," he mused. "You're playing well with a team. Multiple non-sarcastic remarks since I landed, and you are stuck to that woman like glue."

"What of it?" Lucas asked, turning on the smaller man with a glare.

"Just an observation." Nash moved away, hands up in surrender.

"Well, observe someone else."

"Tanvi is also very attentive. She may gripe about you treating her like a child, but she looked to you before agreeing to leave. Suggesting, she also assumed and or wanted you to go with her."

"I'm the guy standing between her and a serial killer. I saved her life. That's all perfectly normal."

Nash's lips formed a deep scowl as he considered. "I don't think so."

"You've been here two minutes. What could you possibly know about Tanvi?"

"I read her file. She's afraid of commitment. Afraid of being viewed as weak because of her sex and race. Also hates that she had to move back home because her ex broke it off and kept the rent-controlled apartment."

"You're kidding."

"No, I always read the files on the people I'm going to be working with."

"Of course you do," he said, rubbing his eyes. "This is why people think you're weird, Nash. And that's why people don't like you."

"I think it's because they're afraid I'll make them feel stupid."

Lucas thought it over a moment. "Nope. It's because you freak them out with your weird, stalker-esk behavior. You shouldn't know someone has commitment or any other issue until you get to know them."

"That's terribly inefficient." He shook his head. "By knowing things like that ahead of time, I can treat them in such a way that they feel comfortable, and we can work well together from the start."

"Inefficient or not, it's how people like it. I mean, if your way was working, people would feel more comfortable around you. But they don't."

He cocked his head to the side like a bird analyzing a leaf to see if it was, in fact, food. "Should I not tell them?"

"That's a start," Lucas laughed. "You could also try letting them show you who they are. People are more complicated than their file."

He clapped Nash on the back and moved to see what was taking Tanvi so long.

Lucas left Nash to contemplate his new insight into people to find Tanvi. She was standing with Frank and ADA Fiona Kincade.

"We can take the death penalty off the table if the information he provides leads to Julie Martin's safe return," Kincade was saying.

"That's it?" Lucas asked as he approached. The woman turned on him, but her dagger-filled stare melted as soon as she gave him a once-over.

"That's the best we offer serial killers and rapists."

"I doubt his lawyer's going to bite," Lucas said, leaning against a desk. Tanvi moved to stand next to him, her arms crossed over her chest.

"I agree we can't let him go, but we need to find Julie."

"That's what you have to work with, so take it or leave it."

Tanvi stepped forward, and Lucas placed a hand on her back. She stopped but glared at the ADA. The woman smirked at them before taking her leave.

"Think he'll go for it?"

"Only one way to find out," Frank said. He gave the window a sharp knock to let Taylor and her client know they would be entering soon.

"We'll present it like we worked hard for it, and it's a miracle he got this."

"Not exactly a lie," Tanvi said.

Lucas opened the door, standing back so Frank and Tanvi could enter first, then he followed. The woman sat there with a smug look on her face as she waited.

"We'll be leaving shortly," she told Joe.

"No," Tanvi corrected. "He needs to be processed, and a hearing will be scheduled for the kidnappings. Also, we have his DNA on two murder victims. So, he's facing the death penalty."

"When were you planning to tell us that?"

"Now," they all said in unison.

"This is absurd. I never kidnapped or killed anyone!" Joe balked.

"The evidence says otherwise," Frank said, looking at the file in his hands. "I just spoke with the ADA. The best we can do is take the death penalty off the table. *If* you give us information that leads to the arrest of your accomplices and the safe return of Julie Martin."

"The lawyer in training," White said with a smile.

"Say nothing," Taylor urged, impatience filling her voice.

"Yes," Frank said, eyeing Taylor. "She was about to graduate law school. A promising career from what I could tell."

"Carl hated her the most, I think," Joe said, ignoring his lawyer.

"Mr. White," she hissed.

"You're awfully quiet now, Agent McGinn," Joe taunted. "Don't want to show me any more of your scars?"

"I showed you mine," Lucas said from his place, leaning against the wall. "Now, it's your turn."

"Mr. White, I can't help you if you keep talking."

He looked at her defiantly.

"I was the first one Carl picked up," he said, looking right at his lawyer before shifting his gaze to Lucas. "I was working my way through the bars up in Fort Wayne--"

"Mr. White, I really need you to stop talking."

"Before this, I never hunted where I lived. Using my charms to get women to agree to a date. Carl caught me one night. Asked me if I was interested in playing a game with like-minded men."

"What did he catch you doing?"

Joe looked innocently at them. "Dating, of course."

"Who else did he get?" Tanvi asked.

"First, the Hatter and the White King."

"Who chose the nicknames?" Tanvi asked.

"Carl did. I suggested codenames, but he picked Alice and Wonderland. That movie always gave me the creeps."

"You played black in the chess game. Were you alone?"

"No, the March Hare and I are black. I abduct and entertain the women, and then the March Hare does the killing. And the Cat likes to have his fun with them, too."

"I need to speak to my client."

"If your counsel was paid for by someone else who's in here for the same or similar crimes, it would be best for you to seek some alternative representation," Tanvi offered. "Especially since Carl and the Hatter are the ones we really want. But you will be put to death if Julie dies."

"The March Hare is going to be sore if not mentioned."

"I need a moment with my client." Taylor barked.

"Do you need a moment with your attorney?" Frank asked.

"I better," Joe grinned at them.

"You can avoid a lethal injection if you provide us with enough information to save Julie," Lucas reiterated as they left. "Make sure she's looking out for you, not your buddy in the next cell."

On the other side of the window, Nash was watching the interview take place. He waited until they'd left the room and the door clicked closed before speaking. "He's not frightened at all."

"Well, saying death penalty versus actually being dragged to the chair are different," Lucas offered.

"No, I mean, he thinks it's funny," he said. "He laughed, 'the March Hare will be mad,' and 'Carl really hated her.' Why does Carl hate these women? Does he pick? Are they trying to find women who Carl will hate? There's something there."

"But the victim profile is all over the place." Nightingale was now looking at the photos on the wall behind them.

"Is it?" Nash asked. "Julie Martin. She was born into poverty. Went to a terrible school. Most of her peers dropped out, went to jail, or started having kids. Julie manages to get her bachelor's degree, is attending law school, and is engaged to a wealthy businessman. She bettered herself. Tamika Jackson, she beat back an intense drug addiction and was about to start on a path to help others do the same. She would have had an incredibly fulfilling career. Again, she would have bettered herself. All these women were bettering themselves. Each one was overcoming adversity in one way or another. Extreme adversity."

Lucas looked at Joe through the window. "Joe's white. Carl's Indian. The girls are all over the spectrum."

"That's just it. We're spending too much time on race," Nash said. "He won't give you information on Julie to save his life. He can't. The ADA stipulates that she is returned alive. But the fact that Tanvi was nearly abducted, and the teen, also abducted in here, in this square—it's Black's turn. So, Julie is more than likely dead."

He moved through to the other room and looked at the board. "She's a rook, so from her starting position, she will turn up in this area if she's been killed. And if he's doing what I think. King side castle."

"I'll send out patrols. Plain-clothed officers. Maybe we can catch them trying to dump the body," Frank mentioned, picking up the phone. "Foster, we have something, we need all hands on deck."

Tanvi slid her hands over her shoulders in a self-hug. Lucas watched her for a moment. "I think I should take Detective

Nightingale back to the hotel to get some rest. Call us if you find anything?"

Frank nodded.

"I'm fine, really," Tanvi said. "I can stay."

"Go get some rest," Foster said as he entered. "I told you not to come back until tomorrow, anyway."

"If I can help, this is where I want to be," she insisted.

"Well, right now, we need you resting so you can come talk to Carl and Joe again tomorrow."

"And with any luck, this March Hare guy," Nash said as he looked over the map.

TWENTY-SEVEN

TANVI SAT ON HER BED, RESISTING THE URGE TO GO TO LUCAS. SHE felt like he needed her, just like she needed him. But that was ridiculous. She'd been fine, better even, before he showed up and pissed her off every single time he opened his stupid mouth.

And he'd been fine without her. But the way he spoke today. Was he lying to get a confession? It wouldn't be the first or the last time a cop did that. Every time she closed her eyes, she saw the bullet hole tattoos. Did they really cover cigar burns? What about his other tattoos? What other dark secrets were they hiding? She stopped pacing and looked out the sliding, glass door, intent on grounding herself with the magnificent view of the sky. But right outside her window was Lucas McGinn, propped against a support pillar, staring up at the full moon as he took a drag off a cigarette. A habit she found disgusting, but it tugged at her curiosity. They'd been together for the majority of his time here, and she'd never so much as seen a lighter or pack of matches. Unable to stop herself now, she went back through her room to the adjoining door. His balcony door was open, and the faint, pungent smell of cigarette smoke wafted inside. The cool breeze chilled her skin as she stepped out. Thunder rumbled in the distance, warning of a midwestern storm rolling in.

"You're going to get an extra charge. This is a non-smoking room," she said as she approached. When he didn't respond, she tried again. "I didn't know you smoke."

"I don't," he said, looking down disdainfully at the remaining half of cigarette before tossing it over the ledge. The tiny ember glowed all the way down to the parking lot below. "I did when I was a kid, and every now and then when I've had a particularly hard day, I pull one out."

He glanced at her before looking back at the moon. He was beautiful. No, that wasn't quite right. He was good-looking for sure. But there was so much pain behind the façade. But looking at him made her yearn to touch him. Be close to him.

"Tell me about this boyfriend of yours," he said as he exhaled smoke. "Your mother thinks he's proof you need a man's man." His brows raised, and there was a hint of laughter hidden in the words. "He did seem a bit, I don't know, whiny."

"You find it amusing that my mom thinks I need a man's man...or that you are one?" She offered him a smile, and he gave her a shy one back. Something she never thought she'd see from Lucas McGinn.

"I like your mom," he said with a sigh. "She's crazy, but it's because she cares about you so much. I bet if you killed someone, she'd be that mom who covers it up instead of making you come forward. Even if it was an accident."

"I can't deny it," Tanvi said, keeping her eyes on the moon. Looking at him hurt. Only a sadist could watch someone suffer like he was. She wanted so badly to reach out and touch him. But that wasn't rational. Was it?

"You still haven't told me about your ex."

She could see he was staring at her from the corner of her eye, and she shivered. Before she could open her mouth to answer, a warm over-shirt was draped over her shoulders. How had he managed to give her his shirt without touching her? And why was she so disappointed about it?

"Henry," she said, as Lucas's scent enveloped her. "He was

training to be a doctor. We had such crazy schedules, I thought it would work. Hoped it would work. But he couldn't handle it. It was okay for him to work late or skip out on dates, but if I missed something, it meant a year's supply of passive-aggressive notes and comments. I didn't even care that he cheated on me. Outside of the inconvenience of needing an STD screening, it was a relief.

"My parent's love for each other is—ridiculous," she mused. "They met young, married young, completely accept each other for who they are. They still dance in the kitchen and make love. I'm supposed to want that—"

She paused as he turned away from her, leaning over the rail. She fought the urge to look at him.

"And?" he prompted. "You don't?"

"I don't know," she admitted. "I thought I didn't." She looked at him sheepishly. One half of his mouth turned up in a small, encouraging smile.

"You're allowed to change your mind." He shifted to look out over the parking lot again. "You could find a nice guy like your dad, settle down, and—have a great life."

The problem was, she didn't want a nice guy like her dad. She wanted someone who would challenge her ideas, push her to think about everything she knew. Someone she could grow with. Fight with. Her gaze landed on him again. She wanted Lucas McGinn.

"I told you mine," she said with a laugh, trying to change the subject. "Tell me yours."

She slid her hand over his arm and pulled it towards her so she could run her fingers over the bullet hole tattoos. They were covering up raised scars—the size and shape of a cigar's ember. She shook her head. How could this happen to a child?

"That's a long, ugly story," he said, turning his wrist so she could inspect his other tattoos. Only one wasn't hiding a scar.

"It's your story," she said, meeting his emerald gaze. "I'd like to hear it, if you want to share it with me."

He gave a heavy sigh, pulling his arm back and stepping away from her. Her heart sank at the distance between them.

"My parents were like yours. They loved each other more than any couple I'd ever known. Except maybe my dad's parents. My mom was alone in the world, but my dad was all she needed. My dad was a Marine, though. And that job comes with risks. He died during a training exercise when I was nine. My mom received a pretty good life insurance settlement, but she was far from a financial genius, and she had twelve kids. It disappeared quickly, spent on food and clothing mostly. Even with her working long hours while my older sisters watched us, money was tight. She did the best she could. But she was tired. The kind of tired that only death can cure. During the summers, we'd go to New Hampshire. To my grandfather's farm. Those summers were the best of my childhood.

"During one, my mother met a man by the name of Lionel Gauvin. He was kind, and he had money. A lot compared to my mother. He wanted to take care of her. And us. He made promises and moved us into his home in Boston. Things seemed to be taking a positive turn—until the following summer. When he told my mother we were to stay in Boston. We were a family now.

"She argued, saying it was the only time we saw my dad's family, and we loved it up there.

"I don't know what happened that night. But we didn't go to New Hampshire that year. And we weren't allowed to call our grandparents unless he was on the line with us. I knew this was bad. I told my mother to leave him. That I'd get a job to help out. Dustin and Matt wanted to, too. We started washing cars in the neighborhood to earn money, show her we were serious--"

"Dustin and Matt?"

"My triplet brothers."

"Last question--"

"We're identical."

She couldn't believe it. There were two other gorgeous men out there just like him? Impossible. No one was like her Lucas.

"Anyway, my mother was never the same after that night. She told us we weren't going to see our grandparents and that we needed to just accept it. She *begged* me to accept it. I couldn't. I wrote them a letter explaining as best I could.

"Next thing I knew, my grandfather was on the doorstep. He told her he was here to collect all of us who wanted to go for the summer. I packed a bag as she screamed at him. We all piled into this huge van he rented, and we were off. I could breathe again. I'd saved us. For the summer, at least.

"A few weeks later, mom and Lionel showed up on the farm. Lionel said they were going to take us home, and if my grandfather pulled another stunt like that, he'd file kidnapping charges. There was nothing my grandfather could do. I didn't know what was coming, but even if I did, we didn't have any proof.

"I'd later learn they waited five weeks because that's how long it took my mother's face to heal from the beating she'd received when he discovered we were gone. That was the last time she'd take a hit for me."

Tanvi sucked in a breath. He refused to look at her, and she was glad. He'd gotten angry the last time she'd shown any kind of pity, and she knew her face was projecting her sorrow.

"I knew something was wrong. Mom wasn't mom anymore. I'd learn later the hell she endured because of me. It's why I pay her rent to this day. Even though she still calls him. Still visits him in prison.

"But I'm getting ahead of myself. The abuse started when we got home, but it wasn't from Lionel. It was from my mother. If me, Matt, or Dustin acted up, she'd put us all in the closet. We'd be in there for hours—days, sometimes. Dustin would lose it. He couldn't handle the tight spaces, and he'd panic. So, I started distracting him with games and stories. War stories with Marines like my dad used to tell us. Matt would stay silent the entire time we were in there. Like he was watching a movie. No crying, no pleading. He'd just survive it. When Lionel would realize we were gone, he'd come 'rescue' us. He'd tell us he didn't know why our mother was so cruel, and he'd talk to her about it. But we needed to do our best to follow the rules. He was trying to get us on his side by having *her* torture us.

"Dustin and I lost it. We knew we'd end up in there even if we didn't do anything wrong, so we decided to make it worth it. I'd act out. I hit, spat, threw things. I hated her. I wanted my mother back. The strong woman she was before. Not this shell of a person who had to hurt us to make it through the day. We skipped school, started smoking, boosted cars--"

"How old were you?" Tanvi's heart broke at his retelling. He spoke with a nonchalance he couldn't feel.

He chuckled as he took another cigarette out of the pack and put it between his lips. He didn't light it, though. The white cancer-causing stick bounced between his teeth as he selected his next words. "Twelve. Lionel can't handle it. He starts in on us as soon as we get home at night. I guess we stole his buddy's car. It was a shame. If we'd known, we would have torched it, too. That's when I got these." He held out his forearm with the bullet hole tattoos. Despite the pain he must have felt receiving the burns, there was mischief in his eyes as he thought of the car ablaze. He took the cigarette and held if between his fingers. Eyeing it as he spoke. "It went on like that. He was a creative son of a bitch. But we wouldn't stop. If anything, the beatings encouraged us. There was nothing he could do to make us comply. So, the summer after I turned thirteen, Lionel announces we're going back to New Hampshire for the summer. He's arranged everything. We were off the wall, excited. I stopped all the bad behavior. Dustin kept up. He's addicted to it by then, I swear. We're packing, and Lionel tells us the girls aren't going. It's a guys only trip. We all faltered, even my little brothers. We knew he was planning something, and it wouldn't be good. Matt, Dustin, and I came up with a plan. Our older sisters were fighting tooth and nail to get all of us to go, but that wasn't working. So, Matt agreed he'd stay behind. Dustin and I would take our younger brothers up to New Hampshire, and we'd get help. We had proof now. We had the stories, the ER trips, scars, and the fact that mom had been the perpetrator of a lot of the abuse. We had her. Mom couldn't promise to leave Lionel, and make it go away.

"So, we went." He took a deep breath, rolling the cigarette between his thumb and pointer finger. "After a couple weeks of talking to the authorities, my Gramps getting a lawyer, and going over everything, Matt stopped answering my calls. No one was answering. When I went back to get him and the girls, they said he ran away. They assumed he was in New Hampshire with us. My older sisters had that same broken look my mother now sported, and my younger sisters? They wouldn't talk to or look at me. After a few months in New Hampshire as the investigation was ongoing, they started to talk.

"It took five years, but they eventually found Matt's body buried in the backyard. My little sister said Lionel came into her room one night, and Matt was already in there. He knew something was going to go very wrong that night. And he was right. Lionel broke each one of my sisters. He sold them to his friends as he'd been doing with my mom for God knows how long. He saw her and her daughters as a way to make money. He told me later, that he would have sold me and my brothers, too, but Dustin and I were so wild, he didn't want to risk it. That's why he sent us away. He tried 'saving me' from my evil mother—tried beating me, tried everything he could to keep me down. And every step of the way, I met his efforts with a bigger 'fuck you.' When he told me that—when he admitted to killing Matt— I leaped over the interview table, put him in a guillotine choke, and was going to kill him. The detectives and lawyers in the room got me off of him, but you know what? Not killing him, that's my only regret in life. He's sitting in a jail cell, fucking the weaker inmates without a care in the fucking world. And my brother had to rot in an unmarked grave for five years. My sisters survived unimaginable horrors. And he gets to breathe."

Tanvi placed a hand on his back and closed her eyes as a tear rolled down her cheek. She could feel the rage burning in his green eyes and the sorrow that filled his heart. It radiated off him, making part of her afraid. She couldn't speak. There were no words for what he'd just told her. "I should have killed him right off. As soon as I knew something was up with my mother."

"You were a kid," she said after a moment. "It was your mother's responsibility to protect you. She failed. Not you."

"I should have been the one to stay. I should have spoken out at school or written Gramps another letter. I could have done *something*."

"Of course," she said, and he glanced at her, pain replacing the rage in his eyes. "As an adult, looking back, you can see all the things you could have done. But you were a child, and you didn't have the gift of hindsight or all your accumulated knowledge. You were going through something no child should ever have to go through, and you did the best you could."

His gaze dropped to her lips, and her heart thundered in response. She looked away from him.

"You only see the good in people."

She blew air through her teeth in a forced laugh. "I'm pretty sure you scolded me for not seeing anything but stereotypes not too long ago."

"Fine, you see the good in me." He slipped his hand around the back of her neck and turned her head to face him. "How do you see good in me?"

"I see the good you're doing...the good you're striving to do. I see it because you are a good man, Luke." She felt her heart taking the plunge she'd promised herself she'd never take.

"I'm broken," he said, the last word breaking into a laugh. "I joined the military to kill the bad guys. I joined the FBI to kill the bad guys some more."

A little smirk came over her face. "How's that working for you?"

"Great, 'til you showed up." He let her go, and she felt his absence like a hole in her heart.

"What did I do?"

"You make me want to live in the light again. To not stay in the darkness. I don't want to kill the bad guys. I want to keep you safe. Keep you smiling," he scoffed at himself. "Pretty stupid, huh? You hate my guts, and all I want is to make you smile."

Her heart ached at his words. "I don't hate you."

He raised a brow. "You have to say that. I'm your security."

She slid her hand into his and pulled him back towards the hotel room. He tossed his unlit cigarette and followed her with a curious stare. She locked the door and sat him on his bed. Biting her lip. She knew he was leaving. Knew he'd never truly be hers. But maybe Adina was right. Having him for a short time was better than not having him at all.

"What are you doing?" he asked, a nervous laugh escaping his control.

"Taking a risk," she said as she straddled his lap.

He shook his head as a growl rumbled up from his throat. "I can't give you what you want."

The pain in his eyes broke her heart.

"All I want is tonight," she said, running her hands through his hair. "I wish there could be more. I do. I wish we could spend the rest of our lives getting to know each other. But if all I can have is tonight, I'll take it, savor it. And I'll look back on it fondly."

He squeezed his eyes shut and sighed as he slid her off his lap and stood up. She could tell he needed the distance to think straight, so she stayed put on the bed and waited. Like he was a feral animal pacing in a cage.

"You'll think back on it, and you'll hate me." His eyes met hers. "Tanvi, I strive to make people hate me. It makes it easier. But—" He looked away. "I couldn't bear you resenting me."

She stood and made her way slowly to his side. Slipping her hand into his, she pulled him to face her, then slid her other hand up onto his cheek. She pulled gently until he looked her in the eye. "I'm telling you right here, right now. I know you have to go. I'm not happy about it, but I'm okay with it. I don't want to look back on this and regret not letting you in." She placed his hand on her bare chest just above her swooping neck line so he could feel her heart racing. "Feel that? That's for you. I need you, need your touch." She slid her other hand into his hair and pulled him close so their foreheads were touching. "I... need to give you this." She was vulnerable, nervous, and exposed, her emotions shining on her face for him to see. She'd torn her wall down in surrender, and her body ached as she took in his scent.

His breathing was labored as he looked at her, searching her face.

"Fuck it," he said, running his fingers through her hair and pulling her to him. He smashed his face into hers with more need than she could have imagined. His other arm wrapped around her waist to pull her in. She pressed herself against him. Her body had craved this for so long, and she could no longer deny him. She needed this, needed to feel him. He ripped open her blouse. Buttons flew around the room as he destroyed the shirt. She dropped it to the floor and pulled her tank top over her head. His gaze on her like he was a pirate, and he'd just found the treasure to beat all treasures. He fell to his knees and kissed the bare skin of her stomach. They both moaned as he yanked at her belt and peeled her pants off. She scooted up on the bed, and he greedily ripped her panties from her body, spreading her legs before she had time to even think about what was happening. His mouth was on her, teasing and tasting. Enjoying every second of it. He ran his hands over her skin, building the pleasure. With her raspy, she called out his name.

TWENTY-EIGHT

Tanvi's body squirmed as Lucas devoured her. He needed to taste and touch every piece of her. If he could only have her once, he was going to make it count. In such a short timeframe, Tanvi had become his entire world. All of his desires and fears now lay with her, and he was helpless to fight it. He wanted this to be forever—so badly that it hurt. But they both knew that wasn't possible. His work was with the BAU in Virginia, and she could never leave her family. They were too close.

Grabbing her hips, he pulled her closer to him so he could lap at the tender folds of her core. Each moan, each whimper teaching him how to touch her. How to make her scream his name. And it was what he wanted more than life itself. Sliding one long finger inside her, she gasped and arched her back in response.

He slid his other hand up her body and over her breast. Pushing her bra aside, and pinching her nipple. She exhaled through her teeth as her eyes closed and her back arched.

"Luke," she said, her brows knitted together as pleasure threatened to overtake her. "I need you."

"I'm right here," he said between long, teasing licks.

"No," she sat up, pushing him back. "I need you inside me."

He grinned as he hooked his hands behind her knees and

pulled her back onto the bed. "If I only get one night, I'm taking my time. And you're going to like it."

She whimpered, so he slid two fingers inside, pumping against her warm wetness as she settled back in. He wondered how long she'd endure his teasing before she'd take charge.

Her pleasure building, he inserted yet another finger into her pulsating center. She was tightening around his fingers and her moaning intensified. He knew her climax was close. He swirled his tongue around her clit in time to his fingers. She lifted her hips and sucked in a breath. He quickened his pace as she bit her lip against her moans. He couldn't have that. Pulling at her nipples, he flicked his tongue over her clit. She screamed his name as her pussy clenched around him. She buried her hand in his hair and pulled his face against her as she came. He worked until he'd wrung the last tremor from her body.

Lucas lifted himself up and leaned over her. Still half-dressed. She shivered again as he stared down at her. He'd never seen anything more beautiful.

"Will you fuck me now?" she asked, mischief in her large, brown eyes.

"Do you want me to fuck you?" he asked. His voice hitching at the thought of asking what he wanted to. "Or do you want something else?"

She frowned, tilting her head to the side. "Are you asking if I want—you to make love to me?"

He looked away. He wasn't one to make love. He was one to fuck. Tanvi had changed his world. Visions of her had haunted him. His name on her lips had made his heart race, and *her* name was now branded on his soul. There was no escaping this feeling any longer. All he wanted was to give himself fully and worship every part of her body.

She placed a hand on his cheek, forcing him to look at her. The smile on her face was more than he could bear. She leaned up and captured his lips with hers before pulling back.

"Make love to me, Lucas?" she bit her lip, and he positioned himself between her legs. His jeans still in place she whimpered as she struggled with his belt. He laughed as he kissed her cheek and slowly made his way down her neck. Giving up on the belt, she slid her hands in his hair. Clutching him to her. Pulling back, he removed his clothes, retrieved a condom from the bedside table, and she welcomed him back. Her hands roamed his body, sliding over scars from numerous beatings. But she didn't hesitate on them. Didn't focus on them or avoid them like other women had. No. She was focused on him. All of him. She reached between them and grabbed his shaft. He hissed at the sudden attention, and she let out a laugh. God, he loved that sound. She guided him to her. He slid himself slowly inside her warm, wet, tight center.

"Fuck," he said as he fought his rising pleasure. He wanted this to last a lifetime. He needed to etch everything—her scent, eyes, raspy whispers, soft skin—into his memory. Despite where they would be living or where career aspirations would lead them, they both knew there would be no returning from this moment—this was forever.

"That's what I was going to say." She laughed again, sliding her hands over his hips and pulling him forward. They found a rhythm that satisfied her and kept him in control. Pumping in and out, he stared down at her, enjoying every second. Every single inch. She squeezed her breasts together, teasing him, and he buried his face into her welcoming cleavage, reveling in the feel of her skin against his.

"You feel so good, Tanvi."

She opened her mouth to speak but stopped, and he was dying to know why. What was she keeping from him? He moved faster against her, feeling her clench around him as she moaned. Dragging her nail down his back, she wrapped her legs around his hips. He pounded against her.

"Lucas, yes," she rasped in his ear, pulling him closer as her body convulsed. Waiting until her second orgasm was over, he followed into the bliss of the moment.

• • •

Tanvi lay in the moment before being fully awake. She frowned as she felt the smooth sheets slide over her naked body. She never slept naked. Her eyes popped open as the night before came rushing back. She smiled as she looked to her right and saw Lucas. He was fast asleep on his stomach, arms tucked under the pillow, face hidden.

Her heart soared at the memories of his touch, before plunging at the realization that she could only have him for one night. And that one night was over. The pain caught in her throat, making it hard to breathe. She gathered her clothes as quietly as she could so as not to wake him. Stopping to gaze out the window, she became lost in the lights of the city. A million blinking stars. A beautiful galaxy of people, hopes, dreams, hardships.

They'd slept the day away, and they'd need to head back to the station soon.

Anxiety rose in her chest. She felt helpless, knowing Julie or another woman was in the clutches of a madman.

"What are you thinking about?" Lucas's voice startled her. She gave a nervous laugh as she turned to him. He had shifted to his side, the white sheet covering him from the waist down. He was breathtaking. She wanted nothing more than to climb back into bed with him and forget about everything awful and ugly in the world. "You looked so serious."

"I was thinking about the case. We should get back." She was walking past the bed, toward her room, when his rough hand slid around her wrist. He pulled her to him and planted a kiss on her lips before she could ask him what he was doing.

"If there was something we could do, they'd call us," he said as he pulled her across him and back into the bed. She wanted nothing more than to hide away in his arms.

"You know as well as I do, we can help," she said, looking him in the eye. His gaze drifted over her, and the corner of his mouth quirked up.

"Yeah," he leaned in and nuzzled her nose. "I just don't want this to end."

She placed a hand on his cheek. He leaned in, kissing her neck. She didn't want it to end, either. "I know. But Julie Martin could still be alive, despite Nash's predictions, and I—"

He kissed her long and deep. Just when she was about to give in to him, he pulled back. "Okay, you win. Showers and back to the real world."

TWENTY-NINE

HQ WAS BUSTLING WITH ACTIVITY WHEN THEY ARRIVED. DETECTIVES from all over the city in one spot, ready to put a stop to the 'Summer of Murder' as the press had taken to calling it.

"Okay, people," Frank said, drawing their attention to him, "what do we know?"

"We know Carl is pulling the strings," Tanvi said. "He views himself as the mastermind of the operation. Joe did his part but doesn't seem to care about Carl at all."

"We know Carl has a strange attachment to Tanvi," Lucas added. "And someone tried to kidnap her. Most likely Joe. Carl also likes little girls. Blonde-haired, blue-eyed ones around ten years old."

"We know he's targeting women who are bettering themselves." Nash offered. "The greater the adversity that's overcome, the more Carl seems to hate them. Perhaps because he couldn't overcome his own."

"Joe is part of, if not the whole, black team, in a sick game of chess, where our city is the board," Frank finished.

"Wasn't his mother supposed to come in?" Tanvi asked.

"She never showed," John chimed from his place by the coffee maker. He looked exhausted, with deep bags under his eyes. He must have been working overtime on the case.

"What we have on Joe so far is he's an Indiana native, born in Fort Wayne, and moved to the city when he was in high school. His father was considered a weak man, and his mother ran the show. She was also the main disciplinarian. There were several calls to CPS about her brand of punishment, but nothing was ever found that deemed the removal of the children," John said, shoving his hands into his pockets.

"How many children?" Tanvi asked.

"Three," he said. "Joe was the middle child, and from what his sister said, he was the scapegoat. She won't even talk to her mother because of the abuse Joe received as a child. The youngest child died under strange circumstances, but it was ultimately ruled an accident."

"What were the circumstances?"

"He was found in the backyard, hanging from the clothesline. It was decided he climbed the tree in the yard and fell onto the clothesline, hanging himself. The older sister doesn't think it's possible. Says mom murdered him."

"We need to talk to mom," Tanvi added.

"Agreed," Lucas said.

"Joe's problems only grew as he got older," John continued, pacing as he spoke. "He became a Peeping Tom and petty thief, stealing neighborhood girls' underwear."

"Girls?" Tanvi asked.

"His own age. Fifteen, sixteen, there about." He waited for more questions, but when they didn't come, he continued. "He then graduated to fires. Spent time with a girl known for prostitution, Constance Peura. Her parents kicked her out, and this seems to be how she made ends meet."

"Aileen Wuornos much?" Lucas added.

"You have no idea," John said with raised brows. "They lost touch when she was convicted for murdering a John."

"Is she still incarcerated?" Tanvi asked.

"I'm not sure. I can look into it."

"Do that."

"So, for now," Frank said, "we need to be talking to Joe's mother—"

"There's more," John piped up. "Joe had a relationship with a woman named Maria Delgada. They broke up a couple months before Susan Johnson's body was found."

Tanvi looked at the girl they'd deemed the first. Her photo stuck to the board with a pawn symbol next to it. A teen who'd stolen her older sister's ID to go clubbing. Her financial aid package for Stanford had just come through.

"So, the mother and the ex-girlfriend," Frank said, pulling her back to the conversation.

"Where can we find Maria?" Lucas asked.

"Her last work update was a restaurant. A little, Italian place over on East Washington Street, Luigi's."

"Tanvi and I can take her and the mother."

"Sounds good. Kincaide is on her way over so Nash can go over everything."

As if on cue, Fiona Kincaid entered the room with her nose in her phone as her thumbs flew over the screen. After a moment, she looked up to Frank. "This better be good," she said. "I have court in twenty minutes, and this is not part of my normal prep."

Nash drew her attention to the board. "Looking at the chess strategy the black team was using, I was able to figure out how white was playing—"

"Wait," she said, shaking her head. "We have teams of assholes?"

"Yes, and we've only caught two. We have no idea how many are actually playing at this point," Tanvi added.

"As I was saying," Nash said, drawing their attention back, "the following cases of yours will be impacted by this."

She looked over at the images. "Shit. How certain are you?"

"Very," he said. "I've verified that each received the Cheshire Cat smile and had a chess piece on their person or around the dump site where they were found."

"This one's closing arguments are today. Do you have DNA? I need something strong."

"DNA came back late yesterday," John said. "Another huge thank you to my buddy at the lab. They are all connected through Joe's DNA and a specific toy used. And the white team, all condom lubricant, but a pubic hair found on two of the victims, Ali Kim and Susan Johnson, match."

Tanvi frowned. "A toy?"

"A crude dildo made from wood. Waiting on those tests to narrow down the kind."

"Does Joe have performance problems?" Lucas asked.

"That or his buddy does. Either way, we can use it in our next interview. Unfortunately, his lawyer is pushing things forward before we're ready."

"His arraignment is this afternoon. With these facts, I can get him remanded. But we have to send them over to the defense. This might also get him talking," Fiona said, sounding a bit more hopeful.

"That's all great, but I have more," Nash said. Tanvi looked back at him. "I know what he's trying to do. The black team—that's Joe's team—is trying to do kingside castle. White likely did the same, and Julie Martin's body should be found in this area."

"We're acting like she's dead?" Fiona frowned. "Before it's confirmed?"

"Unfortunately, this game is moving with or without us. So, yes, we need to look at this area and increase patrols as Black continues its attempt to do kingside castle. But we also need to look here for a body. After this move, they could do anything. It completes the opening moves. Black will probably stop copying White since we're onto them, which means our best chance of ending this now is closing."

"I'll keep the increased patrols in the area and send teams to search for Julie," Foster said from his place in the corner.

"I'll go look for Julie," Frank said. "Help coordinate."

Foster nodded. "Nightingale and McGinn can look into Joe. Be back here and ready to talk to him by four this afternoon."

THIRTY

Maria was outside the small, Italian restaurant, cleaning off tables as they approached.

"Maria Delgada?" Tanvi asked as they displayed their badges.

"Yeah?" she said, tucking a long lock of brown hair behind her ear. She was pretty. Far too pretty to be with Joe White.

"We have some questions for you regarding your ex-boyfriend, Joe White."

She crossed her arms over chest and leaned back. "What about that waste of space?"

"He's been connected to multiple murders."

"I wish I could say I was surprised," she said.

"That's a pretty strong statement," Tanvi shot back.

"Care to elaborate?" Lucas asked.

She led them around the corner, away from the dining area, and pulled a cigarette out of her pocket. She held it up, "You mind?"

They shook their heads.

She eyed Lucas. "You got a light?"

He pulled a Zippo lighter, inscribed with an eagle globe and anchor, from his pocket and lit her cigarette. She took a long drag and eyed Lucas up and down again. Tanvi fought the urge to slide her arm around his and pull him close.

"I swore I'd never tell a living soul this," she said. The ember glowed as she sucked on the filter, a wretched, gray cloud of smoke snaking around them. "Joe was sweet when we met. He was older and white, which isn't my type, but I thought, 'My type ain't working out,' so why not? You know? And it was nice. His mother was horrible. I've never met a woman with a worse cruel streak..." her eyes bugged out of her head in emphasis.

"Can you give up an example?" Tanvi asked.

"We're in his house, and she come busting into the bedroom. Screaming about how I'm a whore, and we're both going to rot in hell because he gave into my whore ways. He's weak, and he'll burn for his sins. And on and on."

"Is that why you broke up with him?"

"No, he chased her off, apologized profusely. He promised I'd never have to see her again and gave me three orgasms. So, I let it slide," she smiled. "He was good in bed. Very attentive."

"Then, what happened?" Tanvi asked.

"He's got this friend, new to town, from the Bronx or something. I don't know. Big, black guy. He was ripped, too. No way this guy had a hard time picking up women. Well, one day, we're all hanging out, and he decides I'm going to have sex with him. I said, 'The hell I am,' and he hit me." She ran her tongue over her teeth as she relived the event. "He took what he wanted, I screamed. Joe—Joe watched. When it was over, I left and I never spoke to him again."

"You didn't report it?" Tanvi asked.

"No. Never spoke of it 'til now."

"Did he use anything on you besides...his penis?" Tanvi asked as gently as she could.

"No," she said, looking behind her to ensure the patrons eating a few tables away weren't listening.

"What is his name?" Lucas asked.

"Damon, Damien, or something, he went by 'D.' " She rolled her eyes. "Big D. I don't know his last name."

"Could you work with a sketch artist?" Luke asked, scratching at his chin.

"I'm really not sure, considering that I've worked real hard to forget that man, that time in my life. I'm sorry."

"Don't be sorry," Tanvi offered. "You've already helped us out a lot."

She nodded before crouching down to put her cigarette out on the cement.

"Before we go, though," Lucas began as she stood, "did Joe have any other friends?"

"I don't know their names, but around the time D showed up, he started hanging out with this group, over on Rural Street. I don't know how many, or anything. But I picked him up once, and there were at least five leaving the house."

"Did you get a good look at any of them?"

"Not really. It was dark, and I waited in my car."

"How often did they meet?" Tanvi asked as Lucas was messing with his phone.

"Nightly, for beers after work. It was putting a strain on our relationship before, you know."

"Do you recognize this guy?" An image of Carl lit up Luke's phone.

"I think it was his house, actually," she said with a sad look. "He let people out and went back inside as we left."

"Thank you so much for your time. This has been very helpful," Tanvi said as they turned to leave.

"Hey," she called to Lucas. They paused, turning back to face her. "If you wanted to give me a call when things settle down, I wouldn't mind."

He offered her a smile and his cheeks turned pink. "Sorry, I'm taken."

"The good ones always are," she said, tossing her hair over her shoulder as she returned to work.

As they walked past the edge of the building, Lucas slipped his hand into Tanvi's and pulled her into the alleyway. Pressing her up against the side of the building, he placed a kiss on her lips, pressing his body into hers. He slid his tongue into her mouth drawing a moan form her. She slid her hands into his hair as his hands roamed her body, and she reveled in him. His earthy scent invaded her senses as his tongue danced with hers. When he pulled back, she was left wanting much, much more.

"I've been dying to do that all day," he said as he pulled back, his hips still pressing into her. He gave her a peck on the cheek.

"Have you?" she asked. "Or is this in response to her eye-fucking you?"

"That didn't help, but the urge was there before."

"Nice save," Tanvi said with a smile, it faded quickly. "Maybe she needs a cop type after what she's been through."

"As long as he's a good one."

"*You're* a good one."

"No, I'm not. Not really—" he laughed, nuzzling her neck.

"Well, I like you."

"Yeah, but you're weird. Just ask anyone who knows me."

"I don't think they know you at all if that's the case."

"Eh," he shrugged. "What would you know?"

He moved to kiss her again, and she laughed as she gave him a light shove. "We have no time for fun. We need to get back and get to work. Let's locate Big D and sort out this mess."

With a childish pout, he followed her back out into the street and to her car.

Back at the precinct, they filled in Frank and Nash on what they'd discovered. Before anyone else had a chance to speak, a commotion in the hallway drew their attention.

"The people from the press conference about the murdered women," the man was saying.

"Please," a woman's voice pulled Lucas into the hallway. The anguish that poured out of their voices left him feeling helpless. "Our little girl is missing!"

"I can help you," Lucas said. They turned to him, and light shined in their eyes. "Right this way, please."

"You're with the FBI? We saw you on TV for the first press conference," the woman said. "I'm Debbie, Debbie Cantor, and this is my husband, Jim. Our daughter Miranda went missing."

Lucas raised his hand. "When was this?"

"Mr. And Mrs. Cantor," Tanvi said, approaching them as soon as they entered the squad room. "What are you doing here?"

"Do we know you?"

Tanvi paused. "This is the homicide unit. I've been following your daughter's case."

"The man who was on the news, Carl Singh?" Jim said. "He was our neighbor."

The expression on Tanvi's face screamed, 'Oh, shit' even if the words didn't come out of her mouth. Lucas gave her a questioning look.

"Mr. and Mrs. Cantor?" Frank said, getting their attention and gesturing to an interview room. "Could you please come in here? We can get started."

Tanvi walked over to him pulling a flyer from the stack on her desk, she handed it to him.

It was a missing flyer for a little girl with blonde hair and blue eyes. His heart sank.

"We would have found her. We went through that house with a fine-toothed comb," Lucas said as tears formed in Tanvi's eyes. She nodded as she fought it back. Lucas took her by the arm, looking for a place to hide away. He moved toward the stairwell. "Come on."

As soon as the door clicked shut, she buried her face in his chest and sobbed. He wrapped himself around her and let his own defeat wash over him. He pulled her close with one arm and rubbed her back with the other. He wasn't used to this. He wasn't sure how to handle his own feelings, let alone hers. So, he settled for just being present with her in her grief.

"We don't know anything for sure yet," he consoled as muffled conversation trickled in from the neighboring rooms.

"Like you said, we searched every inch of that house. If she was there, we would have found her. And since she wasn't—" her voice broke.

"He could have kept her somewhere else."

"And she's starved to death since we've had him in jail?" she scoffed. "How is that better?"

"Rook," he said, unable to stop his lip from curving up. "He wanted to be found. He's meticulous in his planning. If she's alive, she's being looked after or has access to food and water."

"And Julie?" Her lip quivered. "Every time Nash says she's dead, it's like another nail being pounded into my heart."

"We have to hope for the best and work the case. So, let's get in there."

"Thanks, you're right. I need to run to the ladies," she said, taking a deep breath and wiping her eyes. "Want to splash some cold water on my face."

"I'll go with you."

"No, I'll be fine."

"Your food should have been fine, too."

"I'll go to the one right down the hall from the squad room. How's that for a compromise?"

"You were going to go to that one, anyway."

"You stay in the squad room. I'll be back in a flash."

He growled as she moved past him, to the door. He followed her as far as the squad room door and then stopped, listening to the conversation pouring in through the speaker. Foster stood there, listening, arms crossed as the parents told their story.

"The detective we're working with won't listen to us. He said

Carl couldn't be involved because the women in your case are all post-puberty or something?"

"While that is true, when we went into Carl's house—"

"I never saw you go into Carl's house," Debbie said, breathing heavily.

"We've been to all of his known residences," Frank assured her.

"I can't believe I didn't notice."

"We were a little busy," Jim suggested.

"What we found," Frank tried again, "is that Carl is attracted to pre-pubescent girls."

The parents' despair was clear even from a distance by Frank's pause.

"We found child pornography and a shrine to Alice and Wonderland in one of his rooms."

"The child—" It sounded like Debbie was going to puke. Once she had control of herself again, she continued. "Was Miranda involved...in any of it?"

"Not that we know of. We have officers going through it now, trying to identify the victims. But, there's a lot to go through."

"Oh, my God," Debbie sobbed.

"I'll give you a minute," Frank said. Lucas turned his attention back to the hall. A man in a hoodie was flying toward the elevators. A hoodie on an eighty-degree day was a bit odd.

The scream that ripped through the calm sent Lucas running straight into the lady's room. He rounded the corner to see Tanvi standing with her hand on her mouth, staring at the scene before her. A Cheshire Cat smile was drawn on the mirror, and on the sink directly beneath it was a woman's severed hand.

THIRTY-ONE

TANVI FOUND LUCAS IN THE HOTEL'S GYM. SHE LEANED AGAINST THE doorway to watch. With each exhale, he counted his reps on the weight bench. Sweat poured down his nose. Fury still burned in his eyes, even after the intense workout. Not that she blamed him. The fact that a hooded figure entered the precinct without being caught on a single camera set her on edge, too. The violation of her sacred space wasn't even at the top of the list as to why it bothered her. They suspected the hand was Julie's, but they can't be certain until the DNA came back. It was the left hand, and it was lacking an engagement ring, so the owner was anyone's guess at this point. And there was nothing she could do about it. So, rather than worry and allow toxic images to fester, she once again sought out Lucas McGinn. *Detective Nightingale and Agent Lucas McGinn.* The thought put a sparkle in her eye. Her heart yearned to give him peace of mind. The same peace of mind he'd blessed her with more than once. To make him smile again.

"You know, body builders can't even wipe their own asses," she said, trying to sound serious.

After two more reps, he replaced the bar and sat up. "Yeah, being doughy was never my thing. When you're an asshole, you have to at least make an attempt to be sexy."

"I know more than a few nice guys who'd disagree with you."

He shrugged. "Maybe in high school and college, he'd be right. But in his thirties? I bet he's married with two point five kids if he's doughy. Rockin' that dad bod and being an asshole at the PTA."

"Is that what you want?"

His emerald eyes met hers, not a deer in the headlights but definitely pained. "I don't know. Right now, I'd like you to make it to the end of this case. Once that happens, ask me again."

"You'd be a great father," she said. Her words hung heavily in the air. Only her fear of commitment steered her toward spinsterhood. She frowned. Even Elizabeth Bennet was open to love. She was just blinded by her hurt pride and missed it in Darcy's eyes. Tanvi looked back at Lucas. Maybe he was her Darcy.

"My dad was amazing, but he died when I was so young, I don't know." He chuckled nervously as he toweled his face.

"Do you want to try?"

"Maybe." He looked at her. "With the right person."

Hope filled her, along with... happiness? She wasn't sure, but she liked the way it tickled her chest. She took a step forward, eyeing him. "In the meantime, do you want to practice with me?"

"You want me to spank you?"

She laughed. "No—well—"

"Ha! You wanna get spanked!"

She grabbed his towel, twirled it, and whipped him in the butt with it. A resounding crack filled the room before she erupted into laughter and ran away, down the hall. He took off after her. She turned to throw the towel at him, sprinting to the elevators. He barely made it in before the doors closed.

"You were actually going to make me wait for the next one?" he asked as he wrapped an arm around her waist and pulled her close to him. He was completely soaked through. And if he was anyone else, she'd have shoved him away.

"I thought you could take the stairs," she teased, staring with doe eyes. "I did interrupt your work-out after all."

"It wasn't cardio," he said before taking her mouth with his. He grabbed her leg, pulling it up over his hip and pressed into her. She could feel his hard cock through her leggings. As she moaned, the door opened, and an elderly couple stood, staring at them. The man looked shocked. The woman was smiling as she pressed the button. "We'll take the next one, dear. Have fun."

Tanvi let out a laugh as Lucas worked on her neck, silencing her and sending chills all over her body. They couldn't get to the room fast enough.

As soon as the door opened, he took her hand and sprinted down the hall. It was all she could do to keep up with him. Apparently, he'd hit his second wind. Tanvi couldn't help but feel like a giddy school girl. People jumped out of his way. She could only imagine the look of determination on his face.

They reached the door, and Lucas put his key in the card reader. It gave an angry beep and flashed red. A grunt of frustration escaped him, and he attempted to use the key card again. Again, it beeped angrily and flashed red. He stepped back to check the room number as she slid her hand down his arm. His attention moved to her as she slid her fingers over the key, taking it from him. She placed it in the lock, waited a moment, and then removed it. The door unlocked, and she pushed the handle down. He pushed her through the door, covering her lips with his and walking her to the bed without breaking the lip-lock.

She started unbuttoning her shirt in the hopes of saving it from Lucas, and he pulled back to pull his t-shirt over his head. He paused.

"I'm kinda sweaty." He turned and left her there, and her jaw dropped. If it had been anyone else, she might have cared that he was sweaty, but not Lucas. And if it had been someone else, she probably wouldn't have followed him into the shower.

Stripping off her clothes, she threw the curtain back. He was under the water, soap in hand, cock at attention. She bit her lip as she watched the water cascaded down his muscular form. God, he was gorgeous. All ripped muscles and tattoos. His eyes drifted down her body as much as hers. Stepping into the shower, she closed the curtain. She slid her hands up over his chest, spreading the suds around. She worked her tongue over his lips before inserting it into his mouth. The pulsing cock entered, between her legs, effortlessly, and she rubbed herself on him as she took his lips into hers. As he lifted one of her silky, wet legs, he plunged himself deep inside her. A gasp escaped her as water splashed onto her now-closed eyes.

"Shit, Tanvi," he huffed between breaths. "You're so wet."

"You have that affect me."

He thrust against her, and pleasure shot through her body. She pulled at him as he pressed her against the wall and put his head on her neck. He bit her lightly as he moved against her.

"You feel so good. *Too good,*" he whispered into her ear. She was coming undone. His touch, his scent. He was making her crazy. She needed him. Needed this.

"More," she demanded.

He laughed against her throat. "More what?" he asked, slowing his hips to draw it out as he kissed a trail down her neck.

"More of you. I need more of you, Luke," she moaned.

"Like this?" he said, lifting her leg higher so he could push deeper inside her.

"Fuck, yes." She clawed at his back. She couldn't get close enough to him even as he pressed her against the wall with his body. He quickened the pace as they splashed and moaned. The man she could no longer toy with and attempt to resist was now pumping himself inside her as her pleasure built, filling her.

"Luke," she called out his name as she felt herself surrender to her orgasm. He gave a laugh as she convulsed around him. He picked her up, wrapping her legs around him, and slammed into her as he fought to reach his own release. She pulled herself to him in time to his rhythm, another orgasm building in her core. She clenched around him as she was pushed over the edge one more time. He joined her this time, and they both panted. His body shook with hers. He held her with one arm and braced the other against the wall as the last tremors of pleasure overtook them.

"Where'd you learn to do that?" she asked, breathless.

He eyed her. "Right here, right now." He winked as he caught his breath.

"What?" she slicked her drenched hair back. "I popped your shower sex cherry?"

"I don't like to share my shower," he said, kissing her nose. "Accept with you, apparently."

"Really?" she asked, a swell of pride growing in her chest. "How come?"

"I don't know." He placed her on the floor and turned to wash. "It always felt like an intrusion if a woman tried to get in my shower."

"I'm sorry."

"No," he turned back to face her. "I was glad. I didn't really want to wait."

A smile tugged across her lips.

LUCAS LAY HALF ASLEEP, LISTENING TO THE SOUND OF THE SHOWER. Focusing on the sounds of Tanvi washing rather than the infuriating truth of the case. Someone had been in the damn precinct to threaten her, and they had nothing to show for it. Except a hand they couldn't identify. A knock sounded at the door, pulling him out of his spiral. Frowning, he got up and slid his pants on. He went into his room and out his door to see Cora standing there, glaring at him.

"You think I don't know where you just came from?"

"I thought you'd be happy." His attempt not to sound like a smart ass was off to a terrible start.

"What if I was her boss?"

"Foster's not that observant. She'd be fine. Plus, he's so old-fashioned he'd never admit to seeing anything as long as it didn't affect her work."

"Get a shirt, and come down for coffee."

"Tanvi's in the shower."

"She'll be fine. Just knock on the door, and tell her where you're going. We'll be in the lobby."

He sighed, not wanting to leave Tanvi unattended, but her mother was right. She'd be fine. And Cora clearly had something on her mind. So, he nodded and did as she asked.

The ride down in the elevator was significantly more awkward than he'd anticipated.

"I thought you'd—you know—be happy about this?"

"It's not you sleeping with my daughter that has me upset," she said, authority in her tone. "Though some form of commitment wouldn't hurt."

He leaned back. He wasn't sure how to do that. Or if Tanvi even wanted it.

"I'm worried about this killer. I've been watching the news, and he's killed so many."

"It's multiple killers," Lucas told her. "It's a strange case. But Tanvi's safe. Don't worry about it."

"With you stuck to her like glue, of course she's safe," she spat as the elevator door opened. "But I have three other daughters."

Lucas frowned. "I don't think he'd mess with anyone who isn't directly related to the case."

"I might be paranoid," she said. "But I keep feeling someone has been in my house. When I get home. And it's not the rat. I called someone about that. They charged me two hundred dollars to feed it for two weeks. Lord knows how much it'll cost when they actually kill the damn thing."

"Did they say if it was breeding?"

She looked up at him, horrified.

"They'll get rid of them for you, no reason to worry." He felt like a middle-schooler trying to absolve himself in the principal's office.

They ordered their coffees and took a seat where he could watch the front door.

"What can I do for you?" he asked.

"I know I put on a brave face where Tanvi is concerned. Suggesting you get her pregnant and all. I hope you understand that was a joke. Not that a baby would hurt her, but someone getting her pregnant and leaving would be—" She shook her head. "Too much for her to bear. She'd never give another man the time of day. She's too independent that way. She doesn't need a man. She wants one. And I want one for her. I'd like him to be you. You understand the demands of her job, and you don't put up with her shit. You're good for her. That Henry was a doormat. No good for someone like Tanvi."

"I wouldn't leave her with a kid. Besides, she's got this covered. You don't have to worry about her," he tried.

"Well, I do," she said, "But that's not why I'm here. I have a bad feeling. Like I said, I think someone's been in my house, and I'm scared for my girls."

"Any way you could get out of town for a bit?"

"I could get Yasmin and go to Reina's, but my husband and Adina, no way."

"We can keep an eye on them."

"Can you?" she asked, not looking impressed.

He scanned the surrounding patrons, leaning forward, over his coffee. "It would be tough," he admitted. "If we put Tanvi back in the house, the risks increase, but if someone's in your home—have you caught anything on the game?"

"I haven't been setting it up during the day."

"Set it up in the kitchen the next time you plan to leave. Try to make it look like it's not on, or hide it. See if your fears are founded."

She nodded. "That's good."

"Plus, you might catch the guy we're looking for and save us all a lot of trouble." He smiled.

"Wouldn't that be nice?" Her smile faded. "Well, no, because then you'd leave."

"I still think you and Yasmin should leave, though." He looked back and forth at the people moving through the hotel. "I'll talk to Frank. Maybe we both stay at your house with your husband and Adina."

She gave a cackle of a laugh. "David will leave before he lets you sleep with his daughter under our roof. He stood outside her door that night you two were drunk until he was convinced you'd passed out."

He shook his head, imagining her father. "He's a good guy."

"He's quite religious. He didn't even want to let her move in with Henry. It's like pulling teeth every year when I put up the Christmas tree."

"Could he have stopped her? From moving in with Henry?" Lucas asked before he could think better of it.

"No. In trying to stop her relationship with Henry from moving to that step, he would have ended her relationship with him. I was able to make him see it."

TANVI HOPPED OFF THE ELEVATOR, READY TO SEE HER MOTHER. SHE found her and Lucas sitting in a secluded nook where he could see the entrance to the hotel. She approached him from behind, a house plant obscuring her from view.

"So, you see, Lucas, sometimes the best course of action isn't to muscle your way through, and hope for the best."

Tanvi paused as her mother's words hit her.

"We don't even know what this is yet. I mean, we're just fooling around. My job, my life, is in Virginia."

Tanvi took a few steps back. She didn't want to hear this. Couldn't hear this. She slipped back into the elevator and returned to her room as her fear raged in her chest. She knew what he was saying was true. He had never lied to her. But that didn't seem to matter to her heart.

THIRTY-TWO

TANVI DID LITTLE TO HIDE HER ANGER AS THEY RODE THE ELEVATOR, not that he noticed. Lucas stood in the corner, looking at his phone. He'd asked her why she hadn't come down to see her mom, but she'd brushed it off.

"Frank wants us at Joe's house. Look for his mother and see if anything creepy stands out. Nash will meet us with the warrant."

"Whatever," she said, wishing the elevator would hurry. She couldn't be near him like this. She needed to keep her distance, or she'd ever survive when he fled back to Virginia. His eyes shifted from his phone to her, and her heart began to race.

"What's wrong?" he asked, concern showing in his eyes.

"Nothing, I'm just tired," she offered him a smile, but it didn't work. Worry filled his eyes, and she hated herself for avoiding the truth. But what good would it do? They were on borrowed time, and she needed to make sure she didn't fall in love with him.

He stepped in close to her and pulled her against him, wrapping his arms around her. God, he smelled good. Felt good. She fought it before giving in to the hug.

"What's got you flustered? Are you worried about catching these guys before they take someone else?"

She shrugged, knowing that if she spoke, her tears would flow, and the ruse would be over before it began. A pang of guilt shot through her. Women were losing their lives, and here she was, worried the guy she liked was going to be leaving town.

"Don't worry, Rook," he said as he placed a kiss on her forehead that nearly did her in. "We'll catch these assholes. You practically know what they're doing before they do."

"I wish that were true," she said as the elevator opened. She pulled away from him, determined to keep her distance for the rest of his stay.

Joe's house was immaculate. It looked the way you'd expect an older woman's house to look. Ornamental rugs, glass cases placed throughout with her many treasures on display. What Tanvi didn't see was any hint that Joe lived there at all.

"They share this place?" Lucas said as he entered, echoing her thoughts.

"Supposedly."

"Mrs. White?" Lucas called out. "Mrs. White, we're here to do a wellness check? You were due at the Police Station to talk about your son and never showed?"

Silence greeted them. Lucas pulled his gun and headed for the stairs. "Mrs. White?" Tanvi turned to enter the kitchen, which was empty. The bread on the counter was moldy, so she opened the fridge. All take-out containers. *Hmm.*

A panicked cry filled the silence. She raced to the stairs to see Lucas sprawled across the landing with a calico cat on his chest. It purred and rubbed on him as he fought to catch his breath.

"You think they steal part of your life every time they terrify you, and that's how cats end up with so many?" he asked. She laughed and the cat set about cleaning itself, still perched on his chest. Tanvi plucked the feline up and placed her in the living room.

"Need me to protect you?" she asked.

"Please," he said as he took the hand she offered. As soon as his hand slid into hers, she knew she'd made a terrible mistake. The memory of his touch and screaming his name as she convulsed flashed through her mind, followed by a scene of him holding her tightly. His hands found her hips, sending jolts of pleasure through her as he slipped by to take point.

"I could have done it," she protested.

"I know," he said, giving her that damn smile before continuing up the stairs. At the top, nothing looked amiss. They made their way to the bedroom at the end of the hall. "Mrs. White?" he called. When there was no answer, he pushed the door open, leading with his weapon. He fell back against the door with a look of disgust on his face.

"What?" All of Detective Nightingale's training and experience moved through her in waves with each beat of her heart. With all senses tingling and on high alert, she entered the room slowly, only to be met with a perfectly orderly room. Bed made, curtains drawn. And there, on the bookshelf, was a 3D model of Joe's mother's head. "I think that's an urn. The sister didn't say she was dead, did she?"

"No, but she wouldn't know unless Joe told her." He pulled out his phone and held it to his ear. As he waited to speak to Frank or Foster. She looked around the room. On the bedside table was a journal. Lifting it, she opened to the middle. The long, elegant script covered the pages.

Lord, what will I do with this son of mine? What did I do to deserve such terrible offspring? He's still with that whore. Who sleeps with a man like that, with his mother in the next room? And the friend he has. He scares me. I've told Joseph I don't want him around here, but he doesn't listen to me anymore.

• • •

TODAY, JOSEPH INFORMED ME I'D BE MOVING TO A HOME. I WON'T GO, I tell you. That boy is despicable. To hide me away like some dirty secret. Like he wasn't the product of his father's disgusting weaknesses. Like he wasn't born an abomination. He's always been this way. Always been a disappointment. Always been disgusting. When he was a boy, I threatened to cut it off! He went white as a sheet, crying, "Please, no, mommy!" Maybe I need to remind him who I am. Maybe I will cut it off! He loves it even more now as a man with a whore to stick it in whenever he likes. Yes, I think that's it! Ha!

UNABLE TO READ ANY MORE OF THE MAD RAMBLINGS, SHE CLOSED THE journal with a dull *clap*. Joe was sick, but so was his mother.

"Hey, Frank, the mother is dead. At least, I assume her ashes are in this urn. It looks like her face—I don't know, his sister didn't know she was dead."

Tanvi handed him the journal. "There's confirmation of the abuse in her journal. She kept up until she died, it looks like. And she has more on the bookshelves."

Tanvi eyed the shelves. It looked like she had a few journals for every year since she was a girl.

Lucas put a hand on her shoulder. "We've got a warrant. Looking for proof, he killed his mother and was involved with Carl. Includes electronics."

She nodded as she looked out the window. There was a man in a car on the other side of the street looking up at her. He looked an awful lot like Maria described Big D. He looked at her and leaned back in his car. The sirens from the other units coming to assist with the warrant sounded in the distance, and he started his car.

"Lucas!" she called, running to the stairs and leaping to the landing, then to the ground. "Car now!"

Tanvi raced out the front door, praying Lucas was with her as she hopped into the driver's seat. He was there as she started the engine and threw it into drive. He slapped the dash light on as she caught up to the strange car. Rather than pulling over, the car sped up through a red light.

"Hold on!" she called as she floored it. He braced himself as they barely missed a sedan crossing the intersection.

Lucas picked up the radio and called in the pursuit, the units behind them spreading out as they tried to box him in. Lucas called out the locations as Tanvi forced him into a corner. Two other police cars blocked his escape. He lost control of the car and slid into a light post. Tanvi locked up the brakes and turned the wheel, drifting to a stop just behind his crumpled wreck of a car. Tanvi sprang forward with her gun aimed at the man in the car. As always, Lucas was right there. He paused by the trunk, putting his ear to it.

"There's someone in here."

"Come out with your hands up!" Tanvi said, as the other officers surrounded the car. The door opened, and the man fell to the ground. "Hands on your head."

He complied, and Tanvi checked him for weapons as one of the officers cuffed him.

"And what exactly did he do?" Foster asked as he approached.

"He matched the description given to us by White's ex-girlfriend."

"If you're wrong," Foster said through clenched teeth. Lucas popped the trunk open with a crowbar, not giving Foster a chance to finish. A woman with tape over her mouth and her hands tied launched herself out of the confined space and into Lucas's arms.

Tanvi glanced at Foster. "That good enough for you?"

"Good work," he grunted. "I want your report on my desk before you leave tonight."

THIRTY-THREE

TANVI WAITED IN THE ER FOR THE DOCTORS TO ALLOW HER AND Lucas to speak to the woman from the trunk. Minutes felt like hours as the ER doctors kept them from what could be a crucial piece of the puzzle. All they had so far was her name—Lilliana Diaz. And Nash said he was trying to move his queen side bishop if he took her from work. If taken from home, it was unrelated. But Tanvi doubted that would be the case. Luke stepped out to get lunch. The boy was a bottomless pit. Couldn't even think about food at a time like this.

Movement caught her eye. Henry approached through the double doors, and she cursed her luck.

"Are you here for Ms. Diaz?" he asked.

"Yes, we need to speak to her."

"I'm afraid we had to sedate her," Henry said in that same tone he'd always used when disappointing her. Like she was a child, and he had to get rid of her as quickly as possible. Honestly, he wasn't even a good roommate.

As if on cue, Lucas approached with a coffee for her and sipping his own. "What's the deal?"

"He sedated her," Tanvi said, scowling.

"So, when can we speak to her?" Lucas asked Henry.

"Not today." Henry gave a fake smile.

Lucas looked him up and down, then his gaze shifted to the nurse leaving the room Lilliana was in.

"So, tomorrow?" Tanvi asked, stepping away from Lucas. As soon as Henry's eyes shifted from Luke to Tanvi, the agent made his move. He tapped the nurse on the shoulder and was speaking with her while Tanvi dealt with Henry.

"You should call first, though. She's very distraught."

"You know she was kidnapped, right? She needs, and may even want, to talk to us."

"Yeah, she's been through a severe trauma. Her psyche is in a fragile state, so it'd be best to wait until she asks for you."

"It's up to us to go in and initiate the conversation. If she doesn't like it we leave but then she has our cards," Tanvi scoffed. She couldn't believe this. If the patient declined to speak to her, sure, step in and be doctorly, but to deny them access was unheard of.

"Maybe that's how things used to be," he smirked. He glanced over to see Lucas had vanished as the nurse led him into Lilliana's room. Tanvi pushed past him. Hopefully, the nurse wouldn't get into too much trouble.

Lilliana was sitting up in the bed, a light blue hospital gown covered her, and she had an IV tube in her hand. A bandage around her head, but other than that, she looked unscathed by her experience.

"Thank you," she said to the nurse as Lucas sat down to speak to her.

"I'm SSA Lucas McGinn," he said quietly. "And this is Detective Tanvi Nightingale of the IPD."

"I've been asking for you," she said as Henry entered the room. Tanvi turned on him. He took two steps back out of the room, and Tanvi grabbed the door.

"I'm sorry, I need to speak to the doctor real quick. I'll be right back in." She gave them a tight smile and closed the door. "Fragile psyche? Are you freaking kidding me? If you're actually protecting your patient, then you can stonewall me all you want. But if you ever deny a patient access to a detective for petty, personal shit again, I'll go to the medical board. Time is always of the essence in cases like these. And you damn well know it. But because what? It's me, you decide to be an ass?"

"It's not you," he muttered, looking at his hands. Pushing his glasses back up his nose. "I broke up with Carla. I love you, Tanvi. I was lost, and your job is difficult. But I think if we got back together, we could make it work."

"Are you kidding me?"

"No, if you quit your job, I think we can be happy together."

"I don't like you enough to take you back without conditions. But you think telling me to quit my job would help?" she scoffed. "I can't believe I ever thought I could be with someone like you."

Tanvi shut the door in Henry's face. *What the hell was that?*

"So, you noticed him around the bar a few nights before the incident?"

"Yeah, and before that, there was this older, white guy who was giving me the creeps. I had no reason to fear him, it was just a feeling."

"Do you think you could pick him out of a lineup?"

"Probably. I mean, it was only a couple times, and I was performing."

Lucas pulled his phone out of his pocket and pulled up an eight-person lineup that included Joe's photo.

"Three," she blurted without hesitation. "His eyes. They stayed with me, I guess. It was like he was hyper all the time. Anxious and worried, but fixated on me."

Tanvi frowned. So, was the teen he snatched by the precinct just an opportunity too good to pass up? Frank interviewed her. She hadn't noticed anything strange leading up to her abduction, but she was so young, they figured that was why.

"Thank you," Lucas said. "Did he drug you?"

"No, he waited in the alley, outside the club, and grabbed me early this morning. I've been in that trunk all day. I thought I was going to die from the heat."

"He never brought you anywhere?"

"He just drove around. He'd stop for a while and then we'd be going again. It was terrible." She turned to Tanvi. "If you hadn't spotted him, I think I would have died in there. It was so hot it was hard to breathe."

Tanvi exchanged a look with Lucas. "I'm glad I could help."

"IF JOE WAS THE SUBMISSIVE, WHY WAS THIS GUY SO LOST WITHOUT him?" Tanvi asked as they walked down the hospital corridor, toward the lot.

"Frank called. There's another dungeon in Joe's house, like there was in Carl's. I think it has more to do with him trying to make sure it was safe than him being lost." Lucas said, offering her a smile. He wrapped his arm around her. She shrugged it off as she thought about their perps.

"I think it's time to see if we can make Carl sweat."

"Okay," he agreed.

"It looks like we're pretty close to ending this thing. I mean, what are the chances we can't get one of these guys to flip?

Lucas leaned against her car door and looked her over. "Is that what this is about?"

"What?" she asked, feigning confusion.

"You've been acting weird all day," he said.

"I have not."

"You just shrugged my arm off."

"We're in public, Lucas. I can't have people thinking I'm sleeping my way up the ladder."

"I'm on a different ladder," he scoffed.

"Still, with your connection to Frank, I just can't risk it. I've tried too hard to get where I am to watch it slip away because I slept with the hot FBI guy is just...."

"What?" he asked. "Please, enlighten me."

"You wouldn't understand," she sighed. "Being a woman in this field—"

"You put the limits on yourself," he gestured wildly. "Being a woman in this field doesn't matter. It hasn't mattered for a long time. What *does* matter is how hard you work. Foster rides your ass, sure, because he can see the greatness in you. And so can every other guy in that station. They're all waiting for you to take their damn jobs. Frank included. Frank would just give it to you with a smile on his face because that's the kind of person he is. But, Tanvi, all this crap about being a female detective and having more difficulty than your male counterparts, it's in your damn head, honestly. If a young guy came in with half the talent you have, they'd treat him just as bad. Worse even. They're scared. Of *you*."

"And you'd know that after being here for a week. You magically know everything about everything?"

"I spent the first few days observing. You might not have noticed, but that's all I did. Observed and pissed you off. 'Cause I'm a fucking natural." he ran his hands through his hair as he walked in a circle.

"Yeah, you really are." She rolled her eyes. "You need to find another ride back."

"I'm your protection!"

"I'm going straight to the station."

"The station you were almost abducted from?" he barked.

"You would throw that in my face."

He let out a frustrated grunt as he took two steps away from her, then turned back. "When I'm in charge of your safety, yes, I will throw that in your face. We're so close here, but we need to be smart."

"And I can't because I'm a woman?"

Lucas bit his knuckle. "You're impossible!"

She leaned into the annoyance. If he hated her, it would make it easier in the end. In her heart of hearts, she knew—she needed to let him go. Getting in her car, she turned the ignition and sped out of the lot, tears flowing.

THIRTY-FOUR

LUCAS CURSED AS TANVI TORE OUT OF THE HOSPITAL PARKING LOT.

"It's for the best," Henry's voice was like gas on a flame. He turned to face the doctor. "We're getting back together. We just made up in the hallway."

"Yeah, and I'm the tooth fairy," Lucas scoffed. "You're a real piece of work. You think I can't hear through the fucking door?"

Henry swallowed hard. Lucas walked past him, stopping to give the good doctor's shoulder a squeeze. "Do us both a favor, never address me again?"

"That'll be hard if you intend to stay in her life," Henry said as he turned. "She's just confused. Once she's away from you for a minute, I'll have her back. Where she belongs."

Lucas turned to look the little weasel in the eye. "Who says I'm leaving?"

Henry's eyes grew. "She seemed pretty certain you were."

"Maybe I'm gonna surprise her," he said with a smile. His phone rang. He answered it, keeping his eyes on Henry. "McGinn—yeah, thanks, bud."

He hung up his phone and walked back out, into the lot. John's car turned in, and he waited for him to get to the main entrance, where they stood.

Lucas opened the car door. He paused, one leg in the car. "In Boston, your car would be torched, and I'd have all your little nurses spying on you for me. Just in case you might decide to be an asshole to Tanvi. I'm giving you the 'I'm new in town' special. Don't make me regret it." He ducked into the car, and John was off.

"What was that?" John asked. "Isn't that the infamous ex?"

"Yeah, apparently, he thinks I'm standing between him and happily ever after with Tanvi."

"Right, because the fact that she didn't even like him had nothing to do with it."

"Or that she just told him it was never going to happen."

"You think he could be trouble?"

"No. He just realized what he lost, and he's desperate to get it back. If trying to tell me off is the worst he does, she won't even know he's acting up."

"Good, 'cause we have bigger fish to fry," John said.

"Yes, we do."

"So, what's going on with you and Nightingale, anyway?"

"I have to leave. She's upset but, refuses to talk about it. Women."

"You have to leave?"

Looking out the window, he watched the world go by in one big blur. "I should leave. But what am I going back to? A team that can't stand me, no family, nothing really. She has this amazing life here. Her family is close, barbecues on Sundays, her little book club with her sisters and her mom. What if I stay?" He looked at John, who glanced at him from the road.

"You think it could work?"

"I'd be in the FBI field office. If I could get placement here. We wouldn't be working together like we are now, but I would be here. We could make that work."

"Yeah," John grinned. "You could."

"Why are you smiling at me like that?"

"It's a beautiful thing when a man realizes he's in love."

Lucas's jaw hit the floor. How the hell had John figured it out when Tanvi hadn't?

"Don't look at me like that. Giving up your dream job for a chance with a woman? An incredible woman. But still."

"I mean, I had the dream job, yet I feel like I've been lying to myself for years. Like, if I could just get the job, everything would be perfect. And then, I got it, and I have this goodie two shoes so far up my ass, I can't breathe."

"That sounds unpleasant."

"Not the word I'd use."

They pulled into the parking garage for the precinct. Nightingale's car was parked in her spot.

"I don't suppose you saw her make it into the building?"

"Yeah, I was right about here," he pointed to a spot in the lot. "And she was storming past. I asked where you were, and she said, 'At the hospital and in need of a ride.' And she kept walking. Right inside."

"Thanks."

"Look, man." He put the car in park. "Don't tell her you're going to stay until you know you're going to stay. Adina told me Tanvi's never been like this with a guy before. Ever. You have more cards in this scenario than you think."

TANVI WALKED INTO HQ AND GASPED. JULIE MARTIN'S CRIME SCENE photos were brutal. Ramirez had joined them with the photos and what he had on her abduction.

"What the hell?" she said, looking over the scene, her arguments with Lucas forgotten.

"He's escalating. Unfortunately, we have the two black players and neither white. And they're pissed," Frank huffed.

"I wouldn't expect them to stop just because the game is off," Nash added from the corner. "They may even decide to play against each other or themselves. It's pretty commonplace to practice against yourself."

"We need to find them now," she said. "There's no need for much of a cooling period here."

"You're right."

"What did we get from Joe's apartment?"

"Let's wait for Lucas," Frank said.

"Where is he?" Nash asked.

"I may or may not have left him at the hospital," she said, her eyes squeezed shut. "It's fine, John just went to get him."

Frank eyed her, Nash laughed. "You would not believe the places that guy has been stranded. If he could just shut his mouth every now and again."

"He's physically incapable of it," Lucas said as he entered. Nash's smile grew as he went back to his board. "What'd you guys find in Joe's house, and has anyone talked to our newest perp yet?"

"Yes, and a lot," Frank said. "The man who you two arrested was Nickolas Preston. He's asked for a lawyer and is insisting he only delivered the girls. Waiting on DNA to see if he was part of the rapes."

"There is evidence of condoms. Even without DNA, he could be involved."

"True," Frank said. "And flipping his apartment may result in the condoms being found, but that's still circumstantial."

"As for Joe's house, it has a dungeon in the basement. He also had a model of the chess game, I assume, for strategizing. He also has Alice in Wonderland paraphernalia, but it's all the White Hare and the White Rabbit. That seems to be their team."

"So, who's on the other side?" Tanvi asked. "The Hatter and?"

"It's crazy town," Frank said. "I have no idea. There are numerous players in Alice in Wonderland. There are kings, queens, crazies, and then, if we consider the film adaptations."

"Is that all you've found so far?"

"Yeah, the team brought a lot back to go through, and the

house won't be finished being processed for another couple days."

"What about Nickolas? Is his lawyer his own?" Lucas asked.

"Yes."

"So, he could be our weak link in the chain," Tanvi noted.

"Agreed. So, we need all our ducks in a row before we talk to him."

"In the meantime, John found Carl's mother." Frank said.

"Yeah," John added. "I found Carl's family. His father died when was he was young, but his mother is in New York. She remarried and had three more children after Carl."

"Is that all you were able to find?"

"His juvenile records are sealed."

Tanvi turned to Lucas. "Know anyone in New York who could help with that?"

"I do," Frank said. "You two get on a plane. The ADA will be there to pick you up when you land."

He already had the phone to his ear.

"Is that wise right now?" Tanvi asked as he waited for an answer.

"You two getting rest and more information on Carl before you talk to him? Yes, I'd say that's wise."

"But—"

"They all lawyered up, they wont be ready to talk to us for a while yet and we have to bring the DA up to speed. Leave tonight, Interview tomorrow get back here. It's perfect."

She looked to Lucas. She was finally in a good place. Far from him and he was as mad at her as she was at him.

"Jimmy, I need a favor," Frank spoke into the phone. "Can Raf meet my people at the airport and facilitate the unsealing of some records?--- Yeah. We'll need a room to interview a family member as well.---Thanks, man. I miss you, too. We'll catch up one of these days." He gave a hearty chuckle before putting the phone back on the receiver. When he looked up to see them still standing there, he glared. "Go pack an overnight bag, and get your asses on a damn plane."

THIRTY-FIVE

THE EARLY MORNING FLIGHT FROM INDIANAPOLIS TO JFK MEANT Tanvi had slept, technically. Not that two hours was much sleep. And it didn't look like Lucas had even gotten that. She gave his arm a squeeze as they departed the nearly-empty plane. The sun was up, and a haze began to fall over them. They were both exhausted. "I need coffee," she said as they entered the airport and made their way to the exit.

"I need a coffee IV," Lucas replied with a chuckle. Her gaze lingered on the blond 5 o'clock shadow he'd neglected. It gave him a rough air she couldn't get enough of. Shaking her head, she walked in front of him, toward the exit. A man stood by the door with a cardboard sign that read "Nightingale/McGinn."

"Are you my people?" he asked, looking over a pair of sunglasses at them.

"I'm McGinn," Lucas offered his hand. The man took it with a nod.

"And you must be Nightingale," he said, turning to Tanvi. "Not sure when being insanely attractive became a requirement for law enforcement, but okay."

"Really?" she snapped.

"What?" he asked with a laugh. "I was talking about *him*."

She frowned.

"I've heard a lot about you," Lucas said. "Jimmy Guerin?"

"Close. I'm his husband, Raf. The DA of New York."

"Why wouldn't you send someone for us?"

"I owe Frank," he said as he led them out of the building, to the parking garage. "Jimmy is picking up the former Mrs. Singh now. She remarried twice after her husband's death. She's Mrs. Brown now."

"Is that all you know?"

"For now." He popped a mint into his mouth and then offered one to each of them.

"Thanks," Tanvi said. "How much did Frank tell you?"

"Enough to know I want this guy caught as much as you do."

The ride through the city was long. Tanvi picked at the sleeve of her shirt as they got stuck in yet another traffic jam.

"Does Jimmy miss the FBI?" Lucas asked. "He wasn't in very long, from my understanding."

"He'd never tell me if he did," Raf said, offering a small smile. "You'd have to talk to him. I suspect he does, though. Why do you ask?"

"I've bounced through more than a few careers in my time. Wondering if it's time to move on," Lucas mused, watching buildings pass out his window. She fought the urge to turn and ask if he was really considering quitting the FBI. Did that mean he could stay? She didn't dare hope.

"It's different when you *choose* to leave," Raf said. "I've walked away from many solid career paths. When you're forced out, it's different. Harder to let it go. Jimmy was forced out, so I'm sure it still eats at him."

"I've heard the story," Lucas said.

"I haven't." Tanvi chirped.

"He was working with Frank when they made a call to follow a mother into a building being used as a human trafficking hub.

Frank was going in no matter what, and Jim wouldn't let him go by himself. He just wouldn't. Couldn't. They were fired shortly thereafter." Raf explained.

"For saving a woman and her child?"

"For ruining a trafficking sting the FBI had been setting up for years. I believe it was something like five years that some of the guys had been undercover. The shit they'd seen, and then to watch the case go up in smoke because of Frank and Jim? It wasn't pretty." Lucas added.

Tanvi sat quietly. She couldn't imagine. Didn't want to imagine what they saw being undercover in a place like that.

"Anyway," Raf began as they pulled into a parking spot in front of the station in Manhattan, "here we are. Jimmy's got Mrs. Brown inside."

He parked, and they all got out. Tanvi took extra time to stretch before they headed up the stairs. Following Raf through the building, they were led to a squad room. A short, blonde woman with a shoulder holster over her cream t-shirt approached.

"Mable," Raf said. "This is Agent McGinn and Detective Nightingale."

She gave them a nod. "Detective Knight," she offered. "Your witness is through here."

They followed her into a honeycomb of doors until they reached where Mrs. Brown was being kept. A lean man stood watching her through the one-way window.

"Jim," Raf said. He turned to look at them with a start.

"Hey," he said as his eye caught Tanvi. "Wow."

Raf smacked him in the stomach. "Stop it. You're taken."

Jimmy offered her a shy wave. "Your witness is a chatty one. As soon as I told her it was about her son."

Tanvi waved back and gestured to Lucas, who Jimmy seemed equally thrilled by.

"McGinn," Jimmy said with a smile. "Heard a lot about you."

"Not all bad, I hope?"

"No, it was definitely *all* bad."

"Teresa?"

"How'd you guess?" Jimmy jested. "Don't worry. I wasn't her favorite either."

"Let's get this over with and get back," Tanvi interrupted.

Jimmy opened the door and gestured for them to enter first. "Mrs. Brown, these are the investigators who would like to talk to you about your son. Detective Nightingale and SSA McGinn. If it's all right with you, I'll go get you some tea."

"That would be lovely, thank you." She was a tiny woman. Her light brown skin sagged with age as she clasped her hands on the table in front of her. Her black hair was pulled back into a braid and had large patches of silver around the edges.

"Mrs. Brown," Lucas said as they sat. "We're investigating a series of murders in Indianapolis, and your son, Carl, turned himself in."

"I'm not surprised," she said with a shake of her head.

"Can you tell us why that is?" Lucas asked.

"He's had issues ever since he was a boy," she insisted. "It got to the point where, when he was big enough, I was worried about the other kids. I have three others, you know. And he was setting fires, and I caught him with girls' underwear," she shuddered. "I had to do what was best for my other children. So, I asked for help. I was directed to a psychologist who, after talking with Carl a few times, told me in-patient care in a youth home would help rehabilitate him." Her lip began to quiver, and her voice shook.

Tanvi slid a box of tissues across the table. "Take your time."

She wiped at her eyes with the tissue and focused on folding and unfolding before continuing. "They all said he'd be cured, and I was relieved. Because he wouldn't be my responsibility for a little while. I thought, it'll be good for him and me. I'd get a break and be ready to handle whatever they couldn't fix. Well, they tell you not to visit for the first month. They need that time to adjust, but I wrote him letters, and at first, he wrote back. But then, he stopped, and I just figured he got sick of me and wanted to do his own thing. But when I went up to see him." She shook her head and closed her eyes tightly. "He wasn't even in there. He was a shell of a boy. Sunken-in eyes, pale. I knew something was terribly wrong, but when I asked him, he'd look at the guard in the corner. I went after them. He's still never told me the details, but he was horribly abused in there, and I got the place shut down. But not before it turned out a heap of predators. All the kids sent there were already prone to 'deviant behavior,' as they called it back then. To hurt them like those people did. It's almost guaranteed."

"You said you got the place shut down. Were you able to get Carl help after that?" Tanvi asked.

"He was sixteen by then. He wasn't going anywhere he didn't want to go or doing a damn thing he didn't want to do." She gave a gentle smile with watery eyes as Jimmy brought in her hot tea.

For a moment, Tanvi sat staring into the steam rising from the teacup. She rubbed her tired eyes and leaned forward to listen as Mrs. Brown continued.

"I had to kick him out of the house often, too. I paid for his apartment for a while. But then, he was arrested for hurting a little, blonde girl who lived in the building. I stopped paying, and he moved out. The little girl was too traumatized for a trial, and I haven't seen him since."

Tanvi glanced at Lucas.

"How was he at making friends?" she asked.

"That was something he was always good at. But not in a way that makes you proud as a parent. He'd get friends, and then he'd manipulate them. Get them to do whatever he wanted. It's why I started trying to get him help in the first place. I found him in the boiler room of our apartment with a few other kids. He was making them do awful things."

"What kinds of things?" Tanvi inquired, not really wanting to know but needing to.

"I HOPE THAT WAS FRUITFUL," JIMMY SAID AS THEY EXITED THE ROOM, his inherently cheerful nature at odds with what they just heard.

"It was," Lucas nodded. Tanvi was still pale. "I think we need to get back to the hotel."

"No," she shook her head and plastered on a fake smile. "I'm fine. We should go out. Get pizza or bagels or something Big Appley."

"How about a cop bar with great burgers?" Jimmy offered.

"No one likes that place," Raf protested.

"Everyone but you likes that place," Jimmy laughed. "And I'm starving."

Lucas looked at his watch. 12:01.

"Well, it is afternoon. And our flight back isn't until tomorrow, evening."

"Yes!" Jimmy bounced down the hall.

"How old is he?" Tanvi asked.

"At heart?" Raf grinned. "Sixteen. In reality? He's pushing fifty."

"I mean, it's good he's retained a youthful attitude."

"Yeah, but wait until we have to spend the day in the ER because he tried to jump a parking meter or hood-slide a freshly waxed cruiser or… Well, you get the point."

She smiled at him, and Lucas found the expression curious.

"You like him," she said as if it were a secret. "Not in the 'we're stuck together way,' but in the 'you really like him always and forever' kind of way."

"Guilty," Raf said. "Now, we better catch up so I can head off any potentially bone-breaking stunts."

He rushed down the hall, and Tanvi and Lucas followed after.

"What are you thinking about?" Lucas finally asked as they reached the city streets. The sounds of traffic and the low hum of countless people talking elevating the noise level.

"Carl," she said. "He didn't stand a chance."

"Yes, he did," Lucas replied. "I was involved in a sting operation to take out a brothel, essentially. These guys convince young girls, teens usually, but some older, that they love them. Then, they start selling them for money. It happens all over the US and the world. They get them pregnant and use the babies to control the mothers. It's--disgusting. So, we get word from a nonprofit who helps parents when this stuff happens. Local cops ask us to come along because there's evidence the guy moved the girls from out of state. We get there, arrest three men, and there are women and children everywhere. This place is packed. As we're processing the women, this little girl sits down in front of me. I think she's a child to one of these women. Nope. She's twelve years old, pregnant, and a victim of trafficking herself. The things they did to this little--" he paused as emotion threatened to cut him off. "You'd think she'd be messed up the rest of her life. She's not. Her child went into an open adoption, and she was adopted by one of the cops who helped with the sting when her mother gave up her rights. She now works finding these guys on the internet and getting them arrested. She's amazing. I know it's not the same as what happened to Carl, but there are choices we all make. The moment you choose to be responsible for your own life. Hell, I could have decided to be angry and bitter and play the victim. No one who heard my story would fault me for it. But what would that do? Nothing for me. I'd be a drunk in some bar, telling everyone about my horrible past. No, thank you. I'm not a victim, and neither is that girl. We survived. Carl could have, too."

"But he didn't," she said quietly.

"And that's not your fault."

"Did you have someone?" she asked. "Like that girl who had her adoptive parents."

"My grandfather. Sure. That didn't stop my brother from getting into the organized crime game."

She gaped. "Your brother is a gangster?"

"In Boston, part of the Irish. His misdeeds slowed considerably when he realized my prints were in the system."

She laughed. A smile spread over his face. He loved that laugh. He loved this woman. The thought hung in his mind. *Shit.*

LUCAS EYED TANVI AS THEY RODE THE ELEVATOR TO THEIR ROOMS. New York City bustled around them the whole way from the bar, and somehow, he'd never felt more alone. She had said they'd just have one night together, but after the shower he'd thought maybe she wanted more. She'd let her guard down after the interview, but now she was icier than the North Pole at Christmas time. A stone wall of silence was erected between them. She hadn't said a word to him since their food was delivered. Not that Jimmy and Raf left much time for other conversation.

He trained his gaze on the numbers, counting the floors until they would reach the eleventh. They stepped off the elevator, and she led the way through the honeycomb of hallways until they reached their rooms. He waited for her to unlock her door.

She paused, noting him behind her, and glanced at him for the first time in what felt like ages. Her eyes didn't meet his, though.

"Aren't you going in your room?"

"I want to check yours and the adjoining door first," he replied. Did he need to do any of that? No, but he didn't know how to talk to her. What to say or how to say it. So what if he loved her. She didn't care about him. She was making herself perfectly clear. *Wasn't she?*

Tanvi opened the door and stepped inside. He followed her in, checking the bathroom and frowning at the shower. An image of her naked and dripping as he made her cry out his name flashed in his mind. Closing his eyes, he willed the image away before heading for the adjoining door. He unlocked it and opened it to see her pulling out her pajamas. A pair of silky shorts with lace trim and an old sweatshirt.

"Heading to bed?" he asked, arms crossed as he leaned against the doorway.

"Yeah." She offered him the most fleeting of smiles. "Travel makes me tired."

"You wanna call Frank and give him an update?" he asked. "I'm gonna hit the gym. Work off some pent-up energy."

"Good idea," she nodded. "I can make the call."

"I can never sleep after an interview like that," he mused, staring at the floor, though he wasn't sure why. He glanced at her, but she refused to look at him, clutching her sweatshirt in a white-knuckle grip. Who was he kidding? He wanted her to ask him why. What had affected him about Mrs. Brown's revelations? He wanted her to care. Like she had the other night. Needed her to. And he hated that most of all. He closed the door and grabbed his gym bag before heading out.

After his workout, Lucas felt more certain than ever he needed to talk to Tanvi. What the hell was going on? One second, she was hot and the next she was ice cold. He grabbed the knob on the adjoining door, but it didn't budge. He froze. She'd locked him out. Stepping back, he blinked a few times. She'd chosen to stop him from entering her room. Knocking would be pointless. He could threaten to break the door down, but to what end? Maybe it would dull the ache he suddenly felt growing in his chest. A flash of anger overtook the pain. He preferred anger.

Clinging to the burning emotion, he pounded on the door.

"What?" she sounded startled.

"Why is this door locked?" he barked, his anger already fading. He was an asshole. She'd probably been sleeping.

It clicked open. "I didn't like it unlocked without you in your room." Her words were strong, but the red rings and puffiness suggested she'd been crying.

"Don't do that again," he snapped before allowing himself to soften. "You scared me."

She took half a step forward, arms lifting to slip around his waist. But she caught herself and stepped back. "Sorry."

What the hell was this?

"I didn't mean to scare you," he offered. "Good night, I guess."

She met his gaze for a moment, torment burning in her brown eyes. He knew it was mirrored in his own. Why was she doing this? He moved forward, lifting a hand to touch her cheek. She took a quick step back, out of reach. He let his hand drop.

"Good night, Lucas," she muttered, closing the door. He heard the lock click into place. *Fuck.*

THIRTY-SIX

THEY ENTERED THE NIGHTINGALE HOUSE AROUND MIDNIGHT. TANVI wanted to stay here the night and see her family before returning to the hotel tomorrow. Plus, her bed. She needed a night in her bed.

Tanvi held a finger over her lips and pointed to the couch. Nash lay sound asleep in the living room. He must have left the guest bedroom for Lucas after his travels. The entire day had been terrible. They hadn't spoken at all besides simple organizing. She wanted to talk to him. To tell him not to leave. To give them, give whatever this was, a chance. But that was insane. He had a life in Virginia. Who was she to jump in and demand he uproot everything he'd built?

She moved into the kitchen and whispered, "You better be nicer to that boy from now on."

The only response she got was from the cabinet as it creaked opened. She grabbed a glass and filled it with water. Desperate for something to do. If she wasn't careful, she'd say everything she was thinking.

He crossed his arms over his chest, leaning against the doorway. Watching her, she could feel his eyes watching every step she made. He'd been watching her every move as they'd awkwardly explored New York City, waiting for their late-night flight home. He hadn't spoken unless it was in response to her, and even then, only when she asked him a direct question that couldn't be answered with a shrug or nod. He hated her. She could feel it. She was afraid to look at him and see it burning in his eyes. She shouldn't have taken him to her bed. She knew it was a bad idea, and still, she'd done it. Now, she'd have to live with the consequences. Sadness threatened to overtake her, and she took a shaky breath before sipping her water. That was a lie. She couldn't regret their time together. But it still hurt like hell knowing it was about to end.

His rough hand slipped into hers, and she squeezed her eyes shut.

"T?" he finally said pulling to him. There was more pain in that one syllable than she could imagine.

Her eyes flew open, and she glanced up at him. She saw the same pain she'd been feeling for the last couple of days in his eyes. "What, Luke?"

"Why'd you kick me out?" he asked, pulling her to face him when she tried to look away again. "I know you said it was just one night. But—"

"I can't do this, Lucas," she warned as tears built in her eyes.

"What?" he asked. He paused, but she couldn't answer. Tears were choking her, so he continued. "Because what we're doing now is *killing* me."

She studied his face as her mind struggled to find the right words.

"You showed me what it's like in the sun and then banished me to the shadows."

Her heart was breaking as she watched him. He was so confused.

"You have to leave," she said. "We need to be realistic."

"Who says I have to leave?"

"You did. To my mother."

"You missed the rest of what I said," he offered, gently pulling her to him. She stuck her feet to the floor and looked up at him through her lashes. "I don't have a life there. I have a job, sure. One I like, but my future in that job depends on things I'm not sure even Frank can teach me. I don't know if you noticed, but I've got kind of a thick skull."

She gave in, letting him pull her against him. He kissed the top of her head. "What are you saying?"

"I'm saying, don't cut me out. I can't handle it. I don't *want* to handle it."

She pushed him back. "Luke, if I don't push you away, and you leave me—"

"I can't promise the future," he admitted. He didn't know what would happen. If he could find work here, if he minded being out of the FBI...He just didn't know.

Her mouth pulled into a frown, and she looked at the floor as she crossed her arms. "I'm sorry. I can't."

She took two steps past him, and he grabbed her arm, pulling her to him. He kissed her. Hard. It wasn't a meaningless kiss. It was full of his pent-up emotions and conveyed to her the pain in his heart and the longing for her in his life. It was painful yet beautiful. She dropped her guard, pulling him to her. In that moment, she gave herself fully to him, consequences be damned. His tongue swept over hers as he grabbed her hips and pulled them to his. She pulled her mouth away and gasped for air. He kissed a trail down her neck to her collar bone.

"Lucas," her voice breathy. "Please."

He paused. "You want me to stop?"

She couldn't bring herself to say yes.

He pulled back to study her face. "Should I go? Do you want me to stop?"

"No," she admitted. "I just *want you*."

His devilish smirk would have made her drop to her knees if he hadn't already been holding her up. "You already have me. You've *always* had me."

She frowned. "Even on that first day when I yelled at you?"

"Especially on that first day." He nuzzled her nose.

She stepped away from him, and he stood, watching her. Waiting to see what she wanted to do. His patience and reserve filled her chest. Who was she kidding? He was already killing her. She might as well enjoy the time they had.

Slipping her hand into his, she pulled him towards her bedroom. He pushed her door open and yanked her inside after him. Greedily, he pulled her into him, sliding his hands over her body as his tongue explored her mouth. He made her feel beautiful, wanted, needed. How was she going to get by without him?

Pushing that thought away, she shoved him backwards onto her bed. She climbed up his body slowly, she knew what he wanted but it was her turn to take control. She pulled her shirt over her head and tossed it to the side. He pulled her, but she refused to budge. He cocked his head to the side, unsure of how to interpret the situation.

"It's my turn to have my way with you," she said with a raspy voice. He threw his head back and ran his hands over his eyes with a groan.

"Uhmm, that was only fun when I was the one doing it," he griped.

She laughed. "You'll have plenty of fun." She tugged at his belt.

"Why do I have so many layers?" he fussed, he sat up and tugged his shirt off. She gave him a warning glare. "What? I'm helping."

Her angry gaze fell to his strong chest and abs as she pushed the now-open belt out of the way and popped the button on his pants. He smiled down at her.

"See, you like it when I'm naked."

He wasn't wrong. The cocky bastard.

Tanvi reached into his pants and found what she'd been after. A long, thick shaft, ready to play. She pulled it out and stroked it, watching the need on his face grow until she was sure he'd take over. When he didn't, though, she rewarded him by taking as much of his length as she could into her mouth. He moaned at the intimate contact, his shaft growing even harder inside her mouth. Satisfaction swept through her at his reaction, urging her on. She wrapped her hand around the base of him, pulling and massaging in time to her sucking. Swirling her tongue around his mushroom tip.

He wrapped his hand in her hair, tugging lightly. His other hand on his thigh, his fingers digging into the meaty flesh. She knew he wanted her to go faster, deeper. But he didn't force it. So, she took him as deep as she could, before pulling back. He released her hair as she stood at the foot of the bed. His hard cock begging for more, and his emerald gaze not even trying to hide his disappointment at the space between them. She undid her bra and tossed it to the side, his eyes getting hopeful as she unbuttoned her jeans and slid them and her underwear slowly down her legs in one swift motion. She hopped back on the bed, straddling his hips and letting her warm, wet core slide over his cock without taking him inside just yet. She leaned over him to grab condom out of the bedside table. He slipped it on as she continued to tease him.

He whimpered as she set herself down on his abs, letting him feel how wet she was for him.

"You're killing me, Tanvi."

She put her finger to her lips as she leaned forward. Her dark, curly hair forming a curtain between them and the outside world. "What do you want, Luke?"

He grabbed her ass and locked his emerald gaze on hers. "You."

She faltered. If she didn't know any better, she'd think he wanted more than her body. And the longer he held her gaze, the more she thought that was exactly what he'd meant. Unable to think about that right now, she reached between them and gave him what he wanted, sliding his long, thick cock deep inside her. They both closed their eyes and hissed at the sensation. Emotion surged within her at their physical connection, and she realized how much she needed the emotional to go with this. She opened her eyes to look down at him and saw what she wanted burning in his eyes. Even if she was misreading him. She'd take it for now. So this moment could be perfect.

He rocked and lifted his hips in time to her, pushing deeper and hitting just the right spot to send pleasure shooting through her, and she gasped as her hands rested on his chest.

"Stop," she said, her breathing shaky. He froze.

"I'm supposed to be teasing you," she laughed.

"You helped when it got to this part last time," he argued. She pushed his hands off her hips and pinned them above his head. He caught her nipple between his lips, giving it a light pinch.

"You're impossible."

"I can't help it. You put the perfect woman naked and on top of me."

"Tsk, tsk," she slid her hands down his muscular arms, digging into his body with her nails.

"You're killing me, T. I'm dying here, please, have mercy on me."

"I'm just trying to see how much I can torment you before you get frustrated enough to take over," she laughed.

His eyes grew, and a playful smirk again crept over his face. "You little minx." He threw his hips to the side, rolling with her until he was on top. He buried himself deep inside her as he held both her hands above her head in one of his. Sliding the other over her body as he kissed her neck. Working to give them both the release they were looking for. He slid his free hand between them, finding her clit with his thumb and sliding it in small circles in time to his thrust.

"Lucas," she moaned in his ear as he sucked on her neck. "That feels so good!"

He chuckled at the encouragement and moved faster. Driving them both to the edge. She froze as his touch pushed her to new heights. The pleasure was so intense, she bit his neck to keep from screaming as her body fell into convulsions. He moved faster to join her in the perfect moment of physical pleasure. Bliss quickly dissipated and gave way to a terrifying reality—she was falling in love with him.

TANVI HELD THE DOOR AND TWISTED THE KNOB SO SHE COULD SHUT IT silently without waking Luke. Quietly, she padded down the hall. Voices filtered in from the kitchen, causing her to pause.

"...they got in last night. And if they think for one second they didn't wake dad up, they're insane," Adina was saying.

"I didn't hear anything," Nash replied.

"You sleep like a rock. I got up to talk to you last night, just before they got in. I even poked you."

Tanvi took a step closer. Why would Adina wake Nash up to chat?

"You did?" He sounded flattered, and Tanvi knew exactly what Adina was up to. *Sorry, John, looks like you snooze you lose.* "What for?"

"Nothing," Adina snapped. "Just thought I heard something."

"Uh huh."

"I did," Adina argued. "Stop looking at me like that."

"Good morning," Tanvi said as she entered.

"Get any sleep?" Adina asked by way of attack. She was desperate to get Nash off her back.

"I did," Tanvi smiled. "The flight was pretty awful, but Lucas made up for it later."

"You better not have had sex in my house." Her father's voice startled her, and she spilled the coffee she was about to drink.

"Of course not, Daddy," she said with an innocence she hoped would save her from their onslaught. "Lucas gave me a back rub."

Adina and Nash struggled to keep their laughter under control.

"A back rub, huh?" David said, eyeing his daughters. "Lord, help me."

"Good morning," Lucas said as he entered.

"For you," David snapped. "I hear you're quite the masseur. Perhaps you can give me a massage later."

Lucas frowned. "I only do women."

David glared at Tanvi while Lucas looked around her father to raise a brow at her.

"It's a Boston thing, Dad. Cultural differences." Adina added.

Without a word, David turned to Lucas. "If you stay here again, you'll be in the guest room."

"Of course," Lucas mumbled, putting a hand on his neck. Stifling a laugh. "Last night was an accident. We just fell asleep."

"I'm sure."

He left, and Lucas removed his hand and pointed to a giant hickey on his neck. Tanvi sucked in a breath through her teeth. Shit!

Nash and Adina lost it, cracking up so badly that Adina snorted, which brought an entirely new bout of the giggles.

"You guys are terrible," Tanvi said, chuckling.

"Not as bad as you," Adina said, wiping her eyes. "You know how Dad feels about premarital sex, and you did it in his house, no less!"

Tanvi smiled at her little sister. She had one of those bits of information on her parents she wasn't sure if she should tell her sisters. "Wanna know a secret?"

Adina eyed her sister suspiciously. "No. I don't do secrets."

"It's not one you'll have a hard time keeping." Tanvi leaned in close to whisper. "Mom and Dad had premarital sex."

"What?" Adina yelled.

"Shhhh!" Tanvi shushed her, holding up her hand.

"No, they didn't," Adina whispered. "Dad—almost the orthodox Jew—had premarital sex?"

"Mom said she wouldn't marry him without knowing they were, you know, compatible."

"No way." Adina looked around the kitchen, and Tanvi wondered if she'd done the right thing. After all, Adina was planning to wait until marriage. She'd done well so far, but Tanvi and her mother both had the same concern—what if she married someone who was a selfish lover? Tanvi's gaze fell to Nash, who was eyeing Adina. Just what was he deducing from her secret?

"We need to go," Lucas said, glancing at his phone. "Everyone's mobilizing at HQ."

"Do you want me to stay?" Nash asked Adina.

"No, I'm heading to class anyway. I'll be fine."

"Text me regularly throughout the day," Tanvi instructed.

THIRTY-SEVEN

"In other news," Frank was saying as they entered the squad room, "Joe wants us to tell him how his mother is doing."

"Do we have the urn?" Lucas asked, drawing his and Ramirez's attention.

"Yes," John added from where he slipped in behind Luke.

"I say we bring mommy in the room."

"Okay, who's talking to which suspect?" Tanvi said.

"You and Luke can go in with Carl," Frank said. "What did you find?"

"He never stood a chance. Deviant tendencies, sent to home that was supposed to help, but they abused him, sexually and otherwise. He started offending at as a teen. The girl was too traumatized to testify and mom stopped supporting him after that."

"Damn," Nash said. "You can use all that though."

"That's the plan," Lucas said.

"Nash and Ramirez will take Joe and his mother, and Foster and I will go in after Nickolas. We'll hit him hard. He's nervous, which makes me think he's the submissive, but that doesn't make sense either."

"Does anything make sense in this case?" Tanvi asked.

"I'll try to sort that out on Joe's end, too. If he's the dominant, he'll be furious that Nickolas was caught. I should be able to see the aggression."

"Agreed."

"Okay, people. Game time. We can leave here heroes or failures today. Will we sleep soundly, knowing these monsters are off the streets or waiting for the next call about a body?" Frank asked, pointing to Julie's mutilated body. "We can look forward to more of this if we're waiting for a call."

Tanvi looked at the woman in the photos. She was covered in blood, naked, and tossed in the trash, her legs spread to humiliate her further. Her dead eyes still filled with the horror of her last moments.

"That's not happening again."

"Hello again, Carl," Tanvi said as he was shuffled in, looking at her and McGinn. He sat next to his lawyer, Ms. Taylor.

"Well, I'll be," he said with a smile. "I was teasing before about you sleeping with her, but I'd say it's happened for sure now."

"We're here to talk about you," McGinn redirected. "We caught another one of your little buddies. And this one's gonna sing for us. No doubt."

"Then, why are you in here with me?" he said, looking between them. "You must need something, so this isn't as open-and-shut as you make it sound, Mr. McGinn. Oh, no. It's not over yet, and you've shown me your hand—"

"On the contrary, Carl," Tanvi interrupted, enunciating his name. "This is your opportunity to be honest with us and get the death penalty off the table."

He looked at his lawyer. She sat forward. "That's not the best you can do."

"After your client orchestrated eleven murders that we know

of? Not to mention the child pornography?" Tanvi said. "That's the absolute best we can do. We also had an interesting chat with your mother."

"No way you get a taste of that," he pointed to Tanvi while speaking to Lucas. "And don't come out with some kind of attachment. How many times did you have her? Each one will eat a little bit more of your soul. Until she owns you."

"Carl," Lucas sighed. "You can help us and yourself, or you can keep this shit up and take the fast track to a lethal injection."

"You need me even though you've caught two people?" he pretended to think. "That means the Hare and the Hatter are running loose and probably terrifying you. Not going to lie, that Hatter is absolutely mad. I wouldn't want to see what he'd do without a leash. Well, again, I flew him in, you know. From where he was playing, he had free rein. Had to promise him a challenge."

"Flew him in from where?" Tanvi asked.

"Wouldn't you like to know?" A sinister laugh filled the room. "The Cat will be very upset to see you two are getting carnal, though. I know that will irritate him. You'll be able to tell in his victims." The smile that spread over his face made bile rise in her throat.

"Your guy is flipping on you right now," Lucas said, again pulling the conversation away from their sleeping habits of late. "I'm here to offer you a deal."

His lawyer sat up. "What are you looking for?"

"If he tells us the names of the other people involved, *all* the other people, we'll take the death penalty off the table." Lucas slid the folder from the DA's office across the table. The lawyer looked at it and whispered in his ear. His smile still in place.

"It's a good deal," Tanvi said. "You should take it."

"You think I have no more cards to play while yours are all on the table. But I have an ace up my sleeve." He threw his head back and laughed a laugh that went straight to the pit of Tanvi's stomach.

THIRTY-EIGHT

"We missed something," Tanvi said, anxiety threatening to consume her as they left the interview room.

"He's fucking with us. It's what he does." Luke put his hands on her shoulders. Before she could stop herself, she turned into his comfort and allowed him to pull her into his chest. "We're fine. Do not let this guy get under your skin. We need clear heads."

She took several deep breaths, taking in his scent and letting it calm her. He was right. There was no reason to be nervous, let alone panic. Still, there was a tiny ball of anxiety rising in her chest, threatening to pull her down, into a spiral. She stepped back just as Frank and Foster entered.

"He's ready to talk," Frank said. "Discussing the deal with his lawyer now while we wait for the ADA."

"Great," she said, unable to hide her worry from her voice.

"What?" Frank asked, his happiness retreating.

"Our interview didn't go so well." Lucas ran his hand over his face.

He played the recording for them. As soon as Carl started speaking, Foster hit pause. "Is there something going on between you?"

Neither of them moved. Frank would know if they were lying, no doubt, but could they fool Foster?

"There's the potential for something," Tanvi admitted. Lucas latched onto it.

"Yes," he nodded.

"Do not fuck up this case," he said, looking them each in the eye before hitting play again.

When it got to the laugh, Tanvi stopped it not wanting to hear it again.

"That's when we left," she said.

"I think he is toying with us," Lucas said, looking at her instead of the men he was speaking to.

"It's certainly possible." Frank said.

Before they could continue, John ran into the room. "Joe's house, it's burned to the ground, along with two other houses on the street. The fire chief says it's arson. They used the accelerant in Joe's house only."

"He's got more people, and he's speaking to them somehow." Frank rubbed his eyes, fatigue was setting in. The case was wearing on all of them.

"Or they had contingencies in place." Tanvi chewed her bottom lip. "How are we still one step behind these assholes?"

"Is Nash still in with Joe?" Lucas asked, moving to the observation area for that room. He flicked the switch so they could hear.

"Yeah, they had to wait 'til we were done with Carl. One lawyer, remember?" Tanvi said, joining him.

"I want to know how my mother is," Joe was saying.

"Why won't you answer the question?" his lawyer was saying. "He's clearly very distraught. You aren't going to get anything out of him this way."

"I need you to answer my questions first," Nash said. "When is the last time you saw your mother?"

"The morning before you hauled me in here for no good reason."

"Kidnapping a teenager is 'no good reason'?" Ramirez asked

Joe said nothing, looking at the table.

"When is the last time you spoke to your mother?" Nash asked.

"That morning," Joe said, clearly getting agitated.

"Why isn't he just saying it?" John asked as he joined them.

"If he thinks she's alive and Nash forces him to accept she isn't, he won't be any help."

"That's fine," Foster said. "Our guy is prepped and ready to sing. We don't need Joe."

"It could also help him with an insanity plea," Tanvi said. "Which I don't really care as he's locked up, and they know the history."

"What is in your mother's will, for her last wishes?" Nash asked gently.

"Why do you need to know that?" Joe asked, looking to Ramirez, then back to Nash.

"Because you're going to be here a while. It's really just a precaution," Nash said, a little too convincingly. Lucas noted the ease with which Nash lied.

"She has a plot, she wants to be buried in, by her church."

Nash looked at the photo in his hands. Joe's mother's 3D-printed face used as an urn. He slid it across the table. "Have you ever seen this before?"

Joe looked at it and started laughing. "What is that? It's absurd! Did mother have that made?"

Nash looked to Ramirez. "Joe, we just got confirmation. Your mother's ashes are in there. Along with some of a cat. Her pet?"

Joe's eyes widened, and he stood up, slamming both fists on the table while screaming at the top of his lungs. The lawyer shot across the room as he turned and screamed at her. He hurled his chair at Nash, but Lucas knocked it away. Nash's eyes locked with Lucas's briefly before Lucas was pinning Joe to the table, Ramirez helped. Two other officers entered to drag Joe out. The lawyer followed, hollering about the IPD abusing her client.

"I just handed them an insanity plea," Nash said. "I deserved the chair to the face."

"No one deserves a chair to the face. And frankly, if they get the plea, we know it's not a ploy. That wasn't fake."

"I should have eased him into it." Nash put his head in hands.

Lucas sat down next to him, placing a hand on the smaller man's shoulder. "Nash." He waited for him to look up. "Crazy is crazy, and hindsight is twenty-twenty."

Nash didn't look convinced, but he'd heard him. "Why are you being nice to me?"

Lucas sat back, looking at the large mirror he knew hid the woman of his dreams. "I'm an asshole, and not even I would blame you for what happened here."

TANVI WATCHED LUCAS COMFORTING HIS FRIEND WHEN HER PHONE rang.

"You going to get that?" John asked as he entered the room.

"Nightingale," she said, giving John a look.

"Do not react. You're being watched." She froze, listening to the male voice. "It's my unbirthday. Guess how I'm celebrating."

"I don't know." She said, looking around. John frowned at her. She shook her head, and he took a few steps away. She turned the volume up on her phone, still searching for who was watching her. *Maybe it's a hoax,* she thought.

"I got myself a present. In a way, you got it for me. You see, we wanted *you*. But that was only until I met Adina. Your younger sister is the most beautiful thing I've ever seen. The smile on your pillow? It was meant for her. I've wanted her the whole time. It's the damn Cat who likes you."

"Is the Cheshire Cat working with you?" she asked. John turned, eyes wide.

"He's not on my team. The point of this call is simple. If you don't want Adina to end up like Julie, you need to meet me. I want a trade."

"What do you want?"

"You, but not like you think. Like I said, I like Adina. But I've had her. So, you'll do for the body dump."

Tanvi closed her eyes as the weight of his statement hit her. Head on a swivel, Lucas's eyes met hers, and she wished he could actually see her. Tears were forming in her large, brown eyes.

"Suck it up, Nightingale, or I'll kill her. I don't want to, but I'll do it."

"Don't," she said, wiping away her tears and hiding behind a wall of hair. "Where?"

"I'll text you. Come alone, or she dies bloody."

She hung up the phone and stared at it until the text emerged on the screen.

With a sniffle, she looked up to see if anyone was paying attention to her. John was.

"I'll tell Lucas where you went," he said simply. She gave him a small smile. He was smart. He'd help her out of this mess. Right now, she needed to get to Adina. She put her phone on the table, the text with the address still on the lock screen. After he nodded she picked it back up and raced out of the room.

THIRTY-NINE

"Thank you," Nash said, pulling Lucas's attention back toward him.

"I've got your back."

They stood as the lawyer came back in.

"What the hell was that?"

"We found Mrs. White's cremains in the urn while doing a wellness check, prior to it burning down," Nash replied.

She crossed her arms over her chest. "I want a copy of this tape."

"Done," Lucas said as Nash faltered.

"I want a speedy arraignment. My client needs medical care."

"If you speak to the ADA, we'd be more than happy to cooperate," Lucas offered.

She nodded and headed out of the room.

"Why were you so accommodating?" Nash asked.

"They're not equipped to handle him here. Let the psych facility have him. His buddy's ready to talk. We don't need him. Just waiting on the ADA to come with the papers. She'll be here soon. We'll have all the names, and then we can put this whole thing behind us," he said, leading Nash out of the room. Frank was waiting for him with a smile.

Frank clapped Nash on the back. "You live, and you learn. Don't sweat it. If it turns out we have to get more from him, you'll get a second chance."

"I don't want a second chance."

"Yes, you do," Lucas said, punching him in the arm. "Not right this second, but you'll want it in a day or two."

Foster entered the room, his eyes darting around to see if everyone was present.

"What is it?" Frank asked.

"When they were bringing Carl back to his cell, he killed them and escaped. The surveillance disc was wiped He had to have had help."

The room went silent. Lucas looked around.

"Where's Tanvi?" he asked. After several shrugs, he noticed John looking nervous in the corner. "I'm going to go find her."

He eyed John, who nodded and followed him.

"What's going on?"

"Adina was taken, and I think Tanvi went to trade herself for her sister. He said she was being watched, and they'd kill Adina if anyone found out. I don't know what to do. Adina means the world to me, but Tanvi will die if they take her. Honestly, who can we trust here?"

"Take a deep breath," Lucas said, placing his hands on John's shoulders. "Where are they?"

Lucas tested the knob on the door to the roof. When it opened, he breathed a sigh of relief, his weapon in hand. He aimed it out the crack in the door and then pushed out, sweeping the roof. There were various heating and cooling elements, as well as some small outbuildings and a large sign on one side. But other than that, the place was empty. He made his way around until he'd reached the edge. Far below him in an alley, he could see Tanvi. He frowned. She was looking around and then ran to a body that was lying down on the pavement. It must have been Adina.

He heard the distinct sound of a slide being racked back and a bullet being chambered. He looked up to see what looked like a preppy frat boy.

"You've got to be kidding me."

"Nope," he smiled. "Drop your weapon."

Lucas placed his gun on the gravel covered roof.

"Kick it over to me."

"You've seen too many movies."

"To get close enough to you for you to pull some kung fu shit? Yeah, kick it over." Lucas did as he asked and pulled his pack of cigarettes from his pocket. If he was going out, he'd at least have a nicotine buzz.

"What the hell are you doing?"

"Having a smoke," he said around the filter as he lit it. before holding the pack out. "You want one? You seem a little on edge."

"I'm the White King. Hatter says you beat him to his prize."

"Please tell me you aren't talking about Tanvi."

"He didn't want her until the Cat showed interest. And then, you swept in and scared him off. But I still thought he'd get there first. Who knew she hated herself enough to give it up to someone she can't stand."

Lucas exhaled smoke as the little turd's voice got on his last nerve. "You know, you talk an awful lot."

"So I've been told," he grinned. "We were going to win, you know. I have way more kills under my belt than Joe. Doesn't that shit get you BAU fellas hard?"

"No," he said, putting his thumbs in his pockets and letting smoke snake out his nose. Calmly, he rocked back on his heels. Over the ledge, he could see an ambulance and police cars approaching Tanvi. Good, she was safe. "It gets *you* hard. Killing pieces of shit like you? That's what does it for me."

A grin spread over his face. "So, you are like me."

Lucas laughed. A deep and throaty. "No. You like killing

people who can't fight back. Even now, you wanna take me, right? You're going to knock me out first. And while I'm out? You'll tie me up. Because you're a pathetic piece of shit who can't fight someone his own size."

Something struck his side, and electricity bounced from vein to vein through his body until something struck him in the head. Everything went black.

TANVI SAT ON THE CHAIR WITH HER HEAD ON THE BED AS SHE WEPT. Adina's injuries were severe, and she was fighting for her life even now. Tanvi didn't know the extent of her injuries since everything started to spin after the doctor said the words "medically-induced coma."

Two hands slid over her shoulders, and she looked up, prepared to see Lucas. She was met with her father's brown eyes instead.

"Daddy," she said, standing and pulling him into a hug as she lost the battle with her tears.

"Shhh," he said, holding her close. "Our girl is too strong for this to stop her. She has things to accomplish. Lives to change. She won't throw in the towel over this."

"They hurt her dad," Tanvi growled. Rage replacing her fear. "They did things we can't imagine."

"I know. I spoke to the doctor. But she's a fighter. Like you," he said, his voice wavering as his own emotions threatened to overcome him. "What's the matter?"

"Besides the fact that one of my sisters ended up like this because of me?"

"Yeah," he asked. "I know you well enough to see the disappointment when you look at me."

"Oh, dad, don't think of it like that."

"You thought I was Lucas, didn't you?"

"I thought he'd be here."

"Maybe he's off arresting the animals who did this to your sister before they do the same to you."

Tanvi looked at Adina. The ventilator in her mouth and the machines keeping her asleep so her brain could heal from the trauma. Tanvi wanted to arrest them. She wanted them to resist. This had to end, once and for all.

A knock on the door sounded. Her heart leaped until it opened to reveal Nash.

"Come on in," her father said. "Adina needs all the prayers she can get."

Nash looked guilty. "I've never prayed before."

Her father gave a knowing smile. "If you're willing to change that, I can show you how."

Nash nodded.

"Any word from Lucas?" Tanvi asked.

"I thought he was here. I'm sure he will be soon." Nash offered her a smile. She answered with one of her own that she couldn't get to meet her eyes.

Her mother entered the room with Reina and Yasmin, and they surrounded Adina, praying out loud, between stories, laughter, and tears.

FORTY

FRANK ENTERED THE HOSPITAL WITH A BOUQUET IN HIS HANDS. Rachel picked them out for Adina. It was times like these, he was even more thankful for her presence in his life. He hated hospitals and situations like this.

He entered the room to see all the Nightingales present, along with Nash, asleep in the corner. Tanvi was draped over her battered sister's bed. Adina lay on her back with a tube in her mouth and various wires going to machines that beeped and whirred. Her face was black and blue, her neck was in a brace. It was a devastating scene, not unlike seeing someone broken and barely clinging to life after a head-on collision. Thick, hard, white casts concealed her left leg, right wrist, and left arm. They'd really done a number on her.

Tanvi stirred as he placed the flowers on the bedside table. She looked around, noting the rest of her sleeping family members. She touched her mother's shoulder, and Cora took Tanvi's seat next to the bed, placing one hand on Adina's arm and laying her head down. Tanvi stepped around the bed and led Frank back out of the room.

"Thank you for coming," she said, wiping sleep from her eyes.

"Of course," he said. "You know what you did—"

"Was dumb, yeah. I can't figure out why they let me go," she said. "I was there to trade. It was in the block for his move, where she was found. So, I don't understand it."

Frank thought it over. "He called you, said come alone." He looked around. "Where's your shadow?"

She frowned.

"Lucas?"

"He didn't show. He hasn't even returned any of my calls."

"What?" Frank asked. "He disappeared from the station before you called the ambulance."

"What?"

"It wasn't about you at all. They wanted him. Why? You're Alice, and this is all about the damn book."

"It's about Alice's experiences in Wonderland. He was my lifeline." She couldn't breathe, she slid down the wall to take a seat on the cold tile floor. "They're severing my lifelines."

"Okay, I need to know everything."

Frank's phone jingled in his pocket, and he pulled it out with a huff. "Tench—you have got to be joking. Well, McGinn is missing. From the trap we thought was for Tanvi—no, I'm not fucking kidding. — I don't know. Get everyone together. We'll be there in ten."

LUCAS WOKE UP WITH A HEADACHE THAT COULD RIVAL EVEN HIS BEST post-St. Patty's Day celebrations back home in Boston. He hadn't celebrated with his siblings in years to avoid just such a hangover. Also, to avoid the inevitable jail time.

The smell assaulted his stomach. It was thick with dirt, fresh blood, and the rot of decaying flesh. He coughed as he fought to open his eyes. His lids felt weighted down, only opening for a few milliseconds at a time before dropping closed. There was no light at all, and he knew he was in a dungeon, like the one he'd first kissed Tanvi in. A smile spread over his lips, and the skin cracked, the pain bringing him back into his present situation.

The door opened, spilling light into the room. It burned his eyes. He squeezed them shut with a groan.

"You're awake?" The female voice took Lucas by surprise. He squinted against the light to see who was entering, pain shooting through his skull. There were two of them, and they were silhouetted by the door. The second person closed the door, and they turned on an overhead light.

The woman was Constance Puera from Joe's past. The man didn't look familiar at all. He cocked his head to look at Lucas.

"It is a very merry unbirthday indeed." He licked his lips.

"Remember, he's not just here for you. We have to break Nightingale with this one," the woman said.

"But he's so delicious. He screams masculinity. All we have to do is emasculate him, really."

Lucas scoffed. The chuckle turning into a deep, rolling laugh that bounced off the walls. The movement stretched his ribs and relaxed him, despite the situation.

The woman looked him up and down, disgust shining in her cold dark eyes. "You think something's funny?"

"That fact that you think you can break me," he said. "It tickled me just here." He pointed to his ribs. She hauled back and kicked him where he'd pointed.

He grunted as he rolled away, more laughter bubbling up beyond his control. "Good start. And here I was worried you were going to be all obvious about it."

The Hatter moved forward. The look in his eyes was more than enough to wipe the smile off Lucas's face, so he fought to keep it in place.

"You're curious," he said, still licking his lips. "I can be creative. I'll break you."

"Everything you can think of," Lucas said, leveling him with a serious stare. "It's already been done to me."

The man was obviously a sadist, a mad sparkle in his eyes.

"When you were young and helpless. It'll take on a whole new meaning now that you're a big, strong man."

The Hatter whistled as they left. Lucas looked about his prison for anything to help him escape. The light went out, the door clicked closed, and he was surrounded by darkness again, panic threatening his composure. He forced it back down.

"WHAT DO WE KNOW?" TANVI ASKED AS SHE MOVED THROUGH THE police station like she was on a mission. All that mattered was Lucas. A knot of guilt in her stomach threatened to undo the clarity of the task at hand. And the asshole in the next room was the closest thing they had to answers.

"What's important is what we don't," Nash said as he struggled to keep up with her. "Why did he take McGinn? We've been assuming you're Alice. He's all but called you Alice, so why take Lucas?"

"Nickolas Preston is ready to talk, but Nash is right—we need to go in there with a strategy."

"I have one," she said. "Find out where they took him. Get Joe ready, too. We may need him."

"We definitely need a strategy. If his lawyer will even let us talk to him."

"An agent of the FBI has been taken hostage. Can we at least pretend this is an emergency?" Tanvi whirled around to face them.

"We're all as worried as you are, Tanvi," Frank said, placing a hand on her shoulder. "That's why we're being so cautious about not burning a bridge that could lead to his safe return."

"You know what they're doing to him."

"We know nothing," Nash interjected. "They've never taken a male before. All we can even guess is he's probably not having the time of his life right now."

"They killed some of the girls quickly. Mercifully. You said that could be because they fought back or didn't." She threw her head back, starting at the ceiling as her voice grew louder. "We know he'll fight back, and we've got autopsies—so, which was it?"

"They fought," Frank answered. "Hard."

"Okay. Enough with this bullshit. We're going in, and we'll come out with answers. For Lucas."

"For Lucas," they said in unison.

TANVI ENTERED THE ROOM TO SEE THE MAN AT THE TABLE, THE TOP half of his long dreadlocks pulled back in a half-ponytail while the lower half hung over his shoulders. His eyes were on the table and he refused to look at her.

"You agree to the terms of the deal?" she asked.

"We do."

"Well, they're changing," she said without blinking.

"Wait a minute. You can't just—"

"I just did. Now, listen up. Not only do we need to apprehend the other perpetrators of these crimes, but an FBI agent has been taken. He *will* be returned safely, or I'll ensure that you rot in a cell for the rest of your life. The faster you tell us everything you know, the more likely it is that we will be able to save his life, and you could maybe not spend the rest of your life in prison."

"Hold on—"

"No," he said, interrupting his lawyer, fidgeting with his hands on the table. "I'll do it. They told me about this part."

"Who's they?" Tanvi asked with a pen ready.

"I don't know their real names. They used fake ones," he said.

"Okay," she said. "Give me the aliases."

"The leader was the 'Caterpillar.' The guy I worked with—Joe —he told me his name, but he wasn't supposed to. He was the 'White Rabbit.' The girl he worked with—"

"A girl?"

"Yeah," he said, eyes wide. "She is fucking crazy."

"What is she called?"

"The March Hare."

"Okay. Can you describe her?" she said, shooting a text to Frank.

Tanvi: Get a photo lineup with Constance Peura in it in here ASAP

"White, she looks beat up, meth head skin and teeth. Her hair was dyed pink but faded. I don't know what it was before. Dark roots. Maybe dirty blonde? Probably not black."

"Thank you," she said.

"How did you get involved with these people?"

"My cousin," he said. "Big D, he was one of them, he said he just got paid to deliver girls. I know it's wrong. I should have called the cops. Honestly, I know that now, and I knew it then but I didn't realize how involved he was and—"

"I need to speak to my client."

"We're not worried about that right now," Tanvi said. "Your cousin's name."

"Damon Johnson," he said.

"Any relation to Susan Johnson?" she asked, eyeing the victim's photo.

"Yeah," he said. "I didn't know about that until the last guys came in to talk, I swear."

Tanvi nodded. "Okay, who else was there?"

"Mad Hatter and the White King. They were on the other team. Playing against Joe and the girl."

"Did you know what they were playing?" she asked.

"No, they talked in riddles all the time."

"Did you ever meet them anywhere other than Joe's house?"

"No."

"Thank you."

Frank knocked before entering. He placed the photo lineup on the table.

He pointed to the photo of Constance before they even got to ask him if he recognized anyone.

"It's her, she's the March Hare."

"Would she be with the others now?" Tanvi asked.

"I don't know. She's crazy and doesn't care for Carl. But she'd know where they are. She'd know the plans," he offered.

Tanvi left the room with Frank and headed to the HQ.

"We need more," she said, shaking her head and rubbing her eyes. Exhaustion threatened to overtake her ability to stay calm. "We knew most of this already."

"Constance being involved is new," Frank offered. "We can put an APB out and try to find her."

"I don't think she'll be cooperative. We need to know where they are right now."

Her voice cracked as despair enveloped her. A sob caught in her throat.

"Hey, we'll find him. He's tough. He can handle this."

She took a deep breath. "He shouldn't have to. He's been through enough. God, what I put him through."

"Tanvi," Frank said, putting both hands on her shoulders and forcing her to look at him. "We will find him. If we keep it together and stay on track."

"How?"

"There are two witnesses we have yet to speak to. The teen Joe was trying to abduct. I contacted them as soon as I knew Lucas was missing. They're willing to talk, given the circumstances. And there's one more."

She closed her eyes.

"Adina."

FORTY-ONE

McGinn sat on the damp, dirt floor, the cold penetrating his bones and making every past injury ache. He pulled on his chains half-heartedly until they were taught and then moved back, toward the wall where they were anchored.

Shifting earth drew his attention to the door before the blinding light spilled into the room. He at the light as he stood. Two figures entered.

Eerie cackles echoed off the walls, and Lucas's blood ran cold.

"Carl?" he said, knowing he was right.

"Lucas, my boy," Carl shifted so the light was on him instead of behind him. His twisted grin promised a world of pain. "You caused me so much trouble, I decided you'd be more fun to kill than Tanvi. Plus, she'll never drop this case if I take you from her. That excites me in a way few things do nowadays."

"She's stronger than you think," Lucas said straighten his shoulders to look down on Carl. He was a solid two inches taller than Carl, and he knew it would piss him off. But he had nothing to lose. "You know, I could kill for a cigarette."

"You really shouldn't smoke," the woman said with a maniacal laugh. "That shit will kill you."

"Slower than you, I'm sure," he said, never taking his eye off Carl.

"If Tanvi wasn't so tenacious, I could truly take my time with you. You're my first kill in this game, you know."

"You said I could do it," the woman hissed.

Carl shot her a glare, and she slunk backward, her eyes lethal. Lucas took note.

"Ladies, ladies," Lucas said diplomatically. "There's enough of me to go around."

"There won't be when I'm done," Carl promised, a toothy grin spread over his face. "I'm going to make you wish you'd never been born."

"You're about twenty-five years too late for that. But I appreciate the effort." Lucas smiled at him.

Carl's face fell. "Somehow, I thought you'd clam up in here."

"It's not in my programming," Lucas shrugged.

"It will be," Carl said through gritted teeth, his impatience growing. "We'll wait just a little longer for you to get hungrier. Weaker. Then, the games will begin."

"Promises, promises."

Carl back handed him. He straightened from the blow and spit blood onto the floor before smiling at the smaller man.

CARL CURSED AS THE DOOR CLOSED BEHIND HIM. HE NEEDED THAT asshole to be afraid. Sure, he preferred little girls, but all he really needed was for his victim to be afraid. The fear in their eyes drove his creativity for violence.

"You said I could kill him." The feminine growl made his eyes roll. Her lack of vision was her most infuriating trait.

He turned on her, pushing her to the wall and invading her space. "You can torture him to your black, little heart's content, but if you kill him, you'll be the next one in that room. And if you think for one second everyone in this thing hasn't been watching you and hoping to take you down, you're wrong. Even Joe wants a piece of you."

She shuddered, still he was almost certain she was playing him. But she was sufficiently scared, or at least silent, for now.

Carl looked down the hall to where his prize was waiting. *His* Alice. He put a grin on his face and strode down the hall.

TANVI ENTERED THE HOSPITAL ROOM, AND HAPPINESS FILLED HER heart. Her sister was sitting up and enjoying a pudding cup.

"Are you sure that's kosher?" Tanvi teased.

"Har har," Adina said before wincing and placing a hand on her temple. "This headache is no joke, though."

"I thought you'd be in the coma longer honestly."

"They're still monitoring me really close. Every hour. I'd kill to be back in the coma. Get some damn sleep."

"Don't joke," Tanvi said her heart hurting. "They drugged you."

"Twice," she said, knowing Tanvi didn't mean the hospital staff. "Once, before I got to the—place—and then before they took me out."

"Do you remember anything about the trip in or out?" Her attempts to mask the desperation in her voice were failing miserably.

"What happened?" Always the astute listener.

"They took Lucas."

She leaned forward. "Why?"

"To get to me? To show him he's not as tough as he thinks?" she shrugged. "I don't know, and I don't care. I just need to find him."

"But he has a penis."

"Thank you, Adina," she barked. Then understanding hit her. "How long were you there?"

She sighed, putting her pudding cup down. "Eight hours? Maybe more. Maybe less. Everything's a blur. They said my memory could comeback in pieces. But I remember enough."

Tanvi swallowed hard. "What did they do?"

She ran her tongue over her teeth, taking a deep breath, fighting the images that were no doubt now flooding her mind. She'd been saving herself for marriage. If they did what Tanvi suspected, this would not be comfortable.

"Exactly what you think they did," she said, unable to meet Tanvi's gaze.

"I'm so sorry, Adina."

"Don't," she snapped as tears fell from her eyes. Her bottom lip quivered, but aside from that, she refused to show her pain. "I'm not some broken, little victim for you to save. I'm me. Your sister. You slut."

"Goody two shoes," Tanvi said, unable to hold back her smile.

"Horrible driver."

Tanvi gasped as a laugh escaped her control. "At least I *can* drive!"

"Public transportation is there for a reason."

"Yeah, for losers like you who can't drive."

"For heaven's sake!" Their mother's voice interrupted their sisterly squabble. "Tanvi Nightingale! Don't you think your sister has been through enough?"

"It's okay, mom," Adina said through her laughter. "I actually need one more minute with T., please. We'll be nice, I promise."

Tanvi crossed her heart and offered her mother her pinky. Cora glared as she walked back out. "I'll be right outside. I'll hear if you're nasty to one another."

"Of course," Tanvi nodded. Their mother left, and she turned back to her sister. "Adina, I'm here when you're ready. I won't think any differently of you." She stopped talking as Adina looked at her. "Did you remember something?"

"First, don't tell mom. I already talked to dad, he's running interference with the hospital staff. I can't handle it. If she were to find out."

Tanvi nodded. She wasn't sure she agreed but it wasn't her body. "What can you remember?"

"As we were leaving. The drugs hadn't fully kicked in yet. I could see the house. It was green a dark forest green, with white trim. With a front porch that had white columns. I remember thinking, it was such beautiful place, for something so horrible."

"I'll catch these guys." Tanvi promised.

"I'd rather you kill them." Adina said, her tone filled with conviction.

She placed a hand on her sister's cheek, unsure of what to say.

"They took Luke so, maybe they're already dead."

LUCAS GRITTED HIS TEETH AGAINST THE GUTTURAL PAIN OF THE HOT poker being pressed into his side. Carl stood back, watching as the Mad Hatter did his work. Bile rose in his throat, but he refused to give them the satisfaction of knowing how much it hurt.

"What's the matter, Carl?" Lucas said between heavy breaths. "You let this little piece of shit do all the heavy lifting?"

"I like to watch," Carl said. "I always have. It's not the act itself that makes me feel powerful—it's the look of pain in your eyes. In a little girl's eyes. I'm not much of an adult torturer. There's something special when they're young. Innocent. They think the world is all sunshine and rainbows until I come along. You know the feeling I think. Did he rape you too?"

The shockwaves of pain were washed away by rage. "You better kill me now, Carl."

"Not quite yet," Carl grinned. Lucas's own reflection stared back at him in Carl's glasses.

"Remember, I told you."

Carl's mouth was agape, a confused look overtaking his face. "Told me what?"

"I'm going to kill you," a smile tugged at his lips. "You're not getting a trial. No chance for a deal. I'm putting a bullet between your eyes."

"What, no torture?" Carl was enjoying the exchange. As was Lucas.

"No," Lucas said, standing up straight, despite the pain. "You'd enjoy that too much. I'll kill you, and then," he couldn't stop his own grin from spreading, and a laugh escaped his control. "Then, I'll erase you. Joe will go down as the mastermind of this fucked-up game. Not you. No one will remember your name. No one."

Carl grabbed the poker from The Hatter and stabbed it into Lucas's thigh. He screamed out before staring Carl down.

"I will fucking kill you," he whispered the promise. Carl removed the poker, sending another jolt of extreme pain through his body, before leaving the room.

The Hatter looked after Carl, cocking his head to the side. "I've never seen him lose his composure before." He looked back at Lucas.

"It's kinda my thing," Lucas said, trying to put weight on the injured leg and hissing in pain.

"Rape is *my* thing." The psycho sounded as if he was sharing his love of football. "I'm not one for all this torture. I like to hurt women, sure, but if you cut them, if you damage their physical form—" He shook his head like it was unthinkable.

"What about kids?"

The man's eyes shot up. "I'd never hurt a child."

Lucas eyed him. He was probably lying, but just in case. "Then, why let *him* hurt them?"

He walked forward with a knife, placing it on Lucas's arm. He sliced into his flesh slowly. Lucas gritted his teeth through the pain, holding his gaze. The Hatter leaned in, whispering in Lucas' ear. "He's a pussy. He drugs them. Not only can they not fight back, they don't even know what's happening."

"Oh, they know. They fucking know."

The Hatter took a step back, his scowl deep as he contemplated the words. "Scream, like I hurt you."

FORTY-TWO

TANVI WALKED BRISKLY TOWARD THE SQUAD ROOM HQ. WORRY FILLED her at the realization of Frank's absence. He still hadn't returned, and she had to compare notes. Hopefully find Lucas's location.

"Tanvi?" The voice caught her off guard. She looked behind her to see John running to her. "I know where they are."

"Where?" she asked as he struggled to catch his breath.

"Shit, you walk fast," he said as he gulped air.

"Where, John?"

"I texted it to you," he said. "I was able to figure it out—"

"John, you're amazing, and I love you, but I don't care." She gave him a kiss on the cheek and raced back toward the garage. She skidded to a halt.

"What?" John called to her from his spot.

"I need to tell Frank before I go anywhere," she said, rushing back to HQ. "We can't do this without backup and extra units."

"I'll get them," He waved her off and started down the hall. "You go, I'll get them. They'll be five minutes behind you. Scope it out, see if I'm even right."

She nodded and raced down the hall, fear and excitement warring for control of her. She needed to save Lucas. She couldn't lose him. She'd barely found him.

THE HATTER DUMPED LUCAS IN A HEAP ON THE FLOOR BEFORE leaving him in the dark. Dirt and grime scraping his burns, he bit back a cry as agony sliced through his side and leg. The scorching sensation felt like millions of fire ants stinging him directly on exposed nerves. He barely felt the stinging from the cuts. It was the burns that he could feel every tiny movement or brush against them made them feel new again.

He shifted on his side, huffing as he attempted to breathe through the pain. His hand hit something small and metallic. He froze, slowly splaying his fingers. Excitement shot through him as he realized what he'd found. A hair pin. Careful not to rattle the chains too loudly, he sat up, gripping the pin with both hands. He nearly cried out in joy as relief flooded him. It was two pins connected to each other. He pulled them apart, carefully placing one between his teeth while he stretched out the other. He swapped pins and repeated this action. Tugging the cuffs on his feet to him, he worked the pins inside the lock. A *clink* sounded as the metal fell away from his aching skin, ripping a layer of skin off as it went. But he didn't care. He would soon be free. Working the pins in his handcuffs proved more difficult, but he'd been here before—that place where you cannot give one inch, or you'll be destroyed. He panted and winced, working the pin, the other in his teeth. After what seemed like hours, he was finally free. He was fairly certain he knew where the camera was. Carefully, he laid himself down to appear as if he were still restrained. He placed the pins in his cheek and closed his eyes. When he woke, he was going to kill these assholes.

TANVI PULLED UP TO THE CURB, A FEW HOUSES DOWN FROM THE address John had given her. Sure enough, the house Adina described was in front of her—green with white trim. It looked nice. Like it was well cared for. She shook her head, trying not to draw attention from the neighbors.

She slipped out of her car and paused, realizing Frank needed an update. Hopefully, he'd see her text immediately.

Tanvi: John's address was spot on. This is the house Adina described. How far are you? I'm going to check it out.

Unwilling to wait for a reply, she silenced her phone and stuffed it in her pocket. Creeping along the cars on the street, she scanned for any movement in the house. Nothing. Still crouched down, she crossed the street and made her way into the backyard. A white, gauzy curtain moved in one of the upstairs bedrooms, and she paused. It looked like it was from air conditioning or something, so she continued on. The yard was empty. Muffled voices filtered up from the basement as she approached the small window. Crawling closer, she leaned in. They may have been speaking in tongues for all she knew. There were no clear, distinguishable words to make out, but there were at least two different voices. Neither of them sounded like Lucas. Maybe this was a normal residence. Second-guessing herself, she moved into the backyard, looking for any signs of Carl or the others. She crept up on the porch.

Peering in the back, she noticed a sliding, glass door. On the counter, she could see a photo of Carl and his ex-wife. She didn't need anything else. With a tug of the handle, the door shifted and moved smoothly through its track. After slipping inside the house, she slid the door closed behind her. It got stuck. As she turned to free her jacket from the track, a weight slammed into her, and she was greeted with the awful, crazy eyes and white hair of Joe. Joe White.

SCRAPING WOKE HIM. RECOGNIZING IT AS THE DOOR, HE OPENED ONE eye to look through his lashes.

"Wakey, wakey, tough guy," Constance laughed. "I get to kill you now, but you're so pretty. I have a few things I want to do first. We don't take men, ever, so you're kind of my only chance."

Before she could close the door. He lunged, his burned leg screaming in protest as he grabbed her by the hair and slammed her head into the stone wall. Constance screamed as he moved behind her, sliding his arm around her throat. The blood choke stopped her oxygen supply, ending her life within minutes, she clawed at his arm, ripping open his cuts and burns with her nails until she stopped. Limp in his arms, he held on a little longer. Just in case.

He let her body fall to the floor as he looked into the next room. With no idea what to expect, he made his way slowly into the rest of the house every movement sending pain through his body. Like the last one, this room, too, had been built into a basement. There was a commotion upstairs that sounded like a fight, and movement to his left, in the shadows, drew his attention. He moved back into the shadows. The Hatter approached with a girl who looked like she was about ten in his arms. He stood in the doorway of the room, rocking back and forth as he saw the body of the March Hare. He put the girl down and scratched his head.

He looked back at the child, and Lucas cursed his luck. Stepping out of the shadows, Lucas called to him. "Hey, buddy, what are you doing?"

"You killed her." He pointed to the Hare's body. Lucas gave a curt nod. No point in lying. "Why?"

"She was going to kill me."

The Hatter's breathing started to come in short bursts. He was furious. "She was my best friend!"

More muffled sounds. Where were the stairs? He didn't have time for this.

"You wanna kill me?" Lucas goaded. "Come on!"

The Hatter ran at him, grabbing Lucas about the waist. He hit the ground hard, the wind rushing from his lungs from the impact. He pushed through the discomfort, throwing his hips, he positioned himself on top of his opponent and pinned the Hatter. Straddling him, Lucas threw one punch after the other, putting all his weight behind them. A flurry of punches connected with the pathetic creep's face and head. His blocks were useless. Lucas was weak but adrenaline flowed into him. He could still beat this asshole into a bloody pulp. When the thud of a fist hitting a face was replaced with the wet slaps, he sat back. Breathing hard, and covered in blood. The little girl was crouched behind a book shelf, blinking at him, and he cursed himself again. She shouldn't have seen that.

He reached out for her, and she eyed his blood-covered hand.

"Are you Miranda?" he asked through heavy breaths. The adrenaline was fading. He needed to get her out, now. "I'm from the FBI. Your mom sent me to find you."

She looked up at the mention of her mother. "What's my mom's name?"

"Your mom?" Smart kid.

She nodded.

"Debbie. Debbie Cantor."

She took his hand, and he stood, being careful of his wounded leg.

Joe launched himself on top of Tanvi, slipping his hands—which were not old and frail like she'd imagined—around her neck. He squeezed, and she took a deep breath as he failed to close her airway. The harder he squeezed, the crazier the look in his eyes. Fighting the panic threatening to take over, he'd perfected his hold. She couldn't breath. She felt around for her gun. It landed nearby—she'd heard it hit the wall and slide. Her pinky touched the handle. Pushing her legs out, she moved them just a little closer. He was so focused on her eyes, he failed to realize she'd reached it. She put it to his head and squeezed the trigger, fear shooting across his face just before the bullet.

Coughing, she scurried out from under his body as panic filled her. She took greedy breaths, desperate to get the hell away from him. Her gun still in her hand, a shadow fell over them.

Tanvi turned to see Carl in the doorway. A sickening smile spread over his face as he took in the scene.

"You're really in this for keeps, huh?" he said as he walked past her to kneel by Joe. "You really did a number on him."

She aimed her gun at him. "You're under arrest." Her voice came out in a painful whisper.

Carl looked up from Joe and stood.

"Don't move!" she ordered as loudly as she could, her throat screaming with pain.

"You don't want me," he grinned, moving past her, back toward the door. "You want him."

A man stepped forward from one of the rooms. John lifted his head and looked her right in the eyes. "I-I don't understand."

"He's the Cheshire Cat." Carl laughed. "It was his idea to put the Post-it notes down for you to follow. He's the one who led you to me. I may have planned this, but he pulled it off."

She shook her head, gun still aimed at Carl.

"And if you want Lucas alive," Carl whispered, pausing to allow his words to sink in, "you'll kill John, right here and now."

She looked at John, who appeared more surprised by this turn of events than she did. She slid the gun from Carl to John. His eyes pleaded with her.

"T, please, I just did what I was told."

"Did you rape my sister?" she rasped. John looked away. It was all the confirmation she needed. She started to squeeze the trigger. The door to the basement flew open beside her, making her jump.

Lucas stood in the doorway. He was covered in blood, sweat, and dirt. She couldn't even make out what his injuries were. His right arm was behind him at an awkward angle. As he stepped forward, she noticed a little girl behind him, clinging to his arm.

"No," Carl screamed as he saw the pair. "She's mine!"

Before he could step forward, Tanvi pivoted and pulled the trigger. The first shot hitting him in the temple, the second and third hit his chest. By the time he'd hit the ground, she'd unloaded the clip on him. The girl screamed, and Lucas held her close.

Fear shot through her as she searched for John, ignoring the look in Lucas's eyes. She ran to the hall, but John was gone, only an open front door giving her a clue to his whereabouts.

With a curse, she pulled her phone from her pocket and called Frank.

"We're almost there," he said by way of greeting. "John didn't tell me shit."

"He's the Cat," she tried to say. Her voice a hoarse whisper.

"What?"

"He's the Cat. The Cheshire Cat."

"I can't hear you. Tanvi?"

Shaking her head as anger and betrayal coursed through her, she fought to speak. Lucas came up behind and took the phone.

"She said, 'John is the Cheshire Cat.' He's in on it. And he's escaped. Put the word out."

His strong arms wrapped around her as she sobbed. It was over, he was safe. She pulled him to her and kissed his dry cracks lips.

"What have they done to you?"

His breathing was heavy but there was a glint in his eye. "Nothing that hasn't been done before," he said through deep breaths.

FORTY-THREE

TANVI SLID FROM HER HOSPITAL BED, LARGE, RUBBER BOTTOMED SOCKS covered her feet as she padded to Lucas's room. The sound they made making it hard to sneak around.

The little girl and the hospital staff had done an excellent job of keeping her from Lucas. Her mind raced with what he might have been through. She was wracked with guilt. Her sister's rapist had escaped. He was still at large, as far as she knew, though there was an APB out on his car, and he was on the FBI's Most Wanted list.

She hesitated just outside Luke's door. It was left ajar, her hands on the cool, heavy wood. She froze. What if he blamed her? It was her fault he was caught. Tears stung her eyes at the betrayal. How could she have done that and not even realized it for an entire day?

"Are you gonna come in, or just stand there and breathe heavy?" His thick Boston accent made her laugh even as the tears fell. Her throat ached at the strain.

Pushing the door open, she entered. He sat up as soon as he realized it was her.

"Tanvi—" Her name on his lips was like heaven. She wanted to listen to him say her name for the rest of her life. "I didn't know if you were okay. They wouldn't talk to me. Shit." His gaze fell to the bruises on her neck.

Her hand shot up to cover them.

"Don't hide from me," he begged. He was wiggling, clearly wanting to go to her, but he was stuck to the bed, between his injuries and the monitors. "Are you okay?"

She couldn't speak past the lump, never mind the pain in her throat. Instead, she made her way to his bed and climbed in. He pulled her to his chest and grunted as she made contact. She pulled back, frowning at him. He cupped her cheek in his hand and wiped her tears away with his thumb.

"Don't worry about me. I've been through worse." He pressed his forehead to hers. She soaked in the moment. His closeness, tenderness. She was in love with him, and she couldn't even say it. "I love you, T."

A sob broke out, hurting her throat as she tried to tell him she felt the same. He laughed at her flailing display. "Not exactly the reaction I was hoping for."

She looked away, trying to figure out how to say this. A smile broke across her face as she held up her hand. Sign language for I love you, then pointed at him.

"You love me, too?" he asked. She nodded. "That's nothing to cry about." He pulled her to him again, pressing his lips to hers. She opened her mouth, and he slid his tongue inside. He groaned against her, feeling her hands over his ribs. He shifted, hissing in pain. "Don't worry about it."

She glared before pulling his hospital gown up. Her breath caught in her throat at the sight. Where there weren't bandages, there were deep purple bruises. She looked up at him, more tears welling in her eyes. "I did this," she mouthed, pointing at herself.

"Hey," he said making her look at him. "I'm glad it was me."

She looked away. Leave it to him to use her own logic against her.

"Hey," he grabbed her chin and pulled her back to look at him. "If we went back in time, I'd do everything exactly the same."

She sobbed into his chest, trying not to hurt him more than he already was. When she was spent, she tried to get up, to go back to her room.

"Where are you going?" he asked, his eyes barely staying open.

Lifting a weak arm, she pointed to the door.

"Stay."

She padded back to the bed and climbed in. It felt like home as he played with her hair. This was exactly where she was meant to be.

"This could be our last night together." She could hear the sadness in his voice. It was mirrored by the pain in her heart. Virginia *is very far away.*

"We could make it work," she croaked. Every burning word was worth the pain.

"Yes," he whispered, but she could feel his reservation. If she could barely make time for her boyfriend in the same city, how could she make time for one who was hundreds of miles away? Maybe there was no "happily ever after" for cops. She breathed in his warm, masculine scent. There was *right now.* And she was going to enjoy it while she could.

SUN SHONE IN THROUGH THE WINDOW, PULLING LUCAS FROM HIS PAIN med-induced coma. He fought to open his eyes. The weight on his chest was pure heaven. The warm rosey scent of Tanvi flowed over him and he tightened his arm around her.

Stretching, she bumped one of his burns. Pain sliced through him, and he sucked in air sharply. She froze. He lifted her arm, and she pulled it back to her. "Sorry."

Her voice sounded somewhat better, but her eyes were still red and puffy, like she'd cried intermittently throughout the night.

A knock sounded at the door, pulling his attention away from her. A nurse entered, looking at a chart.

"All right, Mr. McGinn, we need to clean those burns and re-bandage them, and—" she paused at the sight of them together in bed.

"She's—with me," he said, feeling childish. "My girlfriend."

"She really can't be in bed with you," she tsked. "Keeping your burns from getting infected is bad enough—oh," she said, pointing behind her with a thumb, "is she in room 411?"

Tanvi nodded.

"What's with the Post-it note?" she asked.

They looked at each other, and both tried to get up.

"No, Mr. McGinn." The nurse tried to push him back into bed, but he wasn't having it. He moved her aside and hobbled after Tanvi. They both stood in the doorway and stared at the yellow note on her pillow. The distinct Cheshire Cat smile.

"We need the footage from the cameras in this hall, now," Lucas barked at the nurse.

"You need to get back into your bed. Now."

"A serial killer got into this hospital last night," he barked. Her eyes got wide.

"I'll go get security."

"You do that." Tanvi clung to him as they both stood silently. If he never let her go, John couldn't get her.

BY THE TIME LUCAS'S BURNS WERE CLEANED AND RE-BANDAGED, Frank had arrived at the hospital.

"We have confirmation," he said, offering them a photo of John at a toll booth headed out of the city at four in the morning. "He must have left right after leaving the note."

"This isn't over. He has some kind of obsession with her," Lucas said.

"Don't upset my patient," the nurse hissed.

"I think it's a little late for that," Frank replied.

"Damn straight it is. No one threatens Tanvi. Not while I'm alive."

"You won't be alive much longer if you don't chill out," The nurse said through clenched teeth, her patience thinning.

Tanvi sat, looking out the window at the parking lot. Her face devoid of any expression.

"Why didn't the toll operator call it in?"

"Didn't see the bulletin until the end of her shift," Frank answered. "At which point, she called and got the photo from security. Or rather, started the process so it wasn't deleted. I don't think he's coming back."

"How can you say that?" Lucas asked.

"He wanted to scare you. To make sure he stayed in your thoughts. He's either going to set up shop elsewhere, or he's done. It was his last hurrah."

"You think she's safe? Her family?"

"I've asked for a protective detail for a while to make sure, but yes. I do."

Lucas sat back. He hated this. His gaze fell to Tanvi. He couldn't leave her here. Not like this. Not with this much uncertainty.

FORTY-FOUR

It had been a week since the incident in the hospital. Lucas was finally being released. The doctors were happy with the look of his burns, and he'd been given leave to go home. Frank stood outside the hospital, waiting for him to come down. He'd agreed to drive him to Tanvi's, where her mother insisted he stay since the FBI would no longer be paying for his hotel room.

A black car slid up next to him as he took a cigarette out of his chest pocket and put it between his lips. He didn't light them anymore, but he liked to chew on them every once in a while. And the last few weeks had started a craving unlike anything he'd experienced in years.

A long, slender leg emerged out of the car. He turned as he realized who it was.

"Teresa?" he said, confused. She grabbed the cigarette from his lips and tossed it into the bushes.

"You still haven't quit?" she asked, pulling him into a tight hug.

"It's been a rough couple weeks," he said in his defense. "What are you doing here?"

"I'm here to collect my agent," she said like it was obvious. "Boss wants me to fire him."

"What?"

"From what we can see, he hasn't learned a damn thing from you."

"He's a hell of an agent, Teresa. He's got instincts and balls to follow through. Hell, without him, I could have lost all of them. Tanvi, her sister, and the little girl."

"He's selfish. Not to mention reckless," she argued.

"John was the problem, not Lucas."

"He played Lucas like a fiddle."

"He played all of us. Keep in mind that McGinn and Nightingale cleaned up the mess, but he played us all."

The doors opened, and Lucas stepped out. He had a pair of crutches and squinted against the light.

"This would have gone down a hell of a lot worse if it wasn't for that agent," Frank said, keeping his voice low. He nodded his sincerity. "You remember that when you're making your decision."

"Prentis?" He hobbled over. "What are you doing here?"

"I've come to get you," she said. "You're needed back in Virginia. Frank, Nash, and Tanvi have all spoken very highly of your work here."

"You spoke to Tanvi about me?"

Frank glared. She'd just played him. She was getting good in her old age.

"Yes, prior to coming down."

"I was planning to transfer," he said. "Here. And not go back."

"That won't be possible," she said without explanation.

"Either way, I need to talk to Tanvi first."

"I'll drive him over," Frank said. "I'll text you the address."

She nodded.

LUCAS WATCHED AS THE TALL CITY BUILDINGS SHIFTED INTO SMALLER apartments and houses as they approached Tanvi's neighborhood. Why didn't she tell him Prentis had called her?

When they pulled up, there was a giant "Welcome Home, Lucas" sign hung above the door. His heart swelled.

"They really like you."

"You kill a couple rats, and they accept you as one of their own," he joked. "I guess families are weird."

"You have a family."

"Now, I do." A warmth grew in him at his own words as he pushed himself out of the car. Teresa wasn't far behind. Adina and her mother left the house to help him in. "Don't worry about me."

"We're not worried," her mother said with a knowing smile as she took his arm. "We're caring."

They helped him through the front door, and everyone whooped and hollered at him. They were all very careful not to hurt him as they hugged and kissed him, surrounding him with affection and appreciation. But the one he really wanted to see was nowhere to be found. "Where's Tanvi?"

"In her room." Her mother looked nervous. "She's been off. Ever since a call from the FBI."

He sighed. "I'll take care of it."

She beamed. "I knew you would."

He made his way down the hall as Frank entered the house, presumably with Prentis not far behind.

Placing his hand on the knob, he turned it and entered Tanvi's room. She was still in her bed. He made his way around to look at her. She wasn't sleeping, she was just laying there, staring at the window, a lost expression on her face. Her eyes flicked to the foot of the bed, where he stood, broken, bruised, but delighted. She shot up. "You're here."

Her voice was stronger than it was before, but her eyes were still full of tears. He sat down next to her. "Of course, I am. Where else would I be?"

"In Virginia."

"Why would I be there?"

"That's where your job is."

"But it's not where you are."

"You're going to stay?"

"I haven't told Prentis yet. I mean, I tried—"

"You need to talk to her. Before you make a decision."

He rubbed his tired face. "What do you mean? I thought we'd decided."

"I can't make this choice for you. You'll hate me." She was panicking. He could see it like a slow motion crash, and there was nothing he could say or do to make it stop. "You'll resent me."

"No, I—"

"Luke," she said. But it wasn't the way that made his heart soar. In fact, it did the opposite. "Don't."

"Don't what?" he barked. Tears prickled the back of his eyes. He couldn't remember the last time he'd cried. But if this was taken from him, he didn't care.

"Don't make me the bad guy."

He looked away from her for a long time, trying to figure out what was happening. "Are you telling me to go?"

Her lips pressed together in a firm line. "I'm telling you not to stay. Not for me."

"Why are you doing this?"

"One of us has to face reality," she spat.

A tick worked in his jaw as his heart broke. He stood without another word and made his way to the door. Slowly, he turned around, no idea of what to even say.

His mouth opened, but no words came out. He put a hand over his mouth as he took a deep breath. "I still love you."

He didn't look at her. He just left. Closing the door behind him he could have sworn he heard her sob. Fighting the need to console her, he entered the living room and couldn't face her mother or sisters. He looked at Prentis. "Let's go."

"What?" Frank and her mother said at once.

"Where are you going?" Frank asked.

"Virginia." Ditching the crutches, he stormed out of the house, his thigh screaming with every step, but he didn't care. He'd do anything to distract himself from the pain in his chest.

Teresa followed him out of the house and into the car she had waiting.

"Do you have things to pick up?"

"No," he said. The truth was they were in that house, but there was no way he was going back in there for some clothes. He'd miss his gun. Maybe he could get Frank to ship it to him.

TANVI LAY IN HER BED, STARING AT THE CEILING FOR WHAT FELT LIKE days. Frank had come in, asking her questions, but she'd just ignored him until he went away. Then, her mother came in. She was yelling, but Tanvi couldn't hear her over the heartache. Lucas left. It was for the best, especially considering the promotion he'd receive. He'd be a team leader just like he'd wanted, and she couldn't leave her family. This was the only way forward. If it didn't kill her, she'd be amazed.

Her door opened, and Adina entered. The smell of warm, sticky cinnamon buns filled the space. A smell she would normally relish turned her stomach. Adina placed the buns on the bedside table. Tanvi rolled away from them. The bed dipped as her younger sister climbed in. She snuggled up to Tanvi, resting her chin on her big sister's shoulder.

"You wanna talk 'bout it?"

"Not really."

"Can I talk then?"

Tanvi shifted to look her sister in the eye. Adina sat up, cross legged, her hands in her lap before letting out a ragged breath.

"He raped me," she said, looking at her hands. "John did."

She paused, taking deep, shaky breaths. Tanvi had guessed as much but hearing it was different. She went into detective mode for both their sakes. "Was he the only one?"

"No," she said around tears. "But he's the one—" She looked away as her voice broke.

Tanvi scooted closer, placing a hand on Adina's arm.

"He's the one who knew I was waiting."

Tanvi sucked in a breath, knowing there was nothing she could say. She pulled her sister into a hug as she cried. Each shake of her little sister's body brought more tears to her own eyes. Before long, they were both sobbing. After a long while, when all their tears were spent, Adina sat up, rubbing her eyes. She grabbed a tissue and blew her nose.

"Why didn't you tell me sooner?" Tanvi asked.

"I didn't remember until I saw him on the news. The doctor said memories would come back in bits and pieces. I have huge chunks that are just—gone."

She nodded, grabbing a tissue to blow her nose. Adina eyed her.

"Just ask," Tanvi said, placing her hands in her lap. "Whatever it is, you want to ask. Just ask."

"Why'd you tell Lucas to leave?"

She took a ragged breath as more tears threatened to escape. "I had to." was all she got out before sobs took over.

"Why?"

"He was getting his promotion. And they don't offer it here. It was only if he stayed in Quantico." She shook her head. "I can't take what he's been working so hard for. I can't be the reason he misses out on that. I can't. Sure, he likes me now, but he'd hate me soon enough."

Her sister took a deep breath. That wise sister look she'd mastered in high school. It meant she was right. Whatever she was about to say. "No, he wouldn't."

Tanvi shook her head. "You don't understand."

"You didn't read Pride and Prejudice, did you?"

"Not all of it," she admitted.

"You sacrifice for the ones you love. Not in a way that makes you bitter or fills you with regret. But to make them happy. Darcy finds Lydia and pays off Wickham so Lizzy can be safe. At huge cost to his bank account and his ego."

"It's his job, Adina. It's not a love story with a perfect ending. Men need a job, they need to be able to support themselves or they grow angry and bitter. You saw how dad was when he was between jobs, during the recession. It nearly killed him when mom went to work."

"Because he wanted to keep her home with us, where she wanted to be. Not because she was earning money." Adina laughed. "Mom and dad are the perfect example of give and take in a relationship. He loves his family but he moved here to be near hers. She loves bacon but she doesn't eat it because it matters to him."

Tanvi looked away, anger flaring.

"You're scared, Tanvi," Adina said, not holding back. "You're afraid of what will happen if you let him in. But, Tanvi, that's the best part. Just talk to him." She handed Tanvi her phone. Sixteen missed calls. All from Lucas.

She swiped up on the screen to unlock it. One voicemail. Adina stood, heading for the door. "Call me if you need anything."

Waiting for the door to click closed, her hand trembled, nearly dropping the phone.

"Hey, Rookie, I'm fast approaching creepy stalker territory here with the once-every-hour calls. I'm in Virginia. Have been since you banished me. Not sure what I'm supposed to find here, honestly. It's the same shit that drove me crazy before I met you, but now—now, I know what it's like to be with you—well, it sucks. I miss you. I love you. Call me back. Let me come home."

Tears fell from her tired eyes as she collapsed back into her bed. A chime sounded from her phone. Another voicemail. She looked at the screen, surprised to see Frank's name instead of Lucas's.

She put the phone to her ear.

"I don't know what Teresa said to you, but I thought you should know. They're going to fire Luke. Nash just called me. I hope this changes your tune, but if not, this is my last call on the subject. Have a good life, kid. You know where to find me if you need me."

FORTY-FIVE

LUCAS PUT THE LAST OF HIS THINGS IN THE FILE BOX HE WAS USING TO pack up his desk. Nash stood nearby with that awkward, 'I don't know what to say' look.

"Don't sweat it, Nash," he said as he turned to leave.

"I'm grateful to you," Nash finally said. "I just, I can't believe you won't be here anymore."

He looked around the office. No one else seemed to notice. "You're the only one to care, though."

"Nah, I'm just the only one who's sad about it," he laughed." The party is at three."

"Heh-heh, sure. I'm proud of you, little buddy."

"Why do you have to call me that?"

" 'Cause you're tiny. A little bean pole of a guy, and what else am I gonna say to a dude with three more degrees than I do, who could probably teach NASA a thing or two? I mean, come on. I need the low-hanging fruit."

"No, you don't," he said. "You just don't want to be mean."

"Hey," he stepped closer. Looking around to make sure no one could hear them. "Quiet with that shit. I have my reputation to think about."

"Call me if you ever need anything." Nash offered his hand.

Lucas took it with a smile. "You too. I mean it."

"Thanks."

The Virginia heat was oppressive as he walked outside. He resisted the urge to look at his phone, mostly because he'd thrown it into the corner of his bedroom this morning when he'd realized she wasn't going to respond.

As he approached his car, he saw a person leaning against it.

"Hey, get off my c—" the words died in his throat as she turned to face him.

"I thought this might be yours."

"How did you know?"

"A sixties muscle car?" she scoffed. "It wasn't that hard."

"Why are you here?" he asked, afraid to get his hopes up.

"You wouldn't answer my calls."

"Sucks, doesn't it?" he bit out. He wanted to pull her into his arms, but he was terrified this was some kind of trick. Was she here to tell him to go to hell?

"What do you want Luke?"

He froze his box of stuff half way into his backseat.

"I asked you if you wanted to be married, with two point five kids once. You told me to ask you once I survived the case. Here I am. The case is over, mostly. And I need to know."

He turned to look at her. What was she saying? "I still don't know. If I marry you are you going to shut me out. Cut me off every time you get pissed or think you know what's best for me? Ignoring me for weeks at a time doesn't exactly say 'healthy marriage' does it?"

"I'm sorry, I thought—" she dropped her gaze. "Frank told me you were fired, and I came straight here. Well, not straight here. I called Teresa and her bosses, and after yelling at assholes for a few hours, I realized Foster was way easier to manipulate, so I got you a job as a detective. If you want it."

"You got me a job?" His eyes sparkled.

"I mean, I didn't know what to do. Teresa said you were

getting your promotion, but you got fired. Because of me. I just can't—I'm so sorry. Can you ever forgive me?"

He shut his door and took a step closer to her, pinning her against his car with his body. He dipped his head down and took her lips. God, he missed this. She opened her mouth to him, and he swept his tongue inside. He needed this. Needed her. Everything else be damned.

She pushed him back. "You aren't mad?"

"Mad that you pushed me away and refused to talk to me for over a week, yes. *Never* do that again."

"No, I mean, about your job."

"Yeah," he sighed. "About that. Frank played you."

"What?"

"I got the promotion," he said. "And then, I gave my notice."

"Why?"

"Because that promotion is nothing if you aren't by my side."

She stared at him like she still couldn't believe it.

"I love you," he tried again. "I want to spend the rest of my life with you. I don't care if I have to be a fry cook to do it."

She grinned. "Okay, SpongeBob. Let's go home."

His heart soared. "For real?"

"No, for pretend," she laughed. "Let's go!"

"Hold up," he said, pulling her back to face him. "I have to make a stop first."

She frowned.

"I have to save my brother's ass in Boston. It could be risky and illegal. You should go home. I'll meet you there after."

She smiled at him, pulling him close. "I'm never letting you out of my sight again, Mr. McGinn. Besides. I have to meet your family, eventually."

"Ha, ha," he gave a fake laugh. "Do you, though?"

Her smile was contagious. "I love you, Luke. Your family is a piece of that."

"You say that now."

"I already did a background check on all of them. I know what I'm getting myself into."

"Are you for real?" He pulled her against him, reveling in the feel of her in his arms once again.

Tanvi stood on her tiptoes, kissing him passionately. The kiss told him everything he needed to know.

The End

Tanvi and Lucas will return…

EPILOGUE

TANVI THREW HER BAGS INTO THE CORNER OF THE HOTEL ROOM AS SHE flopped down onto the bed. Lucas was behind her, falling on top of her.

"You're too heavy!" she squealed, trying to escape.

"Don't wiggle like that. You'll make me hard and I don't have the energy to fuck you properly right now."

She laughed as she slid herself free. "That was the longest drive of my entire life."

"I've never had the ETA get pushed later and later the closer I physically got to the destination. It was like we were stuck in some kind of time warp."

She eyed the clock. "That was supposed to be a seven-hour drive!"

"I know! I've done it a million times, fucking New York Traffic and then Connecticut. What was with Connecticut? It was like the nine layers of hell."

"Lets never drive anywhere ever again."

"Agreed." He said, turning over to look at the ceiling. "Accept we have too."

"What? No. Why?"

"My car," he looked at her, sincerity burning in his eyes. "I can't leave it in Boston. I love my car."

She wined. "Fine, but you have to make it up to me."

A wicked grin came over him. "Deal."

He grabbed her and pulled her to him.

"I'm gross we've been stuck in the car for hours," the protest was weak.

"I love you Rook, day or night, fresh from the shower or a thirteen hour car ride."

She laughed as he pushed her shirt up and kissed a trail down her stomach. He tugged her jeans off and buried his face in her core. She moaned as pleasure shot through her body. His tongue swirled and licked her until she was ready to burst.

"Come on," she tugged his face. "I want you inside me when I come."

He stepped back to remove his clothes. She'd never get tired of this view. He laid himself down between them and slid inside. She cried out as he filled her to the brim. "You feel so good Luke."

He bit her neck as he pumped himself inside her. Her hands roaming his scars as her pleasure built. His bare skin sliding over hers, she dug her nails into his back, urging him to go faster. She came with such force she screamed as her body convulsed around him. He didn't stop, pushing on towards his own release.

He collapsed on top of her, and she wrapped herself around him. Pulling him tight. She held him with her entire body. Feeling every inch of him.

"You're such a liar," she teased.

He lifted his head, revealing a frown.

"You said you didn't have the energy to fuck me properly."

"I really didn't," he chuckled as he trailed kisses down her neck. "But I seem to have found a second wind."

She opened her mouth to speak, but pounding on their door stopped her.

"Go away," Lucas yelled, not bothering to pick his head up from her breast where he was about to get her going again.

The pounding sounded again, this time it didn't stop.

"I'm going to kill them." Luke stood and walked to the door. Swinging it open as she dashed for cover. "What?"

"Get dressed you perv!" the voice sounded like Lucas's. A lot like Lucas's. She grabbed the blanket off the bed and wrapped herself up to lean around the corner. The man before him looked identical to her boyfriend. "Seriously? Who answers the door like that?"

"Someone who's in the middle of—" her cheeks burned and Lucas must have realized his mistake. He followed Dustin's eyes to where she stood in nothing but a sheet.

"That's your girlfriend?" Dustin said, a smile spreading over his face.

"Don't look at her, don't even talk to her," Luke snapped.

"Dude, she's a ten, a fucking eleven even. How did you, the biggest asshole in the fucking world, bag a girl like that?"

Luke shoved Dustin back out of the room and locked the door.

"He has to be allowed to talk to and look at me if we're going to help here."

Dustin pounded on the door again. "Get dressed love birds, we have a reporter to rescue and I can't hold this fucking Seal off much longer."

"We'll be out in a sec," Luke tossed Tanvi her pants as he found his own.

"Was that code or something?"

"He's working with a former Navy Seal. Things here—" he froze as he buttoned his pants. "There's a decent chance things are going to need to happen outside the law."

"And if I can't?" she asked.

"You'll be working with Remi. He's a local cop."

"And what exactly will you be doing?"

"What I have to."

WANT A BONUS EPILOGUE?

YOU CAN WAIT UNTIL THE CHASING THE LEAD SERIAL IS FINISHED AND Copy Cat is out to learn more about Luke and Tanvi, or you can check out this bonus epilogue!

Download Now!
https: / / BookHip.com / LJSPLML

SNEAK PEEK: BRUTAL OBSESSION

COMING 2022

WOODBRIDGE, VIRGINIA
Spring 2020

TOBIAS NASH SIPPED HIS COFFEE AS THE LATE MORNING SUN WARMED his skin. Seated on the patio over looking the bay, he'd enjoyed an early lunch. A spring chill clung to the air but the day was too nice to stay cooped up. He frowned as he read the findings of the latest peer reviewed study on treatment and rehabilitation of psychopaths. The author's interpretations felt, forced, almost like they were looking for political brownie points rather than facts. Turning back to the front page, he looked at the authors names. He'd reach out to Cindy to discuss it further after he was done work today.

A knock sounded at the door, pulling him back to reality. Glancing through the large french style patio doors to the main entrance, another reason to appreciate the open concept his designer had insisted on, all he could see was a red dress clinging to curves.

Prepared to tell the woman he wasn't going to buy anything he made his way through the house. Opening the door, he nearly fell over. Words of protest forgotten as recognition hit him.

"Surprise!" Adina Nightingale flung herself through the doorway and into his arms, her body pressing against his as she squeezed him. The warm scent of hibiscus that clung to her flooded his scenes. Her hands roamed his shoulders and arms as she stepped back. "Wow, have you been working out?"

"Y-yes, I find it easier to focus on my reading if I listen to it while exercising." He gave her a once over, she looked fine. "Is every thing okay? Your mother? Tanvi?"

"Aren't you happy to see me?" her sparkling doe eyes cutting him to his soul.

"It's not that," he chuckled. "Of course I'm happy to see you. It's just—unexpected."

He never thought she'd be here. In his dreams she showed up plenty but this was reality. He bit his cheek to be sure.

She looked around his house. "I'm gonna have to tell you aren't I?" she looked over her shoulder at him. "Or you'll figure it out?"

"It's kinda what I do," he admitted. He looked on the step and she had three suitcases. His heart pounded. How long was she planning to stay? She couldn't really be here for him. She was running from something. But at least, she'd run to him. He grabbed her bags and moved them inside for her.

"Thanks." She said, turning to face him, but her eyes were on her feet.

He cocked his head to the side. This was strange behavior for her. Slipping his hands into his pockets, he waited for her to speak.

"Mom, found out," a tear spilled onto his tile floor and understanding hit him. "She keeps looking at me like I'm a wounded animal. I wish she'd just put me out of my misery. I couldn't take it anymore. And you said I could visit. So I—" her eyes met his briefly, "should have called."

"What about your studies?"

"I haven't been able to focus, since. I even switched, religious studies. That helped some but my mind wonders to dark places as

I read." She looked up at him. Tears in her eyes. "I'm broken. Used."

His heart hurt and he was over come with an urge to pull her into a hug. He fought it back. Licking his lip as he looked away. God forbid he look at her the way her mother had. "You're not broken. And that experience, could even help you relate to victims. It could give you a real advantage."

She smiled, wiping the tears from her eyes. He couldn't help but return the expression. "See! This is why I had to come here. You're so practical. No emotion about it. Tanvi would have beat around the bush for hours trying not to call me a victim."

He slid his hand over the back of his neck. Was victim a bad word? "Well, you're more than a victim, Adina, you know that. I don't need to coddle you."

She stepped in closer to him and he fought the urge to retreat. Forcing his feet to stay put. This was crazy, he'd dreamed about this woman for months. And now here she was. *Get your head out of your ass man!* "I know. But you're the only one who makes me feel like that's true. So here I am. Taking you up on your invitation. I didn't interrupt anything did I? You don't have a woman here? Or you know, at all?"

He chuckled. "No, no women for me." Not since he'd first laid eyes on the woman before him. He couldn't be with someone without thinking about Adina, and that didn't seem fair to the other party.

"Just me, then," she beamed and pulled him against her again. This time he gave in, pulling her to him and turning into her hair. God, she smelled amazing. Felt even better.

"You also give the best hugs." She said as he held her tight. His chest warmed and smile spread over his face.

"Does your mother know where you are?"

"I'm not speaking to her." She stepped back, and he missed her warmth immediately. *Dammit,* had to go being practical again. "Its not that I'm mad I just can't handle the pity in her eyes, in her voice. I'll tell her, I will. I just need time."

"Would you object to me calling her?"

"As long as she doesn't come here."

He weighed his options. Could he keep Cora from coming here? He wasn't sure. The woman was a mama bear in every definition of the word. Fear shot through him. If she found out she was here and knew he didn't tell her, he might not survive to find out what Adina really wanted.

"Are you busy today?" she asked. "I know it's Friday but—"

"I'll need to go to work for a while but I can leave early, maybe we could get dinner?" He offered.

"That sounds great."

"Can I show you the guest room?"

"I could get a hotel," she offered. "I know I should have called."

"Don't be ridiculous," he smiled at her, putting his curiosity aside so she could see how happy he was to see her. "I wouldn't dream of making you stay in a hotel, especially when you were so hospitable."

She laughed. "That couch is a modern-day torture device, but I can't get away with boys in my room like Tanvi can."

He frowned. Was she saying she'd wanted him in her room?

"Where's your room?" she asked peeking up the stairs.

"Adina?" he asked, she paused in her exploration of his home. "What exactly do you want from me? A place to stay? Company? Help figuring out your mother? Not that I'm not extremely happy to see you, but I feel like there's something you're not telling me."

Adina let out a sigh. "I just need some time. To figure out my next move and be around someone who treats me like me."

Tobias nodded. He could do that for her. He could keep his feelings buried and be the man she needed him to be to get through her trauma. Then he could say goodbye. Couldn't he?

THE DEPARTMENT OF SECOND CHANCES

A SERIES OF STAND-ALONE NOVELS

What's in a Name? (Frank and Rachel)

Grin (Lucas and Tanvi)

Brutal Obsession (Adina and Nash coming 2022)

Department of Second Chances Serial

Chasing the Lead (Paige and Noah-intro Dustin McGinn)

Playing the Songbird

The Devil She Knows (2022)

Redeeming the Devil

PRETTY, GRITTY, LOVE STORIES TM

Angela Breen is a romantic suspense author with a passion for true crime. She likes blending her interests in her writing. Love stories are rarely picture perfect. They can be both pretty and gritty and those are the kinds of stories Angela likes to bring to life.

When she's not writing, reading, or sailing, she's homeschooling her three children and joking around with her Marine Corps Veteran husband. Laughter is the best medicine.

To learn more visit AngelaBreen.club

www.ingramcontent.com/pod-product-compliance
Lightning Source LLC
Chambersburg PA
CBHW030340310726
48979CB00001B/120